Praise for *Stealth*

Readers of war stories expect to be taken to the stark heart of a soldier's experience without being overwhelmed by the gruesome.

In *Stealth*, Robert Stermscheg manages that tricky balance deftly, illustrated particularly well in "An Unlikely Hero." This chapter depicts a surprising take on war's dramatic intersection of terror and the potential for heroic action as the protagonist staves off friendly bomber fire with split-second ingenuity and a broom. Even the most seasoned war-story reader has got to be captured by such a stand-alone scene.

~ Marjorie Anderson, English professor

Stealth is a first-rate combination of riveting action, believable characters and great story telling! Stermscheg spins a classic tale of WWII heroism both in the skies above and on the ground below, sharing both their triumphs and tragedies. Stealth is a compelling WWII thriller that needs to be not only on every WWII buffs reading list but on anyone who enjoys a great story.

~ Paul Byers, author of *Catalyst* and *Shattered Sky*

STEALTH
Robert Stermscheg

Published by Siretona Creative.
www.siretona.com

Distributed to the trade by The Ingram Book Company.

Updated interior, March 2022

Cover design: Travis Williams

Photo credits

Front cover:
WWII Airman Officer Portrait by Avid Creative on istock
Cloudy Sky by Nikolay Vorobyev
Crashed B-26 from U.S. National Archives
Horten bomber by Ratpack223 on istock

Back cover:
Storm Clouds by Luke Stackpoole
Konzerthaus Berlin by Ross and Helen Photographers
Author portrait: Robert Stermscheg

ISBN 978-1-988983-24-0 (paperback)
ISBN 978-1-988983-25-7 (ebook)

Dedication

I'd like to dedicate this book to my wife, Toni.
Your encouragement has allowed me to stay the course.

Table of Contents

Foreword

My father was an ordinary man who overcame many challenges as a POW in a German stalag during World War II.

He persevered with a dogged determination, not dwelling on his present circumstances, but pursuing a brighter future for himself and his family.

My dad had actually trained to become a pilot in the Slovenian military, but as a result of rising tension with Germany, pilot trainees were redeployed to the army.

I've followed in his footsteps with a fascination and interest in aviation. In 2011, I watched a video by the National Geographic Channel about the Horten brothers and their delta wing design. I was hooked.

I wanted to share the two brothers' ingenuity in overcoming many obstacles. Truth, when combined with fiction, has a way of capturing a reader's interest. I have always enjoyed reading and translating historical fiction, so it made sense that this cast of characters and exciting plot would evolve around the Horten bomber. I believe this story will resonate with World War II history buffs and I hope it gets you hooked on the Horten brothers, too.

Robert Stermscheg
December 2021

To learn more about my father and the Horten bomber, visit my website: www.robertstermscheg.com.

Germany: The Third Reich, 1943

Hermann Wilhelm Göring reclined in a plush armchair in the study of his opulent hunting lodge, dubbed Karinhall. Located a mere fifty kilometers from Berlin, it was named after his first wife, Karin Göring, who had succumbed to cancer in 1931.

Once Nazi Germany's second in command and the *Reichsführer's* trusted confidant, Göring found himself suddenly out of favor with the country's volatile dictator, Adolf Hitler.

As a World War I veteran and decorated flying ace, Göring wasn't about to let himself slide any further down the proverbial Nazi pecking order, least of all having to bow down to that bootlicker Martin Bormann, now ingratiated into Hitler's inner circle.

Although the thought was an irritant, much like a burr underneath a saddle, Göring pushed it aside, choosing instead to focus on what was directly in front of him: a painting. An exquisite painting. The *Reichsmarschall's* hardened countenance began to soften, the firm lines on his pudgy face replaced with the beginnings of a smile. He had good reason to smile. He was appraising—drooling would be more accurate—his most recent acquisition: Henri Matisse's *Still Life with Sleeping Woman*. Göring was well-known to have a penchant for obtaining beautiful things, including quality art works, procuring them at the expense of desperate families trying to escape the clutches of Nazi Germany.

Göring intertwined his large, meaty hands behind his head and leaned back, the armchair groaning in protest under its master's bulk. His gaze took in every detail of the artist's strokes, the bright, vibrant colors, and the lively composition displayed on the canvas, invoking a host of emotions generated by the impressionist's hand. The visual appeal of the exquisite painting was stunning. Truly a masterpiece.

He reached out for the riding crop on his desk and, with a swirl, he allowed his imagination to envision the artist's strokes.

The all-too-familiar shrill ring of the telephone interrupted his revelry, rudely replacing his lapse into Matisse's make-believe world with real-life matters that couldn't wait. He cursed out loud. He had left explicit instructions with his secretary not to be disturbed.

"My sincere apology for interrupting you, Herr *Reichsmarschall*," his secretary announced from the next room. "Colonel von Stahl insisted on speaking with you right away."

Göring glanced back at the painting as if weighing his options. Then he sighed in submission and instructed her to put Stahl through. He listened with detachment to the latest military reports until Stahl came to a sensitive topic: the loss of German aircraft.

"They shot down how many?" Göring bellowed into the telephone, taking out his unhappiness on the bearer of such bad news, the officer on the other end of the line. Colonel Gerhard von Stahl was a career military officer from a family that spanned three generations of military men and had grown used to Göring's outbursts. He still winced at the reproach.

"Too many, sir," Stahl replied apologetically. "I was informed only minutes ago. Including last night's mission, the Allies have shot down 271 bombers and twenty-two escorts this month alone. In total, we've lost 293 aircraft, not to mention the loss of pilots, a number of whom died as a result of—"

"*Ja, ja.*" Göring placated him with a dismissive tone, more concerned about the impact of aircraft losses than loss of life. "I'll be briefed on that later. But what are we going to do about it, Stahl?"

"I will naturally confer with my staff to see what can be done."

Göring's heavy breathing magnified his impatience, the irritation unmistakable. "Make sure you come up with something, and soon."

Before Stahl could reply, the marshal had disconnected.

Though concerned with losing qualified pilots, Göring was dealing with more pertinent matters. His latest meeting with Adolf Hitler hadn't gone well. Der Führer was particularly troubled over the lack of planes to maintain bombing runs over England. Göring wasn't sure why Hitler was so fixated on the campaign. He could be very obstinate about such things.

A small imperceptible smile formed on Göring lips as he thought back to a recent briefing conducted on the feasibility of the Me 262 fighter. The general who had conducted the meeting was a fine pilot, a decorated ace, much like Göring had been. More importantly, the man was well-respected by his fellow officers—a natural leader.

But that wasn't what interested Göring at the moment. His latest brainchild was a daring and outlandish plan, considered by many to be desperate and unattainable—inviting designers to submit proposals for a revolutionary plane capable of flying at speeds of up to a thousand kilometers per hour while carrying a one-thousand-kilogram payload over a thousand-kilometer distance.

When Göring had first floated the proposal, many engineers, especially Messerschmitt and Heinkel, had scoffed at it. Naturally, behind Göring's back. But then his chief of staff,

Kurt Diesing, had told him about two distinguished Luftwaffe pilots, Reimar and Walter Horten, who coincidentally were also aircraft designers.

Göring had never even heard of the Horten brothers, and his initial reaction had been to dismiss them outright. The notion crossed his mind that Diesing was merely pacifying him. But then Diesing had shown him some of their preliminary designs and advised him of their earlier work with gliders. That had quickly reined in Göring's skepticism.

Now, six months later, and faced with further criticism from Hitler, Göring examined the Hortens' drawings with renewed interest. Not bothering to call his secretary, Göring placed a call himself to Diesing's office: "Kurt, arrange for an immediate meeting with those two designers—the Hortens."

Diesing seemed initially surprised, but then made the necessary arrangements to carry out Göring's bidding.

Propping his big boots on the polished oaken table in his office, the *Reichsmarschall* lit a cigar and gazed back at the Matisse painting. *If Diesing believes in these designers, the least I can do is take a closer look,* he thought. *Their plane just might be the weapon I've been looking for to get Hitler off my back.*

And take a look he did. In fact, he was so impressed that he did more than that. Following his meeting with the designers, Göring opted to forego further evaluation of their designs and gave the go-ahead for the development of a full-scale prototype and, pending his approval, the immediate production of twenty aircraft. Göring at last got what he desperately needed: hope. Hope for a desperate Germany, and hope for his sagging career.

CHAPTER I

France: Beauvais Field

Captain Jack Swaggart yawned and looked east towards the unfolding dawn. Although the rising sun registered with his visual senses, what he saw in his mind's eye nearly overshadowed the splendor of cascading yellow and red emanating from the rising fireball.

It was a late October morning in 1944 and Jack, a pilot of the U.S. Army Air Force's 322nd Bombardment Group, was preparing for another important mission. Only thirty-two years old, he had been recently promoted to serve as the new squadron leader, replacing Captain Bill Worthy, whose plane had been shot down during a recent mission.

Standing at just over six feet, Jack stretched and glanced at the row of hangars. Two months ago, they had been moved to Beauvais airfield, a recently acquired base in northern France, roughly eighty kilometers north of Paris. He thought back to the previous night's briefing, when Colonel Harwood had informed them that they needed to make another bombing run on the Berlin marshaling yards. It seemed the German military had stepped up their production of aircraft parts, as well as that one essential component of all moving machinery: ball bearings.

It would be a dangerous mission, as daylight bombing raids increased the risk of exposure to enemy fighters. Frowning, he reflected on his last mission, two weeks ago, an attack on Nazi factories in a major German city—either Mannheim or Ludwigshafen—he couldn't recall which, although the details had been meticulously entered in his flight logbook.

A squadron of B-17 Flying Fortresses had left Norfolk, England on a similar morning only to run into heavy flak over Germany. Of the seventy-two bombers that had departed Thorpe Abbots Airfield, only fifty-eight had returned. Captain Bill Worthy had been among the missing crew. The two had been high school friends, even training together in Nebraska.

When Jack had first learned of Bill's overdue status, he had naturally grown concerned. He'd waited near the control tower, as a gentle breeze blew in from the southeast. He'd fumbled with his cap, twisting it into a scrunched-up mess, unable to evade the feeling of helplessness that crept up on him. He had needed to do something, anything—but really there was nothing to be done, other than offering up a heartfelt prayer.

Jack recalled—for what must have been the thirtieth time—looking up at the operator manning the tower and noting the concern in the man's eyes and a slow shaking of his head.

Suddenly, a few specks had appeared on the horizon, the first sighting of stragglers who had managed to make it home. Each plane exhibited different signs of damage, some minor, like bullet holes in the empennage or a fluttering aileron. One lucky pilot had managed to fly his aircraft all the way with a large chunk missing from the starboard wing! Fragments of sheet metal were flapping haphazardly around the large hole in a bizarre attention-grabbing look as the airplane stubbornly continued toward home, the crew ever mindful of its precarious and dangerous plight.

But Bill's plane, *Sizzling Sue*, wasn't among them.

Jack's only consolation was that another pilot had witnessed several men emerge at the last second from the crippled plane, bailing from the out-of-control spiral. Out popped a small dot, no larger than a volleyball, followed by a second, then a third. Those balls tumbled, quickly separated, and began a metamorphosis that within seconds transformed each one into a large, white parachute. That singular comforting thought gave him hope that Bill was one of the lucky ones who had made it out alive.

If he had, though, he was now a POW at one of the many *Luftstalags*[1] throughout Germany. As an officer, Bill would be treated a little better than the enlisted men, but it was no picnic no matter where he was confined.

Jack shook himself, brushing aside the cobwebs of his musings. Activity was picking up at one of the nearby hangars. Two mechanics were quietly starting work on the number two engine of *Heavy Strike*, a four-engine behemoth of a bomber. Its protective cowling lay nearby on the tarmac, dwarfing the mechanic's gray toolbox which sat propped open on a handcart. On the other side, under the port wing, Jack noticed a worker in coveralls refueling the plane. The man cranked the lever of a hand pump over and over, humming to himself and oblivious to work going on around him.

Jack watched as his own airplane, a B-26 Marauder nicknamed *Lucky Lady*, received attention nearby. A red-haired young man sporting an abundance of boyish freckles was riveting new sheeting on the left side of the fuselage. The damaged section lay discarded on the tarmac, a vivid reminder of how close a German anti-aircraft battery had come to crippling him on his last mission. Jack winced as he remembered the deafening explosions from that sortie. Shells had exploded all around, some below and others above, buffeting the aircraft with sheer force, the black puffs of smoke a chilling reminder of their potency.

The explosions were powerful enough to rattle one's teeth, eliciting curses from some and hastily offered prayers by others, each man hoping the next concussion would be the last. Miraculously, they had made it through, running the aerial gauntlet and making it all the way home to their base in France.

Jack momentarily closed his eyes, driving the harrowing memory from his mind and replacing it with more pressing matters.

Each aircraft down the line was being prepped for the upcoming mission so it could stand up to the rigors of flying six hundred miles into enemy territory. The plane needed to perform not just adequately, but flawlessly, ensuring it would take the crew and payload to their destination and back.

Jack had already performed the walk-around, only one part of his pre-flight check. Although he had performed it many times, there was no room for complacency. He had visually checked the undercarriage for leaks, loose hoses, and anything that seemed out of place.

He was about to move on to inspecting one of the huge Pratt & Whitney engines when he spotted an overloaded Jeep manoeuvre around a fuel truck and come to an abrupt halt. Five men, including the driver, were cramped together inside the Jeep, reminding Jack of his father's '29 Ford pickup back home. First to disembark was Second Lieutenant Oliver Smith. Then came Lucky, Shore, and Romeo. Each enlisted man had inherited a handle or nickname, a term of endearment meant to identify them, typically in a humorous way.

Together, they formed an intricate fighting unit, each man vital to the team. "Lucky" was more formally known as Frank Lerner, twenty-two years old with black curly hair, easy-going but smart as a whip, and as his nickname implied, lucky in most things, especially poker. Stemming from Boise, Idaho, his main duty was that of nose gunner. Normally seated within the confines of the "bubble," a Plexiglas canopy in the nose of the aircraft, Lerner had a spectacular, panoramic view in front.

"Shore," aka Gregg Fallon, also twenty-two, was tall and slim and possessed boyish good looks. He never missed an opportunity to crack a joke. He occupied the gun turret amidships, known as the dorsal turret, and hailed from Lexington, Kentucky.

"Romeo," known as Stan Koslawski, the oldest of the crew at twenty-five, was of medium height and considered himself a ladies' man. Sporting a pencil-thin mustache that provoked many a comical remark from fellow mates, it often didn't translate into favorable results with the opposite sex. He was the tail gunner and had to keep a watchful eye out for enemy fighters that attacked from the rear. He called Trenton, New Jersey home.

Jack appraised his crew with a sense of pride. Each man was outfitted in a leather jacket and boots, reminding him that it was damn cold—and dangerous—at 20,000 feet.

"Morning, Cap!" a voice called out to him, bringing him back down to earth. "Did you check on that faulty altimeter?"

Jack turned around and came face to face with his navigator, Second Lieutenant Giuseppe "Joe" Rossi, a small but wiry man of Italian descent. Joe had wisely decided to walk to the tarmac, forfeiting his seat in the crowded Jeep.

"Sure, Joe," Jack replied. "I spoke to one of the Limey techs and he assured me it's been recalibrated. By the way, how was your date last night?"

Rossi grinned, the memory still fresh in his mind. "Not bad. She couldn't keep her hands off me." Joe's New York accent was unmistakable.

Jack shot him a questioning look and was about to respond when he was interrupted by the unmistakable voice of their bombardier, Oliver Smith.

"Meaning you didn't get to first base, right?" Smith said mischievously. He grinned from a distance, leaning against one of the plane's huge tires.

"Was it that obvious, Ollie?" Joe replied with a wince. "Well, truth be told, we danced together for half the night and just when things were looking up, two of her girlfriends came over and rescued her. French dames!"

"Well, Joe," Jack replied laughing, "at least you were

dancing, unlike the rest of us." His expression turned business-like. "Anyway, I've done the walk-around and Chuck will do it again. Joe, you and Ollie get settled in upstairs and check your equipment. It's going to be a long flight."

Both men nodded and, without another word, they climbed aboard *Lucky Lady* using the forward access hatch ladder.

Jack monitored their progress when something unusual caught his attention: a uniformed officer pedaling an unconventional bicycle toward their aircraft. A grin broke out on his face and he cupped his left hand over his mouth so as not to burst out laughing.

He readily identified the exuberant cyclist as Charles "Chuck" Boyer, his long-time friend and co-pilot. The tall and lanky Omaha native had a penchant for being different, highlighted by this morning's choice of transportation. Jack recalled that Boyer had called it a velocipede.

Boyer looked pathetic; his tall frame hunched over the handlebars as his long legs worked the pedals. The tire rim seemed out-of-round, causing the front wheel to wobble, threatening to upset the rider's balance at any moment. To make matters worse, his bony knees nearly collided with his chest with each upward stroke, giving him the appearance of a dressed-up orangutan who had, for the fun of it, climbed onto a bicycle and, after managing to work the pedals, set the machine in motion, only to realize his folly as it picked up speed, causing him to hang on for dear life.

Charles Boyer, nonplussed by his mode of transportation, came to a controlled though abrupt stop and quickly dismounted before the velocipede had a chance to tilt. He disengaged himself from the contraption and handed it over to an amused mechanic.

"The front wheel still wobbles, Jimmy," Boyer offered.

"Aye, I can see that, sir," the man replied.

Shore, never missing an opportunity, guffawed to his buddies, "Jiminy Cricket, would you look at that contraption?"

"Uh-huh," Romeo said. "I've seen one just like that on Coney Island back home, you know, the amusement park?"

Lucky slapped Shore on the shoulder. "Get ready. I can feel Romeo about to thrill us with another one of his famous escapades."

"Hey, guys, no fibbin'," Romeo countered, only pretending to be offended. "It was a couple of years ago and I was out on a date with a new girl. There I was showing, her the sights when this clown comes out of nowhere riding that whatchamacallit while juggling bowling pins. I had to jump out of his way, pulling my girl with me. She tripped—God's honest truth—and if she didn't fall into a large puddle of water! She was unhurt, but soaking wet and, rather than thank me, she gave me the dirtiest look and told me—"

"Would you look at it for me?" Boyer asked the mechanic, cutting Romeo off mid-sentence.

"No problem, Gov," the little Irishman replied. He patted the seat and took charge of the relic as if it were an old friend.

Boyer, seemingly unaware of the attention he had fostered, walked up to *Lucky Lady*, and rather than saluting, merely nodded to Jack.

"How does she look this morning?" Chuck asked turning to appraise the Marauder. "Lots of miles on the old girl, huh?"

"You tell me, Chuck. The mechanics have worked on it throughout the night. She's just been signed off, though another look wouldn't hurt."

Boyer, no relation to the French film star, had been flying with Jack for more than a year and the two had developed a close camaraderie, not uncommon with bomber pilots. Jack depended on his co-pilot and often asked for his opinion. Their friendship had morphed into one of mutual respect and inherent trust. In a way, they were akin to brothers.

To both men, the B-26 was more than an airplane. It was

a complex machine, capable of inflicting serious damage to any German factory or installation. But it was also home to a crew of seven men. They would be confined in its metal framework for hours and took fierce pride in her airworthiness.

Jack handed the technical logbook to Chuck, who took it without hesitation and tucked it under his arm. His co-pilot started examining the propeller blades of the port engine. Jack was about to climb up the ladder to prepare himself for the mission when he was interrupted by a familiar sight. Another Jeep was meandering down the flight line, driven by a corporal. An officer, holding a bullhorn, was standing next to him and shouting instructions to each flight crew that they passed. Jack had witnessed it before and already knew what the officer would bellow even before he arrived: the mission was a scrub.

Romeo, not yet catching sight of the approaching Jeep, piped up.

"Anyway, you won't believe what happened. There I was, simply trying to help the gal, when we were nearly bowled over by this nincompoop on his bicycle, and rather than thank me she gave me the dirtiest look—"

"The mission's on hold, lads." The officer confirmed Jack's prediction through his megaphone. "Bad weather over Berlin." His driver, a grim-faced Scot, gazed straight ahead while making his way down the flight line.

Jack sighed as he turned back to alert his men.

The response was varied, but for the most part he could see relief in their faces. No one wanted to go to Berlin. It was well-known that the city was heavily fortified. The men scattered like ants, abandoning Romeo before he could finish his story.

Jack decided to walk back to the barracks. On the way, he was hailed by a uniformed female cyclist carrying out a variety of duties. She was a FANY, short for First Aid Nursing

Yeomanry, and was part of a corps of women invaluable to the war effort.

"Sir," she addressed him in a Cockney accent. "A moment, if you please."

As Jack appraised the young woman, he decided she couldn't have been more than twenty years old.

"You're Captain Swaggart?" she inquired.

"Yes, I'm Jack Swaggart."

"Colonel Harwood would like a word with you, sir."

"Where? In the briefing room?"

"No, in his office. I don't think it's anything to do with the mission, sir. That's all I know."

"Thank you, Corporal," Jack replied, dismissing her.

He walked back to the administration building, all the while wondering what Harwood had in mind. Perhaps he had a new replacement for the squadron? Maybe someone had gone AWOL? But then it could have been one of ten different things.

He breathed in the crisp, cool air and watched the departing FANY, already pedaling toward her next assignment.

CHAPTER II

Doodlebug

Lieutenant Jimmy "Bullit" Hooper could hardly contain his excitement as he piloted his Supermarine Spitfire Mk XII at two hundred fifty knots, climbing through five thousand feet on his way to the planned ceiling of ten thousand feet. The twenty-four-year-old was the lone Australian among the British pilots, having enlisted over a year ago to bolster Britain's defenses.

Every pilot had a slightly different outlook, but Jimmy always felt a rush of excitement surge through his veins once he strapped himself into his safety harness. He scrutinized the instrument panel and mentally checked off each instrument: airspeed indicator, manifold pressure, RPM indicator, altimeter, artificial horizon, compass ... he knew each function by heart. Months of study and practice had produced a sense of familiarity and trust. Jimmy, like most pilots, trusted in the reliability of his airplane, instruments included. He breathed in the unique cockpit smell, a combination of grease, lubricant, and high-octane fuel, and grinned to himself, knowing pilots were an odd sort.

It was mid-morning in late October 1944, and he had just left Hornchurch Air Base in southern England along with five other Spitfires, leaving behind the safety of the English coast. They were on reconnaissance patrol, specifically on the look-out for "Jerry," Germany's enemy bombers.

The Luftwaffe had been making a concerted effort to

weaken Britain's air defenses, and Jimmy and his mates had to be vigilant. It had started out as a perfect flying day, though it was probably short-lived as heavy cumulus clouds were beginning to build on the southern horizon.

The flight was headed toward the northern coast of France, recently liberated after D-Day. Jimmy scanned the vast sky above and below, searching for those familiar gray specks that represented bogeys. On his right, his wingman, Pilot Officer Peter "Jelly" Graham, grinned back at him while polishing off what looked suspiciously like a jelly doughnut. On Peter's right was David "Jerry" Beckett. He was born in Berlin in 1913 and had lived in Austria, but was later naturalized British and had taken his mother's name, Beckett.

At thirty-one, Beckett was considered an old man within the ranks of the squadron, yet his boyish good looks made him look younger. Although he wasn't tall, his five foot-nine frame was still squeezed into the small cockpit.

"Alright, gents," Beckett said evenly, trying to keep the apprehension out of his voice, "keep a sharp lookout for Jerry."

They knew just how quickly a Focke-Wulf fighter could pop out of the clouds and line them up in its cross-hairs. Beckett thought back to their last sortie. They had been briefed on a flight of Heinkel bombers flying across the Channel, presumably heading for London. No sooner had he spotted twelve in formation than one of his younger pilots went straight for them. Harry Blight, with little combat experience and itching for that first kill, had failed to scan the skies for the bomber escorts.

He had missed the accompanying *Geschwader*[2] of Fw 190s, flying about three thousand feet higher and riding "shotgun". Before the Englishman knew what had happened, a hail of cannon fire had raked his fuselage and severely damaged the aircraft's empennage.

Luckily for him, he wasn't injured and managed to bail out. David recalled watching Blight's white parachute, as it drifted down toward the choppy, inhospitable, gray sea. That was two days ago. There was still no word if he had survived. Hopefully, he had been picked up by a destroyer or fishing trawler.

Putting the image behind him, Beckett scanned the skies for any sign of the enemy. Pilot Officer Walter Gibbons broke the silence. "It's Jerry," he called excitedly. "Doodlebug below us at ten o'clock."

"Doodlebug" or "Burner" were two of several names ascribed to the V1 rockets Nazi Germany had been relentlessly firing at England. It was an unmanned pulsejet-propelled rocket that was fired from launch pads on the northern coast of occupied France. Once airborne, the rocket could accelerate to about four hundred miles per hour and would follow a prescribed course.

It was Hitler's weapon of choice, his way of striking at the heart of London and sending the defiant Brits a strong message. Thanks to the Allied victory in the Battle of Britain, they had maintained air superiority, forcing Hermann Göring to resort to improvised tactics—unmanned rockets.

As Gibbons peeled off, he recalled how tricky those flying bombs were. He used a diving turn to close in on the speeding rocket. It was a risky maneuver. The rocket was faster, unpredictable, often exceeding four hundred miles per hour as it sped relentlessly toward the English coast. The objective for an enterprising RAF pilot was to close the gap and intercept the flying bomb.

If the pilot waited too long, the solid-fuel propelled rocket would quickly outdistance the piston-powered Spitfire. If he came in with too much speed and opened fire with his 20 mm canons, the shrapnel from the ensuing explosion could be blown back at the pursuing fighter.

All pilots knew the risk of engaging unmanned rockets. Some daring pilots had developed a dangerous technique whereby the Spitfire pulled alongside the rocket and, by encroaching the V1's wingtip with its own, tried to disrupt the airflow over the rocket's wing. The difference in air pressure could cause the rocket's opposing wing to dip, overriding its onboard gyros. The rocket would then lose altitude and splash harmlessly into the ocean. *Easier said than done*, thought Gibbons.

Yet they all knew the devastation one single bomb could inflict if it impacted on a home or factory. A V1 rocket typically carried a one-thousand-pound warhead, some even greater, something not to be taken lightly.

With that thought in mind, he elected to go for the old-fashioned method.

His Red3 executed a perfect turn and quickly descended upon the flying menace, like a hawk swooping down on an unsuspecting sparrow. But this "sparrow" was anything but timid or harmless.

Gibbons came out of his turn and lined up with the cruising German rocket. His instinct told him to abandon his daring plan, but he had committed himself and now all his mates were watching. When he was perhaps two hundred and fifty yards behind the rocket and slightly to the left, he leveled out.

In optimum position, Gibbons opened fire just as the rocket lurched ahead, one of the inherent traits of the pulse-propulsion system. The bullets streaked blindly forward, none the wiser to the erratic rocket, missing the bomb by inches. Gibbons cursed under his breath. These minions of death weren't about to give up easily. He lightly stepped on the rudder pedal, correcting for the plane's drift and fired again. This time the bullets seemed to fly straight up the rocket's tailpipe, and he was rewarded for his efforts by a tremendous explosion.

He quickly dipped his right wing to escape the cascading debris, turning away while pulling up on his control column. The downing of a V1 rocket was a first for a pilot in their squadron.

Gibbons rejoined the formation, his plane apparently untouched by the debris.

He grinned at Beckett, who responded with a big thumbs-up. Just then, they spotted another V1 rocket coming out of the clouds, racing westward and at least a thousand feet higher than their formation. Nothing short of a P-51 Mustang had any hope of catching the errant menace. Beckett radioed the nearest station, advising them of the V1's approximate position and heading.

Their radio chatter died instantly. In silence, each man offered up a quick prayer hoping the rocket's gyroscopes would lead it into the vast English countryside, far from populated London.

⊥⊤

Ten kilometers due east, Luftwaffe Kapitän Helmut Gerber was flying an Me 262 jet, nicknamed *Schwalbe,* level at five thousand meters. Alert to enemy fighters, he spotted the first V1 rocket's premature detonation; it had harmlessly passed beneath his jet only two minutes ago, its flame burning brightly from the tailpipe.

He tried to shrug it off, dismissing it as just another explosion, but the shoulder harness kept him from moving. One thing was certain: he didn't want to be anywhere near one of these deadly bombs. They had an uncanny way of going off when you least expected it—not unlike his squadron commander's temper.

Thinking of the pompous Major Frank von Glitz elicited a momentary smile. Gerber glanced at his new wingman, Second Lieutenant Willie Schmidt, fresh from conversion training. He had previously been flying piston-powered Fw 190s and only recently transitioned to the turbojet fighter.

They're getting younger every day, he mused. *Göring must be getting desperate.*

All at once he sensed something in his peripheral vision. A cold shiver worked its way up his spine, and to his horror he spotted a second V1 rocket scream by no more than fifty meters past his wingtip. *They were supposed to cruise at no more than a thousand meters above sea level,* he recalled. *Why the hell weren't they warned by Command of its course?*

"Scheise!" he cursed aloud in an effort to control his racing heart.

Probably a malfunction, he mused. *Or perhaps sabotage of the onboard altimeter and guidance system.* Gerber cursed again, reminded of the fact that the German High Command had endorsed the use of slave labor to assemble these killing machines. Whether through incompetence or sabotage, the bombs presented more of a nuisance to the Luftwaffe. *But did Göring really care?* He thought not.

Instinctively, he reached for the mike to alert his flight, but it was obvious that they too had already seen it. His other wingman, Andreas Bauman, below and aft of him, had already pushed his control column forward, creating more separation between him and the errant rocket. It seemed to be climbing and accelerating.

It'll never make the coast, Gerber thought, continuing to watch as the menace maintained its pre-set course. *It has burned too much fuel to reach this altitude.*

Sure enough, he saw the flame sputter a few times and then abruptly extinguish. The rocket, its fuel now spent, had no choice but to commence a downward trajectory that would end with a splash in the open sea. Bored with watching its slow descent, he religiously scanned his instruments, including the important fuel gauges. He had roughly three hundred kilograms remaining in his tanks. It was time to head home.

As the lead Me 262 banked to the right, heading for their home base at Uphoven, the ever-cautious Gerber glanced back to scan the vast sky behind him.

As they crossed the French coast below them, he was reminded of the June 6 invasion of the beaches of Normandy. The Allies had not only occupied the beachhead but were moving forward, chewing up territory once occupied by German troops. There seemed to be no stopping them. Along with Sherman tanks, Howitzer guns, and vast supplies, the Americans had also brought P-51 Mustangs, a formidable long-range fighter. The Allied squadrons seemed to have virtually endless resources, while his *Geschwader* was constantly on the verge of being grounded by the lack of spare parts.

Dieter Weiser, flying the lead, was first to contact the tower and make a wide, sweeping turn, descending through the scattered clouds and lining up with the hard-surfaced runway. The landing gear touched down almost perfectly and the airplane decelerated, taking the exit ramp.

Next was Willie Schmidt, who, initially a little high on his approach, flared longer but still landed well. The third was Erwin Ziller, now low on fuel. While circling the airfield, Gerber caught the glint of something off Ziller's right wingtip. As he looked closer, he spotted the familiar green empennage of a British fighter cresting the tree line. The Spitfire was too low to be taking pictures and was likely lining up for a strafing run of the airfield. The Me 262, though responsive and fast during flight, was the opposite during landing—slow and vulnerable to attack, a detail not lost on British pilots.

Weiser keyed his mike. "Ziller, look out!" In that instant, an anti-aircraft gun started firing at the rapidly approaching fighter. *Useless*, thought Gerber. *He's too low and moving fast. Bauman is a sitting duck.*

As if hearing his commander's words, Ziller reacted and pushed his throttle forward, but the transition back into flight mode took several agonizing seconds, the difference between life and death for a fighter pilot.

Weiser threw his Me 262 into a tight, gut-wrenching turn. Although he was out of position and at a tactical disadvantage, he nevertheless fired a burst at the approaching Spitfire. By now, Ziller's jet was accelerating and climbing out over the treetops, but his undercarriage was still exposed. In his haste to escape, Ziller must have forgotten to retract the gear.

"Ziller! Cycle the gear," Gerber yelled into his mike.

The Me 262's design didn't allow for the wheels to come up as quickly as with the Fw 190. The process was excruciatingly slow. To make matters worse, it hampered the aircraft's aerodynamic flow this close to the ground, slowing down the plane.

The Spitfire rapidly closed the distance, its pilot firing a short burst that missed the jet's right wingtip by centimeters. A second volley struck pay dirt; twenty-millimeter cannon fire strafed the Messerschmitt's starboard engine.

Ziller, preoccupied with raising the gear, had his hands full as he tried to evade the attacking fighter. Black smoke vented from the damaged engine's exhaust nacelle.

With the right engine no longer producing full power and the left one at full thrust, Ziller now faced an even greater problem: a thrust imbalance. He had little choice but to pull back the power lever on the disabled engine, simultaneously stepping on the left rudder. The aircraft responded slowly to his mitigating action. Trying to keep his rising fear from turning into panic, he fought for control of his jet, flying dangerously low and operating only on the port engine.

The British pilot broke off the attack and hopped over the trees, heading northwest and out of danger from reprisal, presumably back to his base on the French coast.

Ziller, meanwhile, was in for the fight of his life.

All his training came down to this one definitive moment. He had few options. At this low altitude he couldn't simply abandon the aircraft. Even if he were able to jettison the canopy and jump clear of the aircraft, he would be too low to deploy his parachute and would likely end up crippled or dead. No, he had to stay with his airplane.

As Gerber watched, his only consolation was that it hadn't happened to the new man, Schmidt. Gerber could almost picture Ziller frantically going over his emergency procedures: shut down the starboard engine, keep firm pressure on the left rudder, trim the aircraft for single engine flight, stay out of the trees, and most important, keep the damn plane flying.

Just when Weiser thought Ziller's jet was doomed, its wings leveled and it barely cleared the looming fence of tall, resolute fir trees at the south end of the airfield. Gerber watched in wonder as the crippled jet climbed, the left engine howling in protest, while the right one still spewed black smoke. After gaining sufficient altitude, Ziller commenced a slow turn back to the airfield. He habitually contacted the control tower, startling the sergeant who manned the post, and advised him that he felt he could make it back without jeopardizing anyone's safety.

"Er … land at your discretion, Lieutenant," the controller offered rather than instructed.

Determined to show Gerber that he was a cut above the rest, Ziller took a cautious, wide turn and commenced the landing cycle. Everything had to be done just right. There was no margin for error, no second chance to go around again with only one functioning engine.

Fighting to keep control, he couldn't allow the RPM on the left engine to drop too quickly. He glanced at his checklist and remembered to lower the gear, receiving audible confirmation from the controller. He then lined up once again, coming from the north, prudently checking the direction of the windsock near the runway's edge. The orange tube was a welcome sight, flapping in the breeze as if beckoning him to land.

Gut, thought Gerber, watching the landing.

Every pilot preferred to land into the wind, using the additional lift to his advantage, thereby allowing him to lower his approach speed. But had Ziller landed downwind, it would have extended his landing run and put him in danger of running off the end of the runway.

Ziller compensated for the strong breeze by ever so gently pulling back on the power lever, slowing the jet and allowing it to meet terra firma. The left gear touched first, followed closely by the right and then the nose gear. He eased the control column forward, pulled the power lever all the way back and applied the brakes. The damaged jet raced past the control tower, decelerating slowly, as if part of it desperately clung to flight.

Ziller managed to turn at the end, taking the exit ramp and coming to a stop once clear of the runway. Mechanically, he shut down the port engine and turned off the master switch. Only then did he look around, taking in the resounding cheer that had erupted from the onsite ground crew. He unhinged the canopy and waved at the approaching well-wishers.

A truck raced out to meet pilot and aircraft. Two mechanics in overalls jumped off and immediately attacked the smoking starboard engine with crude handheld fire-extinguishers.

Gerber, still circling overhead, saw exuberant men jump up and down, and decided to contribute by wagging his wings. Quickly scanning the sky, and not finding any more bogeys, he circled for a landing. On approach, he remembered that Von Glitz had requested that he recommend one of his pilots for the new Horten test program. Having just witnessed Ziller's remarkable recovery, he knew just the man for the job.

But before Gerber could give it more thought, a warning light blinked on the instrument panel. He was low on fuel and needed to land immediately.

With Ziller's plane clear of the runway and being towed to a nearby hangar, the controller cleared Gerber to land. He touched down without incident and breathed a sigh of relief.

CHAPTER III

The Sturmbannführer

In an office on the third floor of a brick building on Leipziger Strasse, Berlin, a man sat hunched over his desk and examined the various documents neatly laid out before him. *Sturmbannführer*[3] Heinrich Schinkel, a man in his late forties, wasn't the picture of the Aryan ideal Hitler boasted about in his speeches.

He came from a poor family, had not completed *gymnasium* (high school), and had little social standing—that is, until he had joined the socialist party in 1933. He wasn't especially tall and compensated for it by placing inserts in his shoes. He had a ruddy, worn face, dark brown eyes, and a slightly crooked nose from one too many schoolyard fights. To make matters worse, he wore spectacles that were ill-fitting and kept sliding down his nose. Yet that wasn't the worst of it. His right arm had been amputated below the elbow, the result of shrapnel, courtesy of an exploded American bomb.

Many men would have wallowed in pity or turned to alcohol, prescription drugs, or some other form of appeasement, but Schinkel wouldn't allow his physical impairment to hinder him. He certainly hadn't lost any of his determination or decisiveness. If anything, he had used his handicap as leverage, often catching an opponent staring at the missing limb and taking advantage of the man's embarrassment.

On this particular morning, he was dressed in his immaculate SS uniform, the Iron Cross perfectly centered below his Adam's apple. Many a man had dismissed Schinkel as just another proud, overzealous SS officer. There certainly were plenty of those in Berlin, having been elevated to lofty positions by superiors who were influenced by old friendships or allowed themselves to be bribed.

Not so with Schinkel. He had attained his position neither through favoritism nor bribery. True, he had caught the eye of one or two superiors, but what ultimately elevated him to his current rank was his dedication to the Nazi Party and its tactics, which, when combined with efficiency and ruthlessness, often produced results.

That's not to say that he was a sadist like so many others in Himmler's SS corps. He merely used his ingenuity and resourcefulness to accomplish what needed to be done.

Many underestimated him, calling him uneducated and even sneered at his social status behind his back. They usually paid for it in due course. Few realized that he was often directly or indirectly responsible for missing a promotion or personal calamity.

What mattered most to Schinkel was distinguishing himself through his work ethic and earning the respect of his peers. He relished nothing more than gaining an upper hand over his fellow officers by completing a difficult assignment and thus silencing his critics. He was wise enough not to publicly gloat over his accomplishments yet modest enough to accept his superior's accolades—at least outwardly; privately he grinned at besting the snobbish elite.

Today, Schinkel was reviewing an intelligence report that had been funneled down to him from his superior, Colonel Herbert von Spritz, who oversaw counterintelligence. He frowned as he read the attached note and focused on the lead paragraph.

"I regret to inform *Reichsminister* Göring that there have been recent unexplainable problems at our secret test facility at Göttingen. Aside from the usual bureaucratic delays, acting director Schloss cannot pinpoint the source. The following information, largely unsubstantiated, is only preliminary, and ...”

Schinkel scanned the next two paragraphs, which dealt with what he felt were excuses and supply problems. He stopped reading, wondering why Spritz had saddled him with such a mundane problem. But then he came to the last sentence and mouthed the words as if needing confirmation of what he had just read.

“It is the writer’s opinion that this may involve acts of sabotage.”

The letter was signed by the director himself.

Was this the director’s way of distancing himself from his firm’s ineptitude by laying the blame elsewhere? Schinkel had little patience for bureaucrats. Sabotage. It had an ominous ring to it. Could it really be that? The word itself was pregnant with all sorts of implications, many of them speculative and inconclusive.

He absentmindedly played with a pencil while he considered his options. Perhaps it could be a case for his new underling, Horst Kloster. The man was clever, ambitious and resourceful, certainly qualified for this sort of inquiry. Schinkel thought back to the day, only two weeks ago, when he had first met Kloster. The man had attended to his office at the exact time of his appointment in a crisp new SS uniform.

Rumor had it that Kloster was a ladies man and, unlike Schinkel, he did have the appearance of a natural-born Aryan: tall, just under six feet, strong physique, blonde hair, and gray eyes. He epitomized every feature Hitler praised and often ranted about.

There was, however Kloster’s sudden departure from his fighter squadron. The dossier laid out on his desk was clear enough and singled out Kloster’s qualities: ambition, dedication, resourcefulness. Unfortunately, there were also his shortcomings: arrogance, independence, stubbornness.

Schinkel smiled to himself. What it didn't contain was a reference to Kloster's secret affair with a high-ranking officer's wife. Kloster had lost his wings and been demoted due to the indiscretion. Had it not been for an influential minister and family friend, Kloster would have certainly been court-martialed.

Schinkel sighed. He was tired of investigating the shenanigans of privileged party members, tired of hauling them into his office only to let the senior ones go after an interceding phone call from a senior bureaucrat or high-ranking SS officer.

Yes, Kloster was the man to handle this assignment. That way Schinkel could evaluate his work ethic and see if there was any validity to the complaint.

Leaning back in his chair, Schinkel glanced out the window and took in the splendid view. The neighboring buildings stood untouched by recent Allied bombing, boldly proclaiming German ingenuity, incorporating turn-of-the century architecture.

One structure, however, stood out from the rest. The *Reichsluftfahrtministerium* (Air Ministry Building), constructed in 1935, was solid and resplendent in limestone and marble. Although he wasn't a fan of architecture, he couldn't help but appreciate its magnificence. Then it came to him, like a slap in the face—it embodied what he detested most: bureaucracy. And its master was none other than Göring himself.

Göring! Now there was a manipulator and an opportunist if there ever was one. The *Reichsmarschall*—that pompous ass—was a difficult man to please at the best of times, but he was still revered as a flying ace of the First World War. Even though the Luftwaffe's reputation was on the decline, he still elicited respect from the masses.

But that could quickly change, Schinkel mused, as his eyes glanced up at the Führer's portrait. Rumors were circulating that Hitler was displeased with Göring, blaming him for the latest Allied bombing of German cities.

No doubt that bootlicker Martin Bormann has been planting seeds of mistrust and incompetency in Hitler's ear, all the while portraying himself in the best possible light.

Favoritism! It was difficult to distance oneself from it, and Schinkel prided himself in staying out of the sort of compromising situations that had far too often proven to be the downfall of fellow officers; they were forced to grovel and make amends, either paying handsomely out of pocket or promising to render some favor in the not-too-distant future.

Schinkel vowed never to place himself in a situation that would compromise his career.

⊥⊤

Reimar Horten looked up from the drafting table at his older brother, Walter, as if needing confirmation of what he had just said. Older by a year and a half, Walter was the more serious of the two. Tall, fair, and somewhat stoic, he was a Luftwaffe officer, but first and foremost he and Reimar were aircraft designers.

Walter glanced at the calendar on the wall and noted the date—July 4. Something twigged his memory. Ah yes, Independence Day in the United States. But here, at *Gotha Wagonfabrik*, an assembly plant situated about three hundred kilometers southwest of Berlin, it was just another working day with many issues to resolve.

Walter had just confirmed what they both feared: there was little hope of obtaining the BMW turbojet engines they had requested. Instead, he had been advised by Air Marshall Milch over the phone, and rather bluntly, that they would have to redesign the nacelle openings of their prototype to accommodate the marginally larger Junkers Jumo engines.

Reimar had fought against making a scathing remark to his superior. After all, Milch was himself under pressure. This latest setback bothered him as much as it did the brothers.

He thought back to their initial meeting with General

Kurt Diesing, Göring's chief of staff. Impressed by their unwavering enthusiasm, Diesing had passed around certain segments of their work for evaluation. Only after other senior officials had given their cautious consent had he requested that the *Reichsmarschall* be briefed on the project.

And yet the promised meeting with Göring had been postponed several times before eventually being held one year ago in Berlin. As Reimar recalled, Göring had been mildly enthusiastic at the prospect of their revolutionary design. He had even pretended to know something of their earlier work with gliders and the sweptback wing design. But when he had been advised that most of the fabrication would come from wood, he'd laid aside his reservations and taken the whole proposal more seriously.

Walter and Reimar had been impressed, flattered even, at having gained an audience with the flamboyant *Reichsmarschall*. But looking back, both brothers realized that it was typical of Göring to do what was necessary in order to get what he wanted. He would cajole, coerce, flatter, bribe, and even threaten when necessary; in fact, these were known to be his favorite tactics.

Although initially thrilled by the opportunity to serve the *Reich* with their design talents, Reimar realized they had also become pawns at Göring's disposal. He had been desperate to appease Hitler with new designs and technology by giving him hope of hitting back at the Allies who had enjoyed all the success of late. There were rumors that other designers, like Heinkel and Messerschmitt, also faced pressure to come up with new and better designs. It was likely true. Hitler's appetite for innovation and technology was insatiable.

But ever since then their work had been plagued by delays, bickering, incompetence, and a shortage of parts. Every week, news filtered down about Allied bombing raids on factories that produced ball bearings, sheet metal, and precision tools—anything that was vital to the war effort.

"It's what we feared all along," Reimar said dejectedly. "This will only push the prototype's production further back."

Walter nodded wearily.

"I know. Still, we have to do what we can," he replied, always the optimist. "We should get our men working on it right away. However, I do have one good piece of news."

Reimar looked up hopefully.

"I was just notified that the German Air Ministry (RLM) has agreed to the hiring of a test pilot for our program. His name is Erwin Ziller."

Originally their test pilot had been a highly touted Luftwaffe officer, Horst Kloster. Neither man had any idea why Kloster's name had been withdrawn.

"Excellent," noted Reimar. "I was getting a little worried that we would have to perform double or triple duty, doing all the administrative work, overseeing the design changes, as well as taking the test flights. Now then, let's start on those modifications. But when can we expect delivery of the engines?"

"When indeed, Reimar? Soon, I hope. Leave it to me."

⚔

Jack walked in the front door of the large administration building situated on the northeast corner of Beauvais Airfield. Built at the turn of the century, it had that modern, yet clearly French characteristic of the late Renaissance. Architecture had always fascinated him, even in small towns like Beauvais. Paris was a cornucopia of museums. There were literally a hundred cathedrals scattered about the capital, just waiting to be explored. Too bad there was a war on! Jack sighed, as he climbed the steps to the second floor and proceeded to Harwood's office at the end of the hall.

The colonel was already there. A no-nonsense man, Bill Harwood liked to get things out of the way quickly whenever he could. But that wasn't always possible. Rumor had it he was raised by a hard-nosed, goal-driven father, though his upbringing had been somewhat tempered by the caring and compassion of his mother.

The door was open, and the corporal seated outside at his desk glanced up and motioned for Jack to go right in. Occupied with mounds of paperwork, Harwood glanced up at the sound of footfall.

Jack thought he detected a slight wince in his superior's expression. Probably because here came another interruption to his busy schedule. Then again, Harwood had been the one to summon him.

"Ah, good of you to come, Swaggart," Harwood acknowledged, standing up. He greeted Jack with a firm handshake. "Close the door behind you, will you?"

Jack complied and returned to the desk, wondering if he should take a seat, though none had been offered.

"Ah, yes, please sit down," Harwood said at last. "Tea, coffee?"

"Coffee would be fine. Thank you, sir."

Jack seated himself and scrutinized the man's face, hoping to detect some sign as to what the meeting was all about. There was a knock, and a FANY came in with a tray laden with biscuits, cutlery, cups, and a thermos, which presumably held the promised coffee.

That was quick, Jack thought.

Harwood, never known for coming to the point right away, cleared his throat and stirred two sugar cubes into his coffee.

"So, how long have you been with our outfit?" he asked nonchalantly.

The question surprised Jack. "Umm, a little over a year, sir."

His superior nodded. "And everything going alright here?"

"Sure. All the comforts of home."

"Uh, right," Harwood replied, still getting used to American humor. "I know you boys have to put up with all sorts of inconveniences."

Jack wondered where this was going.

"Anyways, Jack, I might as well get to why I've called you here. I'd like to say this concerns some administrative matter or issue with aircraft parts, but I'm afraid it has nothing to do with that. It's personal."

"I'm not sure I follow—"

"No, nothing to do with your performance or leadership," he added a little hastily. Jack looked at him quizzically.

"It's concerning George Bridges."

"Bridges? The navigator in Stankowski's outfit?"

"One and the same," Harwood acknowledged.

Jack frowned, feeling a little annoyed. Sure, he knew George. Everyone did. George Bridges III, son of a US senator, Ivy League grad—and a loudmouth. To make matters worse, George had been gaining a reputation for bucking authority, handpicking assignments, and using his father's name and position when he couldn't get what he wanted.

Jack knew men like Bridges and had as little to do with them as possible.

He'd run into George at the officer's club not long ago and unintentionally became involved in a dispute. He couldn't exactly recall what had started it, but he had been annoyed at George's lack of compassion, especially his zeal for bombing—killing "Krauts," as the man liked to point out. Jack had advised him to keep his comments to himself, which hadn't gone over too well. George had become prissy and spouted off about Swaggart liking Germans too much.

Later, Jack realized he should have kept his mouth shut. All his well-intentioned comments only got George fired up, n the end, the discussion hadn't accomplished anything, leaving George angry and other men questioning Jack's loyalty which was nonsense.

"Bridges called on me the day before yesterday and complained about you, insinuating you aren't a patriot but a Nazi sympathiser."

Jack was shocked. Before he could reply, Bill silenced him with his outstretched hand.

"I'm just telling you what he said, Jack. Personally, I think it's a bunch of rubbish. We all know Bridges is all mouth and uses every opportunity to boast about his own accomplishments, not to mention his illustrious heritage. My concern isn't your loyalty. I know where you stand. It's the others—men who don't know you as well as I do.

Harwood continued. "You're a squadron leader, and I want them to give you the respect you're due. I sure as hell don't want to lose you out of some blown-out-of-proportion incident or barroom fracas only to have Bridges waiting in the wings. Do you catch my drift?"

Jack nodded, painfully aware of the implications. "Did Bridges make a formal complaint?"

"No, as a matter of fact he didn't; he's too clever for that. This is all informal."

"Anything else, sir?"

"No. Carry on. And Jack, watch your back. Bridges isn't the only one out there looking for quick advancement."

Jack nodded and picked up his forage cap. He saluted smartly and left the office, feeling irritated that he had been called in, but somehow relieved to have been given the head's up. He had to admit that Harwood was right; there was always someone ready to stab you in the back.

CHAPTER IV

The Horten Bomber

Captain James Buchanan, a Canadian attached to the office of the Special Operations (SO) branch in London, England, followed his boss, Colonel Gregory Bartsch, down the hall of a nondescript building to a room that was used for many things: interviews, staff briefings, and lunches with visiting dignitaries. Seated at the table was a man he'd met before, Major Phillip Lowell, of US Army, Intelligence Section.

Lowell proceeded to empty his briefcase, producing a dossier that was labeled with familiar, yet portentous words: TOP SECRET.

The major spread out a few typewritten sheets intermixed with handwritten notes.

"Colonel Bartsch," Lowell began, "as of yesterday afternoon we can confirm with reasonable certainty what we've suspected for some time: the Germans have not only been working on an aircraft capable of reaching the unattainable speed of six hundred miles per hour, but they appear to have a working prototype." He glanced at his notes. "They're calling it the Horten Ho 229." Lowell glanced up to make sure he had their full attention. He had.

"Not only that, but I've been told the prototype has flown successfully in test trials, and it's entirely possible they are close to starting production."

"Major, how is that possible?" Bartsch uttered in disbelief.

"Which part, sir? The information or how we obtained it?"

"Please, Phillip, let's dispense with all this formality," Bartsch implored. "Just call me Greg. All my officers do. I was referring to the validity of your source."

"Sure thing, sir, er … Greg." Lowell grinned. "I prefer it that way too. As I was saying, we stumbled onto this stuff quite by accident. Let me give you a little background. As you know, we routinely come into possession of all sorts of raw material and quite a bit from captured prisoners. By that, I mean that we interrogate German POWs, some of whom claim they have interesting and worthwhile tidbits for us. They all hope to gain favor, but their intel typically doesn't amount to very much. We listen to their stories, ask a few questions and reward them with Wrigley's gum or Hershey's chocolate."

Lowell took a look around and was greeted with suppressed laughter.

"This time we got lucky," he continued. "It seems there was a bit of a skirmish at one of the internment camps. Two Germans from some infantry outfit were going at it—fisticuffs and all that. One of the men had been assigned to an antitank unit against his will. If you recall, the Nazis have been desperate to find capable men and have resorted to cannibalizing factories and non-essential production sites."

Buchanan had heard much the same from other sources. Within the ranks of the German Command, a few realistic generals knew that the war was lost and had tried to implement an organized retreat, hoping to save as many lives as possible. They were focused on preserving a crumbling Fatherland.

"It seems that no matter where you turn, there's always some animosity within the ranks," said Lowell. "Anyway, two men got into a fight but were quickly separated. When one of our corporals led them to the solitary wing, one of the two combatants, speaking passable English, asked to meet with an officer privately. To make a long story short, this prisoner,

Walter Jüngheim, in exchange for better treatment, was willing to supply our side with what he claimed was vital military information."

Bartsch leaned forward. "And was it?"

The major's grin spread from ear to ear. "We hit the motherlode."

"Go on," the colonel encouraged a little less skeptically.

"Jüngheim, aside from being a soldier, is also a skilled carpenter and had been employed by an unknown and relatively new outfit, something called the *Horten Flugzeugwerke.* It's situated near a small town called—" He glanced down and consulted his notes. "A town called Gotha. He'd been there for about a year. It was a secret project that dealt with the manufacture of a revolutionary jet aircraft. But get this, the planes are made mostly out of wood, hence his expertise as a carpenter. He was one of a dozen workers employed at the facility, assembling the prototype, as well as fabricating two others."

Buchanan, who had kept his peace until now, couldn't contain his excitement. "You mean there's more than one?" he blurted out. "He didn't by any chance furnish you with any drawings?"

"A few," Lowell replied, rummaging in his briefcase. "Here, take a look."

Buchanan eyed the worn leather case with more than passing interest, wondering what sorts of gems the old satchel contained.

Lowell fished out several sheets of paper, with both Buchanan and Bartsch leaning forward in anticipation, like school boys who'd been handed marked exam papers by their schoolmaster.

What they saw was intriguing, no—breathtaking. They peered at the crude, hand-drawn sketches for several minutes without saying a word. Even the secretary glanced up, her writing hand poised.

There on the table, were several rough-drawn diagrams of a delta-wing aircraft. One of the sketches was taken from the side and showed a gray-colored warplane with tricycle landing gear and a bulbous nose topped with what resembled a Plexiglas canopy. The other diagram showed the aircraft from the front, looking head-on; the plane had twin-jet intakes, each one mounted within the wing, flanking the fuselage.

Buchanan was first to find his voice. "Is this for real, sir?" he asked looking up. "I mean, is this verifiable?"

"Real, yes. But verifiable?" questioned Lowell. "Hmm. That may take some doing."

"Well, this looks like something right out of a comic book, Phillip," Bartsch exclaimed. "It's like something Buck Rogers would dream up."

"Believe me, sir, you haven't been the first to suggest this is outlandish," Lowell assured him. "But the more we probed, the clearer the picture became. This man is either a clever manipulator, or a liar, or maybe, just as he claims, he's a craftsman who has collaborated with others in bringing a revolutionary design to fruition.

"Gentlemen, this aircraft has fulfilled—correction, is fulfilling—Göring's demand for an airplane capable of carrying a one-thousand-kilogram payload at the unreachable speed of one thousand kilometers per hour over a distance of one thousand kilometers."

Lowell surveyed the room before he continued.

"Yes, those were Göring's own specifications. If the numbers are anywhere near this man's claims, we need to move fast. This could change our whole strategic bombing campaign. Can you imagine what happens to the next flight of B-17 Flying Fortresses that run into ten or twenty of these swept-wing menaces? It would be nothing short of catastrophic."

Buchanan nodded sombrely. If it were true that this new aircraft could attain those projected numbers, the Allies had nothing to match it. They had nothing that could even come close.

"So far we've had to contend with the Messerschmitt Me 262 fighter," Bartsch noted. "Thank God there haven't been many to deal with. But this new bomber could dramatically change things."

"So where is this Gotha?" asked Buchanan.

Lowell consulted his notes again.

"The installation is called Göttingen. It's a small facility, about two hundred fifty kilometers southwest of Berlin."

Buchanan's mind returned to the matter at hand.

"Colonel, if I may, I'd like to consult with a colleague of mine, a fellow pilot, Captain Jack Swaggart. He's an American, a group captain, and has security clearance. He's flown a number of missions into the heart of Germany. As a serving frontline officer, he would certainly be interested and may be able to shed some light on this."

Bartsch glanced at Lowell, who nodded his approval. Both men then rose, signaling the end of the meeting. Speaking quietly, they exited the room.

Buchanan waited until the secretary had gathered her notes and then followed the two men out of the conference room. On the window, raindrops were slowly sliding down the glass, but his mind wasn't on the weather; he was thinking about the new German threat.

Will Hitler never stop? he thought to himself. *The deployment of V1 and V2 rockets wasn't good enough. Now he's going to resort to using formidable technology to thwart the Allied advance.*

Buchanan eventually left the building. Not used to carrying an umbrella, he did what most foreigners did: shield himself with whatever he had at hand—in this case, a newspaper—as he dashed down the steps. Dodging a turning Bentley, he crossed the street and made it to the tube station just before the rain intensified from a light rain to a full downpour.

╫

Andreas Bauman fingered the edge of the envelope with his left hand. And although there was no return address, he recognized the distinctive writing. It contained a letter from his girlfriend, Hilde, written perhaps two weeks ago but it had only reached him yesterday. The lingering trace of perfume strengthened his resolve to see her.

"I miss you so much," he read again, realizing how much he missed her too. The problem was that he had been stationed at Uphoven Airfield, while she worked in an office in Oranienburg.

How long has it been since we've been together? he mused. *It must have been on her mother's birthday, back in July.* Andreas had been planning on another visit. He was due some leave and wasn't going to take no for an answer. If that pompous Major von Glitz didn't grant it, he had resolved to go over his superior's head.

The sound of knocking on the door startled him. When he answered it, rather than seeing von Glitz, a friendly looking face poked his head inside.

"Reimar!" Andreas called out, acknowledging his friend and fellow pilot.

"It's good to see you too," Reimar Horten confirmed. "I just came back and heard what happened yesterday to Ziller. *Pech!* Anyone else, and the Luftwaffe would have been short one Messerschmitt—and a damn good fighter pilot too."

As the two men shook hands, Reimar spotted the blue notepaper in his friend's hand.

"From Hilde?" he asked.

"*Ja.* It came by post but only reached me this morning. She misses me terribly." Andreas smiled sheepishly. "Well, I miss her too."

"Uh huh." Reimar nodded, remembering the day when his own girlfriend, Matilde, had introduced Andreas to her friend, Hilde. Andreas had fallen for her, while Reimar had eventually moved on from Matilde.

Andreas carefully folded the letter, but before putting it away, he glanced back at his friend, debating whether to say what was on his mind.

Reimar beat him to it.

"I know that look," he said making him feel at ease. "Go ahead, Lieutenant, state your request."

Though still hesitant, Andreas decided to plod on. "You're flying back, to Oranienburg soon, aren't you?"

"Indeed, I am."

Reimar had recently gained prominence due to his secret design work for RLM. Despite his rank of captain, he now had the privilege of leaving town at a moment's notice to attend unspecified, often secret meetings. No one knew where they took place, or with whom.

It was rumored that Reimar and Walter had actually met with Göring and been awarded a prestigious contract. The two brothers had kept quiet about their work, only revealing that it was for the glory of the *Reich*.

"Coincidentally, I have room for one more," Reimar added. "I'm flying the new Dornier prototype. And you're coming with me."

He said it so matter-of-fact that Andreas had trouble believing it.

"Andreas, it's true. It's been arranged. I went over von Glitz's head and persuaded General Diesing to sanction it. You're no longer part of JG26. You've been transferred to JG44, effective immediately. You'll be stationed at a base near Oranienburg, where I suspect you'll have plenty of opportunity to see your little *frauchen*. Here are your orders. We leave in the morning."

✠

Buchanan, by now used to the subway system, caught the right train and exited the station ten minutes later close to his flat. He walked down the street, his mind already on the next day's meetings, when he heard the whine of sirens signaling only one thing—another air raid.

Buchanan looked up into the early evening sky and sensed something wasn't quite right. As he ran for the nearest bomb shelter, he thought it odd not to hear the typical whistling sound of falling bombs. Just then, there was a massive explosion nearby.

Exposed and unprepared, James was nearly knocked off his feet. He staggered and grabbed a nearby lamppost for support. His vision blurred and his ears rang from the bomb's concussion. Struggling to clear his head, he glanced down the street. Everyone seemed to be moving in slow motion.

Aside from the momentary lapse, he seemed to be unhurt.

Buchanan stood motionless, trying to regain his bearings while quietly listening for successive explosions. There were none. It dawned on him that it was likely an unmanned V1 bomb that had struck a building close by—too close for comfort.

Instead of going to the shelter, he walked to the site of the explosion to see if he could help. He saw what once must have been a three-storey apartment block, now reduced to two. The entire top level had been blown away, reduced to rubble. Broken glass and debris littered the street around him.

A wall had collapsed, showering a parked car with bricks and debris. It dawned on Buchanan that the car may have been occupied, and so he walked around to the driver's side. A gloved hand protruded from the window at a strange angle. As he got closer, he realized in horror that someone must be inside. There was no moaning, no calls for help.

Suddenly, fearful cries for help from further up the street distracted him. A nearby building was on fire, likely the result of a burst gas pipe. Decisively, he left the incapacitated passenger and darted into the block.

With nothing but a handkerchief covering his mouth, James gingerly climbed to the second floor, testing each board on the way. He tried the first door and found it locked. He stopped to listen for voices—there, down the hall. He raced to what he judged to be the middle and tried another door, which yielded. The room inside was in total disarray, and in a bizarre way, it vaguely reminded him of his boyhood home back in Winnipeg, Manitoba, where he used to play-fight with his younger brothers. He forced the memory to the back of his head.

In the corner, he spotted an ornate dresser that had fallen over, its drawers having spilled out, relinquishing its fine linen. Threatening to tarnish the material was thick, black smoke seeping under an adjacent door.

James stepped over a chair and began to lift a fallen lampshade when he spotted a stocking-clad leg. Clearing away more debris, he found a young girl, perhaps thirteen years old, wide-eyed and in shock. She mouthed something, but the words stuck in her throat.

As carefully as he could, Buchanan picked her up and retraced his steps out into the hallway. Sheltering the young victim with his trench coat, he raced down the hall and out of the burning building.

Hacking and coughing, he made it across the street and stopped to catch his breath. He sat down on a vacant bus stop bench and examined his young charge, still cradled in his arms. The girl's breathing was rapid but not out of control.

Her clear blue eyes peered at him expectantly. "Where's my mum?"

Buchanan surveyed the pandemonium around them, with people running and calling out to loved ones.

"I'm sorry, I don't know where your mother is. My name is James, James Buchanan; I'm a Canadian."

The briefest smile played on her pale lips. "Yes, that would explain your accent. I'm Katy."

A fire brigade, with sirens blaring, rounded the corner, accompanied by passersby running behind it. People came rushing out of a nearby bomb shelter, eager to check on the damage to their property, others willing to lend a helping hand.

Even though Katy was breathing normally, James decided to alert a matron and have her take over. Seeing the young child, the woman bee-lined for him and took charge of Katy until her mother could be located.

"Don't worry, sir," the kind woman replied, "we'll look after her."

⚓

"Sorry to trouble you again, Captain," Bill Harwood began without his usual preamble. He looked uncomfortable. "It's, uh … it has to do with matters back home. Your home."

Jack Swaggart had just entered the colonel's office—the third time this month—and he instinctively felt something was wrong.

Harwood picked up a sheet of paper from his desk. It appeared to be a telegram. "I'm afraid I have bad news for you, Swaggart. Here, take a look for yourself."

Jack felt his stomach churn, as he took the typewritten message from Harwood's outthrust hand and turned it over to read the few scant lines.

The message had been forwarded from London's War Office, but it stemmed from the United States. He'd seen many messages like this, all starting out with the usual introduction: "I regret to inform you …"

He braced himself, knowing it dealt with his family. His father, William Swaggart, had tragically died in a farming accident. There was a date, but no further details. It ended with condolences from the Secretary of War, Henry Stimson.

Jack tried to take it in. He'd received correspondence from his father only three weeks ago, wherein he proclaimed he was in good health. As it happened, it had been an accident, not a physical ailment like a heart attack. Farmers faced many hardships, not the least of which were accidents around the farmyard. But the fact his father had died, that he was all of a sudden gone? It was hard to digest, never mind accept.

"I'm sorry," Harwood said, his words almost sounding intrusive. "I wish I had more information, but that's all there is. Is there something I can do for you? You're welcome to use my personal telephone to call home." He glanced at the wall clock. It was 3:12 p.m. "That would make it shortly after eight in the morning back in the States, Washington time. Earlier still in North Dakota."

Jack nodded absently. "Yes, perhaps I'd like to place that call now." Harwood stood up, and gently placed his hand on Jack's shoulder.

"I'll arrange it with the switchboard," he said gently. "If you'll supply me with the number, I'll get one of the FANYs to call the overseas operator and put it through here the moment there's a connection."

"Thank you, sir."

Harwood left the office, gently closing the door behind him, leaving Jack alone with his thoughts.

CHAPTER V

A Pompous Mayor

Otto Saufman, deputy mayor of Oranienburg, reclined in his comfortable office chair as he gazed out the window. It was a great view, unobstructed, allowing him to take in the activity in the courtyard below. He had chosen this office not out of convenience, for he labored every day to climb the stairs to the second floor, but because its larger size gave him a feeling of importance and caressed his overinflated ego.

Saufman had moved into the mayor's office on short notice. "Hastily appropriated" would be more accurate. The mayor, the real *Bürgermeister*, had taken an unexpected leave of absence for health reasons, and naturally Saufman had wasted little time moving his belongings upstairs.

Not that he deserved it. He wasn't particularly bright and certainly no businessman. Saufman was fat, lazy—and worst of all, a womanizer. He was approaching fifty, was of average height, and had a growing beer belly.

But he had two things going for him: he was a member of the Nazi regime, and he knew how to manipulate people. He liked to observe the activity in the street below, often postponing non-political appointments so he could bask in his own importance, enjoying their discomfort and frustration in having to wait.

His regular secretary, Maria Kunz, was currently on maternity leave. Prior to her leaving, she had suggested a replacement: Hilde Augsberg, a friend. After having met the beautiful and single Hilde, Saufman wasted little time in appointing her as his interim secretary. To leave the impression of fairness, he interviewed two other qualified women, but since none matched Hilde's figure and dazzling smile, he limited the process to one afternoon of interviews.

Saufman had just sent Hilde out to purchase some fresh-baked buns at the nearby bakery and looked forward to watching her return across the square. He was becoming infatuated with the young woman, and it didn't seem to bother him. Married and the father of two grown children, Saufman was unhappy with many things, his wife included, and relished diversions where he could spice up his mundane existence.

So far, his personal wealth and his involvement with the Nazi party gave him a measure of satisfaction in his otherwise boring, regimented life. Due to his high standing in the party, Saufman was able to access items like real coffee, butter, chocolate, and even silk stockings—luxuries no average German could easily obtain.

At the regular party meetings, many were left to wonder how a buffoon like Saufman could attain such a lofty position. What they didn't realize was that Saufman's brother-in-law was related to Kurt von Rundstein, Himmler's second cousin. What Saufman couldn't accomplish because of his lack of business acumen, he made up for by employing backroom tactics like flattery, bribery, and threats.

Equally opportunistic but less well-connected party members had tried to sidestep or outmaneuver Saufman only to be left on the outside looking in, and in some cases, recipients of a late-night visit from the feared Gestapo.

Naturally, such unfortunates quickly came to respect Oranienburg's pompous deputy mayor. One thing was clear: Saufman wasn't to be ignored and certainly not to be underestimated.

Hilde Augsberg walked to the bakery, happy and relieved to be out of the office. She enjoyed the opportunity to breathe in the cool October air and soak in the sunshine.

It hadn't taken her long to figure out the truth of her boss' whims. She had only been employed in the mayor's office for three weeks when she had caught him looking sideways at her with lustful eyes. She now ignored his stares as much as possible and made sure she didn't dress provocatively.

It didn't help. Hilde was young, attractive, unmarried, and as far as her boss was concerned, highly desirable and available. He had tried getting her to go out to lunch with him, and thus far she had managed to put him off. She had come to realize he wasn't going to give up easily.

As she stood in line at the bakery to pay, all sorts of thoughts plagued her, not the least of which was whether she had made the right decision in accepting the job in the first place.

Without warning, she felt a man's strong hands around her slim waist and she was about to scream, thinking Saufman had slipped out of the office and managed to sneak up behind her.

She spun around, on the verge of calling out for help, when she recognized a familiar grin.

"Andreas!" she exclaimed, wrapping her arms around his neck. "When did you arrive?"

"Late last night," he managed, before peppering her with kisses. Seeing Andreas in the flesh made Hilde temporarily forget her troubles with the deputy mayor. She paid for the buns and they sauntered back to the office arm in arm.

"I caught a ride with Reimar," he volunteered.

"Ah, your old friend from flying school?"

"Right. He's no longer on active duty, though. He's involved in developing new concepts for the Luftwaffe. He's become sort of a whiz, he and his older brother, Walter."

"How come I've never heard of their work?"

Surprised at Hilde's interest, Andreas continued. "That's

because their designs are relatively new. Most of their work has been with gliders. I haven't seen much myself. My superior, General Galland, isn't too impressed with their conceptual work, but that hasn't diminished Reimar's enthusiasm."

"I see," she said absentmindedly, looking at a display in a nearby shop window. "So, how long will you be in town?"

"How long do you want me to stay?" he teased, softly stroking her cheek. They continued along in silence, each occupied with their own thoughts.

As they came into view of city hall, Andreas bid his farewell with a peck on her cheek and rushed off to catch a tram. Hilde watched him leave, then forced herself to think about her impending afternoon at the office. Before walking inside, she peered up and caught a glimpse of Saufman staring down from his office window. Had he seen Andreas? If he had, no doubt the old man would feel all sorts of jealousy.

⚔

"How much for that hat?" asked Lieutenant Horst Kloster, while browsing inside the little boutique in Oranienburg.

"A good choice, Herr *Oberleutnant*," replied the shopkeeper. "Forty-six Reichsmarks. Shall I box it up for you?"

The SS officer nodded imperceptibly, undaunted by the high price. As he turned over the money, his eyes caught movement outside the store window—a young woman walking past with a tall Luftwaffe officer. Although he didn't recognize the officer, Kloster noted the unique shoulder flash on his uniform signifying that he was part of the elite *Jagdgeschwader* 44 unit, a newly formed jet-fighter squadron that had been initiated by veteran Major Novotny.

Kloster had met the famous ace at a party function in Berlin earlier that year. Novotny was quite revered and stood in the same league as General Galland. Kloster couldn't help wondering where the young Luftwaffe officer was stationed.

Germany was retreating on all fronts, and that included

the Luftwaffe. From what he knew, the latest jet fighters required a lot more runway for takeoffs and landings, so not just any old airfield would do. Dismissing the thought, he scanned the crowd for the departing young woman. Truth be told, she was of far more interest to him than the man she accompanied.

Kloster caught a glimpse of her blue dress in the crowd ahead and stepped up his pace, not wanting to lose sight of the pretty fräulein. As he worked his way closer, he saw her enter the city hall.

Ah, he thought to himself, *she must be one of the clerks. I'll have to make her acquaintance someday—but not today; too many things to do.*

Smiling to himself, he turned and sauntered toward his parked car, a 1942 Daimler, with his package in hand.

The car was parked on a side street where he had disembarked thirty minutes earlier, but the driver, Helmut Köhler, was nowhere in sight.

Kloster swore softly, debating whether to go look for the man or just wait. But then he spotted his driver's fair hair overtop the headrest. Köhler's head moved ever so slightly, then slumped forward and with a jerk came up again.

He couldn't believe it. The man was dozing off in the front seat! Köhler had clearly ignored his instructions to stay awake and remain alert. *How could he be so stupid?* Horst thought, suppressing his anger. *And sleeping in daylight for all to see.*

Quietly, Kloster opened the rear door and slammed it, the sound reverberating through the car and startling the driver.

"Köhler!" Kloster shouted. "Wake up, you imbecile. Can't you see it's broad daylight?"

He leaned in through the open passenger window, fixing his gaze on the hapless chauffeur. Shocked, Köhler was left to squirm in his seat.

All blood seemed to have drained from Kloster's face, his nostrils flaring from the sudden intake of air. His eye color, once a pleasant gray, darkened and seemed to change into an ice-cold gray. And the mouth, only a moment ago smooth and genial, now contorted, as the upper lip twisted into a scowl, projecting a verisimilitude of his true inner self.

"What if a Gestapo buffoon should catch you sleeping on duty?" his menacing voice chided. "Do you think they'll merely shrug it off?"

Köhler seemed about to reply, his foolish words already forming on his lips. But Kloster wasn't finished.

"You damn fool!" the officer hissed as he drew his arm back and slapped the driver across the face. "They'll relish the opportunity to inform a superior who will then waste little time in calling my office—or worse, notify Schinkel directly. Is that what you want?"

"No, of course not, sir."

"I should hope not. Well?"

"I'm sorry, sir." He recovered quickly. "I must have dozed off. It won't happen again."

His left cheek still stinging from the rebuke, Köhler propelled into action, remembering his duty just in time. He opened his door and jumped out of the car, hurrying around to the back. He took a deep breath, the once threatening visage having retreated into shadow as he withdrew from the window. He opened the rear door for his superior.

Kloster grunted as he got in and placed the package on the seat beside him. He unfolded the newspaper he'd purchased and began perusing the headlines.

Köhler gently closed the rear door and returned to the front seat, preparing to get under way.

"Where to, sir?" Köhler ventured once he'd calmed his racing heart. "Back to the office?"

"No. I have an errand. Stop by at the mayor's office, the *rathaus*."

"*Jawohl, Herr Oberleutnant.*"

✠

Captain Jack Swaggart scanned the cloudy sky through the cockpit window. His flight of B-26 Marauders had dropped their ordinance on the railway yards situated on the west side of Berlin. The flack hadn't been too severe; he was thankful to get away unscathed. *Too easy,* he thought.

The day had promised to be a good one, weather-wise, but the soft white cumulus clouds had given way to layers of stratus, the once pleasant broken skyline changing to an inhospitable gray. A cold front was advancing faster than projected, threatening their return to France.

Jack glanced to his right and fixed his gaze on the bomber past his wingtip. He spotted his wingman, Lieutenant George Freeman, and was reassured by his presence.

"Free Spirit," Swaggart said, keying his mike. "Let's make a quick turn to the northwest so we can get away from this cold front before it overtakes us."

"You won't get any arguments from me, *Lucky Lady,*" Freeman replied quickly.

"Right. Let's steer, uh … 290 magnetic for now. Inform the rest, will you?"

"Yes, sir. I'll get my Louie on it," he said, referring to his co-pilot. "Do you think we can—?"

Freeman's words were cut short by a deafening explosion. It seemed like Jack's airplane stopped in its tracks. Smoke started to spread inside the fuselage making it impossible for him to see anything, much less gauge the extent of damage. One thing was certain: Jack's plane had been hit by antiaircraft fire.

Dammit, Jack thought. *We're hit and damaged who-knows-what, maybe the entire empennage—and judging from the sluggish feel of the control column, it's serious.*

"Holy crap, Jack!" Freeman called out. "You've lost nearly half of the left elevator assembly. The rest is probably hanging by a thread. It looks really bad."

"Thanks for the good news, George," Jack replied sarcastically, trying to keep the fear out of his voice. "That means we won't make it back. You'll have to take over and carry on without us."

"But, sir, we can't leave you behind."

Jack sighed. "I wish that were an option. Get into the 'soup' and out of this flak. You'll have to get the rest home. No arguments."

"Right. Good luck, Jack."

Just then, Jack remembered his front gunner, holed up in the nose of the aircraft. "*Lucky*, are you still alive down there?"

"Sure, sir," Frank Lerner replied. "But if it's all the same to you, I'd rather come up and ride it out up there." Lerner climbed up the access ladder and made himself as comfortable as possible behind the navigator's station.

Jack reduced their speed and fought the unstable controls of his crippled B-26 as they headed north, already losing altitude. Out of the corner of his eye he saw Freeman's plane, along with the other eight Marauders, continue their turn to port, settling on their prearranged course.

Foreboding settled in the pit of his stomach as he felt the weight of responsibility for his crew of seven sapping more strength from his already tired muscles.

Jack had no illusions about what awaited them. Assuming he could land the plane without killing them all, the next step would be evading the enemy. But they'd be crash-landing in the heart of Nazi Germany, so he didn't like their chances.

Jack surveyed the sky again. The once-broken cloud layer was now overcast. He could make out stratus and nimbostratus clouds, suggesting rain, maybe even freezing rain.

Damn, he cursed to himself. *That's all I need—ice forming on my wings.*

They had lots of fuel, though. Theoretically, as long as

the tail assembly held together, they could evade the German defences for a while. No sooner had the thought entered his mind than a red light started to flash on the instrument panel.

"We'll have to shut down the starboard engine," Boyer muttered from his co-pilot's position, loud enough for Jack to hear. "I can't cross-feed from the left tank. That flak must also have ruptured one of the fuel lines."

Steeling himself to look at the fuel gauges, Jack saw what he feared most: the indicator needle hovering just above empty. The starboard wing tank's fuel was virtually depleted, while the left held enough for maybe another thirty minutes of flying time. Maybe, if their luck held.

So much for assuming he had plenty of fuel. It certainly wasn't enough to get them back to France. He had to face the grim facts. The weather was encroaching on them from the northwest, they had little fuel left, and the airframe could start coming apart at any moment. Their only real option was to ditch somewhere in the countryside, preferably in a relatively flat meadow or a farmer's field and take their chances while he still had some semblance of control.

"What do you think, Chuck?" Jack asked Boyer.

"I'm with you, Jack. We've lost a thousand feet already. Let's get this fat lady on the ground as soon as we can."

The right engine sputtered, losing RPM, the result of being starved by the dwindling fuel supply. Jack's head snapped to the right and gazed at the offending engine. As if sensing criticism, it resumed its steady drone, yet both men knew they had minutes, perhaps seconds, before the inevitable occurred: engine failure.

As pilot-in-command, Jack had the final say and wasn't going to waste more time by fretting about things that were out of his control.

"Alright, Chuck, we don't have much time," Jack decided. "It's going to be unpleasant either way. I'll look for a decent field, while you alert the crew. We just might get lucky."

While Boyer extricated himself from his confining harness, Jack was all business, checking and rechecking the gauges while keeping the plane in the air. At the same time, he sought any place that could double as a makeshift landing field.

As if things couldn't get any worse, a Luftwaffe fighter appeared out of nowhere, the Me 109 bearing down on them from two o'clock high.

Jack braced himself for the hail of bullets, but strangely none came. The German fighter raced past the aircraft's nose, slightly above and to port, then banked sharply to make a tight turn so as to approach them from the rear.

Great, Jack thought, *he's coming around for a better shot.*

Once the fighter had completed its turn, the unthinkable happened. Instead of lining up the crippled bomber in his sights, the pilot reduced his speed and came alongside the B-26. Jack recognized it was a later version of the Me 109, the "Gustav," and could clearly make out the man's goggled face staring back at him.

The Luftwaffe pilot saluted smartly and then peeled off, disappearing into the low cloud cover.

Stunned, Jack sat motionless as he processed this unexpected act of chivalry. He breathed a sigh of relief, allowing his heart rate to slow. Of all the ugly stories he'd heard about Nazi cruelty, this act of mercy was an anomaly. Just then Boyer returned to the cockpit and resumed his seat. He glanced at Jack.

"Are you alright?" Chuck asked, sounding perplexed. "You look like you've seen a ghost."

"You're not far off the mark, Chuck. I'll tell you about it later. What's the damage like back there?"

"Well, the elevator assembly is pretty badly banged up. I'm surprised it hasn't broken off. The rudder has a few holes in it, but it should hold up a bit longer. A couple of cables have snapped, too. Our problem is the fuel, or lack of it. I can see it streaming out a hole in the starboard wing."

Jack nodded and mechanically checked the fuel gauges.

The port engine fuel gauge registered close to empty, while the starboard hovered just above the red line.

"How are the boys holding up?" he asked, momentarily taking his mind off his most pressing problem.

"Good, actually. Lerner's left arm was hit by shrapnel. Missed his head by inches. No wonder they call him Lucky! Fallon managed to bandage it up. The rest are fine."

"That's a relief. Okay, back to business. Let's see if we can find a place to set her down."

Both men scanned the vast countryside. There wasn't much snow yet, leaving many fields bare and exposed. They were down to two thousand feet, skirting the bottom of the clouds and losing altitude.

"Over there, Jack," Chuck said pointing to a landmark ahead. "Just past that farmstead. There's an unploughed field and I don't see any obstructions. I think we can make it."

"Alright. Say a prayer while we go over our emergency procedures."

Boyer nodded as he fished for the tattered manual underneath his seat.

⯓

Horst Kloster walked into his spacious apartment, located within sight of Berlin's fashionable Unter den Linden borough. He closed the door and removed his forage cap and uniform tunic, stowing them in the closet. He then removed his gleaming leather boots and placed them side by side next to the closet door.

Catching his reflection in the door's mirror, he stopped to appraise his profile. He was loath to admit he was narcissistic, but sometimes he couldn't help himself. He smiled at his own reflection.

He frowned, though, when the insignia on his collar caught his eye. It was a reminder that though he held the rank of lieutenant, he no longer served with the Luftwaffe.

His thoughts turned bitterly to the event not long ago that had changed the course of his career.

He'd met Lottie at a social event and had been captivated by her beauty. Regrettably, she was married to a Luftwaffe staff officer. Lonely and bored, she was looking for a little romance and Kloster had been all too eager to oblige.

He had allowed himself to succumb to her charm, and they'd spent a romantic weekend in the Austrian Alps, only to be exposed and betrayed by a nosy maid, leading to an embarrassing confrontation by Lottie's angry husband.

Kloster had to live with the consequences, though it could have been far worse. If it hadn't been for General Stückheim's intervention, he might have faced a court-martial. In the aftermath, Kloster had kept his rank, but he had lost his placement as test pilot.

He glared at the mirror, contemptuously scolding the image facing him. "How could I have been so stupid?" Next to the mirror, the Führer's portrait added insult to injury with a disapproving look.

Kloster, not a fan of self-recrimination, shrugged it off and walked over to the bureau. He retrieved a bottle of schnapps and poured a good measure to wash away the bad taste in his mouth.

As he sipped the smooth-tasting liquid, he casually observed the activity in the street below. A vendor was selling roasted chestnuts wrapped in paper bags. Two young boys were kicking around a bald and deflated soccer ball. A couple meandered down the sidewalk arm-in-arm.

Kloster froze. When the woman turned her head, laughing at something her male friend had said to her, he recognized her. It was the same young woman he'd seen previously in Oranienburg. He supposed they had ventured to Berlin for a brief excursion, perhaps attending a family function.

The man was tall and wore a brown fur-trimmed coat. Judging by his upright and well-paced gait, he was likely an officer or businessman. The more Kloster thought about it, the more it seemed to him that he recognized the man as well. Andreas Bauman. Even out of uniform, the man stood out.

A strange feeling worked itself up from Kloster's heart. Although he couldn't explain it, he felt perturbed. It surprised him. But then, was he jealous of Bauman or just feeling sorry for himself? He couldn't say.

Kloster retreated from the window, yet the sensation lingered. He sat on the divan and took another sip of schnapps. It tasted good and he allowed the golden liquid to linger on his tongue.

His attention was drawn back to the framed picture of the Führer. Though many had labelled their leader as cold and calculating, those were the qualities that appealed most to Kloster. He, too, could be opportunistic and calculating.

Kloster relegated his disappointment at leaving the Luftwaffe to the back of his mind, settling on a new objective. In his search, he'd learned the identity of the test pilot who had been selected to replace him: Erwin Ziller. The man presented a challenge but Kloster felt he could pull it off. Getting rid of Ziller would present an opportunity for Kloster to perhaps return to his former glory. Once again, he could become a prominent officer in the Luftwaffe.

Admittedly, he lacked one thing: a viable plan. *No matter,* he thought. *After all, I have time, ingenuity, and resources.* The lack of humility escaped him.

He toasted Ziller in absentia, grinning as he anticipated the havoc he would cause on the young pilot's career. He knew just the man he could involve in his little caper.

He picked up the telephone and asked to be connected to an outside number.

"Guten Morgen," the friendly operator answered. "How may I direct your call?"

"Bitte, Fräulein," Kloster replied, "I'd like to speak to Herr Saufman."

CHAPTER VI

Father Hiller

It had been a quiet October morning at The Church of St. Nicholas in Oranienburg. The parish priest, Alfred Hiller, had reviewed his homily and left the rectory. He felt optimistic, even invigorated, as he readied himself to take on the day. Despite the recent daylight bombings of Berlin, the German populace remained confident in their leader, the Führer, and refused to give in to the sentiment of some who declared the war was lost.

Hiller stopped in front of the beautiful stained-glass window overlooking the vestibule. Bright light, diffused and filtered by colored glass, cast a magnificent aura on the statue of St. Nicholas.

What could be more pleasing than that? he mused.

He slowly made his way to the confessional. It had two cubicles joined in the center by a third intended for the cleric. It allowed Hiller to alternate between the two sides when hearing confessions.

The curtain was open on the left side, but the one on the right had been drawn shut.

The priest glanced at his watch and saw it was 8:40 a.m.

An early riser, he thought. *I just hope it's not Frau Sonnenberg again. Can't she keep some of her complaints to herself? She pretends that she's confessing some minor sin when it's nothing more than disguised gossip about her neighbors.*

He sighed as he opened the door to the central cubicle and seated himself. He coughed discreetly to alert the parishioner he was at his station.

"Good morning, Father," a man's voice intoned. "Forgive me, for I have sinned."

Pleased that it wasn't Frau Sonnenberg, Hiller surveyed the man's profile. He was young, perhaps in his early thirties, and clean-shaven; lower-middle-class, probably a workman.

"Yes, my son," the priest encouraged. "What is it that's troubling you?"

"Well, Father, I … er, I mean I've spoken about things I wasn't supposed to. Secret things."

"Family secrets?"

"No, nothing like that. They're … work-related. I was in a local bar on Friday evening, and I guess I had one too many beers. We were all talking and laughing. One thing led to another, and not wanting to be left out, I told a joke about another man, an officer."

"That doesn't sound too bad. Was the officer there?"

"No, Father, but I should have stopped with the joke. I suppose I wanted to look important, to be noticed by my friends. I had overheard a conversation this officer had and I shared it with them."

"I see. And that disclosure was bad?" Hiller asked, hoping the man would open up.

"Well, if it gets back to him, it would be. He doesn't take kindly to being talked about behind his back."

Most men wouldn't, Hiller thought to himself. "Alright. You never mentioned his name, so I suppose—"

"I would rather not identify him, Father," the man blurted out.

"Very noble of you," Hiller nodded.

"I'm afraid I've already said too much, Father."

Hiller, now a little annoyed, had to remind himself that he was in the confessional to listen, not there to sound out a parishioner. He waited patiently, but the man offered nothing more. Either he was reluctant to elaborate—or worse, frightened.

"Well, the best you can do now is leave it with God. Say three Our Fathers, and in the future refrain from repeating private conversations in a beer hall."

"Yes, Father, I'll do that."

The man made the sign of the cross and quickly left the cubicle.

Hiller opened his confessional door just in time to see the man leaving. In the dim light, he was able to make out the man's features. He could have been mistaken but he thought it was Helmut Köhler, known to be a driver for senior members of the secret police.

How interesting, Hiller thought to himself.

As he walked past a pew, he thought he recognized another man, an infrequent visitor, on the verge of leaving.

"Ah, Herr Kolbe, is it?" Hiller said, smiling at the man. "How nice of you to stop by."

Fritz Kolbe, forty-five years old, going bald and diminutive in stature, was currently a resident of Potsdam. Formerly a minor government official, he had distinguished himself through his work ethic. If Hiller recalled correctly, his task was to sort through and appraise recent cables, then forward the most relevant ones to a high-ranking Nazi official who often had direct contact within Hitler's inner circle.

Curiously, Kolbe had never joined the Nazi party, even though becoming a party member would have ensured more recognition and future plum appointments. Perhaps he had his reasons.

Kolbe glanced up at the smiling priest towering above him and returned the greeting.

"You don't come here often," Hiller remarked, more out of curiosity than politeness.

"Sadly not, Father. My work at the Foreign Office keeps

me quite occupied, so I have little opportunity to get away. I just visited a sick friend and on impulse decided to drop by."

"Well, I hope she—"

"Umm, he—" Kolbe coughed, interrupting the priest.

"I'm sorry," Hiller apologized, "I shouldn't jump to conclusions."

Kolbe got up from the pew, smiled awkwardly, and crossed himself. The priest watched with interest as the man headed for the side door.

╬

Hilde paced in the foyer of her mother's house in Oranienburg, her face tense.

"Mother, I'm worried about Aunt Eva," Hilde began. "It's not like her not to call. When was the last time you heard from her?"

Gertrude Augsberg looked up from her knitting. "Let me see now. It was only last Thursday that she called. I'm sure she's fine. The phone lines are probably down again, that's all. If it'll make you feel better, I'll call her tonight. She's probably out right now."

Hilde smiled. "I'd like that. Thank you." She knew her mother cared as much about her own sister as she did.

Just then, they heard a knock on the door. Gertrude put away her knitting needles and got up to see who it was. It turned out to be a neighbor, and the two women became engrossed in conversation about food shortages.

Later that day, close to suppertime, Gertrude placed the call to her sister. The line connected right away, and when Eva answered Gertrude cupped the mouthpiece and, turning toward her daughter whispered, "See, there's nothing to worry about."

But no sooner had she spoken the words than her demeanor changed.

"You don't say," she continued. "I'm sorry to hear that,

Eva. What? Yes, I heard that cough. You poor dear. Alright, I'll let you go and perhaps Hilde can come see you tomorrow or the next day. Good night."

Gertrude turned to look at her daughter again.

"It seems you were right. She's been ill and didn't call so we wouldn't worry. It sounds like a bad cold. The poor thing is all by herself."

"I'll make arrangements to go visit her," Hilde replied. "I'll talk to Andreas about it tonight."

Over supper that evening, Hilde voiced her concern about visiting her aunt. Andreas agreed to help in whatever way he could. He thought he could persuade Reimar to let him use one of the base's chauffeurs to take Hilde on her excursion. He readily agreed that as long as he didn't need it for official business, Andreas was free to take it and the accompanying chauffeur.

⚜

After several days of frustration, Hilde finally managed to arrange the visit. They had initially planned to go on Sunday, but a sudden snowstorm made the road impassable for anything but a tank. Then Reimar's car was not available on Wednesday or Thursday, leaving only Friday, only to be told there was a fuel shortage. Friday turned into Saturday.

Gertrude called her sister on Friday evening, confirming her daughter's visit the following day. Although she had hoped to accompany her daughter, a persistent cold persuaded her not to go; she didn't want to infect Eva with another malady. Naturally Hilde was disappointed, but eventually had to accept her mother's decision.

Promptly at ten o'clock on a beautiful late October morning, a sleek black Mercedes pulled up outside the Augsberg home. Hilde had been pacing in front of the window, hoping Reimar Horten hadn't changed his mind about the use of his car. The sight of the automobile rekindled her spirits.

"*Mutti*, it's here," she called out excitedly to her mother. "Captain Horten kept his word."

Hilde hurriedly put on her gray winter coat and rushed to the door. She opened it expecting to see Reimar's personal chauffeur, Fritz Pfalz, a man she had seen once or twice. Instead, a tall officer, a lieutenant, smiled back at her.

"Guten Morgen," he smiled. "Fräulein Augsberg, isn't it?"

Composing herself, Hilde replied automatically. "Er … yes, how can I help you?"

"Well, perhaps I can help you. Isn't this yours?" he asked, holding out a small, wrapped package.

Hilde looked dumbfounded, but then recognized the wrapping. "Why it's the wrapping used by Frau Bresslauer at the Chanté boutique."

"Indeed," he replied. "Coincidentally, I was shopping there a few days ago, when the owner mentioned you were a frequent visitor. It seems you had left a package behind. I saw you leaving the shop, and naturally I offered to return it to you."

Hilde relaxed and smiled at the officer's gesture. "How kind of you, Herr Leu—"

"Please, my name is Kloster. Horst Kloster. It was no trouble. Perhaps I'll see you again, Fräulein."

He clicked the heels of his shiny leather boots, spun around like he was on a parade square, and headed for his waiting automobile where a uniformed corporal was waiting to close the door behind him.

After Kloster had left, Hilde stood motionless and watched the departing car, holding the package in her hands.

Her mother came up behind her and asked. "Who was that, dear?"

Hilde turned around and replied awkwardly. "An officer. He said his name was Kloster and he dropped off this package. I was at the boutique last week, on another errand for that pompous Saufman. I must have left it behind."

"But how did he know where you lived? I should imagine he would normally have dropped it off at city hall."

"That's exactly what I was thinking. Why would he drive all the way out here?"

They heard another vehicle drive up, adding to their consternation. They glanced at each other, thinking the same thing but not voicing it. *Did the lieutenant return?*

Hilde, still standing beside the partially open door, peered outside and spotted an older black Opel. The driver got out and approached the house. It wasn't Pfalz.

"Rudi!" Hilde called out excitedly, recognizing the familiar face as he exited the car. "What are you doing here?"

Rudi Schultz, a friend and former classmate, gave her a big grin. "You'll have to put up with me, Fräulein," he explained. "It seems Pfalz had been celebrating last night and overslept. He woke up with a splitting headache. He's lucky he still has a job. Anyway, he begged me to cover for him. Since I didn't have anything up today, I offered to help out."

"That's nice Rudi, but where did you get the uniform?" Although Rudi did work for the Wehrmacht in the capacity of a clerk, he wasn't a regular soldier, and thus not entitled to wear the uniform.

He grinned, as if reading her mind. "Don't worry Fräulein Augsberg. It's all taken care of. Pfalz loaned me his uniform and even paid me."

Hilde didn't look reassured. "I don't know, Rudi. What if—?"

"It's alright, Fräulein. Lieutenant Bauman knows all about it. So, are you ready?"

The mention of Andreas' name wiped away the last of her doubts.

"Give me two minutes," she called over her shoulder, running back into the house. She gathered up several items: a shawl and mittens her mother had knit for her aunt, a warm blanket, and a basket of food. She pecked her mother's cheek and headed outside, climbing into the backseat of the waiting car.

Rudi whistled to himself and looked forward to the outing as he pulled away from the house. He wasn't aware of the old motorcycle equipped with the sidecar that followed at a distance as he drove out of the city.

⚔

Otto Saufman wasn't happy. If asked, he wouldn't have been able to quite pinpoint the source of his foul mood. But one offense stood out above the others; he felt that he should be able to command more respect from his subordinates, his private secretary included.

He licked his lips, thinking back to the last time he had watched Hilde step onto a chair to retrieve a book he had purposefully left on a higher shelf. *Mmm*, he thought to himself, *she does have great legs.* He had to come up with a way to get more acquainted.

Regrettably for him, she was often in the company of her boyfriend, Lieutenant Andreas Bauman. If he were merely just another flyer, that wouldn't have presented much of a problem, but Bauman was in an elite JG unit, headed up by Major Navotny, a man who carried considerable influence with the Luftwaffe.

Saufman sighed and stepped away from the window, slumping into his reclining chair. He unlocked his desk's bottom drawer and fingered a handwritten note that had been delivered only that morning. One of his contacts in Berlin had come into possession of information that would prove to be invaluable to a man like Saufman. He licked his lips as he re-read the last two lines:

"It's quite certain that this young boy is one-quarter Jewish and not of Aryan lineage."

Saufman glanced at the name of the boy in question: Adam Rosenbaum. He was tempted to scoff, thinking Rosenbaum to be an ordinary German name. Yet Saufman's source—very reliable in such matters—had assured him this was not the case. Young Adam Rosenbaum was, none other than *Oberleutnant* Horst Kloster's nephew, and he actually went by the name, Adam Kloster.

Saufman glanced up and whistled, a wolfish grin spreading from ear to ear. Whereas Kloster had recently called upon him to ferret out dirt on a fellow officer—which Saufman was more than happy to accommodate—he now had a formidable advantage over Kloster and would use it to squeeze lots of Reichsmarks out of him.

Saufman picked up the phone and dialed a familiar number in Berlin. After three rings, a female operator picked up and asked who he would like to be connected with. *Hilde*, he thought, licking his lips.

"*Oberleutnant* Kloster, *bitte*," he replied.

"*Ja,* the lieutenant is in. Who shall I say is calling?"

"Herr Saufman, deputy-mayor of Oranienburg."

"Right away, your Worship."

Saufman smiled at the use of his formal title, imagining the expression on Kloster's face when he delivered this latest bit of news.

CHAPTER VII

Crash Landing

Jack Swaggart looked around at the carnage his crash-landing had caused. The bomber had ploughed a deep furrow in the farmer's field; the left wingtip demolished a wooden shed in the process. Jack could make out a few handheld implements strewn on the ground. Less than twenty feet away, an abandoned tractor faced-off with the nose of the airplane, as if daring it to advance. But unlike the old tractor, the Marauder would never see action again.

He thought back to the rough landing and vaguely remembered lowering the flaps. The rest was a blur. Jack said a quick prayer, thankful to be alive. He glanced to his right and was about to ask Boyer if he was okay, when he noticed his co-pilot was slumped forward. He reached out and touched Boyer's shoulder.

No response.

Frantically, Jack grabbed Chuck's left wrist and felt for a pulse. It was there—slow but steady. His friend was alive.

"Thank God," Jack mouthed in relief.

Suddenly excruciating pain shot through his right ankle. Judging from the intensity, he knew it must be badly sprained, perhaps even broken. Despite the pain, he manoeuvred himself to get a better look behind him. He spotted Ollie, his bombardier, still buckled into his seat but leaning back awkwardly.

"Ollie, how—?"

But the unnatural position of Ollie's head made him pause, the words sticking in his throat.

Jack tried to get up when the man's head turned unexpectedly. His heart lurched with relief—but then he realized it was nothing more than a result of the aircraft settling on the half-frozen field. Ollie's listless eyes stared back at him and Jack had to fight off the sickening feeling in his bowels.

Once Jack managed to get to his feet, he limped over and tenderly closed the airman's eyes. Nearby, Joe Rossi was slumped over his table and appeared to be breathing normally. He had probably been knocked out during the rough landing. But at least he hadn't been killed.

With relief, he heard moaning coming from the left gunner's position. Another man was alive.

"Lucky," he said as he approached Frank Lerner. "Are you okay?"

"Yea, sure, Cap," the gunner replied weakly. "Not one of your better landings, huh?"

"I know. It couldn't be helped." He peered down the fuselage corridor and, aside from some smoke and sparking wires, all he saw was darkness. No flames.

He couldn't see any of the other men—yet. "I'll go see about the rest of the crew."

Jack used a flashlight to guide his way down the narrow corridor. The last thing he wanted was to step on an injured airman who had been catapulted from his seat by the plane's impact.

The small beam of light found Romeo crumpled on the floor, moaning and holding his head. He'd received a deep gash to his forehead and was bleeding. Jack recalled seeing the first aid kit on the floor and turned around to retrieve it. He hastily unpacked the box and found some gauze and bandages.

He knelt down beside Romeo and propped him up into a sitting position. He held a compress pad against the wound.

"Keep this in place until we have time to get a better look at it," Jack offered.

Romeo nodded imperceptibly.

Jack worked his way down to the back and spotted Gregg Fallon getting up, gingerly placing his weight on his feet. The rear gunner seemed okay, with no sign of external bleeding.

"Shore," Jack called out to the him. "You—feeling alright?"

"Sure, Cap. Nothing broken."

"Good. Go check on Romeo. He's got a nasty cut to his forehead."

"Right, sir. I'll get right on it."

Jack slowly turned and hobbled back to the cockpit. The ankle didn't feel any better. The recent exertion had pumped more blood through the joint, causing further discomfort. When he reached the bombardier's station, he grabbed a nearby blanket and draped it over Ollie's body. Then he sunk down opposite him, trying to size up their situation.

He knew they were deep in enemy territory. His best guess was that they had come down about forty miles north of Berlin. Since they'd crashed due to fuel exhaustion, there was little fear of fire, and they would be warm as long as they stayed inside the plane and out of the cold north wind.

However, German search parties were another matter. Sooner or later, one was bound to turn up. He didn't relish the prospect of spending the rest of the war in a POW camp. But what could he do? He couldn't walk far, and he certainly didn't want to burden any of his men by slowing them down. The only viable solution was to let Boyer or Rossi take charge, depending on which was in better shape.

Jack noticed Joe begin to stir, as if having read his mind. He got up and shuffled over to the radio operator's cubicle. "Welcome to Germany, Joe. Bit of a rough ride, huh?"

"No kidding, Jack." He rubbed his eyes and stretched before looking around. "Is everybody okay?"

"Almost everyone." Jack looked away, unsure what to say. "Ollie didn't make it. I think he broke his neck. Chuck was also knocked out, but I think he'll come around. Romeo got a nasty cut, and I sprained my ankle. The rest are fine."

"Ah, shit," Joe managed.

Both men stared at the floor, not wanting to break the silence. There was nothing to say.

After a decent pause, Jack stood up. "I'd better check on Chuck."

He shuffled up to the cockpit, relieved to discover that Boyer had awoken.

"Well, good thing you're here," Chuck rasped. "I thought you guys had left me here all alone to fend off Jerry."

"I'm glad you're alive, Chuck. How do you feel?"

"Okay, I guess. I must have hit the instrument panel and got knocked out. What about the rest?"

Jack recounted the same report, including the bad news about their bombardier.

"That's a damned shame," Chuck managed, biting his lip. "The old boy deserved better."

"I know, but we have to face the facts. We're behind enemy lines, and Jerry's bound to come calling. We need to formulate a plan."

Boyer nodded. "Problem is," he said looking at Jack's foot, "you won't get far with that bum ankle."

⚜

Back in London, Bryan Shelby was already at his desk when James Buchanan arrived in the morning. As he entered, Buchanan involuntarily glanced up at the wall clock to see it was 7:15 a.m.

"Good morning, Shelby," Buchanan greeted as he hung up his wet trench coat. "Another fine day in store."

Shelby grinned, acknowledging the fact that most foreigners, especially the Americans—with the Canadians lumped in as well—weren't used to the constant barrage of rain.

"I've heard it's supposed to stop later this morning," Bryan quipped.

"Then maybe we'll get some sun."

"Yeah, sure. I wouldn't hold my breath," Buchanan said, making a face. "So, what have you managed to come up with so far?"

"Well, I was going over some preliminary numbers on the production estimates. Our man in Germany seems to be pretty sure. Too bad there aren't any accompanying photos. Still, if they manage to manufacture more of those Me 262s, we're going to be in trouble. Although we're getting more P-51s from the Americans, the Mustang is no match for the speed of that new fighter. That Mess—er, Messer—what's the designer's name again?"

"Willy Messerschmitt."

"Right. He sure came up with a brilliant design. It would be something if we could get our hands on one of those planes."

"You can always pray." Buchanan sidled up to Shelby's desk and picked up one of the documents.

"Alright. I'm going to see if I can reach my old friend, Jack Swaggart." He picked up the telephone and issued instructions to the operator, indicating that he wished to speak to the commanding officer at Beauvais Field in France.

Buchanan was still examining the sketches when the operator rang back. She asked him to wait, while he was connected. But rather than Swaggart's voice, he was greeted by an unfamiliar Scottish brogue.

"This is James Buchanan," he said. "I wished to speak to Captain Jack Swaggart."

There was a brief pause before the Scot, one Lieutenant McTaggart, advised him that Swaggart's aircraft hadn't returned from its latest bombing run. He apologized for not having more information.

Buchanan automatically thanked him and clutched the receiver, the gravity of the man's words sinking in. He stood there, unmovable, as he cradled the phone.

"James, what's wrong?" Shelby asked.

Buchanan finally glanced at his friend; his concern evident.

"Jack's plane didn't make it back last night. I'm told it's overdue, meaning it probably had to ditch. Or worse, it was shot down. They won't release the information right away, certainly not over the phone."

"I'm sorry."

Buchanan nodded, not sure what else he could say or who he could confide in.

╬

Hilde Augsberg enjoyed the car ride, despite the cloudy morning. It was good to get out of the city. As she watched the passing scenery, she thought about the upcoming visit with her Aunt Eva. It had been too long since they had seen each other.

They had just passed the village of Liebenwalde and now found themselves in the open countryside on the way to Zehdenick. The fields and patches of forest were a welcome sight, beckoning them to stop. Hilde thought back to a happier time when she had stopped somewhere in the area for a picnic lunch. She recalled the peaceful scene: she and Andreas sitting on a bright checkered blanket, sipping Zinfandel as Andreas regaled her with tales of his flying sorties.

The combination of pleasant memories and the steady rhythm lulled her into a trance-like state.

"Fräulein Augsberg," Rudi interrupted. "There's smoke up ahead."

As the car crested a hill, they could plainly see smoke coming from the vicinity of some sort of man-made structure, perhaps a barn or shed in the middle of a farmer's field.

Hilde paid closer attention as they drew near. She was able to make out a wreck, as well as debris from a downed aircraft.

"Rudi, it must have crashed," she said excitedly. "We need to stop and offer what assistance we can."

Rudi glanced at her in the rear-view mirror, not at all pleased with the prospect of stopping.

"But surely the Luftwaffe is aware by now that one of their planes has crashed and will send their people to check it out."

"I'm sure they will, Rudi, but that's no reason for us to just drive past. Someone may be badly hurt. I insist we stop."

Rudi shrugged his shoulders. "Of course, Fräulein. I suppose there might even be a reward."

The car slowed and they turned onto a dirt track that would lead them up to the barn. As they approached, Hilde could see that the crash-landing had virtually obliterated the plane's markings.

Once Rudi had come to a stop, Hilde wanted to get a closer look. She scrambled out, not waiting for Rudi to open the door and hurried toward the scene.

She nearly collided with a uniformed man who was doing his best to hobble out the barn's open door. He seemed just as startled to see Hilde as she was to see him. Hilde instantly liked what she saw in his soft, brown eyes. In fact, his solid facial features suggested a man used to giving orders, though not in a take-charge-no-matter-what kind of way.

She peered at the soldier's peaked cap and leather flying jacket and, for the first time noticed something different, something—she didn't quite know what. Then it dawned on her. There was no cross or swastika; in their place on the lapel were two shiny silver bars.

Recognition dawned on her. This was an American airman.

Just then Rudi rounded the corner, calling her name. He stopped dead in his tracks, recoiling not so much at the appearance of the uniformed officer, but by the pistol in the man's right hand.

"Halt!" the American officer called out.

"Nicht schießen!" a startled Rudi managed, slowly raising his hands in the air.

Hilde, no less startled, found her voice and appraised the armed aviator.

"Bitte, Herr Kapitän. We're not with the military," Hilde pleaded.

The American looked at her questioningly, unconvinced. He didn't budge, and kept his pistol aimed at Rudi. Were it not for the seriousness of the situation, Hilde would have laughed aloud, realizing her stupidity. Rudi was wearing his friend's uniform: a German uniform.

She tried again, this time in fairly fluent English.

"He may be wearing a German uniform," she explained pointing to Rudi, "but Rudi is not with the military. He's just my driver. Do you understand?"

The American smiled. "I most certainly do. But is that really true, Fräulein?"

Hilde frowned. She noticed the way the officer was supporting his right ankle and realized he must be in pain. She quickly deduced that he had likely sustained an injury in the crash.

"You're injured, Captain," she replied. "Please, allow me to help. We're not here to detain you."

Whether it was the familiarity of hearing her speak English, the kindness of her entreaty, or simply the appeal in her eyes, the American nodded and lowered his pistol.

She smiled and pointed to a nearby wooden crate, motioning for the officer to take a seat.

"My name is Hilde," she said. "Hilde Augsberg. And this is my friend, Rudi Schultz."

Rudi had located a second crate and dragged it over, allowing Hilde to take a seat opposite the officer.

"Howdy!" Rudi replied with a smile, choosing to remain standing.

Jack glanced at him quizzically but kept a neutral face.

"Captain Jack Swaggart, United States Army Air Force," he said at last.

Hilde motioned towards the downed aircraft. "And that must be your airplane."

"Umm—that's right, what's left of her. We named her *Lucky Lady*. We had just completed our bombing run, when flak damaged her tail." He glanced at the ground, perhaps gauging how much he should reveal. "You see, we had no choice but to ditch. One of my men died in the crash," Jack added, biting his lower lip.

"I'm sorry," Hilde replied, surprised by his vulnerability. She actually felt sorry for him. Curiously, a recent memory washed over her and it seemed as if time stood still.

She had been with her mother, having taken the train to Berlin to meet friends and do some shopping. They had barely left the station when the air raid sirens went off.

Trapped outside, the two women hunkered down in the entrance of a shop. Fortunately, the incoming bombs were destined for a ball-bearing factory and posed no immediate danger to them. After the wail of the nearby siren had died, Hilde and her mother cautiously emerged from their place of refuge.

In the aftermath, Hilde viewed the surroundings, trying to get her bearings, when suddenly a large bomber came into view overhead. One of the engines was on fire and part of its right wing had been sheared off. Small debris was separating from the plane as it spun out of control, losing altitude. She noticed small objects separate from the aircraft—but they weren't objects.

Within seconds, the first one seemed to elongate and grow in size, like a butterfly escaped from its cocoon, quickly transforming into a bright, white covering—a parachute.

The airman, his body rolled up in a tight ball, had pulled his chute's ripcord once he was clear of the doomed bomber, thus releasing himself from its confinement. The other parachutists immediately followed suit.

Mesmerized, Hilde watched as four small white plumes descended in unrehearsed unison. She briefly wondered where they might land and if they were prepared to face an inhospitable, bitter enemy.

However, fate hadn't prepared her for what she was about to witness.

Emerging from the broken cloud layer, a German fighter promptly appeared. Hilde was able to tell that it was one of the newer planes, signified by its yellow cowling. Its pilot, perhaps the same one who had brought down the bomber, executed a sweeping turn and, rather than follow the descending bomber for the coup de grâce, made a beeline for the four parachutes.

"Dear God, no!" Hilde cupped her mouth with her hands and, like her mother, voiced words that barely escaped her throat.

In horrified disbelief, the two women witnessed the murder of four Allied airmen that day. Though they had escaped their doomed plane, they were now completely helpless in the sights of their German executioner.

Hilde heard the deadly cannon-fire and as soon as it started it was all over. The bullet-riddled bodies of the dead airmen descended uncontrollably. The first parachutist collided roughly with the metal awning of the shop that only moments ago had provided shelter. The impact whipped him around and against the store's plate glass window, shattering it with a loud crash.

Unable to bear watching any further, Hilde turned her face from the horrific scene. In that instant, she felt utter grief and recoiled at what it meant to be German, shocked to have witnessed such a brutal act, committed by an officer of the revered Luftwaffe.

The two women embraced, hoping to console each other at what they'd witnessed. Nothing could have prepared them for such an event. With tears streaming down her cheeks, Hilde fought to compose herself and steeled herself to leave this place and face the rest of the day. Arm in arm, the women had stumbled away from the scene.

"Fräulein?"

The American's voice brought her back to the present.

"Ah—and the rest of your men?" Hilde's words tumbled out as she tried to concentrate on the matters at hand. Seeing the wariness return to his expression, she quickly added, "I only want to help. That is why we stopped, *ja?*"

"The rest left without me, a few minutes ago. They didn't want to leave, but I insisted that they go. I would only slow them down, you see."

She nodded thoughtfully.

And then it came to her. Here was a chance for her to help, to perhaps expunge the memory of that senseless act she had witnessed. Caught up in the moment, Hilde didn't think what consequences might come as a result of her actions. After all, she was about to help the enemy. Instead, her intuition propelled her into action.

"Captain, how can we help?" she asked, as she removed her gloves.

He hadn't expected that. "Help me, an American?"

"*Ja.* Perhaps it's hard for you to understand. But I've witnessed atrocities committed by my own people. I really do want to help."

It was a strange sensation she felt. Perhaps her willingness to help stemmed from an inner compulsion, in some way hoping to atone for the deaths of the airmen. Yes, part of it was a desire for atonement, but another part of it had to be with her need to stand up for what was right. And to Hilde, part of standing up was doing what she could, rather than simply arguing over the merits.

She thought back to the day after the harrowing Berlin scene, when she had the opportunity to discuss it with Andreas. She had fallen into his arms as the whole ordeal spilled out of her. His comforting words helped and had provided some consolation, as much as she could be consoled.

But she knew his profession and that his job involved patrolling the skies over the capital. Deep down, she had hoped he didn't share any complicity in that despicable murder.

Hilde didn't pursue the subject further, but if she had she would have realized that her attitude toward the war, toward the air campaign, was changing. Like it or not, Andreas was part of the Luftwaffe. But then, later, she had felt something within her, something intangible, as if she were distancing herself from him. It was no more than an impression and she had been reluctant to dismiss it.

Jack nodded, not wanting to reject his new-found benefactor.

"Well, my ankle is badly sprained, probably broken," he offered. "A tensor bandage would help."

At last, here was an opportunity to be useful in a small yet tangible way. Armed with new resolve, Hilde turned to face her driver. "Rudi, please go to the car and check the trunk for a first aid kit. Failing that, bring anything we could use as a bandage."

Rudi, who had been leaning against the wooden barn door, promptly came alive and, without saying a word, disappeared behind the barn.

"You see, Captain, he's *really* not a soldier," Hilde assured Jack. "The car is borrowed, as is the uniform. It helps if we get stopped. You see, not many German civilians have use of a private automobile these days."

"I can see that you're quite resourceful."

"Don't worry, Captain. I don't intend to leave you stranded. We'll be back in the morning. I promise."

Out of the corner of her eye, she caught him glancing down at her right hand—at her finger. She pretended not to notice. European tradition held that a wedding band adorned the third finger of the right hand. A wistful smile slowly spread across his face but was quickly replaced by a grimace, as new pain shot through his injured ankle.

CHAPTER VIII

On the Run

Charles Boyer, now in charge of the airmen, checked his compass and looked to the northeast. He had suggested looking for help at the nearby farmhouse, but Jack had talked him out of it, citing that it was much too risky.

In the end, Boyer and Rossi decided to head toward the small forest. They still had several hours of daylight, and with the small number of rations they'd retrieved from the airplane they had a chance of surviving one or two days without having to scrounge for food. They were relatively unhurt, save for Romeo's cut. Boyer, who had suffered a mild concussion, now tried to shrug it off.

That was the good news. As for the bad, none of them knew more than five words in German and they had only three pistols and five magazines between them, barely enough to keep a few wolves at bay, much less a unit of German troops.

"Alright men," Chuck said. "Lucky, you help Romeo, Shore will fall in behind you both, with Lieutenant Rossi taking up the rear. Let's try to make that forest before Jerry shows up.

Shore sighed. "So, this is why we signed up with the Air Force, so we can hoof it when we run out of gas. We should have stopped for gas back in Berlin."

They plodded on through the field and before long

reached the edge of the forest. It wasn't the dense foliage Boyer was accustomed to back home, but rather a scattering of fir trees. At least it was enough to keep them hidden. They marched on without speaking, each man occupied with his own thoughts. Boyer's musings however, drifted back to the man they had been forced to leave behind.

Will Jack make it? God alone knows.

Eventually they came to a clearing, and spotted a small shack nestled among the trees. It probably served as shelter for local hunters. They quickened their pace and made a bee-line for the small structure. Boyer cautiously advanced the last few yards, motioning the others to hold off while he checked it out. He walked around the structure looking for footprints or other signs of life. Not finding any, he approached the front door with his pistol drawn for good measure.

Gingerly, he opened the wooden door and peered inside. Empty. Relieved, he called over his shoulder for the rest to follow. It was as he had surmised, a shack used by the locals, perhaps during inclement weather. In any event, it seemed perfect for their little troop.

He scanned the interior. It contained a small table with two chairs near the door, with a rough-hewn bed in the corner. The bonus was a small stove with piping that vented through the roof. Boyer instructed Romeo and Lucky to look for firewood but to remain in the immediate vicinity.

Twenty minutes later, and with daylight fading, the men were either seated or stretched out on the floor, eating their meagre rations, while the little stove cast warmth. They wouldn't have to spend the night outdoors after all.

The driver of the BMW motorcycle lowered his binoculars and watched the black Opel turn off the highway and head down the dirt road. Feldwebel Wilhelm Vogel had been following the vehicle ever since its driver had picked up its female passenger back in Oranienburg. Vogel too had seen the smoke rising near the barn, and he had correctly surmised that it was coming from the wreck of the American bomber.

Attired in a black overcoat that protected him from the wind, he didn't look like a typical soldier. He had a beak-like nose and thin, bloodless lips which he tried to hide through a well-groomed moustache. But what really stood out were his cold black eyes. His penetrating gaze spoke of an inner longing, of a determination most men wouldn't have attributed to him.

Vogel, formerly a sergeant in the *Wehrmacht*, had been promoted and recommended to join the Gestapo. Seizing the opportunity, he'd found himself working for Lieutenant Horst Kloster. Vogel was no fool and quickly realized that the way to impress men like Kloster was by obtaining results, not by bootlicking.

Having been entrusted to follow Rudi Schultz, he saw it as an opportunity to distinguish himself. The same could be said for his escort, Kurt Weber.

Vogel thought it wise not to follow the car to the barn. Instead, he kept his distance, parking behind a tree and out of view of anyone looking back his way.

"Kurt," he called to his *kamerad*, who was surveying the scene. "Use your radio to monitor the local army frequency and see if the command post at Liebenwalde has received reports of an American bomber crashing near here. If they have, you can bet a truck is underway to round up any survivors."

Vogel watched as Weber manipulated the frequency control on his portable radio set. "Herr Feldwebel, our troops are coming," Weber reported back. "They should be here in about fifteen to twenty minutes. A Lieutenant Zonder is leading them."

Vogel nodded, thinking about what to do next. Rudi Schultz had turned down this track and should have returned by now.

The fact he hadn't done so suggested he and his passenger had encountered someone. He picked up the binoculars again and was surprised at what he saw. Near the far side of the barn, a man in a German army uniform was speaking to what appeared to be a foreign soldier. Perhaps an American soldier.

Vogel rubbed his eyes and peered through the lenses again. As he adjusted the focus, he made out the German's features, leaving little doubt he was looking at Rudi Schultz. The enemy airman's face wasn't visible, but his peaked cap and flight jacket made it abundantly clear he was either the pilot or co-pilot.

What is Schultz doing talking to an American pilot? he thought. Vogel had to make up his mind quickly. He doubted he had the authority to take any prisoners back for questioning. No, he had better just make a detailed report and brief his superior at an opportune time.

He waited long enough to see that the American didn't get into the vehicle with Rudi, and then he watched as the Opel headed back to the main road and headed north, presumably towards Zehdenick.

Vogel waited another minute, to make sure Schultz didn't change his mind and come back.

"I know what you're thinking, Kurt," Vogel said once his partner returned. "I'd like nothing better than to go there myself and round up the Americans. But there are only two of us, and we might be outnumbered. We'd better wait for our troops to show up. I'll brief Lieutenant Kloster when we get back."

Without waiting for a response, Vogel started up the motorcycle and donned his goggles. He slowly backed the motorbike from the confines of the trees and, once clear, turned onto the main road and headed back to Oranienburg.

╬

Back near the barn, Jack lowered his binoculars, evaluating what he'd just seen. Although the men on the motorbike weren't in uniform, it was possible they were plainclothes policemen, or worse, Gestapo agents.

The first man, the one with a beak-like nose and moustache, appeared to have been the one in charge. Jack reasoned they must have been alerted to the crash. Perhaps they'd even observed the crash-landing. And they almost certainly had witnessed the encounter with the man and woman in the Opel. Without a doubt, they would be reporting the encounter to the authorities.

Jack made a mental note to inform Fräulein Augsberg and her driver of the danger awaiting them. For now, his main task was to make himself scarce.

He hobbled over to the tractor, covering up his tracks as well as he could. He settled himself in behind the large rear tire, hidden from view by discarded machinery. He took out the thermos of coffee and sandwiches left behind by the young German woman.

He knew the German troops would search the aircraft, barn, and immediate area. The fact that his crew had left their bombardier in the plane and not buried him should help with the deception—implying they had all left in a hurry. He had agonized over leaving his friend in the plane, but what choice did he really have? Hopefully the Germans would concentrate on the tracks left by his crew.

Now, if they brought dogs, his little ruse would end quickly enough. He tried not to think too much about what might happen if he were captured. He offered up a quick prayer for Boyer and his men, hoping they were putting distance between themselves and the pursuing Germans.

⚔

Rudi slowed down and left ample room to pass the tractor and hay wagon ahead of them on the narrow road. Once he was past, he sped up again and grinned as the car picked up speed. He tried not to think of the implications of helping the American pilot.

He spotted a sign advising him they were only three kilometers from Zehdenick. It turned out to be a quiet village, seemingly unmolested by the ravages of war. But Rudi knew that wasn't the case; although the village hadn't been bombed—there had been no reason to fortify it since there weren't any military bases or industrial buildings nearby—everyone in Germany suffered from the shortages, these villagers included.

Hilde supplied Rudi with instructions from the back seat, and in short order he had pulled up to an old stone building with an ornate sign out front bearing number 43.

"This is it, Rudi," Hilde exclaimed. "Remember, not a word to my aunt about the American, *ja?*"

"Of course, Fräulein."

She climbed out the back before Rudi could open the door for her. Hilde walked up to the front entrance. She didn't even get a chance to knock before the door was opened by a middle-aged woman, her face beaming with genuine delight.

Slightly older than her sister Gertrude, Eva Poller was the taller of the two, with a trim figure that was still capable of catching a soldier's eye. Her face, though pale from her recent sickness, radiated at the sight of her niece. She was wearing a red dress, one that was still considered fashionable in Berlin. She had even managed to apply a trace of makeup.

"Hilde, my dear," she said happily, wrapping her arms around her niece, "It's so good to see you."

"It's good to see you too, dear aunt." Hilde took in the sweet aroma of baking that drifted toward her. "This is my driver, Rudi Schultz, compliments of Lieutenant Bauman."

Frau Poller nodded politely at the escort and, after hanging up their coats, ushered both inside her kitchen for a light lunch of salami, Swiss cheese, and fresh-baked bread. The meal was augmented by a sweet sherry that Eva had been saving for such an occasion.

Rudi eventually became bored of listening to the women's gossip and excused himself, explaining that he wanted to get some air. He retrieved his coat, sauntered down the street, and had no difficulty in finding the local pub. Though the lights were dimmed, the raucous noise confirmed its location. Inside, several older men sat at a table, playing a game of cards, laughing in turn. Rudi nodded towards them and had barely sat at an empty spot before several boisterous soldiers came in and seated themselves nearby. He had no wish to take part in their conversation and occupied himself with a local newspaper, yet he couldn't help overhearing the emerging discussion.

"I'm spitting mad," one of them said. "I had a date lined up for tonight, and now we have to get ready to comb the countryside for some downed American flyers."

"What's so urgent?" another piped up. "They're probably holed up in a farmer's barn, trying to keep warm."

"I agree with you, Hans. They won't be going far. They aren't foolish enough to spend a cold night outside. Tomorrow morning, some farmer will spot them and turn them in."

"Exactly, Fritz, only our Lieutenant Zonder has other ideas. I guess he's trying to impress his superiors."

"Those Yankees probably bombed one of our cities before crashing. Serves them right, *nicht?*" He checked around for agreement and got a few nods. "So then, let me tell you about Gretel. She's the one who likes men who—"

The speaker lowered his voice, the boast clearly meant only for those at his table. As if on cue, his four companions erupted in boisterous laughter.

Rudi quietly got up and paid the innkeeper for his beer.

As he walked out the door, he heard the same soldier defend himself: "Honestly, Willie, that's what she said!" More laughter followed.

Rudi walked back to the house, finding that a plump woman—a neighbor as it turned out—had joined the women. He nodded politely at her and seated himself in the corner of the kitchen. He sighed and once again picked up the discarded newspaper. It was going to be a long evening.

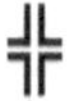

Jack had dozed off, but he awoke to a relatively quiet countryside. He glanced at his wristwatch and was shocked to find that only twenty-five minutes had elapsed. The pain in his right ankle had brought him out of his slumber. He bent down and touched his foot, relieved to find that the swelling hadn't gotten worse. Out of habit, he removed a stick of Wrigley's from his flying jacket and popped it in his mouth. As he was savoring the taste, he reflected on the plucky young woman, grateful for her help.

Somewhat protected from the cold wind, he glanced up from his hiding place at the sound of a truck engine in the distance and realized it was getting louder. *So, they're coming after all*, he thought. *Those Krauts don't waste any time.* Even though smoke was no longer rising from the wreckage, the searchers had little difficulty in locating the crash site.

In no time at all, a *Kübelwagen*, a small military car, pulled up near the barn, closely followed by a large truck. Jack listened as instructions were shouted; men jumped from the truck and busied themselves following orders. He also listened for the sound of barking dogs and, to his relief, didn't hear anything.

The officer in charge arranged for a systematic search of the area, assigning several men to scour the barn while he led others in investigating the downed bomber. Jack watched the soldiers go into the aircraft, then emerge a short time later carrying Ollie's covered body on a makeshift stretcher towards their troop transport. A part of Jack was grateful that they hadn't left his body inside the plane, becoming an invitation to carrion, even wild dogs on the prowl.

Just then he heard an excited soldier alert his superior that he'd found something.

Jack listened as the lieutenant and several men headed over to where the soldier had called from. Judging from the direction, it was likely they had discovered his crew's tracks.

As the soldiers discussed their find, the officer stepped back a few paces and came into Jack's line of sight. He seemed to be satisfied that the survivors, save the one casualty, had all headed northeast.

The lieutenant called for the rest of the soldiers to join him in a semicircle where he outlined his orders.

Although Jack could hear every word, his limited knowledge of German, coupled with the local vernacular, didn't allow him to grasp the full meaning of what was being planned.

After a few minutes, four soldiers marched off in double time, following the departed airmen's tracks. The rest headed for the barn. Although Jack couldn't see them, he guessed that the officer had returned to his scout vehicle, while the rest of the soldiers climbed back into the truck. He heard both vehicles start up and then drive toward the highway, heading north.

Not to be fooled, Jack remained hidden, just in case a sentry had been left behind. After about twenty minutes, and not finding the slightest indication of activity, Jack left his shelter and hobbled toward the barn. He carefully peered around the corner and was relieved to find that all was quiet, with no soldiers lurking nearby.

He was about to head for the open barn door when he felt a gentle hand on his shoulder. Forgetting about his sprained ankle, he spun around and fumbled for the pistol he had earlier tucked into his waistband.

Fear flooded over him like a tidal wave, but then it subsided just as quickly. Instead of facing a uniformed soldier, Jack found himself face to face with a boy of no more than fifteen, dressed in shabby clothes.

The youth was tall for his age, thin and wearing a creased jacket, crumpled corduroy pants, and worn leather shoes. Jack got the distinct impression he had probably slept in his clothes.

Jack's instinct told him he wasn't a farmhand and didn't belong to the family that owned this land. Not sensing danger, he left the pistol tucked in his pants and scrutinized the young man in front of him.

"Don't worry, I'm not with them," said the boy. "I mean the Germans, Captain."

Jack was left nearly speechless, not so much at being surprised, but by the young man's use of English.

"Who are you?" Jack managed. "What are you doing here?"

"I should ask you the same, sir," the boy replied, unimpressed. "But then, you're the one wearing a pilot's leather jacket. My name is William Sochalski. I'm a Jew."

Jack took in the news. "Jack Swaggart. As you've already deduced, I'm a pilot and that's my airplane that crashed over there."

Sochalski glanced over Jack's shoulder at the wreckage. "Too bad about the other pilot. Your friend?"

Jack nodded, surprised at his interest.

"Don't worry," the youth said matter-of-factly. "They won't just dump him anywhere. He's an officer. Since he's not a Jew, they'll make sure he's properly buried."

Jack was shocked at the casualness with which the young man spoke of such issues. *But then he probably had to grow up in a hurry and he'd witnessed more death up close than I ever will,* Jack thought.

"Anyway, how did—?"

"How did I end up on this farm?" Sochalski offered. "Same as you—not by choice. I've been hiding from the Nazis for the last week. By sheer luck, I managed to escape from one of their trains when the locomotive stopped to replenish its water supply. My ... parents are still on it."

He stopped speaking and glanced down at his shoes. "I don't know if I'll ever see them again."

Jack didn't know what to say. Not wanting to follow this

line of talk, he switched to more pressing problems. "Are we safe here? I mean overnight?"

"Sure, so long as no more American planes crash in the vicinity."

Jack decided he liked the young man and his strange sense of humor. "Okay. We're probably safe on that one. Er … William, what are you doing for shelter?"

"I've been sleeping in the hayloft for the last two nights, waiting for my chance to make my way back to Belgium. That's where I—my family and I—where we come from."

Jack nodded and sensed that William was wise beyond his years. He was interested in the young man's story. "Tell me about your home. Were you attending school?"

A sadness crossed William's face. "Sadly, no. The Nazis put a stop to that. But I did manage to keep busy by working part-time in my uncle's motorcycle repair shop. He taught me many things, like how to rewind electric motors."

Jack was impressed and wanted him to elaborate, but the young man had other things on his mind.

"I've heard reports that many parts of Belgium have been liberated by the Allies."

"That could very well be," Jack nodded. "I've heard as much, although I can't be certain. My bomber group is based in northern France. That's where I was this morning, at Beauvais. It seems like a long time ago."

Jack was surprised at himself for revealing so much personal information to someone he had only just met, never mind that he was a teenager.

"I'm sure you'll see your crew again, Captain," William replied to the unspoken question. "From all accounts, the Germans are being pushed back on all fronts, especially by the Russians. All you have to do is evade the search parties. I've been lucky so far. The ones that have come this way haven't used dogs."

"So, where will you go from here?"

"That depends entirely on you, sir."

The survivors of the crash spent a relatively quiet night in the hunter's cabin. Boyer awoke first and roused the others telling them to get a move on. As comforting as the cabin was, they had to be alert and stay ahead of the search parties that were sure to come.

Boyer glanced at his wristwatch and was shocked to see that it was already after eight o'clock. He decided to allow the men a quick bite and then head out, probably in a northerly direction. He glanced out the frost-covered window, relieved to see they were still alone, save for the presence of a squawking black crow.

When the men were ready, he cautiously opened the door and peered out. The crow was gone. He took the first steps outside, with the rest shuffling behind him. They had barely covered ten steps when they were nearly paralyzed by a loud shout.

"Amerikaner, Hände hoch!"

Almost immediately, a German officer stepped into view from behind an oak tree. He held a semiautomatic pistol in front of him. To add credence to his challenge, several soldiers clad in white camouflage gear emerged from behind bushes and a fallen tree trunk, brandishing Schmeisser submachine pistols.

Boyer counted eight men, and those were only the ones he could see. Sighing, he realized the game was up. Reluctantly, he lifted his hands in the air. Seeing they were badly outnumbered and outmatched, Rossi followed suit, with the others joining in.

"Oh good," Shore piped up. "I was getting tired of this winter outing. I can hardly wait for some hot food and warm blankets."

Boyer gave him a withering look. "Not now, Shore."

The German officer, a lieutenant in rank, holstered his sidearm and approached, accompanied by a sergeant carrying a machine pistol.

"You will remove all weapons and place them on the ground. Now!" the officer instructed in German. The order was quickly translated into English by the sergeant.

"We've got no choice, men," Boyer said, voicing the obvious.

He unzipped his jacket and carefully, butt first, removed his pistol, dropping it at the officer's feet. Rossi and Lerner followed their leader's actions.

The lieutenant motioned for the rest to comply.

"They're unarmed," Boyer clarified. "We only have three pistols between us, Herr Lieutenant. My name is Boyer. Lieutenant Charles Boyer, 322nd Bombardment Group, US Army Air Force."

The German officer nodded.

"Lieutenant Werner Zonder, Homeland Defence Forces," he replied slowly, but in English. "Is that true, no more weapons?"

Boyer called over his shoulder to his men. "Unzip and open your jackets, slowly. Show them you're not armed. And guys, no heroics."

"Heroics?" questioned Zonder, looking at his subordinate. The sergeant whispered something to his superior. "Very well, Lieutenant Boyer. You and your men are now prisoners of war, prisoners of the Third Reich. And now, you will follow me."

As Boyer zipped up his jacket again, he couldn't resist asking Zonder the obvious question. "Lieutenant, how did you find us so fast?"

A smile crossed Zonder's face as he pointed to the cabin, with smoke still rising from the stack. Boyer nodded, inwardly cursing himself for being so careless.

Zonder, all-business, barked a few orders at his men and led the group back into the trees. As they marched through the forest, Boyer witnessed the results of German efficiency firsthand. Thus ended the airmen's short-lived taste of freedom.

CHAPTER IX

A Missing Pilot

"I have a call for you, Lieutenant Zonder," the secretary said. "It's from Berlin."

'

Zonder looked pleased with himself, expecting to receive accolades for rounding up the Americans.

"Certainly, put it through." He waited for the click. "Lieutenant Zonder here. How can I help you?"

"This is SS *Oberleutnant* Kloster. Good work on capturing the men. I just have one question? What happened to the sixth man? Your report only mentions five."

"That's right, five men, Herr *Oberleutnant*," the other man confirmed, checking his report. "I have three officers listed, one of whom perished in the crash, and three enlisted men. In total, we've captured five Americans."

"Yes, yes, I know what it says in your report, Zonder. But did it occur to you that a standard complement on a B-26 bomber allows for seven men? *Three* officers and four airmen. You're missing one man. What happened to him?"

"I, uh—are you sure, sir?"

"My information indicates there were seven men. With one dead, that leaves six, but you captured only five. Perhaps the sixth man eluded you in the forest."

It was more of a statement than a question. Kloster didn't want to share the source of his information—namely, that

Vogel had spotted a tall officer, likely an American, talking to a young woman at the crash site.

There was static on the line.

"Zonder, are you still there?"

"*Jawohl.* I'm er … thinking."

"Well, I have other things to do than wait while you're thinking. I want you to send out another search party and find the last man. Is that clear?"

"*Zu befehl, Herr Oberleutnant.* I'll arrange it. I'll be in touch as soon as I hear anything."

"Good. I'll be expecting your call. Heil Hitler."

"Heil—" Zonder wasn't able to finish the salutation, for the line had already gone dead.

"Damn Gestapo buffoon!" Zonder cursed into the phone. He was about to expound on it but stopped himself just in time, remembering a fellow officer's admonition about the phone lines being tapped.

He was fuming inside. Instead of recognition for a job well done, he had been criticized for coming up short—allowing one man to get away. The Gestapo lieutenant was insinuating that he had slipped up. But had he? He picked up the file recounting the capture of the crew, and this time read it over more carefully. He recalled visiting the cockpit himself, but not being familiar with the layout, he couldn't envision the placement of the crew.

Zonder picked up the phone and asked to be connected to the Air Ministry. He outlined his request and the officer, a friend, promised to get back to him as soon as possible.

Meanwhile, he pushed back his chair and opened the office door. He leaned out and instructed his secretary to summon Sergeant Holzig, one of the men from the search party detail. Zonder decided to go out for a cigarette break and to check on other assignments, many of which were more pressing than finding a fictitious airman, officer or not.

Half an hour later, Zonder returned to his office and

found a handwritten message from his earlier phone inquiry. The Air Ministry friend had called back sooner than expected and confirmed that a typical compliment for an American B-26 bomber crew consisted of seven men. Zonder wondered how Kloster could have known that.

He was interrupted by the arrival of Holzig. Perfunctorily, he explained the latest development. Zonder could read the doubt in the man's eyes.

"Missing, *Herr Leutnant?*"

Zonder nodded. "Yes. I've just received more information. I've been told there were seven men, not six. We'll have to find him."

"What now, sir? Conduct another search?"

Zonder glared at him. "Yes, dammit man. Tonight! Get on it!"

He instructed Holzig to round up another squad and head back out to the hunter's cabin and conduct a thorough search for the missing airman. The sergeant saluted smartly and hurriedly left the office to carry out his task.

╬

Heinrich Schinkel paced in his office, unhappy with the progress of the investigation. He had sent one of his best men to look into the alleged irregularities at the test facility in Gotha, but so far nothing unusual had come to light. Could the report, as he had suspected, have been embellished to deflect the delays and cost overruns? Perhaps. He decided to give it another week before calling a halt to what had proved to be a fruitless and questionable use of Gestapo resources.

More problematic was that his right-hand man, Horst Kloster, always seemed to be one step ahead of him. *Why do I get the feeling that Kloster is plotting, or even hiding something?* Schinkel reflected on Kloster's work ethic and couldn't come up with anything to complain about. After all, the man was conscientious, a stickler for rules, and punctual. But something about him bothered Schinkel. He just couldn't put his finger on it. *Could it be*—the telephone began to ring, derailing his train of thought.

He picked up the telephone and, after the customary exchange with Brunnhilde, his secretary, he found himself listening to one of Göring's assistants, once again asking for a favor on behalf of the *Reichsminister.* Schinkel sighed and tried to listen to what he knew would be some indiscretion on behalf of a diplomat or senior officer.

"*Ja, sehr gut,*" Schinkel replied into the mouthpiece, hoping that the man on the other end of the line would soon hang up and leave him alone. "I'll see what I can do. Heil Hitler!"

No sooner had he hung up than the infernal instrument dared ring again. He was about to voice his displeasure when he detected the urgency in his secretary's voice.

"I'm sorry to interrupt you again, sir, but *Oberleutnant* Kloster is on the line. He insists it's urgent."

"Of course," Heinrich replied. "Put him through right away." There was brief static on the line and then he heard Kloster's crisp, aristocratic-sounding voice.

"Guten Morgen, *Herr Sturmbannführer,*" Kloster began. "I'm at the police station in Zehdenick. You may recall that it doubles as the local Gestapo office. I'm in possession of some vital information obtained by one of our men, Vogel. Surely you remember him, sir?"

Schinkel thought back to the first time he had met Vogel at Gestapo headquarters. Initially with the *Wehrmacht,* the man had distinguished himself as a clerk, solving the theft of supplies from a commissary. Kloster, or more likely a senior officer, had gotten him transferred to Berlin and pulled a few strings to elevate him to the *Waffen-SS.*

"*Ja,* a clever man. So, what do you have for me, Kloster? I'm busy."

"Right away, *Herr Sturmbannführer.* I assigned Vogel to follow a man we have long suspected of belonging to a group of communist sympathisers."

Schinkel sighed, remembering how many good officers had been wrongly, and probably vengefully, implicated for taking part in the conspiracy to assassinate Hitler in the July '44 plot. It was well-known that the way to gain favor and promotion was to make subtle suggestions about an officer's disenchantment with the current regime and allow for the rumor mill to make any connections, however far-fetched they may be. Once the Gestapo was called in, it was difficult, if not impossible, to clear one's name.

His thoughts drifted to a fellow colleague, a man he actually liked: Kurt Siemens, a captain in the *Wehrmacht*. Schinkel had received a file on the man and been forced to investigate. What should have been routine had somehow gained momentum and eventually turned into an inquisition—all because the man's uncle was one quarter Jewish.

"And what did they come up with, *Herr Oberleutnant?*" Heinrich asked.

"The man may still be a communist sympathiser, but my men came up with something far more interesting," said Kloster. "During the course of their surveillance, they stumb—I mean, came upon an impromptu meeting at a farmhouse. The man they'd been following, Rudi Schultz, was seen talking to a tall man in a flight suit, likely an American pilot. It seems his aircraft had crash-landed in a farmer's field and the pilot remained behind, while his crew walked away. Coincidence, sir? I think not."

"Good work, Kloster. What's your next move?"

"I'm coordinating efforts to capture the American flyer and then bring him to Berlin for interrogation."

"My thoughts exactly. Carry on. Heil Hitler."

"Thank you, sir. Heil Hitler."

Very interesting, thought Schinkel as he cradled the phone with his left arm. *I wonder where this will lead?*

"*Scheise!*" he cursed out loud, but also chastising himself for his clumsiness. He gazed at the empty sleeve, where his right hand should have been. He steeled himself and relegated the thought to the back of his head, as he selected another file.

╬

Jack looked at the slowly rising sun. It was shortly before eight o'clock on a peaceful Sunday morning. A memory of long ago played on his mind, of a time when he was just a boy, no more than nine or ten years old, visiting his grandfather on the family farm in North Dakota.

It all came back to him in a flash. There he was, sitting in the kitchen of the old farmhouse, listening to one of his grandpa's stories while his parents slept. He could almost see Grandpa Walter talking animatedly about the birth of a calf. Jack had been enthralled at the time and the memory of the event brought a smile to his lips. Things had been simpler then.

He nearly forgot about his present predicament. He wanted so much to indulge in the memory, to revisit his boyhood and briefly escape the war. But then Sochalski stirred next to him and muttered something in his sleep, forcing Jack to leave the past behind and face the new day.

At last, a rooster crowed, waking his new companion. Jack watched the boy rub the sleep from his eyes and bid him a good morning, perhaps a strange greeting considering the circumstances they were in.

As Jack listened to what the young man had to say, he became convinced that he was exactly who he said he was—a Jew trying to evade capture. Jack was surprised at how mature the boy turned out to be. Boys his age back home in the States thought about cars, music, and girls, while this young man's thoughts were occupied with his homeland, family, and survival.

In the developing dawn, Jack lay propped up on the straw in the barn loft, thinking about what to do next. As he saw it, he had two choices: he could wait for Hilde Augsberg and her driver to return, or slip out early and get a head start but risk getting captured.

Even though he wanted to leave the barn and the unfriendly homestead, common sense told him to stay put. He was injured, had no identity papers, and was wearing an American flight suit, not to mention the flight jacket that kept him warm but would quickly give him away.

No, he had to remain where he was. Once he'd come to that decision, he shared it with William and that he'd take his chances with Fräulein Augsberg's resourcefulness.

William merely nodded, mulling things over.

Jack heard the sound of an approaching car, forestalling any further debate. Without having to prompt him, Sochalski quickly stood up and headed for the gable window. He returned after a few seconds.

"I don't think it's the Germans," William whispered. "And it's too early for the farmer to be out. It must be your friends."

Friends. The word had a welcome ring to it. Jack nodded, for the first-time taking Hilde and her driver at face value. With William's help, Jack stood to his feet and hobbled to the ladder. Climbing down took even more time than going up the night before—and it was nearly twice as painful.

The vehicle came to a stop outside, and both men distinctly heard the opening of the doors. Light footfalls proceeded a woman's voice whispering through the dim of the early morning.

"Captain. It's me, Hilde."

A strange sensation came over Jack, as if he were meeting a cousin or aunt he hadn't seen for some time.

"I'm here, Fräulein," he whispered back. "And I'm not alone. I have another guest with me—a refugee."

By this time, Hilde had squeezed through the opening and was peering into the barn's darkness. Jack switched on his torch and shone it on Sochalski.

"This is William Sochalski, my new friend," he explained.

"And this is our new patron, Fräulein Augsberg."

The light played across Hilde's face. Was it the illumination or was she wearing lipstick? And if that weren't enough, Jack even detected a faint trace of perfume. Surely, that wasn't his imagination.

"I uh … the Germans would love to get their hands on him," Jack stammered. "He's a Jew."

Before Hilde could reply, her male companion joined the trio. The limited light from Jack's torch was enough to reveal his German uniform. William immediately drew back, fearing the worst, but Jack took him by the shoulder and comforted him.

"It's alright, William. He's on our side."

The comment seemed nearly farcical to Jack. "Don't be afraid. Herr Schultz is a civilian and only dons the uniform to make his job easier."

"That's right," echoed Hilde, holding out her hand. "Please, Herr Sochalski, don't be alarmed. Rudi is my friend. He's no soldier."

Reluctantly, Sochalski came forward and shook her hand. "Nice to meet you, Fräulein Augsberg."

"We have to hurry," she said. "Dawn is breaking fast and we can't risk being seen here a second time. We're heading back to Oranienburg and you're welcome to join us. You see, Herr Sochalski, Rudi has connections with the Resistance and you stand a better chance of survival in a larger center. It's up to you."

William looked from Hilde to Jack and back to her. Undoubtedly, he found something reassuring and quickly made up his mind.

"If you're willing to risk it, I will accompany you," he decided.

Hilde smiled, removing the last of Sochalski's doubts. With the young man helping the hobbling pilot, they followed Hilde outside toward the waiting Opel. Jack hesitated, looking back at the downed bomber.

With William's assistance, Jack slid into the car's back seat with minimal discomfort. William climbed in after him while Hilde found her place up front. Rudi sat behind the wheel, started the engine and without turning on the headlights eased his way along the dirt track. He successfully made it to the paved road and turned south, heading back to Oranienburg.

Jack tried to make himself as comfortable as possible and mulled over the events of the last twenty-four hours. But as they disappeared further up the road, he kept glancing behind him, irritated that he couldn't salvage the photo of his fiancée Nicole, which he'd attached to the altimeter dial. He'd limped back the previous evening to retrieve it, only to find it was gone. He cursed the Germans for removing it.

⚜

Just as the farmer was seating himself at the kitchen table for his morning porridge, one of his farmhands, tasked with milking the cows, came outside to see a black car leave the farm property and reported it to the farmer. The man merely grunted, more concerned with his breakfast than some errant car.

Later that morning, when he was the recipient of an un-scheduled visit by the local Gestapo, his nonchalant attitude changed abruptly. He was more than willing to co-operate. The mere appearance of the Gestapo had an unnerving effect on most people.

CHAPTER X
Test Flight

On a cool, cloudless October morning, Walter Horten was enjoying his first cup of coffee in silence—that is, until he detected the sound of an approaching car. He quickly grabbed a tunic and headed for the side door of the hangar to find a black staff car turning off the paved road and gliding to a stop. It was quickly followed by a second, then a third.

Walter had been preparing for an important visit, but it was scheduled for the afternoon.

A chauffeur emerged from the first vehicle and hurried to the rear, efficiently opening the door and enabling a uniformed officer to alight the sedan. Anyone who knew anything about high-ranking military men in the Luftwaffe would have recognized General Adolf Galland instantly. The handsome general surveyed the empty tarmac and showed surprise at the lack of activity.

Colonel Siegfried Knemeyer, head test pilot for RLM and the vehicle's other occupant, climbed out next and stretched. He caught the look of apprehension in Galland's face.

"Don't worry, General," the colonel began. "The hangar may look deserted on the outside, but I would wager there's a beehive of activity going on inside. We're early, that's all."

Galland nodded as he surveyed the scene but failed to acknowledge Walter's presence in the doorway to the hangar's side entrance.

"Go inside and advise Walter Horten we've arrived," Galland ordered one of his men. "Tell him that the Führer, without consulting anyone, has moved up our timetable. He has insisted that the demonstration be conducted this morning."

He then waved to the driver of the Mercedes directly behind him. A burly, immaculately dressed SS guard got out, took a furtive look around, then proceeded to the back door. He stood back and came to attention as a diminutive figure got out.

The man was considerably shorter than his guard and wore only a black leather coat and peaked cap. There were no insignia on his lapel and no shoulder boards to indicate rank. But his demeanor dwarfed the giant of a guard standing next to him. The penetrating glance, small black moustache, and self-assurance would mesmerize any man. A second guard, even taller than the first, fell in behind their leader.

From the third car emerged the hulk of Hermann Wilhelm Göring. He was so much larger than Hitler that it presented a comical sight. Göring's Luftwaffe great coat was decorated with a plethora of medals and ribbons and he proudly brandished an ornamental riding crop—perhaps, in the absence of a horse, intending to use it on an unsuspecting subordinate. Although he towered over Hitler, Göring subjected himself to the man's authority by clicking the heels of his boots.

"Mein Führer," he began, "this is the airfield I spoke to you about. The hangar and nearby buildings have purposefully been kept in a state of disrepair so as not to attract any undue attention from Allied reconnaissance aircraft."

Adolf Hitler peered up from under his cap, his facial expression unchanged. If he accepted Göring's explanation, it was difficult for Walter to tell from his reserved look—his face often a mask that hovered a shade above displeasure. He merely grunted and waited. The *Reichsmarschall* seemed to go on a lengthy explanation, when he was forestalled by the appearance of a uniformed officer.

Captain Walter Horten stopped short of the leaders, apparently having been briefed on the protocol of approaching the Führer. He clicked his heels, extended his right arm, and proclaimed "Heil Hitler!"

Seemingly impressed, Göring returned the salute. "Ah, Horten, I'm glad you're here. The Führer thought it best to arrive a little earlier so that—"

"*Ja, ja,* Hermann, you can fill him in later," Hitler interjected. He turned to face Walter. "Perhaps you can show us what you've been doing with Germany's Reichsmarks." The interruption was not without effect.

"Of course, *mein Führer,*" Walter replied. "This way, please."

Hitler followed him into the administration building, the two guards automatically falling in behind. As they toured the offices, Walter summarized the design work and the complexities of building not only a working prototype but a fully functional jet aircraft. Hitler seemed to listen with interest, as Walter led them to one of the workshops.

He welcomed the opportunity to show off the importance of the work they'd been doing. When they entered, Hitler stopped to allow his eyes to acclimatize to the artificial light. When a technician wearing gray coveralls came around the corner carrying a box of supplies, he came face to face with Hitler and stopped in his tracks, nearly dropping his tool box while shifting it to his left arm and performing the obligatory "Heil Hitler" with his right.

"*Achtung!*" shouted Hitler's bodyguard.

Those within hearing distance immediately stopped working, as if paralyzed with fear. Seeing the effect his presence created, Adolf Hitler stopped to speak to a workman, reassuring him and praising him for his contribution to the Reich's war effort.

After he had spoken to a couple of technicians, Hitler became restless and asked to see the prototype. With Walter leading the way, they walked into another section of the warehouse, where Hitler could plainly see a jet engine that hung suspended from a mini-crane. Nearby were the nearly completed wings of a Horten Ho 229.

Hitler examined the empennage, yet seemed uninterested in the fabrication and assembly process. He turned around and fixed his gaze on the young designer.

"Herr Kapitän," he said quietly, "I thought your firm had made significant progress on the bomber and that you were undergoing flight testing. Was I misinformed?" Although he addressed Walter, he glared over his left shoulder at Göring.

Before the *Reichsmarschall* could respond, Walter interjected.

"Mein Führer, you were informed correctly. We have started conducting test flights with the prototype. What you see here are components and engines for subsequent testing. We have made some small modifications to enhance the aircraft's flying characteristics. It would give me great pleasure to personally demonstrate the aircraft's capabilities."

Hitler's expression changed instantly, coming as close to what one would consider a smile. "Sehr gut. I look forward to it."

An adjutant approached Göring and whispered something in his ear. The ever-astute *Reichsmarschall* then turned to face his leader. *"Mein Führer,* I've been told there are refreshments in the adjacent building. Perhaps we can go there while our Captain Horten prepares the aircraft for the demonstration?"

Hitler glanced at Göring with approval and motioned for him to lead the way.

Walter excused himself and hurried into a nearby building so he could change into his flight suit. His mind worked feverishly, going over the checklist and other details he had rehearsed earlier with his brother Reimar. He knew what a successful test flight would mean, and he remembered what Göring had said about failure:

"I've entrusted you with this sensitive project. If your demonstration fails to impress the Führer—or worse, if there's a crash—it would most certainly hamper the continuation of the project and seriously restrict further design work by your firm. I can assure you that I would have little choice but to relinquish your services here and both of you would be, er … reassigned to active duty. A posting to the Russian front would be a distinct possibility. I don't think I need to remind you what an unpleasant assignment that would be. Do I make myself clear, Horten?"

What *was* clear was that Göring was protecting himself, and in the event of failure, he would lay any blame directly at the brothers' feet.

For the first time, Walter felt the immense pressure of the whole project resting solely on his shoulders. He and Reimar had debated on who should conduct the test flight. In the end, they'd decided it should be him, even though Erwin Ziller had more time and experience in twin-engine aircraft. Ziller had expressed a strong desire to perform the demonstration, but had to bow to Walter Horten, thus absolving himself of any blame but also depriving himself of any accolades.

Well, it's too late to reconsider, Walter thought to himself. *It's up to me now. Here at last, the designer can showcase what he's been preaching all this time.*

As he put on his specially designed flight suit, the door opened and Reimar walked in. The younger brother wore his customary worried but excited look. Both men, designers and pilots of the Third Reich, knew what was at stake.

Reimar slapped his brother good-naturedly on the back. "Walter, you'll do fine. I checked the instruments, engine inlets, and control surfaces. Then I rechecked them. I personally supervised the fuelling. The weather is acceptable, with a strong but not overpowering breeze from the north. As long as you stay out of the clouds, you won't have to worry about icing conditions." Then he grinned, as if remembering something. "As our former instructor used to say, *mazel tov!*"

That broke the tension. Both men laughed, remembering

the little Jewish gliding instructor who'd taught them years ago.

Reimar ensured the flight suit was zipped up and then slipped the newly designed helmet over Walter's head. It had an innovative, revolutionary design that gave it its unusual appearance. It seemed like it belonged in a Jules Verne novel. He produced his little 35mm Zeis camera and took a picture of the pilot in the futuristic flight suit.

As Walter strode out of the hangar office, he was surprised to see that none of the senior officers were there to watch the prototype get towed out of the adjoining hangar. All but one that is—Siegfried Knemeyer who was intently watching the tractor's progress.

When the aircraft at last faced the taxi strip, a technician detached the towing strut and secured the wheel chocks, while another worker leaned a ladder on the left side of the fuselage.

Walter strode confidently up to the aircraft, climbed the ladder, and seated himself in the cockpit. The technician followed him up the ladder and assisted him with adjusting the shoulder harness and attaching the oxygen supply tube to his flight suit.

In the meantime, Walter scanned the various instruments, familiarizing himself again with their location, as he hadn't flown the aircraft for two weeks. At last, he nodded to the technician, who closed the canopy and slowly climbed down the ladder, removing it.

When all was in readiness, he stepped back and glanced at the pilot. Walter nodded, indicating that he was ready to proceed. He began the start-up procedure, toggling the master and auxiliary switches. Through the canopy, he watched the technician approach the port engine air intake and retrieve the starter handle.

The Jumo 004B jet engine was equipped with a revolutionary auxiliary power unit (APU), the Riedel starter, designed by Norbert Riedel. In effect, the APU was a self-contained two-stroke motor that would run on a gasoline/oil mixture and was situated within the intake housing of the engine.

Walter watched as the technician pulled the handle, starting the small motor. The motor's driveshaft was attached directly to the turbine, and once the motor caught, it would spin up the turbine. Walter felt the vibrations from the turbine and activated the fuel pump, igniting the fuel mixture, while he scrutinized the RPM gauge as the engine spooled up.

Satisfied with the port engine's progress and not finding any warning lights, he watched a repetition of the process with the starboard engine and was pleased to find that it too started as expected. After about two minutes of closely monitoring the vital gauges of both engines, he was satisfied that the time had come.

This is it, Walter thought. *All the design work, the countless man hours of fabricating and assembling the airplane, it all comes down to this critical demonstration. Well, Reimar, here we go.*

Walter released the brakes and slowly advanced the slim throttle's levers. The aircraft lurched forward. Taking another look around and making sure there were no obstructions, he steered the nose toward the runway. As he taxied, he carefully checked the instruments; he saw no warning lights, no pressure drops, nothing that would require his immediate attention. He glanced at the office building and saw what he thought was Hitler's visage near the door. The man was actually watching the airplane's progress.

Walter continued to taxi toward the apron, the small rectangular area where pilots performed a final run-up check. It would be his last opportunity to make sure the two turbo-jet engines were operating normally in preparation for takeoff. Walter, however, decided to dispense with it, thinking back to Göring's warning about the Führer's limited patience. A lengthy run-up, normally a wise procedure with any prototype, might in this case turn out to be counterproductive.

He advised the controller that he would taxi directly out

to the runway and was told he could proceed. Walter checked the windsock and found it to favour a departure to the north, just as Reimar had advised him.

He turned left onto the runway and backtracked to the far end, so that he would have the maximum distance for a takeoff run. He came to the end and turned the aircraft into the wind. He rechecked his instruments and remembered to add ten degrees of flap, giving the aircraft extra lift. As he smoothly advanced the two throttle levers, the Ho 229 started to accelerate down the runway. Everything looked good and—just as important— everything felt right.

Walter reminded himself that the takeoff was the trickiest manoeuvre. Aside from the landing, of course. The pilot had to be mindful of many things: keeping the aircraft aligned with the runway, casting a wary eye on the important engine instruments, and compensating for wind gusts. Then came the vital part: deciding on the right time to rotate the nose wheel of the plane, in effect transitioning from the takeoff roll to flight. Raising the wheel too early could hamper the actual takeoff by extending the takeoff run, even coming close to stalling the airplane.

Walter Horten had never been more ready. He glanced down the runway one last time, before committing himself. In the distance, a red-tailed fox scurried across the asphalt, oblivious to the jet about to race toward him.

He released the brakes and gently advanced the throttle levers, as the twin turbines spooled up, creating thrust. The fan blades bit into the air and propelled the jet forward, pushing Walter backward into the seat. Exhilarated, he advanced the throttles further and the jet raced down the runway.

When the airspeed indicator reached 180 km/hr, Walter gently pulled the control column back and instantly the nose wheel lifted. He trimmed the column for the climb-out and concentrated on the airspeed. Once the speed indicated 195 km/hr, he pulled further back and the plane broke free, lifting off the ground.

Walter inhaled deeply, realizing that he'd been holding his breath. He quickly glanced at the rate-of-climb indicator and confirmed a slight, yet positive rate of climb. The altimeter needle registered a climb of thirty meters. Everything looked good.

Once he had climbed two hundred meters, he reached for the gear lever that would raise the large nose wheel. The two smaller main gear wheels followed suit. Instantly the jet accelerated, no longer hampered by the parasitic drag of the landing gear. When the aircraft had reached three hundred meters above ground, Walter levelled the prototype and trimmed the controls for level flight.

Feeling comfortable and in his element, he relaxed a fraction. He banked the plane into a shallow left turn, intending to change course 180 degrees so he could return to the airfield. The aircraft responded to his gentle touch. Once he was heading south, he levelled the wings and flew directly over the aerodrome, flying the length of the runway, level at three hundred twenty meters. He heard a familiar voice in his headphones, distracting him. It was Reimar.

"Walter, you're looking great. Nice flyby. You should see the look on Göring's face. He looks pleased and probably wished he was twenty years younger and flying it himself."

"Good to hear that," Walter replied. "From up here, it's performing perfectly. No warning lights. Oil pressure is normal and both the exhaust temperature gauges are within limits. It couldn't be better. I'm thinking of doing a high-speed run. What do you think?"

"Up to you. It would certainly show them what we've been talking about all these months."

"Right, then let's do it," he agreed.

The Horten jet had by now traversed the airfield and was close to coming to the outskirts of the town of Oranienburg. He banked the bomber and trimmed the nose slightly downward, thereby increasing his speed. He watched as the altimeter needle slowly dropped while he performed a gentle turn, bringing him back on a reciprocal course. His intention was to drop down to two hundred meters and make a pass at about eight hundred kilometers per hour.

He watched the airspeed indicator register five hundred kilometers per hour. When Walter judged he was about two kilometers from the airfield, he advanced the throttle lever to seventy per cent power. The airplane lurched forward, pressing him into the seat. The airspeed indicator jumped as well, first registering 530, then 560, then rapidly climbing to 610 ... 640 ... 690 ...

Walter held his breath. He levelled off at one hundred ninety meters, a little lower than he had intended. The airspeed kept climbing as the farmyards whizzed by below. As an experienced pilot, he knew he had to maintain focus, especially at such high speeds. There was little margin for error.

After his third scan of the instruments, he dared risk the flyby. Now only about one kilometer from the airfield and level at just under two hundred meters, he advanced the throttle marginally, increasing the speed past seven hundred fifty kilometers per hour. He keyed the mike and as he spoke into it, he hoped he didn't sound like a school kid who had jumped onto his older brother's motorcycle.

"Reimar, everything looks good. The engines are performing wonderfully. I'm going for it."

Just ahead was the aerodrome. He checked for the windsock, but at this speed he couldn't locate it on the field. Walter lined up with the runway, compensating as the wind seemed to have shifted to the northwest. Even so, the airspeed indicator hovered around 815, and inching up towards 830. He passed over the aerodrome, straight as an arrow, racing to the north.

Reimar, stationed in the control tower, was holding a stopwatch in his right hand. He knew the length of the runway, as well as the wind speed. He clicked the stopwatch just as the Horten Ho 229 roared over the north fence. Using his slide rule, Reimar made a fast calculation.

"Ach, du lieber!" He muttered the minced oath to himself. He rechecked his figures and then keyed the mike.

"Walter, what does your airspeed indicator show?"

There was static for several seconds. "I'm not sure the reading is quite accurate. I'm showing 870 at eighty-five per cent power."

"Amazing! I clocked you with my stopwatch and calculated your speed to be close to 880, and that was going into the wind."

"Good. I'm throttling back and I'll do another pass with a tight turn."

Walter pulled the levers back to sixty per cent power, and like before made a cautious but tight turn, heading back to the airfield. He allowed the aircraft to climb to three hundred meters again.

When he was about two hundred meters from the north side of the airfield, he pushed the throttle lever forward and banked hard right. The aircraft responded immediately, banking thirty degrees. He intended to perform a full 360-degree turn, coming out at the same altitude and heading.

As he came out of the turn, he glanced at the temperature gauges and was relieved to find that all was in order. Rather than throttle back, he decided to perform one more manoeuvre. He lined up with the north end of the runway and headed in a southerly direction. With the wind at his back, he pushed the throttle levers forward to the stops and heaved back on the control column.

What he was attempting was in effect a nearly vertical climb, unheard of with piston-powered aircraft. Gravity pulled him down into his seat as the Ho 229 vaulted itself upward. The climb indicator bounced to the top, indicating a climb rate of over two thousand meters per minute. His airspeed jumped to 630 and climbed to 740, before levelling off at 760.

As he continued the climb, the airspeed dropped off, imperceptible at first but then more rapidly. Walter glanced at the altimeter, shocked to find he had climbed past two thousand five hundred meters. Releasing pressure on the control yoke, he sensed less force on his body, but also found he could no longer see the horizon; he was surrounded by cloud.

Several things occurred at once. He eased the pressure on the column, allowing the pitch to return to what he felt was around zero degrees, indicating level flight. The airspeed had dropped off considerably, settling to 320. He gently pulled the throttles back to sixty percent power and prepared himself for a slower, more manageable speed. He popped out of the clouds, flying south at an altitude of two thousand eight hundred meters. The vast farmyards below now looked like postage stamps.

Walter checked the ever-important fuel gauges and determined he still had enough for about thirty minutes of flying time. He remembered that Reimar had insisted on not topping off the fuel tanks, a precaution in case something went wrong. He keyed the mike.

"Well, Reimar, what did you think of the climb?"

"Spectacular. I think even Herr Hitler was impressed. I know you couldn't tell, but from down here it looked like you had achieved a seventy degree climb angle—for the uninitiated, nearly vertical. I don't think Scheidhauer or Ziller could have done any better."

CHAPTER XI

Ho 229 in Flight

Boyer led the way as he and his men followed Lieutenant Zonder onto a well-used trail through the forest. Less than five minutes of walking took them to a country road where a staff car and military truck were waiting for them.

The lone sentry became alert when he spotted his superior leading the search party.

"*Alles in Ordnung*, Kupfer?" asked Zonder.

"*Jawohl, Herr Leutnant,*" the soldier affirmed.

One by one, they climbed aboard the lorry, each man carefully watched by an armed soldier. The men seated themselves on wooden planks, bunched together to conserve heat. Boyer was last to climb up.

"So, where to now, Lieutenant?" he asked.

"Zehdenick, for interrogation." Seeing the alarm in Boyer's eyes, Zonder offered some clarification. "Don't worry. It's only the local police station, not Gestapo headquarters."

Two soldiers also climbed up and seated themselves. The muzzles of their machine pistols were pointed at the floor, but this in no way diminished their threat.

As the truck slowly lumbered down the forest track, no one wanted to be the first to speak. Boyer viewed his men's faces and saw the same emotions in each one: defeat and helplessness. He thought back to Jack, alone now and having to deal with a sprained ankle. Boyer wished they hadn't needed to leave him behind, but they had little choice. It wasn't meant to be.

⚜

Jack rested in the back seat during the car ride back to Oranienburg. Fortunately, they had encountered only one check point, near the town of Liebenwalde. The soldiers there had only taken a cursory look at their vehicle and occupants, and thanks to Rudi's pass and the lieutenant's uniform, saluted and waved them on.

Jack relaxed again and even dozed fitfully. But eventually he was lulled out of his relaxed state by a quiet conversation between Hilde and Rudi. William was gently snoring through it, a good sign he was no longer afraid.

Jack's trained ears picked up a distant yet not too unfamiliar sound. He partially sat up, as much as his injured ankle would permit and glanced outside. It was a bright, sunny day, so Jack cracked open his window. The shrill sound was distinctive and became more pronounced as time went on. He knew it wasn't coming from their car and was too high-pitched to be coming from a tank or military transport.

"Fräulein," he said to Hilde, "do you hear that sound?"

Hilde listened for a moment, half-turning in her seat.

"Yes, it sounds like an airplane. The Luftwaffe has several of those new jet fighters stationed near Oranienburg. I believe they're called Messerschmitt."

Jack had certainly heard of the Messerschmitt Flugzeug-bauwerke and the various sites where the famed twin-engine jet components were manufactured. He'd been briefed on this latest German technology.

Word from other pilots was that you didn't even see them approach, and by the time you identified one the pilot would have already shot up your tail or shredded the engine. While your airplane was on fire and on its way down, the fighter would be lining up another target. They were known to be extremely fast, superior to the venerable British Spitfire, even outpacing the new P-51 Mustang.

Jack peered through the windshield and spotted a rapidly growing speck against the clear blue sky, a speck which abruptly turned and climbed higher in the sky. It was too mechanical, too fluid to be a bird.

No, it couldn't be happening, he thought. A gray-colored delta-wing shape—an aircraft without a doubt—was entering a near vertical climb while the pilot performed a slow roll through its vertical axis.

Jack rubbed his eyes for a better look. This aircraft was like nothing he'd ever seen before. And judging from its roar, it wasn't powered by a reciprocating engine but by some sort of turbine. Fascinated, he followed the aircraft's progress until it disappeared from view, his vision obstructed by the car's roof.

Jack called out for Rudi to pull over, but the alert driver had already slowed and stopped to get a better view for himself. Ignoring his sprained ankle, Jack managed to extricate himself from the rear seat and climbed out. He looked for the aircraft but it had vanished. He was about to ask Rudi if he carried binoculars on him when he heard a rumbling sound.

He turned just in time to see the same aircraft fly overhead, straight and level, no more than five hundred feet above the ground. Instantly, it shot straight up, its wingtips like elongated fingers, reaching for the highest clouds. The roar of twin jet engines was so loud it made conversation impossible.

Jack was stunned. Had he been in England, or back in the States, he would have been thrilled to be privy to such a display of innovation and power. But here, in the heart of Nazi Germany, he was dismayed. Frightened even. He shuddered at the implications.

Once everyone had climbed back into the automobile, they continued on their journey. They were entering the outskirts of Oranienburg when a loud bang interrupted their trip. The car swerved as Rudi fought to maintain control and veered to the side of the road. Everyone held their breath.

Fortunately, Rudi hadn't been driving fast and managed to pull over without striking the curb.

Jack breathed a sigh of relief and patted Rudi on the shoulder. With Hilde's help, he got out of the car to examine the cause of their mishap: a flat tire. Jack hobbled to the back, intending to retrieve the spare tire. Hilde, however, seemed to have other thoughts and waved him off. She gave Rudi a look. He caught the unspoken message and quickly busied himself with the repair. In the meantime, Jack sauntered over to the side of the street and glanced appraisingly at the architecture of a nearby church.

No sooner had Rudi removed the jack and spare tire than a black Daimler pulled up behind their car. Jack was first to spot the two male occupants and deduced that they were likely policemen—or worse, Gestapo.

The men exited the car. Jack withdrew into the recessed foyer of a nearby house and fingered the pistol in the pocket of the borrowed greatcoat. He didn't think he'd been spotted.

As Rudi continued manhandling the spare tire, Jack checked for Sochalski but couldn't locate him. What he did see was the alarm registering on Hilde's face. She was doing her best to look nonchalant, but Jack could tell she was worried.

The taller of the two, perhaps approaching forty years, was clean-shaven save the pencil-thin moustache. He had close-cropped black hair that protruded from underneath his brown fedora. The man was attired in a plain gray suit.

His partner, younger by several years, was considerably shorter and also sported a fedora that practically concealed his round-rimmed spectacles, adding years to his smooth-shaven face. He wore a gray suit with a red tie that added a touch of color to an otherwise plain appearance.

The two men reached the car and had a brief discussion with Hilde, who flashed them a disarming smile. Although Jack couldn't hear what was said, he could easily follow the outcome. The tall one, seemingly in charge, took a no-nonsense approach and wanted to see some identification. Rudi and Hilde handed them their passes, with each man carefully scrutinizing the documents.

At last, satisfied that all was in order, the taller man whispered something to his younger partner. The other agent shrugged his shoulders, but in the end complied and assisted Rudi with the repair, while he himself continued talking with Hilde.

Jack couldn't believe his eyes and nearly burst out laughing. It seemed they were going to get away unscathed. That's when he realized he had left his flight jacket in the back seat of the car. If either man took a cursory look inside, the gig would be up. Hilde and Rudi would be arrested and taken for interrogation. A lump began to form in his throat. Here he was, the recipient of Hilde's generosity, yet his carelessness could end up costing them all dearly.

Jack watched helplessly as Hilde did her best to appease the agents. Was it Jack's imagination or were the men actually smiling? He couldn't help but admire Hilde's calm demeanor in the presence of the Gestapo men.

And then to Jack's relief, Hilde thanked the men for their assistance. He watched them as they headed back to their own car. As the car pulled away from the curb, the younger man rolled down the window and, rather than elicit the customary "Heil Hitler," waved his hand in farewell.

Jack felt himself relax as relief washed over him, much like the effect of downing twelve-year old scotch whiskey. Hilde simply leaned against the car's hood, exhaling her own sigh of relief. Or was it a prayer? He couldn't tell.

Out of the corner of his eye, Jack witnessed Rudi slump against the side of the car and double over. He started to walk toward him, only to stop in his tracks when he saw Rudi retching, throwing up all over Reimar Horten's shiny car. Clearly the severity of the situation had caught up to Rudi.

Before Jack could say or do anything to help, the ever-attentive Hilde kneeled at Rudi's side, comforting him. Sochalski unexpectedly appeared from the alleyway and headed back to the car, carrying a metal bucket full of water. Once Rudi had gotten hold of himself, William quickly cleaned up what was left of Rudi's breakfast and washed it down a nearby drain.

As they got back into the Opel, Jack complimented Hilde on her impromptu, yet convincing performance with the Gestapo men—and he was rewarded with a generous smile.

⚊⚊

"I'm sorry, *Herr Sturmbannführer*," Horst Kloster said into the phone, grateful his apology wasn't conducted in person. "We missed apprehending the American flyer by minutes. A farmhand saw a black automobile leave the scene just before dawn, but he couldn't say how many occupants were inside."

Kloster paused, expecting a reproach from Schinkel—or worse, outright blame for the flyer's escape. Instead, he heard only static. For a second, he thought the line had been disconnected, but then he heard breathing through the earpiece.

"Go on," Schinkel prompted.

"Naturally, I questioned the farmhand further. Although he was intimidated by our presence, he answered my questions without hesitation and I have no reason to think he was being untruthful. The stupid farmer wasn't any help at all. He kept talking about how much he believes in our beloved Führer and how he wouldn't do anything to hamper our cause. In my opinion, he's a stupid, lazy man."

Kloster shuffled some papers before he continued. "I then ordered my men to conduct a thorough search of the barn and vicinity. Nothing. Well, I thought we'd come up empty when a soldier found a discarded silver foil wrapper. Apparently, Americans like to chew gum, and this man, or one of his crew, had carelessly discarded the wrapper." Kloster had a trace of amusement in his voice. "I'm pretty sure that's what we found."

Schinkel grunted, as if expecting more. "Anything else?"

"Yes sir," Kloster quickly added. "Once there was sufficient daylight, I personally had a look at the interior of the crashed airplane and I came across a small photograph in the cockpit. It was wedged between the seat and a navigation chart. It depicts a young American officer, a lieutenant, standing next to a young woman. I compared the man's likeness with that of the captured men, and it doesn't match any of them. Sir, we now know what the missing pilot looks like."

"Good work, *Herr Oberleutnant*," Schinkel said, the tone in his voice less severe. "I'll expect a full report by the end of the day."

"Yes, sir. Heil Hitler."

"Heil Hitler."

Kloster hung up the phone and smiled at the photo sitting face up on his desk. It was quite fortunate of him to have found the photograph. But then Kloster had always depended on a little luck to get him what he wanted.

"Where are you hiding, my American friend?" Kloster murmured out loud, scrutinizing the man's likeness.

He dismissed the young woman standing next to the pilot. He peered closer, memorizing the man's facial features: the firm chin, and although the photo was in black and white, the vivid brown eyes.

Capturing the pilot would give Kloster more than a measure of personal satisfaction, and a pat on the back from the hard-to-please Schinkel couldn't hurt either. It might help him with his plan to oust Ziller from the test program. Things were finally going his way.

╬

Jack watched as Rudi pulled the Opel to a stop outside the Church of St. Nicholas. Although it was Sunday, it seemed that few parishioners had ventured out of doors to attend services. The driver tentatively checked both ways before ducking into the building through a side door. If the Gestapo were watching, Jack thought his actions likely gave him away. But then Rudi was an amateur and no professional spy.

After a minute or so, the door opened again and Rudi appeared, beckoning them to leave the car and join him inside the church. With Sochalski's help, Jack emerged from the back seat, followed by Hilde.

An older, fiftyish man was waiting for them just inside. He had dark bushy eyebrows, a stark contrast to his mild blue eyes, and wore a gray linen suit, augmented by a clerical collar.

"This is our parish priest, Father Hiller," Rudi said by way of introduction.

"Please, come in," the priest greeted them in accented English. "I am merely God's servant. Herr Schultz says that you survived a plane crash and need to—how do you Americans say—keep a low profile?"

Jack smiled and extended his hand. "Captain Jack Swaggart."

The priest smiled in turn, shaking it. "Alfred Hiller." He turned appraisingly to William, only barely visible in the dim light. "And you must be our little Jewish friend."

Sochalski nodded, but didn't saying anything.

"Don't worry young man," said Hiller. "You're safe here. For a while anyway. I'll see what I can do for you. Rudi will help me, won't you?"

Rudi nodded. "But first, we had better hurry. I need to return Fräulein Augsberg to her home, then drop the car off."

Hilde grasped the priest's hand. "Thank you, Father. I'll be in touch."

"Of course, my child."

She turned on her heels and followed Rudi out of the church. The three remaining men watched her leave.

"A good-looking woman," the priest remarked with a trace of amusement. "Don't you think, Captain?"

"Er … yes. And resourceful."

"Indeed. Now, please, both of you, come with me. Some of my parishioners may be arriving soon and I don't want to risk you being seen."

They followed the kindly priest toward the back of the church and down a flight of stairs. He led them to the crypt area and, after carefully checking that no one was inside, brought them into a vacant storage room. Judging from the dust on the shelves, it probably wasn't used very often. Jack spotted spent ornamental candles, stacks of ledgers and la-belled boxes, likely holding church records.

"I'm afraid that this will have to do for now," the priest apologized. "Once I have a few minutes to spare, I'll come down and see to your needs, *ja?*" He smiled and left, closing the door behind him.

"Well, that didn't go too bad, right Captain?" William re-marked.

Jack nodded as he seated himself in a wooden chair, mak-ing himself comfortable.

‡

Father Hiller walked quickly to his private chamber and removed his overcoat. He donned a green robe and tied a col-orful sash around his waist, visible confirmation of his cho-sen profession. He then sat and glanced out the small window, watching a few parishioners walk across the town square, still early for the first service. But his mind wasn't on them, nor on the sermon he had prepared the previous evening.

Hiller placed his fingertips together in contemplation as if he were going to pray; but that was merely an illusion and no prayer was forthcoming. Gone was the warm smile and the genial countenance, replaced by a stern and distant look. A determined look.

He reached for the telephone and placed a call, a formal call. The apparatus at the other end rang several times, with no answer. Pensively, he gazed at his instrument and decided to try another number. It was a business call, not to his ministerial superior, but a superior nonetheless.

"Geheimpolizei," a female voice answered at Gestapo headquarters. "How can I direct your call?"

"Guten Morgen, Fräulein," Hiller began. "Is Heinrich, I mean Major Heinrich Schinkel, available?"

"Well … it is Sunday, you know."

"Yes, but perhaps you could check for me," he said undeterred. "It's quite important that he gets my message."

"I'll see if he's available today. Just a moment, please." Then after a brief pause, the same voice came back on the line. "I'm sorry, but he had to attend an unscheduled meeting."

"Then don't disturb him. But do tell him that Father Hiller called."

"I see. I'll advise him after the meeting, Father," a more respectful voice answered.

"Good. When he has concluded his business, could he call me at the church? It is rather urgent." Hiller supplied the number.

"Very good, Father."

Hiller hung up and left his study. He found a ministerial assistant in the hall and paused to speak with him.

"Matthäus," he said quietly, "would you be so kind as to make some tea? And perhaps add a few croissants? You see, I'm expecting company."

The priest then continued on his way to the rectory. He found the deacon there and explained that he had urgent matters to attend to. He asked him to take the evening service. The deacon nodded and said he would be happy to. Hiller thanked him and, whistling, headed back to his private office.

╬

The military truck rumbled into Zehdenick's town center and stopped in front of a three-storey building. The large swastika flag flying prominently out front told Boyer this wasn't a hotel. He judged it likely to be the local police station.

The guards dismounted and with the business end of their machine pistols motioned for the prisoners to disembark. They were herded through a side entrance where, after a few introductory words by the sergeant, they were taken to a holding cell.

"Well, it's about time," Lucky quipped. "I was just starting to wonder about accommodations."

This got a chuckle from Romeo and Shore. One of the guards struck Lucky in the gut with the butt of his machine pistol.

"No speak," he chided in poor English. "Wait for … *Kapitän. Verstanden?*"

All of a sudden, Lucky wasn't feeling so lucky anymore. He doubled over from the pain and merely grunted in acknowledgement.

"*Sehr gut!*" the guard affirmed and motioned them to take a seat in the cell. Shore helped Lucky inside, while Romeo followed wordlessly. They looked around at the inhospitable holding room. It was small, with one door and no windows. Two wooden chairs and a small table completed the ensemble; not even a toilet to alleviate nature's call; just a bucket.

As officers, Boyer and Rossi were treated a little more cordially. They were led upstairs to a windowless corner room, containing two cots, a small table, and two chairs. Later, a guard brought in a metal tray laden with cups containing a broth as well as sandwiches. There was a metal jug underneath each cot, presumably meant to be used when nature called. The guard then left, locking the door from the outside. Clearly, they were staying here for the night.

CHAPTER XII

Captured

Back in the storage room, Jack noted Sochalski's apprehension as he began to fidget. Still feeling uneasy, William got up from his chair and paced back and forth in the confines of the small room. He confided to Jack that he wasn't sure why, but something about the priest felt … off. Jack listened to his concern but eventually dismissed it, attributing it to the fact the boy was Jewish and was feeling uncomfortable in a Catholic setting.

Jack couldn't have been more wrong.

Father Hiller arrived to collect them and brought them up to his private chamber to enjoy a tray loaded with cups of tea and croissants. They dug into the welcoming food, while the priest left them alone stating he had to see to the service. Jack was starting to relax, enjoying the food while his eyes admired the numerous books on the tiered shelves.

As pre-arranged, Hiller headed to the rectory while the deacon was getting the service underway. He drummed his fingers impatiently, while he awaited the phone call from Schinkel. It was taking longer than expected, so he settled into his armchair and picked up the tea he had set aside earlier.

He made a face. The tea was now lukewarm, but the thought of turning the Jew over to the authorities produced a smirk of satisfaction on his face.

Hiller pictured the scene when the Gestapo would walk

into his study to arrest the Jewish boy. Even though Hiller never uttered that word—Jew—it bore a distinctly negative connotation, which probably reached from as far back as his seminary days. One of his favorite teachers, a Jesuit, had fostered a negative portrayal of Jewry. Over time, with little input to the contrary and growing antisemitism by the Nazi party, it had cemented within Hiller a deep-seated dislike, bordering on hatred.

Then there was the American pilot. Hiller cursed silently, reminding himself of the bomb—an American bomb—that had killed his sister and almost killed himself and his brother-in-law.

How long had it been? he mused. *Nine months? Longer? Yes, nearly a year had elapsed since that day.* But the memory was still raw and vivid. Heinrich, Anna, and he had been enjoying a Sunday evening meal at Heinrich's apartment when they'd been interrupted by the air raid sirens going off. Ordinarily he wouldn't have bothered going to the air-raid shelter, but Anna had insisted.

So, reluctantly they had left the Wiener-schnitzel, roasted potatoes, and red cabbage on their plates and hurried down the stairs. They'd crossed the street and came to within meters of the entrance to the shelter when the first bombs started exploding. Anna would have been one of the first to go through the shelter's entrance, but instead she had stopped to help an elderly lady who had stumbled and fallen.

Hiller clenched his teeth as he remembered what had happened next. Anna, helping the woman to her feet, Heinrich lending a hand, people rushing by. The last thing he remembered was Heinrich shouting for him to get inside. Then a massive bomb—probably a one-thousand-pound bomb intended for the adjacent railway marshalling yard—exploded nearby. The explosion had been deafening and the concussion had knocked the wind out of him. He vaguely recalled staggering backwards and falling to the ground.

He hadn't blacked out, but when the confusion had subsided and the dust had settled, he had spotted Heinrich, apparently unconscious, lying face down on the sidewalk and bleeding from his sleeve. Anna was nowhere to be seen.

He'd struggled to get up and at last made his way to where she had been standing, only to be held back by a uniformed soldier. The man appeared to be speaking to him, but he couldn't hear a word he said. All he could make out was a dull droning sound. Hiller had motioned with his hands, trying to be understood, but the soldier only nodded and held out a handkerchief for him. He was dumbfounded, not knowing what to make of the offering. But then the soldier had pressed the kerchief into his left hand and guided it to his neck, to where he was bleeding.

"No, Father," the man had said once the droning began to fade. "There's … nothing … you … can do. Perhaps … later …"

Sirens from a fire engine drowned out the rest of the man's words. Hiller had looked on helplessly as workers arrived and did their best to sort out the carnage and tend to the injured. Reluctantly, he'd retreated to a temporary first-aid station to receive treatment himself. As it turned out, shrapnel had felled the person next to him, but an errant small piece had struck him in the neck, explaining the blood loss. When he'd felt somewhat like himself again, he had offered what priestly help he could to the injured. It wasn't until the next day that he learned Anna had been killed instantly. Her husband, Heinrich, had survived, although he would later undergo an operation to remove a portion of his left arm.

Ironically, the apartment hadn't been hit during the air raid, the offering of Wiener-schnitzel and its trimmings now cold and unsavory, like his distaste for Americans.

Sturmbannführer Schinkel left the meeting, feeling irritated at being manipulated by one of Göring's minions. Once again, he would have to bow to authority and allow discretion to prevail, enabling a government official to escape the consequences of his carelessness.

He sighed as he climbed the stairs to his office. On the way, he spotted his secretary, the one who usually filled in on weekends, seated at her desk, busy—or at least pretending to be busy, he couldn't tell.

"Major," she addressed him by his less formal title. "There was a phone call for you from … er … a Father Hiller. He left a phone number."

"Danke," he replied, taking the slip and heading to his office. His brother-in-law didn't customarily call him at work, so something important must have come up. He picked up the phone and dialed the church's number.

⛉

William had become more restless as he paced in the priest's study. It was more correct to say he appeared scared. He constantly glanced toward the door, and every time he heard a noise out in the hallway, he nervously jumped. Jack tried to calm him, but he had little success.

"Something is wrong, I know it," William persisted. "Why do we have to wait here for that priest?"

"Remember, William, Rudi led us here and he told us about Father Hiller. He officiated at Rudi's uncle's funeral and he trusts him. Perhaps we can give him a little bit of ours."

It was evident by the expression on William's face that he didn't find it comforting, but Jack didn't press it. They waited in silence for the priest's return.

While William fretted, Jack willed himself to take his mind off their present circumstances. He glanced around the room and noted the typical things one might expect to find in a cleric's study: a framed picture of Pope Pius XII, flanked by two smaller frames depicting members of the clergy. There was a small bookcase with an assortment of hardcover books. Jack, a school teacher back home, was drawn to them and tried reading the German titles. Many appeared to be spiritual in nature.

He straightened up and, by chance, noticed a silver-framed picture of a good-looking woman in her mid-thirties. She wasn't striking, but her face had a warm appeal. The black-and-white photo didn't reveal her eye or hair color, but she seemed to have a fair complexion. If anything, she reminded Jack of someone back home, someone he cared about a great deal: his fiancée, Nicole.

Without further prompting, his thoughts returned to happier times, back to his life in Minnesota with Nicole. He thought of her as his fiancée, and spoke of her that way to his colleagues, but the truth was that he hadn't yet asked her to marry him.

As his thoughts turned to her, he recalled a particular fond weekend they had spent together at a friend's cottage.

Wilbur, an accountant, had been called away on business and had asked if Jack wanted to make use of his family cottage. Jack hadn't needed much time to make up his mind.

And so, he had packed up enough groceries into his '39 Ford to last several days, and before long he and Nicole were rumbling down the highway to nearby Alexandria where they were to meet one other couple, the girls sharing a room and the guys bunking together. They all had a wonderful weekend, getting reacquainted and enjoying the peaceful scenery.

Jack was due to return home in a couple of weeks. It would be the perfect opportunity to spend time with Nicole, perhaps go back to that cottage, and finally get up the nerve to ask her to become his wife.

Reflexively, he reached into his wallet to retrieve her picture, only to remember that he'd lost it in the crash. He was crest-fallen as he realized he would likely never see it again.

Instead, he tried to summon a memory of Nicole, of her fine skin, luscious lips, and the sweetest brown eyes he had ever seen. She was petite and had to stand on her tiptoes to reach him for a kiss. Well, she was a long way from France—well, Germany, and his longing to be back home with her was nearly overpowering.

But then he considered William, all alone, who had lost his parents in the Nazi maelstrom. The dose of reality brought him back to the reason he was here—the reason he was fighting in this war. He felt his sense of duty return.

He stretched and felt the urge to use the bathroom. He got up and told William he needed to relieve himself and would be right back. William nodded absentmindedly, staring out the window.

Jack picked up a walking stick that was propped up against a coat rack and headed out into the hall. Unfamiliar with the layout, he turned the corner and peered down a long hallway. *Is it this way?* he thought to himself. He walked slowly, studying the beautiful tapestries hanging on the wall.

As he walked, he casually glanced out the second-storey window and noticed two gray-colored sedans pull up and park in an alcove at the rear of the church. Nothing unusual about that. He suspected that worshippers with means and influence still drove cars, and perhaps parked at the back to avoid being singled out.

A man in a fedora and dark overcoat emerged from the front seat and walked to the rear of the second car. He opened the door for someone Jack supposed was a member of his family. Jack was about to continue on his walk, but then the second passenger emerged.

Jack stopped in his tracks.

This man wasn't dressed for church but was attired in the black uniform of the feared Gestapo. As the man looked about, it became clear that he wasn't interested in the architecture nor in its history. No, he'd come for something else.

Jack scrutinized him. Although Jack knew the man couldn't possibly see him, he still stepped away from the window as the first pangs of fear shot through him. What were they doing here on a Sunday evening? Was it merely coincidence?

The man retrieved a cigarette case from his inner coat pocket and selected a cigarette. Immediately, one of his companions produced a lighter. Cupping his hands around the lighter, the man lit the cigarette and drew on it, deeply and slowly, allowing the smoke to escape his nostrils.

Before Jack could consider the matter further, the man extinguished his cigarette, and with a nod of his head bade his men to follow. They disappeared from view around the corner.

Jack's heart beat a little faster and the hair at the nape of his neck stood on end. He was beginning to sweat. Instinct told him they had come with a purpose—to arrest someone. He caught his reflection in the window and instantly knew why they were here. They were going to arrest him. In all likelihood, they were pursuing a lead and probably already knew about him, perhaps Sochalski as well. *But how could they have learned about us so quickly?* he debated with himself. The answer didn't really matter.

Jack knew he had to act fast. There wasn't any time to lose.

As he turned to head back to the priest's office, he heard a distant shout. An authoritative voice, followed by another, this one much quieter and diminutive. The second one sounded like William's voice: subdued, pleading.

He was too late. All of a sudden it all made sense to Swaggart. The Gestapo weren't here by accident. Somehow, they had been alerted to his presence. They *knew* he was here. And now they had arrested Sochalski. Poor William.

Angry at himself, Jack clenched his fists in frustration. He should have paid more attention to William's foreboding and realized he had stayed alive this long because he had trusted his instincts.

Jack thought of rushing to the boy's defence, but what could he do? There were at least three, possibly four armed men, while all he had was a walking stick. He realized he had left his pistol in his flying jacket, stashed in the trunk of Rudi's borrowed car. A sickening feeling crept into his bowels. He had been a fool to be so trusting. What he had passed off as coincidence was likely more sinister, perhaps even betrayal.

Betrayal. The word stung as if he'd been slapped.

His thoughts drifted to Rudi, then Hilde. He didn't want to believe they had turned against him and William, but the harsh reality couldn't be ignored. He wanted nothing more than to dismiss the thought. He liked Rudi and there had been something reassuring about Hilde. Damn! And the worst of it—he might never know who turned them in.

Jack didn't need more convincing. *Stick to your gut feeling,* he reminded himself. He kept walking until he found a set of stairs. Not worried about where they might lead, he slowly descended the steps in the hopes of finding a way out of the building. If Sochalski had told them he had gone in search of the lavatory, they would be looking in the wrong place, buying him a few precious seconds.

Jack spotted a small wooden door, hoping it led outside. He was about to reach for the handle when he saw it start to turn. His heart skipped a beat. There was no time to turn back—he couldn't even run. Instinctively he lifted the cane and pressed himself flat against the wall.

The door creaked open, and just as Jack was about to strike the unsuspecting person, likely a Gestapo agent, Rudi Schultz stepped into view.

"Rudi? What ... I mean ... what are you doing here?" Jack almost shouted.

Rudi turned sideways seeing Jack's raised arm and instinctively lifted his own to protect himself. Jack's arm wavered, not sure if he should strike. But seeing the hurt look on Rudi's face somehow convinced him of his innocence. Jack lowered the cane and smiled. "It's good to see you."

"Yes, you too, Herr Kapitän. But I ... must ... must you ... to get out, *ja?*" His expression turned serious. "Gestapo

... here!"

Jack nodded. "Yes, I saw them from upstairs."

Rudi turned on his heel and motioned Jack to follow. They ducked out the door unnoticed and headed down the alley. Jack bit his lip and kept up a good pace despite the pain in his ankle. At least he had the cane for support. They turned the corner, and to his surprise he discovered that Rudi had stopped beside a parked motorcycle with a sidecar. A wisp of smoke escaped the exhaust pipe, suggesting the motor had recently been running. "*Bitte,* for you," Rudi said, handing Jack a military overcoat, a lieutenant's forage cap and goggles.

"BMW?" asked Jack, nodding at the gray motorcycle.

"*Nein,*" Rudi smiled. "Zündapp KS750. Better than BMW."

Jack marvelled at Rudi's ingenuity but didn't question him. He quickly donned the hat and coat, not in the least bit perturbed about the temporary reduction in rank. He felt a strange sort of camaraderie with the man beside him, a man he barely knew. The whole thing seemed absurd. Jack wondered if he'd ever get the chance to tell the tale to his family, perhaps his grandchildren.

He slipped on the goggles and, with Rudi's help, climbed into the sidecar. Rudi then leaped onto the motorbike, flipped the crank handle with his boot and, with practiced movement, kick-started it. The motor turned over but didn't fire.

"Where ... to?" Jack managed.

"Safe place."

Jack wanted to know where, but he also didn't want to hold them up with unnecessary questions. The important thing was to leave the vicinity of the church.

Rudi reached for the primer, made a minute adjustment, and tried again. Jack felt a surge of excitement as the engine fired, its vibrations passing from the chassis to the sidecar. Rudi grinned and donned his own goggles. He squeezed the clutch lever, engaged first gear, and glanced down the lane. He inched forward and, with no Gestapo men in sight, accelerated smoothly away from the church. He turned right at the next street corner and drove towards town center. He calmly shifted up to second, then third, as if he were simply taking his superior for a Sunday drive.

⊬

Father Hiller was furious that his plan hadn't worked out as he had intended. He swore and pounded his desk upon learning that the American pilot had slipped away.

His brother-in-law sat calmly opposite him in the rectory, mildly surprised by the outburst. He showed it by raising an eyebrow. At last, the priest managed to get a grip on himself.

"I'm sorry, Heinrich," Hiller apologized. "I shouldn't have sworn like that."

Amused, Schinkel dismissed the outburst with a wave of his gloved hand.

"Don't worry about it, my dear Alfred," Heinrich replied. "I probably would have reacted the same way. In any case, he'll be rounded up fairly quickly, I should think. How far can he hobble with that sprained ankle? My men are checking the church right now, in case he doubled back. No, I think we'll have him in short order."

Schinkel picked up his tea but his hand hovered in midair before he took a sip.

"Besides, my men already have the rest of the crew in custody in Zehdenick," he continued. "One of my more competent officers, Horst Kloster, the man you saw a few minutes ago, will return and interrogate them in due course. Now, my good Alfred, do you still keep some schnapps in your desk?"

CHAPTER XIII

Kloster Forges Ahead

Pankow, a popular borough for Berliners, was far enough removed from the city to have escaped most of the war-time bombing. Rivalling Potsdam, the city was considered one of the more desirable areas to live, distant enough to elude the capital's politics while remaining easily accessible.

It became clear to Reimar Horten that his brother Walter was going to be occupied with the dignitaries for some time. Still, Reimar felt the need to celebrate the success of the test flight, and so he invited Ziller, as well as Bauman, to accompany him to a local tavern. Reimar travelled with Andreas in a loaner from the motor pool, having loaned out his own car and chauffeur to Hilde. Even though it was mid-afternoon, they found a lively atmosphere in the bar.

The two men seated themselves in the restaurant and hungrily dug into a warm meal of sauerkraut and bratwurst. Ziller joined them in a short while, and, though they couldn't talk openly about their project, they were in a jovial mood nevertheless.

Once they had finished their simple meal, Reimar wasn't as eager to end the evening, much less depart, and suggested a game of billiards.

Reimar walked over to the bar to register his name for the table, with Ziller following close behind. He didn't immediately spot the uniformed officer who had just entered.

Kloster had spotted Ziller, however. Kloster was in a singularly foul mood because the American pilot had eluded him. He remained at his table and nursed his beer, watching the two pilots play through their game. He had half a mind to leave them be, but something within him made him stay.

If truth be known, he was plagued by the mystery of just why he had come to detest Ziller so much, an amiable fellow who was liked by all.

But the explanation was simple. Although both men had excelled in their careers, Ziller had honed his flying skills, while Kloster had honed—well, pursued other interests. Women mostly. Pretty young women, voluptuous women, but worst of all, married women. Ultimately, that had proved to be his undoing. Just when he was slated to accept a test pilot position, his bad luck had surfaced—or so it seemed to him.

Not that it could be attributed to bad luck. Luck, after all, implied that the recipient did not have much input into the outcome of an event or the circumstances surrounding it. It had nothing to do with luck, it was all his own doing. Not satisfied with his current fling—the pursuit of a young vivacious secretary—he had set his sights on her boss' wife. Kloster enjoyed a challenge, but this time his enterprising had wandered too far. His sought-after prize turned out to be the wife of a general who was politically and socially well-connected but also a workaholic.

Kloster, unscrupulous and narcissistic, felt he could give her what the general couldn't—undivided attention. After a number of theatre outings and intimate dinners, he got the bored *generalin* exactly where he wanted her: hungering for more. From there it was relatively easy to bed the love-starved beauty. He pressed on and failed to consider the consequences, not to mention the disgrace if he were caught. As so often happens, the best-laid plans can be thwarted by unexpected events.

"Horst, another beer?" A voice intruded his musings.

He turned around to see the familiar face of Captain Bruno von Holzberg, a former pilot, now assigned to the Reserve Army and stationed in Berlin.

"Bruno, what brings you out here?" Kloster replied, his smile showing he welcomed the interruption.

"Why, the same thing as you, my friend. A nice draft beer and a little *gemütlichkeit.*"

"Of course. Companionship is good for the soul. Have you noticed our old friend over there?" He nodded in Ziller's direction.

von Holzberg turned in his seat and appraised the man. "Ah, you mean Ziller? He's the new test pilot for the Horten project, isn't he?"

Kloster nodded grimly. "*Ja,* but he's not half the pilot I am."

"Perhaps. But you're not flying anymore, remember? So, what's it like working for Schinkel? I hear he's a hard man."

"Actually, he's not that bad once you get to know him," Kloster replied after a moment's hesitation. "He expects a lot, but he's not a bootlicker, if you know what I mean."

von Holzberg nodded thoughtfully.

Though engaged in conversation, Kloster continued watching Ziller's table. When he noted that he and Bauman were about to leave, he decided to give them a parting shot. He excused himself and followed the two men out the door.

"Well, well, if it isn't the esteemed test pilot, Herr Ziller," Kloster called out.

Ziller spun around at the sound of his name. He raised his hand to blot out the dying rays of the sun only to spot Kloster's advance.

"What do you want, Kloster?" Ziller managed, barely keeping his civility.

"Not much. I just wanted to know how you're getting on with the new job."

Ziller's eyes were adjusting to the fading light as he tried to focus in on his adversary.

"It's going well. Flight testing is proceeding slowly, but that's part of the job, right? Why are you so interested?"

"I have my reasons. But then I was a much better—"

"Come on, Horst," von Holzberg intervened. "Let's finish that beer."

Without waiting for an answer, von Holzberg took Kloster by the elbow and was about to guide him back inside.

Kloster, not entirely minding the interruption, started to head back but couldn't resist firing off one last shot.

"Just go easy on that stick, Ziller. You can't manhandle it like you would a woman."

Ziller was about to respond, when he caught a look from Reimar, who had at the last minute decided to follow them out. Ziller reluctantly decided not to take the bait.

Kloster, not feeling the least bit vindicated, returned to the bar with von Holzberg.

"What was all that about, Horst?" von Holzberg inquired.

"Oh, I just had to get something off my chest," he uttered, trying to control his frustration.

"Don't let Ziller get to you," von Holzberg cautioned. "Horst, your turn will come. Anyway, let's drink up. I have to get going."

von Holzberg drained his glass and stood up, glancing at his friend. "Coming?"

"No, you go ahead," said Kloster. "I'll just finish my beer. And—don't worry about me."

von Holzberg nodded and left. Kloster sat alone absorbed in his thoughts. He felt himself being drawn down a path he was all too familiar with—hatred. He hated being made a fool of, regardless of the circumstances. It was no wonder that he came to revisit the run-in with the jealous general.

Kloster had visited Claudia one fine morning, knowing the general would be away attending high-level meetings. The two lovers had just retreated to the bedroom when Kloster heard noises downstairs. The general must have returned home un-expectedly, Kloster surmised. Perhaps he forgot something. He sprang into action and quickly grabbed his coat and boots. Just as he was heading for the veranda, he heard the general bellow from the doorway, "What the hell is going on here?"

As Kloster mounted the railing, he saw the general fumble with his holster. Kloster tossed his boots down into the garden but couldn't resist a furtive glance over his left shoulder. The general, Luger in hand, was actually taking aim at him.

The shot rang out, but missed its mark thanks to Claudia's intervention: a well-placed throw of her shoe that hit the general's right arm, altering his aim. The bullet sailed harmlessly over Kloster's head. He swung himself over the railing and climbed down the front of the façade, leaping the last few feet to the ground. He ventured one last look, only to find an angry man glaring down at him, while his terrified wife struggled to pull him back inside.

Kloster couldn't help the twisted grin on his face. No-one could say he wasn't adventurous. He picked up his mug and gulped a good measure of his draft beer. He replaced the *stein* on the table and ruefully glanced around the tavern, feeling a little sorry for himself.

He noticed two men in civilian clothes seated by themselves at a nearby table. He didn't pay them much attention at first. They were young, probably in their mid-twenties, and sported short, military haircuts. He had seen many like them—pilots or army officers on leave—with money to spend and looking for a good time.

They were engrossed in conversation, elevating their discussion by talking animatedly with their hands. Laughing, one of the men recounted a particularly amusing romantic escapade. Kloster sat there, appearing detached, yet listening with amusement. Laughter followed the conclusion, and Kloster assumed his *kamerad* would try to trump him with a story of his own.

But then the man changed the course of the conversation. It seemed he himself was a pilot and had been flying bomber escort at high altitude, when he experienced a problem with his oxygen supply.

The fresh-faced lieutenant spoke with surprising candour and Kloster had half a mind to chastise him for being so out-spoken in public.

What the hell, let them blow off a little steam. Kloster reconsidered his earlier assessment. *They're entitled to it. Who knows? They could both be dead tomorrow. Defending the Fatherland was no picnic.*

Getting bored, he was about to dismiss their conversation and stood up to leave, when one of the men called out loudly, "I was lucky. I could have been killed. But it wasn't my turn."

Kloster hesitated, as his clever mind clung to the man's comment. Like a slithering snake caressing its eggs, he played it over in his mind, an idea forming. And the more he thought about it the more it appealed to him. What had Bruno said? "Kloster, your turn will come." All of a sudden, he had found the means of getting even with the enterprising Ziller.

Kloster quietly got up, paid his bill, and left the *brauhaus*. He whistled to himself, satisfied that he had stumbled onto a perfect means of stalling Ziller's ascending career. *Well, not just stall it,* he thought grinning at his own metaphor. *I'll end it, and end it with a bang!*

CHAPTER XIV

Making Plans

It was mid-afternoon, when Hilde Augsberg used her latchkey to come in through the side door of her mother's house. She removed her boots and hung up her overcoat, then breathed in the sweet aroma of her mother's cooking. She walked into the kitchen and wrapped her arms around her mother's waist.

"It smells wonderful, *Mutti*," she said, glancing over her mother's shoulder. Gertrude was retrieving a pan from the oven. *"Rouladen?"* Hilde gave her mother a questioning look. "From Andreas?" she asked, already knowing the answer.

"Who else would think of providing for two lonely women? Now, put on an apron and help me with the potatoes. Remember, I have to work tonight."

Hilde did as instructed and the two went about preparing a nutritious meal, a rarity during these hard times they'd been facing in the waning months of the war. While dinner was cooking, they put on some tea and sat near the fireplace, enjoying its spreading warmth.

"Mother," Hilde began, with a hint of trepidation in her voice, "there is something I need to tell you."

"What? Is something wrong between you and that handsome lieutenant?" she asked with alarm.

"No, nothing like that ..."

Knowing her daughter well, Gertrude placed her teacup on the side table and picked up Hilde's hand. "I thought something was troubling you when you walked in. You can tell me, *mein kind.*"

The term of endearment brought back a recent memory, one that reminded her of her mother's unselfishness and deep affection for her daughter.

"Alright," Hilde said. "You've always been supportive of me, even if you haven't always agreed with my decisions." She paused, collecting her thoughts. "Yesterday, on the way to Zehdenick, Rudi and I came across a plane crash. You see, there were survivors, and one man was injured. I ended up helping a downed flyer … an American."

"An … American?" Gertrude stammered.

"Yes, an American pilot."

"But why, for God's sake? You could end up in serious trouble. If that self-serving Saufman finds out he'll use that knowledge as an opportunity to … to advance his career and gain influence in the Nazi party. I've already lost your father to the war and I don't want Saufman robbing a mother of her last joy—you!"

"I'm not worried about Saufman, mother," Hilde said, squeezing her mother's hand. "But you see, I didn't know the plane was an American bomber."

Hilde went on to explain the situation, how she had felt compelled to help and then felt sorry for the wounded officer. She even mentioned the young Jewish boy they had met.

Gertrude's expression slowly changed from one of disapproval to one of interest and lastly admiration. She seemed to be reconsidering her earlier stand.

"Yes, I understand now," Gertrude said. "Many of us have felt for some time that Germany was losing the war, despite what that dummkopf, that *tolpel* Goebbels keeps proclaiming in his weekly broadcast. My dear, feeling sorry for a downed airman is one thing, but to go so far as working against Hitler's regime? It could prove your undoing. And now, you're thinking of helping him more?" She stopped and smiled at her daughter. "I wasn't aware you had such resources at your disposal. What will your faithful lieutenant think?"

"I hadn't thought that part through yet, *Mutti*," Hilde admitted. "But there's more. We saw something strange on the road back to Oranienburg. A jet plane, one unlike anything I've ever seen before, flew directly overhead. The American pilot was equally surprised. During the car ride, he mentioned that many more lives, both German and American, will be lost if the Nazis build more of those types of war planes. He explained how the Allies have ramped up efforts and are determined to end the war quickly. They, especially the British, want to minimize further loss of life. That's why I've decided to help him."

Gertrude nodded thoughtfully, trying to absorb everything her daughter had just told her. "That's very noble of you, but have you really thought this through?"

Hilde frowned, painfully aware of the difficulty of the task before her.

"Still, you may be right, my dear," Gertrude continued. "What's to be done?"

"Well, to start with, we'll need identity papers," she managed.

Gertrude nodded thoughtfully. "Yes, I should think that would be a priority."

Hilde and her mother spent the next hour making plans, then discarding them, and starting afresh.

An unexpected knock on the door sent a shudder through Hilde. She got up from her chair and went to answer it. Expecting an unsolicited visit from a policeman, perhaps from the Gestapo, she cautiously opened the door. A uniformed soldier stood there, wearing goggles. Behind him in the lane was a motorcycle with sidecar, and seated inside the compartment was a Wehrmacht officer.

She relaxed a fraction. At least it wasn't the Gestapo. But then the driver removed his goggles and leather helmet, revealing none other than Rudi Schultz. Hilde smiled with relief. But then, just as quickly, her smile disappeared when she perceived the worried expression on his face.

"They've got him," Rudi managed, looking down at his spit-polished boots.

Hilde's thoughts immediately went to what she'd feared the most. "You mean the American pilot?"

"No, no … he's here with me." He gestured over his shoulder. "He's outside, waiting in the sidecar. "I meant, the boy, Sochalski. They've just arrested him. If it hadn't been for the captain's quick thinking, they would have gotten him as well. I just don't understand how the Gestapo could have known to come to the church and—"

"Not now, Rudi," Hilde interrupted gently. "We'll discuss it later. I take it you brought … Herr Swaggart to hide him in our house?"

Rudi nodded. "I couldn't think where else to bring him on such short notice."

"You did the right thing. Now quick, bring him inside."

While Hilde went inside to inform her mother of this latest development, Rudi went around to the sidecar and helped extricate Jack from the confined space. Thankful to be on solid ground, Jack hobbled after Rudi, all the while glancing at the neighboring houses. But if anyone was watching, they didn't show themselves.

In the kitchen, Jack removed the overcoat and seated himself on a chair. A moment later, Hilde came in from the parlor with her mother and introduced her guests. Jack was about to get up to shake hands, but Gertrude waved him off.

"Please, Herr Kapitän, don't get up," she said with Hilde translating. "You must be in pain. Allow me to assist you. I helped raise two brothers through all sorts of escapades and calamities and I'm sure I can be of assistance to you as well."

Grateful for the offer, Jack nodded and leaned back in the chair. Frau Augsberg removed her apron and knelt down on the floor. She was all business. First, she slowly unlaced the boot and slipped it off his left foot. With the same care, she removed his woollen sock, exposing a swollen white foot that had turned black and blue at the ankle.

Jack grimaced each time she touched the sensitive ankle, but he had to admit to himself that these German women were quite capable and efficient.

"There should still be some warm water on the stove, dear," Gertrude instructed her daughter. She turned to Rudi. "Please, go next door and see if Frau Sonnenberg is home. She has one of those new iceboxes. Ask her for some ice without revealing what it's for."

Rudi, used to taking orders, thought nothing of it and headed out the door on the errand. Hilde returned with a pot of warm water, soap, and a hand towel. Frau Augsberg dipped the cloth in the water, applied some soap, and wrung it out. She proceeded to clean his foot, carefully working her way up to the ankle. The gentle but firm pressure caused Jack to bite his lip, but he didn't move, trusting his new-found nurse.

Gertrude probed around the joint and satisfied with her assessment, looked up at her patient.

"It's badly sprained, but not broken—my opinion. I'm afraid we don't have the luxury of having it X-rayed."

Jack nodded. As if on cue, Rudi returned with a bowl containing several chunks of ice. Gertrude rewrapped them in her hand towel and held it against the ankle. It felt so good that Jack nearly sighed. He couldn't help grinning from all the attention he was getting. First from the lovely fräulein and now from her efficient mother.

While they fussed over him, he thought back to his own mother and his home near New Salem, North Dakota.

He smiled, realizing that it was his grandmother's influence that ensured he had retained some of the German language into adulthood. He listened attentively to the women's conversation, and surprisingly caught more than the odd word. Listening to them talk brought an odd yet reassuring sensation, the familiarity of the German language a welcome throwback to times spent on the family farm.

"There, that should do it for now," Frau Augsberg said with satisfaction as she finished her ministrations.

Rudi looked on with amusement, but then remembered he still had a motorcycle to return and said as much to Hilde. She followed him out to say goodbye. Jack saw her give him a peck on the cheek. Rudi seemed embarrassed by her show of affection, but then just shrugged and mounted the bike.

Jack heard the Zündapp's engine roar to life, then grow more faint as Rudi drove down the lane.

Hilde returned inside, while her mother busied herself in the kitchen.

"Your pilot can rest while I finish the preparations for supper," Gertrude said. "Remember, I have to go to work this evening, so I won't be joining you."

⚔

Gertrude Augsberg, though outwardly composed, felt anything but calm inside. As she walked toward city hall for the weekly cleaning ritual, she replayed the recent events in her mind.

It all seemed so surreal. Part of her was immensely proud of her daughter and the stand she had taken against the Nazi regime. But another part, the emotional one—the mother in her—couldn't help but view the situation with foreboding and worry.

She passed a neighbor in the street, smiling and hoping Frau Schmidt couldn't see the anxiety written on her face. At last, she arrived at the grand building. How often had she walked by and admired the superb craftsmanship, the unique architecture of the building.

But today, she paid little attention to that, instead climbing the steps, noting the Nazi flag flapping in the breeze. It was only a flag, but a shiver went through her nevertheless. The swastika, a solemn symbol, represented the German empire, but more so the enormous war machine, a powerful juggernaut that had conquered most of Europe.

Before entering the building, she caught site of the two gargoyles mounted on the parapet, overlooking the square. For an instant, it seemed as if those stone-faced guardians were about to detach themselves and crash down on anyone not completely adhering to the ideology of the current regime. She had always been fascinated by them, but not today; somehow, they menaced her, as though daring her to stay away.

Gertrude forced herself to look away and focused her attention on the sentry who guarded the entrance. He hardly paid her any attention. After all, he had performed the same routine many times before. He held out his hand, as if receiving the early edition of the daily newspaper, and took the offered document more out of habit than duty, clearly bored by the repetitive job. He glanced at her pass and didn't even bother to check on the contents of her handbag.

She moved aside and nodded politely to the young women leaving the building from the day shift. She watched in amusement as they filed out, talking animatedly about their evening plans. She wondered what kind of an evening was in store for her daughter and her American pilot friend.

She was actually a little early. The head cleaning lady, Frau Burghardt, hadn't shown up yet. Gertrude went to the cloakroom, removed her coat, and donned an apron. She glanced at the posted schedule and headed for the second floor. As outlined, she was to commence cleaning Herr Saufman's office.

She spotted another guard loitering in the hallway, and after bidding him a good evening asked him to unlock the mayor's office. The guard, clearly bored and wishing he were elsewhere, examined her pass and asked to see the contents of her handbag. She opened it for him. After a cursory look that revealed nothing more than house keys, a powder case, a small sandwich, and thermos of coffee, he granted his approval with a grunt.

Gertrude entered the spacious office, placed her bag on a chair, and went to collect a mop and pail. She noted that, like his companion on the main floor, the guard elected to make himself comfortable and perused the daily paper. She switched on the radio, hoping to lull him into *gemüttlichkeit*[4]—a feeling of serenity—thus ensuring he wouldn't be inclined to check up on her.

After cleaning the windowsills, Gertrude took out polish and concentrated on the large wooden desk. She noticed the lower drawer had been left partially open, and in the process of closing it, she spotted a ring of keys atop some papers. It didn't take much thought for her to realize that one of those keys probably unlocked the other drawers.

She felt a pang of conscience as she was about to turn the key in the lock of the topmost drawer. Was this ethical? She certainly knew it was improper, perhaps bordering on criminal, but then two things struck her almost simultaneously. One, she spotted the framed picture of the conceited Saufman shaking hands with Himmler, the head of the Gestapo. Two, the radio station rudely interrupted the melodious sound of Beethoven's Fifth symphony with the all too familiar voice of Joseph Goebbels, the Third Reich's minister of propaganda.

In that instant, she made up her mind to go through with it.

Gertrude crept to the door and peered out. Spotting the guard still reading his paper, she returned to the desk and unlocked the top drawer. She had no idea what she was going to find inside. Perhaps Saufman's little black book, a large quantity of Reichsmarks, and maybe a flask of schnapps. Instead, she found several dossiers labelled "Communists," travel documents, and a manila envelope marked "Private." She glanced at the dossiers and found information on various Communist sympathisers living in Oranienburg. She laid them aside.

Now more than just curious, Gertrude picked up the travel documents. The first was for an older German woman who had requested travel to Paris, France to attend a funeral. A second outlined a professor's request to visit a university in occupied Poland. The third was for a couple wishing to travel to northern Germany. These travel papers all bore the mayor's official stamp; they were sealed and endorsed.

Gertrude was speechless. She recalled seeing the couple mentioned in the travel papers. They had come to Saufman's office over a week ago. Gertrude remembered them specifically because they had just left the building when she had walked in, talking excitedly about visiting family in Neubrandenburg.

Gertrude was puzzled. So why were the papers still in Saufman's desk and not with the couple? She rummaged through the desk and found nothing else that stood out except the manila envelope. Much to her surprise, it contained only one item: a small black book.

Well, well, Saufman does have his secrets, she mused. At first, she nearly dismissed it for an address book, but then she decided to glance through it. Inside it contained a list of names and dates, as well as itemized payments. She flipped to the current month and found the three corresponding names from the travel documents. The first column gave the name, the second the amount paid, and the third a date with a space for a checkmark or comment, presumably detailing when the payment had been received.

She flipped back to the previous month and found five entries, each with names, dates, and a checkmark. It was easy for Gertrude to draw the obvious conclusion. Saufman either received kickbacks for approving or expediting these travel requests, or worse, he delayed their approval until money changed hands.

Possibly there was a more sinister explanation: blackmail.

But she stopped herself from further speculation.

Gertrude didn't think; she just acted on impulse. She placed the first two visas and their accompanying papers back in the drawer, but she pocketed the last one, the couple who were destined for Neubrandenburg. Aside from this, she made sure all the papers were returned to their respective places and locked the drawer. She also remembered to replace the keys in the bottom drawer.

She then commenced cleaning as if nothing had occurred. Later, when all the staff had shown up, Gertrude feigned not feeling well. As she had practically completed all her assigned duties, she was excused from any further work. She removed her cleaning garb and hurried home, wondering how Hilde might be able to use the pilfered travel documents.

CHAPTER XV

The Interrogation

The following morning, Boyer was roused by a different guard. The soldier motioned over his shoulder for Boyer and Rossi to follow, and they were escorted to an office. File folders and a telephone had been neatly arranged on a large wooden table, the only items on it. A comfortable rolling chair was tucked in behind the desk.

A filing cabinet occupied another wall and mounted above it was a framed picture of the Führer. A coat tree flanked the door on one side, while an armed sentry who appeared as stiff as the rack itself guarded the other. Before either man could complete his evaluation of the interior, they were interrupted by the door opening.

A female clerk walked in and, without uttering a word, placed a silver tray on a side table. She then turned and left the room.

Rossi peeked at the basket of steaming buns and silver pitcher that undoubtedly contained tea or coffee. He glanced at Boyer, whose look told him to leave the buns and wait. But before he could object, the door opened again and a German officer entered. The guard immediately snapped to attention, clicking his heels smartly.

The German officer, a captain in rank, acknowledged his presence with a slight nod.

"Gentlemen," the captain said, addressing the Americans

in nearly fluent English, "please remove your jackets and take a seat."

As he gestured toward two upholstered chairs, another woman walked in and took her place beside the officer.

"My name is Horst Kloster, and I am assigned to the Luftwaffe, and this is Fräulein Braun, a stenographer. I've been given the task of, how shall I put it, interviewing you. Don't worry. I'm not with the Gestapo."

Boyer appraised the officer's immaculate uniform. His boots were polished to a high gloss and his pants were pressed, showing one perfect crease. The tunic, perhaps slightly ill-fitting, bore a number of decorations including the Iron Cross with Oak Leaves, and equally important, the shoulder boards confirmed he was a Luftwaffe officer, a *Hauptmann*. Reassuring was the fact that the captain didn't carry a sidearm. Even Rossi relaxed a fraction.

But appearances can be deceiving. Earlier that morning, Kloster had climbed the steps to the town's administration building, nearly colliding with a captain from the Luftwaffe. In a stroke of good luck, Kloster talked the captain into loaning him his tunic—professional courtesy. Kloster reasoned that airmen facing interrogation would feel less threatened being questioned by an officer with the Luftwaffe, as opposed to the ruthless tactics imposed by the Gestapo.

Boyer removed his flying jacket and walked to within three paces of the German and saluted.

"Lieutenant Charles Boyer with the 322nd Bombardment Group, US Air Force." He supplied his serial number. He then gestured toward Joe. "Our navigator, Second Lieutenant Joe Rossi."

"Bon giorno," Joe replied. "Giuseppe Rossi, Lieutenant, U.S. Air Force." He also supplied his serial number.

Kloster appraised each man in turn and returned a quizzical look to Boyer. "You said your name is Boyer, Charles Boyer. I'm a little unclear on that. I thought the French—"

Boyer had gotten used to making explanations. It came with the territory when you shared the same name with a major film star.

"Allow me to clarify, Herr Hauptmann," Boyer interjected. "Well, I'm obviously not a film star and the actor is not with the military. We just happen to share the same name."

Kloster smiled at the explanation. "Yes. It makes perfect sense."

"You speak quite good English, Captain," Boyer offered, hoping to keep the conversation civil.

"Thank you," Kloster replied modestly. "I was able to take several English courses while at the University of Hanover, but that was before the war." He leaned forward conspiratorially. "You see, I also had a friend … umm, a lady friend … who studied overseas and spoke English."

This seemed to break the ice.

"Now, please, take a seat and enjoy the refreshments," Kloster gestured at the tray.

Each man received a cup of coffee and buttered bun. They took the offering eagerly, though each man knew that this was merely the German's way to make them feel at ease. Interrogation was sure to follow.

Kloster began by asking Boyer some routine questions about the mission: flight altitude, number of aircraft, mission parameter, that sort of thing. Boyer guessed that Kloster knew they had been assigned to bomb the railway yards, and so he stated this openly. After a few questions, the German reached into his pocket and retrieved a photograph, showing it to Boyer.

Boyer's eyes widened in surprise, realizing that the image was of Jack and his fiancée, Nicole. The Germans must have retrieved it from the wreckage. It was a clever tactic, one that should have given Kloster the advantage. But before he could elaborate, Boyer leapt out of the chair, catching the interrogator off guard. He reached for the photo, but Kloster pulled it away just in time. In the process, Kloster bumped into the side table and knocked over the coffee, some of which sloshed out of the spout onto his uniform tunic, eliciting a curse.

Kloster glared at Boyer and unbuttoned the tunic. But in so doing, he inadvertently allowed a wallet to slip from an inside pocket and tumble to the floor.

The billfold split open for all to see. Displayed prominently was an identity card bearing the portrait of a tired-looking Luftwaffe officer—an older man with a dark complexion. The picture didn't remotely resemble the younger, energetic-looking Kloster.

Boyer froze in his tracks, then glanced up at the Luftwaffe captain, who seemed unmasked but was trying not to show it. He too couldn't help staring at the open wallet and the revealing photograph. He glared at the guard who, like the rest, was frozen into inaction.

Fräulein Braun had involuntarily risen from her chair, her hand cupped over her mouth.

"Achtung!" Kloster instructed the guard, intending to hold Boyer in check.

The sentry remembered his duty, stepped forward, and prodded the American with the Schmeisser machine-pistol, communicating in no uncertain terms that he was to back off.

Boyer retreated a few steps as Kloster leaned down and scooped up the wallet with the offending photo. He stashed it in the pocket of the borrowed tunic, returning it to its rightful place as if the very act could somehow reverse his blunder.

Boyer was no fool. Although he couldn't explain what exactly had happened, it seemed clear that Kloster was impersonating another officer. Indeed, now that he looked closer it struck him that the tunic probably didn't belong to him; it hung a little loose.

Boyer's face took on a hardened expression as his mind raced to make sense of the interview. He scrutinized the man facing him: tall, with an athletic build, the man exuded confidence and somehow didn't strike him as a typical officer. There was something about this German officer, something that … well, Boyer couldn't quite put his finger on it.

His stern look left the impression he didn't believe Kloster. Who was this man? Was he even a military officer? Was he a member of the police? Could he actually be a member of the Gestapo?

Boyer tried to mask his questions behind a mask of ambivalence. He could see how a man like Kloster enjoyed being in charge of a situation and, now exposed, felt his influence slipping away.

"I'm sorry for startling you, Fräulein," Kloster apologized, addressing the stenographer and bringing a sense of calmness back to the interview. Then turning to face Boyer, he said. "Let's continue, shall we?"

But the damage, however brief, had already been done. Boyer stepped back a pace and folded his arms in defiance. "Who are you, really?" he asked.

"My name is Kloster … and I'm with the Luftwaffe," Kloster persisted.

"Right. If you're a Luftwaffe officer, then I'm Mickey Mouse," Boyer sneered.

Kloster didn't seem to understand the reference and neither did Braun.

"You know, Mickey Mouse, the cartoon character?" Boyer placed his hands beside his head and waggled them like the mouse's big ears.

Whether it was the reference to the cartoon or just Kloster's inability to understand, he took offense and reacted instantly. Faster than Boyer would have thought possible, Kloster advanced two quick steps and delivered an *ohrfeige*, striking Boyer on the cheek with his open hand.

Boyer staggered backwards but didn't fall, holding his ground. The hard slap, though smarting, was meant more as an affront, rather than an outright attack. Boyer's cheek sported a deep red, but his jaw had absorbed much of the blow.

The look of shame on Kloster's face seemed to show he regretted the assault, wishing he'd kept his temper in check. This one quick uncontrolled action confirmed what Boyer had suspected all along; this man didn't belong to the Luftwaffe and wasn't to be trifled with. He had to be careful.

"Sit down," Kloster ordered, fighting to regain his composure. "What do you think this is, a drama club or comedy show?"

Boyer was about to respond with a clever retort, something he'd probably live to regret, but he stopped himself just in time.

As soon as the words had left Kloster's lips, he realized his faux pas. But it was too late. He cleared his throat and tried to appear nonchalant.

"Now, shall we start again, Lieutenant Boyer?"

At this point it was clear that the interrogator had lost any advantage he may have had over the American, not unlike a locomotive, whose tender had been stoked, but had run into an unforeseen obstruction. Kloster was clearly dissatisfied with the outcome and would have liked to continue the interrogation. However, with the damage done, he had little choice but to end the interview in the hopes of resuming at a later time.

╬

In the end, Boyer was spared further interrogation and was escorted, along with the rest of his crew, out the back door of the mayor's office. He was relieved to see that Lucky, Shore and Romeo were no worse for wear. It seemed they had escaped the Gestapo's more sinister interrogation techniques.

As they climbed onto a transport truck, they were surprised to find four other men, British airmen who had been shot down in their Lancaster. As expected, two armed German guards were seated at the rear, mute and inhospitable.

The truck engine roared to life, but just before the tarp was lowered and secured, an officer hoisted himself onto the tail gate. An unwelcome yet familiar face appeared at the back: Kloster.

Boyer swore under his breath. Was it all a ruse, to get them comfortable and relaxed, only to be hauled off the truck for further interrogation?

"Guten Tag, gentlemen," Kloster said mockingly. "Have a pleasant journey. And Lieutenant Boyer, when you get to Neubrandenburg, say hello to Captain Swaggart for me. I expect he'll be joining you shortly."

Kloster grinned and, before Boyer could formulate a response, jumped off the tailgate and disappeared from view.

Romeo started to get up. Likely he wanted to yell a few choice words after the departing German, but Boyer was in no mood for reprisals and glared at him to sit back down.

"Not now, Koslawski!" Boyer hissed, cutting him off. "Do you really want another round of interrogation with the Gestapo?" He glanced around, addressing the rest. "All of you, remain in your seats and shut up."

The only other officer on the truck aside from Rossi, was a British lieutenant. Shorter than Boyer by a good four inches, he wore a beret and sported a huge walrus-style moustache. Boyer hadn't intended to include him or his men in his remarks.

"I say, old boy," the Brit spoke up with amusement on his face. "I sure hope you'll extend us a bit more courtesy. By the way, the name's Cartwright. William Cartwright."

"Charles Boyer, at your service. Sorry about the outburst."

Before anyone else could join in, one of the guards intervened. *"Nicht sprechen!"* he ordered.

The truck driver must have received the go-ahead, because he engaged the gear and eased out of the back lane, heading north into the snow-covered countryside.

Boyer mentally dismissed Kloster's irritating send-off.

Instead, he thought back to the man's last comment, indicating their destination: Neubrandenburg. He recalled that it was one of many Nazi POW camps, and if memory served it also housed an *Oflag*, a facility within the larger camp set aside for officers. He relaxed a fraction, knowing that officers were treated better than enlisted men and weren't subjected to hard labor. He couldn't help but think of the plight his crew faced at the camp.

A gust of wind found a gap in the canvas and invisible ice-cold tentacles robbed the men of what little warmth they had. Boyer shivered involuntarily as his thoughts returned to Jack. He hoped their captain was faring better than they were.

⸸

Horst Kloster wasn't pleased with the airmen's interrogation. He reluctantly returned to his office in Berlin and brooded over the situation. The interview with Lieutenant Boyer had gone poorly, he reminded himself while caressing his right fist. It still felt sore and was mildly swollen. *Not as swollen as Boyer's cheek*, thought Kloster, a malicious grin forming. Rossi hadn't been forthcoming at first, but in the end, he'd turned out to be quite gullible, allowing himself to fall for Fräulein Braun's charms. Americans were weak and nothing more than boy scouts, Kloster scoffed.

Boyer, however, was a different story. He was going to be a tough nut to crack. His intuition had seldom failed him. Well, he still had to report the matter to his boss, Schinkel. Later, over the phone, he outlined the few bits of information he had gleaned from Rossi and commented on Boyer's reluctance to part with anything useful. Conveniently, he left out details of his altercation with Boyer, fearing it would tarnish his reputation. What was the point in rehashing the past?

Schinkel took the report in stride and surprisingly showed little interest. The man merely grunted a few times and then instructed the two officers to be shipped off to Stalag IIA,

Neubrandenburg, in northern Germany.

It was late Monday afternoon and Andreas Bauman was in good spirits. He had the evening off and looked forward to spending a little time with Hilde. Earlier in the day, his superior had advised him that a series of important dispatches would be delivered to Neubrandenburg from the Heinkel Flugzeugwerke in Rostock. Rail travel was becoming more and more unreliable due to increased Allied bombardment, hence the need to send one of his pilots.

His initial reaction had been disappointment, but then he'd recalled that the last man who had tried to get out of a mundane assignment like this had gotten his wish, only to be detailed to a worse task the following day. Bauman wished someone else had been chosen, but in the end had to comply with his orders.

The one good thing about the assignment was that he would have the chance to be reacquainted with an old friend, the Me 109 fighter, an aircraft he had flown many times prior to transitioning to the more powerful Me 262 jet.

Anyway, the less he complained, the sooner he'd be finished. He hated to be away from Hilde, but hopefully he'd be back in a couple of days. With that bit of encouragement, he drove to the Augsberg home, optimistic about enjoying a short yet pleasant evening in the company of his girlfriend.

As he rounded the corner, a gray sedan drove past. Andreas only glanced at the car, but he was startled by what he saw. He could have sworn the passenger in the front seat was the spitting image of Hilde. But who had been the man sitting in the back? Andreas didn't get a good look, but was fairly sure it wasn't Saufman. It nagged at him and he had half a mind to turn his car around, but dismissed it as foolishness and continued on his way.

He pulled around the corner and parked, and with a light

step approached the door and knocked. Gertrude opened it and invited him inside.

"You're a little early," she remarked.

He sensed tension the minute he entered the home but shrugged it off. Although Gertrude was as polite and hospitable as always, she seemed to be distracted.

"When is Hilde expected back?" he asked casually.

Gertrude wiped her hands on her apron and glanced at him with surprise. "She left a few minutes ago. She won't be joining us."

Andreas tried not to look disappointed.

"She won't be joining us?" he asked, needing confirmation of what she'd just said.

Frau Augsberg seemed uncomfortable for the briefest of moments.

"Yes … I thought she told you," Gertrude lied.

"Told me what?" Andreas asked, now perplexed.

"That she was called away unexpectedly. She had to deliver important documents on behalf of Herr Saufman."

"For Saufman? Deliver them where?"

"To Neubrandenburg. It seems that Herr Saufman took ill—food poisoning, I think it was. Apparently, the matter couldn't wait. He insisted that she leave immediately. Tonight."

Bauman took this in, not entirely convinced. He needed to know more. "Did she go alone?"

"No. I believe a colleague is travelling with her."

"That's good. Do you know who?"

"Let me think. If I'm not mistaken, I think his name was … Herr Schuman," she replied, remembering the name that had been written on the travel document. Trying to appease him, she added with a smile. "He's much older, bald, and married. Not as handsome as you, Lieutenant."

"I see," Andreas replied, feigning a smile.

Andreas felt uncomfortable, but it was more than just a feeling of unease. He sensed something wasn't quite right, that he didn't have the whole picture. He needed to find out what was troubling him, but he wasn't going to interrogate Gertrude. He reasoned that this likely had nothing to do with her.

"I'm sorry," he said, getting up from the chair. "I just remembered that I need to deal with another matter. I'm afraid I'll have to head back to the barracks. Perhaps I can join you for supper another night?"

Gertrude nodded. "Yes, Andreas, that would be nice. Please, come again."

Bauman grabbed his coat and headed to his car. He intended to return to the barracks, so that much of his story was true. But first he needed to stop at the Berlin's *Hauptbahnhof*, the railway station.

In his haste to leave, he pulled away from the curb and failed to notice a pothole. The right front tire dipped into it, but rather than slow down, he sped forward, intent on catching up with Hilde. The rear tire followed the track, though. Thinking he had cleared the hole, he stepped on the gas. It was a mistake he would regret.

The sudden acceleration caused the rear end to swerve. He overcorrected and the rear wheel bounced off the curb. He winced, hoping that was the worst of it, but then he heard a bang.

"*Scheise!*" he cursed. "Just what I needed, a blowout."

He pulled over and got out to examine the Opel's damaged tire. It had gone flat in no time, although fortunately there didn't appear to be any damage to the rim. For an instant, Andreas thought of just resuming his trip, flat tire and all. But then he thought better of it.

He surveyed the street. There were no repair shops in sight, and calling a mechanic out from the barracks would absolve him of changing the tire, but it would also take up considerable time, and time was the one thing he could least afford to waste.

He knew what had to be done.

Pushing the frustration to the back of his mind, he removed his jacket and went about retrieving the spare from the trunk. He breathed a sigh of relief when he spotted the necessary tools, including the jack, neatly rolled up in a canvas bag next to the tire.

He rolled up his sleeves and went to work. Just then, a military motorcycle with sidecar roared past, splashing him. Andreas shook his fist at the departing motorist, and as he did so was reminded of one, he'd seen just like it the previous day when he was out for a stroll. He'd had a fleeting look at the driver, but it was the passenger who had caught his attention. A tall man, an officer, who resembled … well, he couldn't quite recall.

As Andreas removed the flat tire, the answer came to him. The driver of that motorcycle had reminded him of Rudi Schultz, who worked at the base commissary and was a friend of Fritz Pfalz. And the man in the sidecar, tall and attired in a lieutenant's uniform, looked vaguely like the man in the back of the gray sedan he'd spotted moments ago. He eventually shrugged it off as coincidence and went about changing the flat.

$$\maltese$$

Horst Kloster sat alone in his apartment, a tumbler of Scottish whiskey nestled in his right hand. A rare find. He leaned over the table, absorbed with examining a schematic he had just acquired. As a former pilot, he was well acquainted with aircraft drawings.

He had obtained, at significant risk, blueprints of the inner workings of a Messerschmitt jet, all part of his devious plan of tampering with an aircraft's oxygen supply.

This is a bit different from the Horten prototype, he reminded himself, as he studied the drawings. Still, it was enough to help formulate his plan for ousting Ziller.

His sabotage couldn't be too obvious, nothing that would be caught by the plane's technicians. But by tampering with just the right valve, he might be able to decrease the oxygen flow while introducing deadly carbon monoxide into the cabin.

Yes, he could make it work. It would require closing one valve and unscrewing a fitting just a few turns from the return-flow tube. Pleased with the discovery, Kloster took a good-measured gulp of whiskey, savoring the golden liquid. The tricky part would be to gain access to the facility where the prototype was hangared. Difficult, but not impossible. A plan was already forming in his mind. All he had to do was obtain copies of inspection forms, alter a few details and then appear unannounced. The other details could be worked out later. He smiled to himself. Yes, it could work.

╫

Twenty minutes later, with the tools and flat tire stowed in the trunk, Andreas Bauman was back in his car and heading to the railway station. He found a vacant parking spot in the military section and quickly pulled in. He placed the Luftwaffe placard on the dash, ensuring he wouldn't get a tow-away notice. He fought the urge to run up the steps and with purposeful strides headed to the large atrium. There, he found the massive billboard displaying the departure times for trains leaving Berlin.

Scanning the long list, he found the one he was looking for: Neubrandenburg, track 17, departing at 19:00 hrs. He checked his watch: 19:21 hrs. He glanced back at the board to make sure he had read the correct line. Track 17 at 19:00 hrs. The departure time, he knew, was arbitrary. With frequent Allied bombing, schedules were no longer accurate and often tended to be pushed back an hour or two, sometimes longer than that.

Once he had cleared the Gestapo checkpoint, he picked

up his pace and rushed to the departure section. As he was in officer's uniform, the attendant didn't try to stop him and allowed him to proceed. Andreas went past tracks 11, 12, and 13. He brushed past a couple sauntering arm in arm and hurried along to 14, 15, and 16. He rounded a concrete pillar, stopping at number 17. He peered at his watch. 19:26. Several people were still milling about the long, virtually empty platform. The train had left.

Disappointment at last sunk in. Trying not to show it, he approached a young woman with a small child.

"*Entschuldigung,* Fräulein," Andreas said, excusing his intrusion. "Can you tell me when the train bound for Neubrandenburg left?"

She glanced at him, took in the uniform and the worried look, and guessed that he had tried to see off a close friend, perhaps a sweetheart.

"I'm sorry, *Herr Leutenant,*" she said, smiling. "I'm afraid you missed it by no more than ten minutes."

"Thank you," he barely managed as he turned away.

Andreas slowly walked back the way he had come, less eager, less hopeful, and still feeling ill-at-ease. Just as he was about to pass the station café, his stomach growled. As if sensing the restaurant's proximity, it was reminding him he had missed the meal at the Augsbergs and hadn't eaten since lunch time. Although his mind was still preoccupied with Hilde's sudden departure, his body urged him to consider more practical matters: nourishment. Rather than head for the kitchen at the barracks, he stopped at the café. It would help him to clear his head and hopefully sort things out.

He stood in line, waiting to be seated, when a man's voice unexpectedly called out to him.

"Bauman! Andreas, is that you?"

Surprised, he turned to look for the man who had called him by name. Two tables over, a lieutenant in the *Schutzwehr,* the military arm of homeland security, was motioning him to come over. The lieutenant was by himself and smiling at the consternation on Andreas' face.

"You don't recognize me, do you, Andreas?"

Bauman scrutinized the face for a few seconds. "Willie, Willie Schmidt? No, it can't be." Andreas shook his head.

"Of course, it's me, dummkopf. Who else?" The man saw Andreas still studying his face and grinned. "Yes, the moustache fools them every time. When I last flew with you, I hadn't grown one yet. But since the crash, I've had to put up with this nasty scar. So, what better reason than to grow this *schnurrbart*, yes?"

Bauman peered closer, past the moustache, and on further inspection recognized his friend's familiar face.

"But what are you … ?" he stopped himself in mid-sentence. He was about to ask Schmidt why he was wearing the uniform of Homeland Security, when he spotted a cane resting next to Schmidt's right leg.

Schmidt had followed his friend's gaze and replied matter-of-factly. "My right knee was banged up a little in the crash."

"I'm sorry, Willie. I hadn't heard."

"Not everyone has," Schmidt said dismissively. "Compliments of a P-51 Mustang's 20mm cannon fire. To tell the truth, I'm lucky to be alive."

Andreas kept staring at his friend. "I had no idea. Since I've been transferred to JG32, I've lost track of our old unit. You know how it is."

Schmidt nodded. "Sure. Then you probably don't know about Weiser either, right?"

"I'm afraid not. What happened to Dieter?"

Schmidt squinted, pretending to look for the waiter. When he glanced back, his easy-going expression had disappeared replaced by a sombre tone.

"Dieter was shot down. I wasn't flying with him that day. I heard about it later. His unit had intercepted a flight of American B-17s over Stuttgart. He shot down two before one of those new American fighters got an angle on him, and despite the Me 262s speed advantage, the Yank fired off a lucky burst that tore off half the left wing, along with the engine. His plane spiralled down. There was no sign that he tried to jettison the canopy; no one saw a parachute. Maybe he was already dead before the jet hit the ground."

Andreas stared at his water glass. What could he say? Another brave man lost. He remembered Dieter, a man known for his sense of humor, always looking at the funny side of a situation. Only there was nothing funny about how things had ended up. Reluctantly, Andreas pondered his own flying career. Was that how he was going to end—shot up by an enemy fighter while defending the Fatherland? And would he have the chance to bail out? A slight shiver went through him, remembering the deadly game he played every time he went into combat.

He glanced up to find the waiter standing there, looking at him expectantly, pencil and notepad in hand. Thankful for the interruption, he gave his order and waited until the man had left the table.

"And you, Willie? You're not even wearing a Luftwaffe tunic. How come?"

Schmidt smiled at him ruefully. "Yes, well, that's how things go sometimes. With Reimar Horten no longer with our unit and our illustrious Major von Glitz calling all the shots, I had little recourse. Once the medical people informed me, seconded by our commander, that I was no longer fit for active flying duty, I was quickly removed and assigned a desk job."

Still not sure what really happened, Andreas cleared his throat, and continued. "Alright. That would explain why you're no longer flying. But as I recall, you had, like me, been promoted to first lieutenant. Now you're sitting here, wearing a second lieutenant's shoulder bars, and no longer in the air force."

"Oh that," Schmidt said, trying to brush it off. "Well, I can thank von Glitz for that. I guess it was that same evening, the one when I got the happy news that my flying days were over. I was in the officer's mess, celebrating my *good* fortune, when that yokel walked in. Squadron Commander or not, I let him have a piece of my mind. I guess it was the schnapps talking. Anyway, I said more than I had intended and embarrassed him in front of the other men. You know, he didn't say one word. He abruptly got up and walked out."

Bauman nodded, knowing what was coming next.

"The following day," Willie continued, "I was summoned to Colonel von Stachel's office. He advised me that von Glitz had made a formal complaint, insisting that I be court-martialed for insubordination. Fortunately for me, Stachel intervened, insisting the matter be dealt with via inquiry as opposed to formal proceedings. The good news is that I was not court-martialed, just demoted. But at the same time, I was ousted from the Luftwaffe, relocated, and given this menial posting. Von Glitz had the last laugh after all."

Schmidt couldn't hold his friend's gaze and looked away, perhaps embarrassed over the way he had handled himself. It had, after all, ended his career in the Luftwaffe. Andreas reached forward and tapped his friend's hand.

"Willie," he said softly, "don't let it get you down. Look at it this way. You're still alive and at the very least are no longer taking orders from that pompous von Glitz."

Schmidt grinned. "You're right about that. I could easily be enjoying the hospitality of a military prison right now. So," he said, looking a little more cheerful, "what brings you here, to the station?"

Caught up with Willie's story, Andreas had nearly forgotten why he had come to the railway station.

"Oh, I er … I came to see somebody off, but by the time I got here, the train had already pulled out."

"Which train?" Willie inquired, happy to be talking about

something else.

"What? Oh, the one to Neubrandenburg."

"Track 17, right?"

"*Jawohl,* how did you know?"

"Well, it *is* my business to keep track of train arrivals and departures, since I've been relegated to this important post in the *Schutzwehr*. The train for Neubrandenburg just left, surprisingly almost on time. The Gestapo are always scrutinizing people, looking important, and generally making things miserable for everyone not with the military. Curiously, they didn't make much of a fuss and allowed it to proceed. Me, I just do my job and try not to get too involved."

Schmidt caught something in his friend's expression and grinned. "So, Andreas, who was she?"

Andreas was surprised at his friend's astuteness. "Was it that obvious, I mean the look on my face?"

Schmidt nodded. "Let me guess. Blonde, slim, carries herself well …" He stopped speaking to see if he had drawn the right conclusion.

Andreas stared thoughtfully, and although he didn't say anything, he didn't deny what his friend had already suspected.

"Wearing a maroon winter coat," Willie continued, "and in the company of a tall man, as I recall."

"A tall man?" Andreas asked quickly. He thought back to his conversation with Gertrude where she indicated that Hilde's companion was short and bald.

Schmidt nodded, thinking back. "Yes, about your height. Quite handsome, I might add. He walked with a bit of a limp. A gimp like me, *ja.* Hold on, I still have the sheet from the checkpoint with me."

The food had arrived, and Andreas was about to take his first spoonful of soup, when Schmidt continued.

"Yes, here it is," Willie said producing several sheets. "My captain insists that we note the names of passengers who are not travelling on official business."

Bauman hesitated. "Not on official business?"

"That's right," he said glancing at the papers in his hand. "*Herr und Frau Schuman*, travelling to Neubrandenburg."

Bauman just about dropped his spoon. "*Herr und Frau Schuman?*"

"Yes, that's what I had written down. Here, take a look." Schmidt passed the papers across for Andreas to see for himself.

"But that can't be," Andreas objected. "Hilde was supposed to ..."

He didn't finish his sentence. He was confused and wondering what was going on. Should he reveal to Schmidt that something was wrong? He decided to hold off and took a spoonful of tomato soup, trying to look unconcerned. "Interesting. Tell me, what did this man look like?"

"As I've already mentioned, tall, brown hair, and he had that superior air about him. You know, like he was a bureaucrat, a diplomat, or an officer out of uniform. He didn't say much. His wife, the pretty one, did most of the talking. Her husband coughed a couple of times. I guess he had a sore throat or cold."

A thought, an improbable thought worked its way into Andreas' head. He had to be sure. "Do you by chance remember the details of their travel papers?"

"Sure. The young woman told me how thrilled she was to be given last minute permission to travel to see her family in Rostock. She explained that her husband had been injured in a recent bombing blast and had leave to accompany her. That would explain the cane."

Andreas nodded absentmindedly, while his brain tried to make sense of it all.

CHAPTER XVI

Escape to Neubrandenburg

Hilde Augsberg sat opposite her new confidant, Jack Swaggart, fingering their false travel papers. As Herr and Frau Schuman, they had played their parts well and passed scrutiny at the Gestapo checkpoint. Now Jack was looking out the window as the train picked up speed, heading into the countryside. It was almost dark and the shadows grew longer with each passing kilometer.

"Well done, *Herr Kapit*—I mean Herr Schuman," Hilde corrected herself. "We fooled the Gestapo. But back at the station, did you notice that young lieutenant, the one standing to the side of the track?"

Jack nodded. "How could I have missed him? He seemed to be more interested in me than you. I wonder if he suspected we really weren't a couple."

"I don't think so," she replied, although she wasn't totally convinced. "If he were suspicious, he would have come over and asked a few questions. As it turned out, he only glanced at the names on his clipboard. Well, don't worry. I'm sure it'll work out."

She had been about to say more but changed her mind, choosing instead to catch a few last glimpses of the countryside before dusk took over.

Jack wasn't about to argue with her. He had to admit, everything about the plan had worked out so far. Perhaps the rest would go just as smoothly.

As he glanced at her again, he realized that there was something about her that drew him in, even though he couldn't quite put his finger on what it was. He forced himself to stop thinking about her. She was a young woman, an attractive—no, a beautiful young woman. But he couldn't just forget about Nicole back home. He had to remind himself to keep his thoughts and actions on a professional level.

He caught an amused look from Hilde and thought she had read his mind. He hoped the flash of embarrassment didn't show on his face.

"I heard it too," she said, then politely turned toward the window.

"Pardon me?"

Slowly, yet persistently, a strangely familiar feeling worked itself through his stomach. Then it came again, this time more pronounced. Hunger. His stomach was growling. Their hasty departure hadn't permitted them to get anything to eat. In all the excitement before their unscheduled departure, Jack had nearly forgotten that her boyfriend, Andreas, had intended on coming over for dinner. He was probably enjoying the nice meal that Frau Augsberg had prepared. Would he buy the last-minute story Hilde had concocted, forcing her to leave on such short notice?

Jack felt a pang of regret, wishing he could have stayed and enjoyed the *knödel*. Not wanting to linger on what might have been, Jack turned his attention back and faced Hilde again and coughed gently to get her attention.

"*Entschuldigung*, Fräulein," he said, speaking German as best as he could. "*Sind Sie hungrig?*"

Hilde smiled at him, pleased at the effort. "Now that you mention it, yes, I'm feeling hungry as well," she said. "Wait here. I'll see what I can get from the next car."

As she rose from her seat, Jack fumbled with his billfold and extracted a few notes, hoping it was enough money to cover the expense. He held them up to her, hoping she would accept the offering. They hadn't discussed money before boarding.

To his surprise, Hilde pushed back his hand, shaking her head, and left the cabin. She closed the door behind her. Jack glanced at the notes, and to his horror realized he was holding several American five-dollar bills. He quickly ripped them up, raised the window, and allowed the wind to scatter the incriminating evidence. He felt foolish, but more than that, vulnerable. It dawned on him how damaging their discovery could have been earlier at the checkpoint.

After a few minutes, he began to relax and even allowed his mind to drift to memories of home. He wondered how his mother was coping now that his father was gone. He took comfort in knowing she had her church friends as well as next-door neighbors. They would see her through.

The compartment door slid open and Jack looked up as Hilde carried in a plate of sandwiches and two bottles of Warsteiner beer. He smiled and was about to ask her how much it cost when she cut him off.

"Don't worry about it, Herr Schuman. I took care of it."

They both dug into the sandwiches hungrily. Jack raised his bottle to his mouth, anticipating the delicious taste of German beer, when the train began to slow. Jack checked his watch, then peered at Hilde.

"It's only been thirty minutes," he said. "Why are we stopping?"

"I'm not sure, but I'll go and find out." She left the compartment, while Jack waited nervously as the train continued to slow, eventually coming to a stop on the tracks. Hilde returned a few minutes later. "The train tracks have been damaged and will have to be repaired. We have no choice but to wait."

Jack nodded unhappily, yet realizing there was nothing to be done about it. While he was finishing the last of his sandwich, Hilde asked him about farm life in North Dakota. Here at last was something he enjoyed talking about. He told her about early morning milking, teasing the cats by squirting them with milk, and even running for his life after provoking an angry steer.

"But you know what I treasure the most?" Jack added. "Sharing the seat with my father while riding an old John Deere tractor."

The mention of his father instantly brought on such a deep feeling that he couldn't continue. Jack thought he had dealt with his father's death much the way he had been expected to—suppressing his feelings and continuing with his job as a military pilot. The only problem with stuffing them, though, was that they could remain in the recesses of his mind only so long; eventually they were bound to come out, unexpected and without any forewarning.

Jack gazed out the window, though there was nothing to see in the pitch-black night. He vaguely heard Hilde call his name, and when he turned to look at her, a tear loosed itself from the corner of his eye and slid down his right cheek. He wiped it away quickly, embarrassed that she had witnessed it.

Hilde was initially surprised at the display of emotion and, like any woman in a similar situation, was immediately drawn to his vulnerability. Jack, not knowing how to proceed, remained silent, yet his eyes spoke volumes.

Sensing that he wanted to talk, Hilde reached for his closest hand. Reassured by her warm smile, he decided to confide in her. He spoke about the unexpected telegram, of the blow that news produced, and how much his father had meant to him. Hilde listened patiently, nodding occasionally, encouraging Jack to continue.

As he told his story she was reminded of her own father, Helmut Augsberg, who, though not dead (at least she hoped he wasn't dead), was confined in a POW camp, somewhere in northern Russia.

Here, at last, was something they had in common. Both were without a loved one they cared deeply about. In a way, it was comforting to know they weren't alone in their grief. Somehow that made it easier to bear. She glanced down at her hand, conscious she was still holding his, and reluctant to let go. He, too, noticed her discomfort and, smiling sheepishly, gave her a slight squeeze before letting go.

After an hour or so, getting a little tired and realizing that the train may not get moving again for some time, they mutually decided to get some rest.

⚜

William Sochalski wanted to get comfortable, but it was quite impossible. The freight car was overcrowded, yet it was cold in the confined space. The frightened eyes of other prisoners darted around, none of them sure where to land. Every once in a while, warm breath escaped a child's nose only to be snatched away by the harsh wind whose unseen icy tentacles swept through the gaps in the wooden slats.

He glanced up at an older woman he had failed to notice earlier. Thin and wearing a worn gray coat, she vaguely reminded him of his own mother. What drew his attention was her kind face, something that was out of place on this train. Funny that he hadn't noticed her before. Feeling a little guilty, he did what his mother would have expected him to do.

He got up and motioned for her to take his place. Grateful, she accepted his offer and allowed him to ease her onto the cattle car's wooden floor. A few of the others actually scowled, wishing he had vacated his place for one of them.

He took in all the harried faces of the captives. Although each was different, they shared one thing: the yellow star of David. They had been herded into this small, wretched car simply because they were Jews.

It seemed like only yesterday that William had slept in the farmer's hayloft—a luxury by comparison. He reached inside his trouser pocket and pulled out the package of gum the American pilot had given him. He opened the foil wrapper and put the stick in his mouth, experiencing the same sweet sensation as that first time, along with a temporary sense of well-being.

William knew his small supply of gum wouldn't last. Who knew? It might even get confiscated during the next search. As he chewed, he exchanged glances with a small boy huddled against his mother.

Feeling compassion, he offered the boy one of his sticks. The boy, no more than nine or ten, accepted eagerly. Having watched William, the boy freed the delicious offering from the wrapper and, imitating him, began to chew. A combination of excitement and satisfaction spread over his young face, eliciting a few weak smiles from those watching.

But then the train's whistle blew twice, putting an end to the smiles and signalling that a stop was imminent. They were coming into another station. As the brakes squealed in protest, William managed to glimpse the station's name: Weimar.

He didn't have time to reflect as the wooden doors slid open and the opening filled with armed guards and snarling German shepherds.

"Raus! Alle Raus!" A uniformed officer bellowed at them to get out.

The men standing near the door climbed down and turned to assist the elderly and infirm. William was further back and had no choice but to wait his turn. He held his handkerchief to his nose, the stench of unwashed bodies, sweat, and fear more prominent than ever.

An older man stumbled and barely caught himself from falling. He stopped to wait for his wife and, instead of taking hold of her hand, was given a swift kick from a soldier.

"Macht's schnell!" the austere guard barked, propelling him forward. "There's no time to waste, Jews."

"But my wife … ?" the man pleaded, but his words fell on deaf ears.

Another man who wasn't moving fast enough was struck in the back by the butt end of a rifle.

An officer stood off to the side, motionless, watching the proceedings. He held a clipboard in his hand, his eyes fixed on the disembarking men. When William's turn came to leave, the officer spotted him and pointed. "This one."

William was pulled aside and ushered toward a waiting truck. The soldiers pulled back canvas covering and shoved him inside. Several men were seated on benches and none appeared to be older than forty. There was room for about ten passengers, but in no time at least twenty were crowded in. Two armed sentries sat at the back, their stern expressions quelling any questions, much less talk among the men.

The truck engine started up and the driver began to navigate through the mass of people. Once clear of the railway station, the truck lumbered toward the town's edge, then picked up speed, heading north.

William had no idea where they were going.

As the truck followed the incline of the narrow road, he caught glimpses outside that showed they were heading into the mountains. He thought he saw a sign that read Nordhausen, though the name meant nothing to him. Eventually the truck stopped and the canvas flaps were folded back to allow the prisoners to disembark.

The first thing that registered with William was the vast number of barracks situated in the flats beside a mountain. An unobtrusive sign declared their destination: Dora-Mittelbau.[5] He gazed up and saw a large manmade tunnel leading into the rock. Before he could contemplate his situation further, a guard shoved him and marched him toward one of the barracks.

Once inside, the guard barked at the captives to undress. Embarrassed, frightened, and having no choice, Sochalski did as ordered. Never before had he felt so helpless, so alone. He had little time to remove his clothes as a guard was always haranguing them to hurry up. Then the guards sprayed the naked men with an unpleasant white chemical from a handheld dispenser. William had no idea what it was for until a man near him whispered, "For lice."

There was more prodding as they were shuffled into an adjoining room where he saw stacks of drab, gray prison clothes. With little time to find a matching set, William grabbed the closest pair and donned it, thereby avoiding being struck by an overzealous guard.

The men were herded in groups of twenty into the nearby barracks. As William entered the nearest one, he was immediately assailed by an unpleasant odor of sweat mixed in with something else—something organic.

While his eyes adjusted to the limited light, he caught the inhospitable looks of the men. Emaciated, they stared from hollow recesses—weary, cautious, even angry. William noticed a pot-bellied stove in the middle of the room, its pin-pricked pipe ascending through a hole in the roof. A small pot sat on the grate with puffs of steam escaping at intervals.

If William had expected to find a cot, he was sorely disappointed. The few beds were already taken and he was forced to find an empty spot with nothing but straw to separate his tired body from the cold, wooden floor.

╬

The truck rumbled on. Although Boyer couldn't see where they were, he could tell they were out in the countryside. From what he could make out, they were headed north. He rubbed his hands together to generate some heat, grateful at least for the warmth his flight jacket provided.

Periodically, the truck driver sounded his horn, and Boyer felt the truck swerve around unseen obstacles. Some of these were probably small vehicles, travelling the same direction, but he also saw people walking by, and from the sounds of it there were quite a few.

After about an hour, the truck came to a halt in a wooded area. The tarp was peeled back and they were instructed, at gunpoint, to pile out. Boyer noted that captured prisoners were also streaming out of two other transport trucks. There were no buildings, but the men were instructed—through hand signals—to relieve themselves where they stood. A few, unaccustomed to the lack of privacy, wandered off a short distance, looking to use the nearby trees for cover.

While Boyer squatted beside a large fir tree, the nearest guard was distracted by two arguing Russians and no one was looking Boyer's way. He quickly pulled up his trousers and darted into the foliage, hiding behind a large bush. He reasoned that if he were spotted, he would simply say that he'd needed privacy.

He waited.

Surprisingly, the rest of the men were rounded up and, without being lined up for a head count, were instructed to mount up again. Boyer watched his men scramble onto their truck, casting sideways glances for their missing leader.

The guards, probably as cold as their charges, didn't want to spend one minute longer than was necessary. Tarps were secured and engines roared to life. Boyer couldn't believe his luck. He was free—temporarily.

"Halt!" an authoritative voice bellowed. "The count is one short. Find him."

A soldier hurried to carry out the order, releasing a large German shepherd from one of the trucks. The dog strained against the long leash, instantly taking to the challenge and doing what it was so good at: finding scent.

Boyer knew the gig was up. The dog would certainly come across him. If he ran now, the dog would surely spot him. Remaining still would produce the same result. And to what end? This escape attempt would do no better than delay the trucks from leaving and infuriate the Germans. Seeing no other option, he stood up. With hands raised high, he slowly walked into the clearing.

CHAPTER XVII

Kloster Acts

Horst Kloster flicked his cigarette against the brick building and watched it fall to the pavement. He rubbed out the last of it with the heel of his polished boot and checked his watch. It was exactly five o'clock, on Tuesday afternoon. As if on cue, Major Fritz Zimmermann, the officer in charge of Luftwaffe maintenance at Oranienburg's military airport, left his office and walked to a waiting Daimler out front.

The alert driver jumped out and opened the rear door for the major. Impressed, Kloster thought back with irritation on his own driver, a man clearly not on par. He would have to do something to motivate him to do better. Next time he wouldn't let him off so easily.

Kloster watched with satisfaction as the car departed for what he knew was Zimmerman's favorite hotel in Potsdam. He had paid good German marks for the information. In his right hand, he carried a leather briefcase that contained a dossier with genuine maintenance records. It also included forged documents he had painstakingly assembled, giving him authorization to inspect the airworthiness of several aircraft. Zimmermann probably would have balked at the impromptu inspection. A stickler for rules, likely he would have insisted on verifying the orders and made a few phone calls, which would have ruined everything, not something Kloster had in mind.

Kloster checked his watch again and forced himself to be patient, not one of his strengths. After several minutes, and not seeing the major's car return for some forgotten item, he walked purposefully across the street to the main entrance.

Catching his reflection in the glass, he habitually straightened out his tunic. Satisfied with what he saw, he opened the office door and closed it quietly behind him. He observed a uniformed clerk seated behind the reception desk, clearly not performing his job. The man was so absorbed in reading his newspaper that he failed to notice or acknowledge Kloster's entry.

It couldn't have gone any better for Kloster. Attired in a borrowed Luftwaffe overcoat, he clicked his heels and thrust out his right arm, bellowing "Heil Hitler!" at the framed picture of the Führer directly behind and above the clerk's head.

The startled Feldwebel dropped his paper and, while attempting to return the salute, knocked over his cup of coffee. Some of the hot liquid spilled on his pants, eliciting *"Scheise!"* instead of the customary "Heil Hitler."

Ordinarily, Kloster would have loved nothing better than to tear a strip off the careless, incompetent clerk, but he supressed the urge today. He needed the man's cooperation to carry out his bidding.

"Sergeant, I didn't come here to interrupt your leisure activity or to watch you make a fool of yourself," he said. "Inform Major Zimmerman at once that I have arrived. I have regrettably been delayed, but I'm ready now to carry out the inspection. Here are my orders."

He took the dossier out of his leather briefcase.

The startled clerk stood up, still reeling from the discomfort of the spilled coffee. He accepted the dossier from Kloster's extended hand and, while perusing the cover letter, tried to formulate a response.

"Herr Lieutenant, I er ... I mean we ... he wasn't expecting you tonight, or anyone else. As you can see it is already 17:12 hours …" He glanced at the clock on the wall and hoped it would lend credence to his words. "I'm afraid the major has left for the day. He never mentioned anything about an inspection, sir."

Kloster nodded. "Yes, yes, I know it's after five." He sighed, feigning irritation. "Then call the major at home, give him my apology for disturbing him, and advise him that I'm here now."

Kloster knew full well that Zimmermann wasn't at home, but the best way to keep up the ruse was to keep the clerk off balance.

"*Entschuldigung, Herr Leutenant,*" he apologized, "but I don't believe the major is currently at home. He indicated he had to keep an appointment but didn't reveal the details. Unfortunately, his subordinate, Lieutenant Hauser, is away as well. Perhaps I can assist you in this matter?" Again, the clerk looked at the clock.

Kloster noticed it too. In the absence of both officers, the clerk obviously hoped the lieutenant would curse at the inconvenience and decide to return another day.

"What is your name, Feldwebel?" Kloster asked, scrutinizing the man's unkempt uniform shirt. The careless clerk must have earlier loosened his tunic after the major's departure.

"*Feldwebel Meisner, Herr Leutenant,*" he uttered as he hastily buttoned up the tunic.

"*Schon gut,* Meisner. Now, go fetch a supervisor or technician who can assist me with going over some of these records. I don't have all night, and I'm certainly not going to come back. I have to be in Hamburg tomorrow and have little time to waste."

"Right away, sir." The flustered clerk dashed out the back door.

Kloster removed his overcoat and hung it up on a nearby hook. A few minutes later, the harried clerk returned with a mechanic in tow. The mechanic, a little shorter than the clerk, was clad in overalls and was wiping his hands on a rag. He snapped his heels together and saluted. "Corporal Stengl. How can I be of assistance, *Herr Leutenant?*"

Kloster nodded his approval and handed him a sheet of paper. "I've been given the task of inspecting several aircraft at this facility. I was informed that Major Zimmerman would assist me in this matter, but I've just been advised that he's already left."

"Yes, sir. I spoke to him less than an hour ago, but he never mentioned an inspection at such a late hour. Most of the men have left for the day, and it will be difficult to recall any on such short notice."

"I see. Well, I don't want to waste your time any more than I have to." Kloster sounded almost conciliatory. He pointed to the hangar door.

"Of course, sir," Stengl agreed. He stopped short. "Will anyone else accompany us?"

Kloster shook his head. "I'm alone and my driver is waiting outside."

"Then, this way, Sir." Stengl glanced back at the clerk. "You can go, Werner. Just make sure you lock up."

Meisner nodded and visibly relaxed. Soon, Kloster was walking past several aircraft, including an Me 109 fighter and an FW 190 fighter/bomber. He pretended to be occupied with papers in his folder while he asked about the maintenance history of each plane.

"The Messerschmitt needs a new propeller," clarified Stengl. "The FW 190 sustained elevator damage, the result of a rough crosswind landing."

Kloster nodded and continued walking down the line. He then came to a stop and turned to face the mechanic. "Stengl, I was informed that this facility is also responsible for maintaining the new Messerschmitt jets, but I don't see any. Was I misinformed?"

"No, sir. They're here. Right this way."

They walked to the far end of the hangar where Stengl slid a connecting door back on an elevated rail system, revealing two gleaming Me 262 jets.

"We only received them last week," said the mechanic. "We've installed the radios and armaments, but haven't been able to add the camouflage paint yet. They should be available at the end of next week."

Kloster followed the mechanic into the building and examined the two aircraft, pretending to verify entries on his clipboard. "This aircraft," the mechanic pointed to the nearest one, "has a minor fuel flow problem on the port engine. I was working on it when I was summoned to the front by Meisner. It's a faulty fuel pump and I should have it repaired by Wednesday, Thursday at the latest." He picked up another logbook and flipped through several pages. "This second Me 262 tested satisfactorily, has been signed off as airworthy, and is deemed fully operational."

Kloster nodded, then asked several questions relevant to the airworthiness of both jets. Stengl did his best to answer the questions. Kloster listened attentively and pretended to verify the information as outlined on his clipboard. "Alright, I've seen enough here."

Looking through a window, he spotted a mechanic parking a service tractor at a nearby maintenance building. It was a non-descript warehouse type structure. Pointing it out, he inquired, "And what about that building there, any aircraft inside?"

"Yes, sir. That's the temporary assembly building for the Horten project."

"Very good." Kloster checked his documents. "RLM wants updates on everything. I'll need to see that as well. Is anyone still on site?"

"All the designers are away, but there's always a sentry on duty."

This was more than Kloster could have hoped for. He was pleased that neither Reimar nor Walter Horten were present. He and Stengl walked from the main building to the smaller warehouse and were greeted by a uniform soldier, an older man, looking to be in his late sixties. Kloster appraised him and wondered if he were going to be a problem.

Stengl outlined the officer's inspection and was readily admitted to the facility. The front section was divided into small, but functional offices. Kloster spotted drafting tables, chalk boards depicting algebraic equations, and mounds of paperwork on most tables. He could envision the beehive of activity on a typical workday, with men bent over their work desks and slide rules crunching out numbers.

They walked down a corridor and, through a connecting door, came into the large workshop that also served as a hangar. One side contained work benches, hoists, and metal shelves. But the bulk of the space belonged to the Horten bomber. Kloster abruptly stopped in his tracks as he came face to face with the Horten brothers' latest working prototype, the Ho 229 V2. Situated at the far corner and despite the dim light, it still looked impressive. Kloster had seen the plans, but to see the real thing up close was something else. He had to supress feelings of anger that Ziller had been picked to fly this new invention. *It should have been me,* he fumed inside. Stengl walked over to an electrical panel and flipped several breakers to illuminate the vast space.

In another section, Kloster spotted another Horten prototype in the final stages of assembly. The airframe appeared to be intact and only the engines were missing. He checked his notepad and walked around both aircraft, making notes. The sentry returned with the message that Stengl was wanted up front by one of his maintenance people. The man excused himself, leaving the sentry alone with Kloster.

"Your name, soldier?" Kloster asked conversationally.

"Holtz. Peter Holtz, sir."

"And this is part of your duties, keeping watch over Germany's latest innovations?"

"Umm … inno … what was that again, sir?"

"I meant that you have an important job watching over our property." Kloster could tell the man wasn't too bright. He spotted the yellow fingers on the man's right-hand twitching slightly.

Just then Stengl returned, apologizing that he was needed back in his own building, but would return as soon as he could. Kloster nodded absentmindedly, giving his assent.

Stengl departed leaving the two men alone again. "Holtz, why don't you take a smoke break," Kloster suggested, "while I complete this mundane paperwork."

Holtz's eyes lit up. He patted his trouser pocket and produced a paper wrapper and a small bag but, to his dismay, found it empty. Kloster, familiar with the sight of hand-rolled cigarettes, fished out a pack of American *Lucky Strikes*—a find from the downed American bomber—and offered Holtz two cigarettes. The old soldier opened his mouth to a nearly toothless grin and happily accepted the offering. Kloster in turn smiled and pointed to the non-smoking sign directly behind him: *Rauchen streng verbotten*. Holtz nodded in compliance and headed for the side door, relishing a break from monotonous sentry duty.

Kloster watched him leave and knew that every second counted. He walked over to the Horten bomber, appraising the stylish wing design. He reminded himself that he had no time to gawk at this latest example of German engineering. Spotting an open toolbox, he removed several wrenches and helped himself to a nearby wooden ladder, propping it up against the fuselage.

Seated inside the cockpit, he fished out the schematic he had studied earlier. Since the bomber was still in the test phase, many of the inside panels were not securely fastened, making it easy for him to remove an access plate on the port side.

He found the oxygen supply line that connected behind the pilot's seat. He selected the correct wrench and partially closed one valve, then unscrewed a fitting just a few turns from the return-flow tube. If his calculations were correct, this would limit the amount of oxygen entering the cockpit, while at the same time allowing invisible carbon monoxide gas to infiltrate the cabin. Kloster replaced the cover plate and alighted from the cockpit. He checked his watch. No more than three minutes had gone by. He looked around. There was still no sight of the sentry.

Kloster replaced the wrenches in the tool box and retrieved his clipboard. He headed over to the second prototype and pretended to make notes. A few minutes passed when he heard the side door close and watched Holtz return, smiling.

"Well, that should do it," Kloster proclaimed to Holtz. "Let's head back to the office."

The two men left the hangar with each of them satisfied: Kloster having tampered with the oxygen supply line and Holtz in possession of an extra cigarette. Kloster informed the sentry there was no need for him to bother Stengl further, retrieved his coat, and walked back to his parked car. Holtz saluted and walked back inside the building.

CHAPTER XVIII
Berlin: Führerbunker

It was late afternoon in Berlin as the sun began to dip in the west, drawing the last of the warmth as it receded behind the skyline. But all of this was lost on the two SS guards stationed at the *Führerbunker's*[6] entrance in the Chancellery Garden. Their chief assignment was to keep close watch on the diminutive man in the trench coat, slowly walking along, lost in deep thought.

The taller of the two elite guards craved a cigarette, his fingertips tracing the outline of the package in his pants pocket. He debated whether he could fish one out without their charge being the wiser.

Just then, the man turned to face the guards, an awkward and rare smile on his lips.

The taller man froze, wondering if he'd given himself away. But to his relief, the man wasn't looking directly at them.

"Komm hier, Blondi," Adolf Hitler called out to his faithful Alsatian as it bounded up the last few steps into the garden. *"Gut, mein kind."*

The dog leapt past the guards and paced excitedly in front of its master, anticipating the familiar pat on the head. Hitler lowered his hand to fulfill the expected caress, then stopped, no longer looking at the dog, but gazing over the east wall, far into the distance. Distracted, the Führer inclined his ear, not sure what he'd heard.

And then the sound came again.

Perplexed, the two guards looked in the same direction, unable to see anything. They had experienced few minutes of relative calm since the last raid by American bombers. Two German Me 109 fighter aircraft had just flown overhead heading west, perhaps ordered into action to reassure the Führer there was still a remnant of the Luftwaffe in Berlin, but the fighters were an unlikely source of the distraction.

No, something else had caught their leader's attention.

Then they heard it too: a distant rumbling. Hitler was keenly aware that the shelling he'd been warned about was drawing closer to the capital. He spun around, startling the two sentries.

"Komm, Blondi," Hitler called out. "Time to go inside."

Clearly the last statement was meant for himself, as his trusted canine had only spent a few minutes in the open air. He walked purposefully toward the stairwell, even as the dog hung back. "Nice day, isn't it Hermann?" he said almost cheerfully to the closest man.

"Jawohl, mein Führer," the soldier replied, snapping to attention.

Hitler paused and glanced over his shoulder. "No use ruining it for Blondi. Let her run around for a while and then bring her below, will you?"

"Of course, *mein Führer,*" came the expected reply.

The Alsatian initially peered at her master, intending to follow him. She quickly changed her mind when the second guard playfully tossed a stick toward the garden's far end, rekindling her favorite game and eliciting a slight smile from her owner.

Blondi bounded toward the wall in search of the stick, while Hitler descended the steps to the lower level, his smile already faded, replaced by the near constant scowl that clung to him like his trench coat.

He was angry at the army's inability—no, it's incompetence—to slow the advance of the Russian forces. *How could the generals be so stupid,* he mused, *not having foreseen the speed and determination of the Soviet advance?* Something had to be done. He would see to it, right now.

Armed with new resolve, Hitler walked through the outer door and down the hall, and entered the first room. He spotted his personal secretary seated at the desk.

"What time is the next meeting scheduled for, Fräulein Junge?" he asked without preamble.

Traudl Junge, didn't bother to look up. "At 5:00 p.m. sharp, *mein Führer,*" she replied calmly.

"*Sehr gut.* Ensure they're all assembled on time. We have much to cover."

Not waiting for a response, Hitler wandered down the narrow, elongated hallway, taking his time. *Perhaps I'll have time to look in on Eva,* he thought to himself.

The German leader, an abstainer from alcohol and self-imposed vegetarian, criticized those who enjoyed such simple things as meat and drink, yet he had his own vices, not the least of which was keeping a mistress for all to see.

Not finding Eva in her outer room, he glanced across the corridor toward the telephone switchboard room. There he spotted Martin Bormann, his tunic removed and sleeves rolled up, in consultation with two senior officers.

Deciding to speak to him later, Hitler headed to his own room and requested a simple tea from his manservant. He then slumped into his chair and absentmindedly gazed at a stack of files on his desk. While waiting for the tea, he picked up a few and flipped through the ones closest to the top.

The first two dealt with important troop deployments. He scanned them but decided they were of no immediate importance. The third folder contained dossiers on his military aides as well as senior members of his entourage. That, too, could wait.

As Hitler selected a file on one of his generals, an envelope fell out. Ordinarily he would have dismissed it, but he elected to pick it up and see for himself. It contained a black and white photo of the general, obviously taken several years ago. The background was an unfamiliar castle.

As Heinz Linge, his valet, walked in with his tea, Hitler casually held out the photo for him to see. "Linge, where do you think this castle is situated? In Bavaria?"

"No, *mein Führer.* It looks like one of the English castles."

Hitler's eyes darted back to the picture, staring at it but keeping his thoughts to himself. "Danke. That's all for now."

Linge nodded and left the sitting room. In solitude, the Führer examined the picture, his mind working feverishly. *That's right, I should have realized it. This was probably taken at a diplomatic meeting back in 1939 before the 'Push' into Poland.*

With his mind already on other matters, he casually tossed the photo on his desk so that it landed upright, revealing the British foreign secretary, Anthony Eden, and beside him the man Hitler loathed above all—Winston Churchill.

╬

William Sochalski awoke with a start from a troubling dream, imagining that he had mistakenly been sequestered in an insane asylum. He allowed his eyes to adjust to the morning light streaming through cracks in the clapboard wall.

As he glanced around him, the vision of the asylum and its restless, noisy inhabitants was replaced with the reality of an even more confining space outfitted with smelly, snoring men. He sat up and grudgingly accepted his new habitat, mindful of one objective: survival.

He was young, and most importantly, in good health. He reasoned he had a good chance of staying alive as long as he didn't find himself in a guard's crosshairs. It was now late November, and he recalled Jack telling him that the war in Europe was running decidedly in the Allies' favor. If that was true, perhaps the Nazis would hold out for another six, maybe seven months. He viewed the squalid conditions, the poor food, and the hard manual labor to come, and all of a sudden six months seemed like a lifetime.

Some of the men went to the back of the barracks and relieved themselves in a metal bucket. They huddled around the small stove, rubbing their hands to keep warm. Then, as if by some unseen signal, they looked to the sole entrance, which opened inward to admit a *kapo*,[7] a prisoner who worked for the guards. The man carried in a pot of coffee and a loaf of bread, placed them on the hearth, and left.

An older man beside William scoffed at the meagre rations. "Don't get your hopes up, young man," he whispered. "It's not even real coffee."

The bread was quickly divided, with one man getting the end pieces and crumbs. Nothing was wasted. Once breakfast was done, there was no time to linger. A guard brandishing a rifle herded them out and marched them across the campsite, toward the tunnel entrance.

⚔

James Buchanan had just returned from a meeting with Anthony Eden. He had been advised that Winston Churchill was returning to London from a meeting at Bletchley Park, the clandestine location of the intelligence service. Many of the war effort's vital services had been moved out of London, the direct result of the Luftwaffe's intensified bombing campaign.

His friend, Bryan Shelby, privy to the prime minister's schedule, had informed Buchanan that Churchill intended to take a rare evening off, having accepted an invitation to attend a performance by the London Philharmonic Orchestra in Tottenham, just north of the city. His advisors had been encouraging him to take in an event such as this, to be seen by the local populace and thus bolster morale.

Coincidentally, Shelby had an aunt residing in Tottenham

and felt it might be a good opportunity to visit. In the process, he hoped to spend a few minutes with the prime minister. Buchanan agreed to join him; after all, he could use the distraction, even if it only meant a lively visit with Shelby's aunt.

"Well, now, look who took a shine to my aunt," Shelby commented, unable to hide his twisted grin. "What will the lads at the office think?"

What indeed? thought Buchanan.

"Corporal, make your way to St. Ann's Road," Shelby instructed the driver. "My colleague is in need of repentance."

"Very good, sir," the driver replied, trying not to laugh.

In just a few minutes, the car deposited the two officers at the side entrance of St. Ann's Church, a stately building that dated back to the 1800s. VIPs were being admitted there. Shelby and Buchanan joined the line and were asked to show their credentials. With Churchill in attendance, security was tight.

The men quickly passed inspection and took seats near the middle of the church, about ten rows back. From here, Buchanan could make out the dignitaries near the front and had no trouble spotting Churchill. As usual, Britain's leader was in deep conversation with a member of his inner circle.

As the orchestra tuned-up, Buchanan noted townsfolk filing in through the main entrance, many looking forward to the symphony, but especially eager to catch a glimpse of the prime minister. The two men shed their uniform coats and settled into their seats.

The conductor stepped onto the dais and, after acknowledging the dignitaries, began the first movement of Beethoven's *Ninth Symphony*. Buchanan, who had been contemplating the war effort, thoroughly enjoyed the concert and felt a tinge of disappointment when the last notes resonated through the hall. After the performance, he remained seated with Shelby and waited for the throng to leave the church.

Churchill made himself available to a select few parishioners and graciously listened to their concerns. After most had left, the two officers picked up their coats and stepped closer to the prime minister. Once cleared by the security detail, Shelby patiently waited for an opportunity to address Churchill. Being in close proximity, he caught a few words uttered by Anthony Eden.

"That's exactly what I was getting at, sir," Eden was saying. "The Germans, though beaten on both fronts, show no signs of giving up. In fact, I've read reports suggesting they've ramped up their development of new and diabolical war machines."

Shelby couldn't have asked for better timing. He inched forward, pulling Buchanan with him. He coughed, catching the minister's attention. Eden recognized him instantly. "Ah, Shelby, good of you to come," he said, motioning him forward. Eden turned to Churchill. "Prime Minister, may I introduce one of my aides from the Intelligence section, Commander Shelby."

Churchill appraised the young man speculatively. "Good evening, Commander. Great performance, wasn't it?"

"Indeed, sir," Shelby acknowledged. "One of my favorite symphonies, even though the composer is German."

"Quite, quite," Churchill reiterated with a smirk. He noted that most of the crowd had left. "Now then, Commander, what have you got for us?"

"Prime Minister, in light of what Minister Eden was just saying, may I introduce Captain Buchanan, our Canadian chap at the War Office."

Churchill glanced up at Buchanan, considered the man before him for a second, and smiled broadly. "Ah, a Canadian chap, here in London. How good of William Lyon Mackenzie King to send us a representative."

Shelby elbowed his friend, hoping he'd get the drift and take up the conversation.

"Mr. Churchill," Buchanan started, "we—that is Commander Shelby and I—have recently come across information that confirms what we've suspected all along. The Germans have been working on another secret project, an aircraft much superior to our piston-driven airplanes. Sir, you're no doubt familiar with the development of the Messerschmitt twin-engine jet fighter." It was more of a statement than a question. He paused, looking for confirmation from Churchill.

The Prime Minister nodded, encouraging him to continue.

"Well, sir, the Nazis haven't stopped there. As you may recall, one year ago we became aware of a new initiative, a directive from Göring himself, challenging German aircraft designers to come up with an innovative design that would satisfy his '3x1000' project."

Churchill's visage went blank for a split-second. Buchanan knew that a man in his position was privy to all sorts of secret information, war directives, government proposals, and even rumors, but no man was able to keep on top of every intercept or every cable.

"Prime Minister," Eden interjected, "Göring has stipulated—well, demanded actually—that their experts come up with an airplane capable of delivering a one-thousand-kilogram payload over a distance of one thousand kilometers. Not only that, sir, but it has to attain a speed of one thousand kilometers per hour, something that no fighter or bomber has been able to achieve."

"Until now, you mean," stated the astute leader. Churchill was no fool and his quick-thinking mind had often left a fellow politician bewildered and on the defensive.

Buchanan knew the prime minister's time was valuable and that he needed to keep it short. "I'm afraid so," he said. "Although their Messerschmitt program has been plagued with various supply problems, that's not the case with this new bomber, the Horten Ho 229. Information has come to light that the Germans not only have a working prototype but that they've conducted several test flights."

He paused for effect. "Sir, we have every reason to believe they intend to put it into production. If successful, it would mean catastrophic losses for our side."

Churchill nodded sombrely. "Then let's hope they don't get that far." He turned to his minister. "Keep me abreast of that, will you, Anthony? And thank you for the update, Captain Buchanan; you too, Commander Shelby. It's always better to be aware of your enemy's plans before they're implemented; rather than being caught off-guard."

With that, Churchill turned and wearily approached the side entrance. He stopped to speak to the conductor, congratulating him on the marvelous performance, and then was whisked out the door by his security team.

On the way back to London, Buchanan and Shelby felt cautiously optimistic that Churchill would now lay more credence to the latest threat. But as so often happens, priorities change and other matters take on a greater importance.

⚜

William Sochalski awoke to shouting, interrupting a dream about his parents. How he wished he could see them again! He rubbed the sleep from his eyes and peered at the *kapo* who had barged into their barracks, his presence proclaiming the start of another long day. The man was calling for the men to wake up while he delivered what passed for food: a sorry-looking broth mixture that vaguely resembled soup.

After the meagre breakfast, those who were able were hustled outside and marched up the mountain, then down the long tunnel to the various work stations. William, due to his experience of working with electric motors, had been assigned to the final assembly site of V1 rockets. For this task, he had been teamed up with a Polish Jew, Urgud Zbignew, a lanky man in his early fifties.

Urgud had been more accommodating than most of the

prisoners, perhaps feeling sorry for the young man. He had filled William in on the various tasks, and more importantly how to accomplish their work without being harassed or beaten by the guards who oversaw them.

William was a quick learner and worked well with the older man, a machinist from Katowice, an industrial city in the Silesian region of Poland. Working side-by-side, William noticed that Urgud occasionally embedded a small ball bearing within a ball of wax no bigger than a large grape. He then attached it to the underside of the instrument panel of the rocket.

When he asked Urgud about this unusual practice during one of their rare breaks, the man coughed to hide his embarrassment.

"I don't mind telling *you*, William, but don't let anyone else know." He leaned in conspiratorially, checking to make sure no one was within earshot. "The wax is there just to hold the ball bearing in place temporarily. During the rocket's launch down its wooden ramp, the metal housing will be exposed to considerable stress and vibration. Eventually the wax will break apart, and the ball bearing will be freed to roll around within the panel's cavity."

William scrunched his eyebrows together, trying to follow the logic, but not coming up with an explanation.

Urgud saw the consternation on his face and started to grin. "Ah, that has you perplexed? Well, you may have noticed that I don't include the little ball in every rocket. Why? The inspectors know some of us try to sabotage some aspect of the rocket, like the gyros, or maybe tamper with the propellant when no one is looking. Regrettably, some do get caught, like poor Victor. You saw him hanging outside our barracks last week, didn't you?"

William shuddered. The Nazis had caught the prisoner trying to loosen a fuel valve. To make an example out of him, they had strung him up with piano wire for all to see. The poor man had suffocated in agony, a vivid reminder of what happened to saboteurs.

"Well, I don't want to get caught like Victor," Urgud continued. "So, I plant my little ball on every third or fourth rocket."

"But I still don't understand …" William trailed off as a guard walked up to them.

"Break time is over, Jews. Get back to work."

Both men got up and shuffled toward their assembly site. Once they were back at their work bench, Urgud coughed to get William's attention. "I magnetize the ball bearings ahead of time," he whispered. "Once they break free, they roll around and their magnetism interferes with the magnetic compass. Simple, no? Well, that's the theory, anyway."

Sochalski nodded, amazed at the older man's ingenuity. But what could he do? He resolved to do what it took to stay alive and held out hope of seeing his family again.

CHAPTER XIX

Saufman's Demise

Otto Saufman grabbed his overcoat and hat and was ready to leave his office. Ordinarily he wouldn't have been at work this late, but an earlier fight with his wife had given him an excuse to linger and catch up on some mundane paperwork. The door to his office slowly opened on its own. A broom handle came into view, followed by a cleaning woman pulling a bucket on wheels. Sensing she wasn't alone, the cleaning lady turned around and found Saufman staring at her.

"My apologies, Herr Saufman," Gertrude Augsberg said when she saw him. "I wasn't expecting to see you today. You see, I'm filling in for another cleaner. I can come back later."

Saufman was about to instruct her to do just that when he reconsidered.

"Wait a minute," he said, replacing his overcoat on the rack. "Your name is Augsberg, isn't it?"

"*Ja,* Gertrude Augsberg."

He nodded his head a fraction, not in acknowledgement but in decision. "Your daughter, Hilde, also works for me—or used to anyway. Where is she now?"

"I ... I don't know. At home, I should think."

"Don't play games with me, woman. We both know she's not at home." Saufman moved toward her, pointing his index finger accusingly, like a teacher addressing a student who's been caught in a lie. "She's up to something, and I intend to find out what it is."

"I don't know anything about her work affairs. I thought everything was alright."

"You thought," he smirked. "Well, everything isn't alright. I'm missing some travel documents and I know who took them—Hilde!"

Augsberg's face paled. "I assure you, Herr Saufman, Hilde would never —"

"Enough!" he interrupted. "I *know* she pilfered them. I've been looking all over for them."

Gertrude couldn't think of what to say, so she remained quiet.

Saufman didn't bother waiting for a response. He walked over to his desk and picked up the telephone. "I know who can get to the bottom of this. The Gestapo."

A horrified look came over Augsberg's face. "No, not them, please." She walked over to the desk to plead with the deputy-mayor.

But he turned his back on her and spoke into the mouthpiece. "This is Herr Saufman. Connect me with the Gestapo."

Terrified, Gertrude tried to snatch the phone out of his hand, but he slapped her hand away like an irritant fly. She was determined now and recovered quickly. In desperation, she used the broom handle to brush the phone's cradle off the desk, forcing Saufman to reach for the tumbling instrument. But in doing so, he overreached, tripped over the cord, and fell to his knees.

Saufman's earlier anger returned in a flash. He struggled to get up, his face unmasked, malevolent. Gertrude dropped the broom, no longer a cleaning implement but an accomplice to the violence she had set in motion. She backed away toward the fireplace with her hands outstretched, silently imploring him to reconsider.

"Now you'll get what you deserve, you, you ... *dumme Gans,*" he hissed, as if emulating a hen.

Saufman tried to grab her, but she eluded his grasp, knocking over the cleaning bucket and spilling its contents on the floor. He lunged for her, slipped on the liquid mess, and lost his balance. He fell backwards and his head struck the corner of the oak coffee table.

Saufman collapsed to the floor and lay still.

Suddenly all was quiet. Gertrude, on the verge of fleeing, stood motionless, her eyes transfixed on the mayor's prostrate form. For a split-second she thought he might be faking, baiting her to check on his well-being so he could grab her. But then she saw blood oozing from around his left temple, slowly spreading and marring the parquet floor's high-gloss finish.

She reluctantly knelt down beside him and only then did she notice his glazed open eyes, staring into nothing. The panic returned and she recoiled from the sight of those listless eyes. She rose to her feet, ready to run, but then she froze, not wanting to look but unable to look away.

Like an actress in a play anticipating her cue, she seemed to wait for direction; but the imaginary director had quietly slipped away, like Otto's soul, leaving her with uncertainty.

Gertrude was no actress, and this was no play. It was real, as real as life gets. And the reality of life dictated no opportunity for rehearsals, no stand-ins, and certainly no postponements. She felt surreal, as if being pulled against her will, the curtain of insanity ready to drop on her.

I have to act, she thought, rousing herself from the lingering effects of shock. *I have to be strong. Yes, strong for Hilde.*

She steeled herself to gaze at Saufman's prone, lifeless body, willing it to move, to breathe, to do anything but lay immobile. The slow, incessant ticking of the grandfather clock in the corner reminded her that time was marching on, that life continued. Yet each time she glanced at Otto's body, she somehow felt trapped by a feeling of timelessness.

Gertrude's gaze swept around the room and landed on the framed portrait of his family on the desk. She felt a pang of regret, of compassion—not for Saufman, the now dead man—but for his wife, Brunnhilde, the mute witness now bereft of companionship, of husband, and the income he had provided.

I have to get a grip on myself, she thought.

Reluctantly, Gertrude bent down and picked up his hand, somehow feeling obligated to check for a pulse. There was none, of course. It was hard to believe, but Saufman, the outspoken deputy-mayor, the fanatical Nazi and loathsome womanizer was dead and would never bother anyone again.

Andreas Bauman landed at the Neubrandenburg aerodrome after an uneventful flight. Feeling more relaxed, he taxied the fighter to the main hangar where a flagman signalled him to stop and shut down his engine.

By the time he had unbuckled his seatbelt and shoulder harness, the mechanic had placed a ladder against the airframe. Andreas climbed down and lightly jumped from the last rung onto the tarmac. It had felt good to be in the air again.

Bauman had been here before and was familiar with the airfield's layout. Pleased to have arrived ahead of schedule, he headed directly to the commander's office.

He seated himself in the outer office and smiled at the secretary behind the desk.

After a short wait, he was ushered into the commander's office. After a brief exchange of pleasantries, Andreas handed over his attaché case to the major, who merely grunted and set it aside. He informed Andreas that he would peruse the contents in due course, but he first had to attend to other matters.

There were other documents on the way, arriving from Rostock, and Andreas would need to take them back to Berlin. Since it would be at least several hours, the major allowed him the use of a car from the motor pool to occupy his time in Neubrandenburg.

Bauman couldn't have been more pleased. He changed out of his flight suit and into civvies: plain gray slacks, a blue shirt, and matching blazer. He was glad he had the foresight to bring along a change of clothes.

After signing out an older model Opel, he stowed his small bag in the trunk, ensuring the spare was inflated and in good shape. Although he would have preferred to stop at one of the local inns for some refreshment, he was eager to head to the railway station and inquire about the train from Berlin.

He arrived at an opportune time, catching the station master unoccupied and reading the morning newspaper. Andreas approached him circumspectly and sat down opposite him. After a minute of pretending to read his own paper, he casually asked when the train from Berlin was scheduled to arrive. The man lowered his paper and peered at Andreas over top of his spectacles.

"It hasn't arrived yet," came the curt reply. The official was a little irritated at being interrupted in his reading. "The train was delayed just outside Berlin—sabotage on the line; or so the rumor went. It took railway workers several hours to repair the damaged track." He glanced at his watch and added, "I expect it to arrive within the hour."

Bauman couldn't believe his luck. He would be in time to see Hilde disembark with her "colleague," whoever he was. He rose and thanked the station master, who had already resumed reading his newspaper.

Andreas headed inside to get a coffee and a copy of the local paper, hoping to use it as a distraction and occupy his time. To anyone watching, he would have appeared calm, but inside he was conflicted. He debated what he should do when he met Hilde. He felt betrayed, not only by the inconsiderate way in which she had left, but by her failure to tell him, her friend.

Bauman was annoyed that her mother assumed Hilde had

informed him, or had it been just a way to forestall him, to prevent him finding out the truth? But what was the truth? What was really going on? If Hilde had been sent out on business, why hadn't she gone with Saufman himself? He suspected Otto Saufman had been trying to get Hilde all to himself and this would have been a perfect opportunity. Something didn't make sense and he had to find out what it was.

At last, Andreas heard a shrill whistle in the distance, and seconds later, the sound of an approaching train. He paid for his coffee and headed for the platform.

The locomotive chugged into the station, pulling nine carriages behind it, each one identical to the rest. Andreas scrutinized the windows, looking for any sign of Hilde. In the process he was joined on the platform by others eagerly watching for family members, friends, and acquaintances.

The train had barely come to a stop when the doors flew open and a horde of humanity disembarked. First came soldiers, then businessmen, followed by women and children, and lastly older people wise enough to allow the younger crowd to get off first.

He did his best to watch those leaving and was fairly certain he hadn't missed Hilde. For a second, he thought she might have gotten off on the other side, but that seemed unlikely. To be sure, he positioned himself for a better view, but was forced to admit that no one had alighted on the far side.

Then Andreas was struck with an uncomfortable thought. *What if she doesn't get off?* He realized he hadn't expected her to stay on. He had to make a quick decision: either continue waiting or get on the train and search for himself. According to the schedule, the train would stop for a mere ten minutes, before carrying on to Stralsund. That left him precious little time.

Something akin to foreboding worked itself up his spine. He fought the growing uncertainty trying to unsettle him. He had to make a decision.

The whistle blew again, reminding people to hurry up. The flagman was poised to signal the engineer. The wheels began to spin in place, sparks flying. Andreas only had a moment now and instinctively headed for the closest ladder. As his hand hovered over the handrail, he glanced up, hoping to see Hilde's smiling face beckoning him to get on board. He envisioned her telling him it had all been a mistake, that she had misrepresented her actions, that she wished to see him.

As the train began to move, Andreas clung tightly to the ladder. What would his superiors say if they found out? He hadn't come to Neubrandenburg to follow his girlfriend, and yet he couldn't jump off now. The train left the station and he was on it.

CHAPTER XX
Erwin Ziller

On a cool, crisp morning, in the town of Oranienburg, with remnants of frost visible on the flowers lining the town square, Erwin Ziller, RLM's test pilot, drove by, eager to conduct another test flight of the Horten Ho 229.

It was just after sunrise, as he got out of his 1939 Daimler, stretched, and headed for the secluded hangar at the north side of the airfield.

Ziller was eager to get started on his preflight check. He nodded to one of the mechanics and headed to the rear of the hangar, where a changing room had been hastily erected. Everything was in a state of flux since the Allies had ramped up their bombing campaign of military airfields.

He changed into his flight suit, made from layered material to protect him against the cold temperatures, and retrieved the unique metal and plastic helmet, an experimental design for use at high altitudes. He declined an airman's offer of coffee, instead preferring to review the latest Horten maintenance report. The mechanics had conducted a thorough inspection of the aircraft and signed off on the its airworthiness. Everything had checked out.

Ziller walked alongside the Horten bomber as it was being pulled out by a small tractor. He slid—caressed would be more accurate—his hand over the smooth contour of the wingtip, looking for anything out of the ordinary: a crease, a loose rivet, even drops of oil adhering to the fuselage.

Now that the aircraft was out in the open and free from the hangar's confinement, the Plexiglas canopy reflected the beehive of last-minute activity around it. One mechanic disengaged the tow bar from the nose wheel, while another secured it and promptly drove the tractor back to the hangar, while a third attached a ladder to the airframe.

Satisfied that all was in order, Ziller climbed up the ladder, and settled himself into the pilot's seat.

Suppressing a grin, he glanced at the instrument panel, familiarizing himself again with the layout. He'd done it many times before, but he had to remind himself that this was no ordinary airplane. The shell consisted of welded steel tubing, but the airframe and wings were a wood fabrication. This ingenious concept, a cost-saving measure, also decreased the airplane's total weight. He had to admit that the Horten brothers' design was ahead of their time.

An airman hovered near the cockpit, watching as Ziller worked through the start-up procedure, flicking switches on the side panel and verifying the response against a checklist that outlined the correct sequence. As the port Jumo engine spooled up, Ziller carefully monitored the instruments, making sure all were functioning properly. He gently tapped the circular glass face of each gauge in the instrument cluster—altimeter, airspeed indicator, compass, artificial horizon—noting with satisfaction that each registered the appropriate readout. Lastly, under the pilot's watchful eyes, a second airman attached the hose for the oxygen supply.

The man then closed and secured the canopy, climbed down the ladder, and removed it from the airplane. Meanwhile, Ziller fired up the starboard engine and monitored the all-important temperature gauges. Satisfied that all the readouts were within specified limits, he motioned the airman to remove the wheel chocks.

Using his mike, Ziller advised the airport controller that

he was ready. Sadly, Reimar and Walter Horten were away in meetings with RLM. The controller advised him of the most recent altimeter setting, cloud base, and current wind speed and direction. Ziller acknowledged the information, released the brakes, and began to taxi out toward the active runway.

Receiving the final go-ahead, Ziller turned onto the runway. He looked around him and relished the moment, remembering all the training and preparation he had undergone to get to this point.

He gradually applied the power levers as the delta-wing aircraft smoothly accelerated down the runway, picking up speed. Once he reached one hundred fifty kilometers per hour, he pulled the yoke toward him and nudged the nose up. Within seconds, the body of the plane lifted off the runway.

The seemingly docile airframe, confined to terra firma, suddenly transformed into a viable flying machine, transmitting exhilaration to the pilot and replacing any further doubt. The Horten bomber, barely airborne, vaulted into the sky from the powerful thrust of its two turbojets, climbing steadily to the planned altitude of five thousand meters.

╬

A black Daimler automobile pulled over to the shoulder of a side road, not far from the airfield's boundary. Horst Kloster, the lone occupant, exited the car and walked across the road to a small church and its adjoining cemetery. To avoid suspicion and perhaps unnecessary questions, he grabbed a small bouquet of dried flowers from a nearby urn and headed into the grounds.

Kloster wasn't interested in any of the grave markers neatly laid out before him. Truth be known, he knew of no one interred there, and he hadn't come to commiserate over the dead. Rather, he was contemplating the soon-to-be deceased: Erwin Ziller.

Alerted by the approaching shrill of a jet engine, Kloster

looked up to see the Horten aircraft leave the military airfield and fly overhead. He smiled, picturing the series of events about to unfold for the unsuspecting pilot: haziness, confusion, difficulty in judgment, drowsiness, and if left unchecked, loss of consciousness.

An elderly woman, hunched over and dressed in black, slowly walked into the cemetery, interrupting his solitude. She was also carrying flowers. She nodded respectfully to Kloster and continued to the next row, stopping in front of a recently dug grave.

Kloster quickly turned away, covering his face so she wouldn't catch his inappropriate smile. To keep up his grieving act, he stopped at an arbitrary gravestone and knelt down to place the flowers. He stepped back in astonishment when his gaze caught the gravestone's inscription: Erwin Leiter – REST in PEACE

Kloster fought to keep from laughing out loud. *Well, well, Erwin,* he thought, reminded of his nemesis. *It seems your namesake is already buried here.* Unperturbed by his own macabre humor, he turned and quickly walked back to his car, leaving the old woman to ponder his ungracious actions.

Climbing through two thousand meters, Erwin Ziller went through his pre-planned maneuvers, intending to test the aircraft's capabilities. He felt more confident with each turn, feeling the plane's responsiveness while pushing it further to discover its limitations.

He was too pre-occupied with the flight to notice the first subtle symptoms of hypoxia: fuzziness, drowsiness, and lack of clarity. He followed up with another tight turn, a reciprocal turn, and then an abrupt drop in altitude, simulating a dog-fighting technique.

Afterward he felt disoriented but attributed it to the extreme maneuver. That proved to be his undoing. A strange, hazy feeling hit him, followed by more confusion. Ziller might have attributed this to a lack of oxygen had it not been for an unexpected development; the right engine suddenly flamed out. Preoccupied with the sudden loss of power, Ziller didn't realize that he was slowly succumbing to the effects of carbon monoxide poisoning. All his mental focus now hinged on trying to restart the starboard engine while maintaining control of the aircraft.

Ziller's thinking became scattered and confused. The first signs of panic hit his groggy, oxygen-starved brain. He was sliding toward a delirious state. He began to hallucinate, and the controller's insistent calls, first a distraction, now became such a nuisance that he switched off the radio. More and more his thinking slowed and, in a final attempt at recovery, his hands fumbled with the latch, trying desperately to unhinge the canopy and escape the cockpit. Instead, he passed out, no longer the pilot-in-command, but a doomed passenger.

Several kilometers to the east, an exuberant Kloster caught sight of the bomber, laboring on only the port engine, bank abruptly and then stall. It began to descend in a wide arc and eventually plummeted toward a snow-covered hillock. Kloster was rewarded with the sound of the crash, and the distant smoke served as confirmation as it rose from a copse of trees. Thrilled that his plan had succeeded, he pondered his next move.

No sooner had he returned to his office than an unexpected opportunity presented itself. He reread the message left by his secretary. It was short and to the point, advising him to contact Colonel Knemeyer from RLM.

Kloster was familiar with the name and his prestigious position as the head of RLM's technical aircraft development. What followed was a brief telephone call, with Knemeyer arranging for a private meeting—just the two of them. Curiously, it didn't take place at any of RLM's facilities, but at

Knemeyer's private residence in Potsdam the next day.

Once the initial pleasantries were out of the way and a servant left the study, Knemeyer came to the matter at hand.

"*Herr Oberleutnant,* I have been instructed by Göring to formulate a plan, in effect conduct a secret mission utilizing the Horten bomber."

He allowed that to sink in, making sure he had Kloster's attention.

"A modified Horten bomber would carry an experimental bomb," Knemeyer continued, "a bomb that is to be dropped on an-as-yet unspecified target. Let me be perfectly clear. This mission has been envisioned by Hitler himself. Does that appeal to you?"

Kloster was speechless. His mind swirled with questions and he opened his mouth to seek clarification but was interrupted by Knemeyer.

"Yes, yes, I know there's much to discuss. Here's what the Führer has sanctioned. Let's review it and then you can voice your concerns." Knemeyer selected a dossier and revealed the main aspects of the plan.

Kloster eagerly leaned in and listened as Knemeyer outlined the specifics. He had to admit the mission was bold in its premise. *But could they really pull it off?* On the whole, Kloster was pleased that he had been considered for such a sensitive project. He was about to voice his concern regarding his current commitment with the Gestapo, but it seemed that Knemeyer had already anticipated the question.

"Don't worry about Schinkel, Kloster," Knemeyer added conciliatorily. "I've already consulted with him and he will make the necessary arrangements when it's time. All he knows is that you—based on your former qualifications—are required for a special mission. If you consent to participate, you'll be handsomely rewarded. In fact, I've been authorized to promote you to the next level: *Hauptman.*"

Kloster was barely able to suppress a grin. A promotion to captain, and then accolades, perhaps from the Führer himself. Without a second thought, Kloster had taken the offered carrot.

╬

It was mid-morning when the train started moving again. Hilde smiled, relieved they were finally getting underway.

After a breakfast of hard-boiled eggs and bread with marmalade, Jack settled into his seat, enjoying a real coffee, not the usual ersatz—a poor substitute most Germans had grown used to.

Before long, the train pulled into Neubrandenburg, but they wouldn't be getting off. They would proceed further on to Stralsund. Once the train left the station, Jack felt the need to stretch his legs and get some circulation moving through his ankle. He rose from his seat and opened the door to their compartment.

But that's as far as he got.

Hilde heard a commotion and watched as Jack was pushed back into their compartment. She turned toward the door and was about to address the clumsy traveller, when she saw who it was. She cleared her throat.

"Um … Andreas?"

All the color drained from Hilde's face as she fought to regain her composure. Her feet felt like lead and her heart skipped a beat.

"What are you doing here?" she managed, her voice barely above a whisper.

"The exact same question I have for the two of you," Andreas replied coolly, then glanced towards Swaggart. "Sit down, Herr Schuman."

Jack, not wanting to create a disturbance, complied.

Bauman stood with his back against the door, blocking their escape. "Aren't you going to introduce me to your *colleague*, Hilde?"

A thousand thoughts raced through Hilde's mind. What could she say? How much did Andreas know? What did he suspect? Did he recognize Jack? Bewildered, she gazed into Andreas' face. The consternation was obvious.

"Well?" he demanded.

"Entschuldigung," Jack said and attempted to pass himself off as a German citizen by addressing Andreas in German, startling Hilde. *"Wer sind Sie?"*

Bauman turned to look at him, a look of vague familiarity forming in his eyes as he regarded Jack.

Jack looked to Hilde, appealing her to take over—his German being too limited. Hilde was struggling to come up with a plausible story. Taking a deep breath, she decided to tell the truth. But deep down she felt afraid.

"Andreas, this won't be easy to explain. And even when I've finished, I'm not sure if you'll understand my reasoning. I don't expect you to agree with it. What happens here doesn't have anything to do with our relationship; however, the outcome may influence it. All I want to say is that I still have feelings for you, and I hope you'll respect what I have to say. I pray you won't do anything rash."

She paused, watching for his reaction. He seemed a little less severe and nodded fractionally, which she took it as a sign to continue.

"Are you armed?" Hilde asked, surprising Jack more than Andreas. Bauman shook his head and she breathed a little easier.

"Alright then. This man," she said, pointing to Jack, "is, as you've already guessed, not my colleague. He doesn't work for Saufman and he's not with the Gestapo. Actually, he's not even German. He's a ... foreigner."

"He's not German?" Andreas asked, looking bewildered.

"Nein. Ein Amerikaner," she replied evenly, then switching to English. "He's an American pilot, shot down a few days ago, north of Berlin. Andreas, I'd like you to meet Captain

Jack Swaggart, US Air Force."

Bauman looked stunned and took a moment to process her words. "I … er … I thought he worked for Saufman. He's an American? A pilot?"

"That's correct," Jack replied in English, giving credence to his nationality. "My squadron is based in northern France, but originally I come from the American Midwest. Please, Herr Bauman, won't you sit down?"

Hilde translated, and reluctantly Andreas seated himself opposite the two. Over the next few minutes, Hilde summarized how she and Rudi had come across the downed aircraft and in the spur of the moment had decided to help the injured American. Jack sat there, focused, trying to absorb the gist of what was said. She left out the part about Sochalski, reasoning that it would only add to the confusion. She explained what had happened at the Church of St. Nicholas, the betrayal, and their need for a hasty departure.

"I can understand your need to help," Andreas said, patronising her, "but surely there are … other people who could have helped. Why compromise your position with the mayor's office and your own safety, not to mention your loyalty as a patriotic German?"

He was, she realized, still in a state of disbelief. But could she change his mind?

"I can explain my reasons to you. There's still time." She sighed. "You see, this has to do with more than just helping one pilot escape from behind enemy lines. It concerns Germany's future. Do you want to hear more?"

Andreas nodded. Hilde reached forward, taking one of his hands into hers. He didn't seem to mind and didn't pull back.

"Andreas, this war has changed our country. And not for the better. Our once idolized and beloved Führer is no longer doing what's best for us. Many of his decisions will have dire consequences, some that you've already seen, like food shortages and the reduction in the average German's quality of life. Other consequences, which I don't fully understand, will have a long-lasting impact on our economy, society, and way of life. I worry we will soon be facing one disaster after another."

Although Jack didn't understand every word, he caught quite a bit and nodded in agreement.

Hilde continued. "Our country is in shambles and Hitler doesn't care! He's bent on revenge, whatever the cost, and if we let him, he'll drag the whole country down with him."

Hilde knew, from previous discussions with Andreas that he tended to respect her views, but as an officer he had taken an oath of allegiance to the military, and specifically to the Führer.

She went on to remind him that since the Stauffenberg assassination attempt, many Germans had become disenchanted with the military. Some had come face to face with the Gestapo's brutality and many had experienced, whether by eyewitness account or testimonials, Himmler's "solution"[8] for gypsies, communists, religious leaders, radicals, and other political factions. And those were German-born people.

She needed to convince him that loyalty to his country outweighed his obligation to the current regime.

"Andreas, I care deeply for you, and I know that you care about our country. Just last week, you yourself said that the war has been lost. What I'm hoping to do, by helping Captain Swaggart, is bring the war to an earlier conclusion, thereby minimizing further loss of life. You've seen what the bombings have done to our cities. But what sends shivers up my spine is what Hitler and Himmler have orchestrated, their ultimate directive in dealing with 'The Jewish question.' I'm talking about concentration camps. Think of it, Andreas. Thousands, hundreds of thousands have been shipped off to these death camps, never to see their loved ones again. It's … barbaric. I'm ashamed to call myself German."

Andreas nodded reluctantly, looking down at the floor.

"But there's more," she continued. "The military hasn't

been satisfied with the air attacks on Britain; they've resorted to bombing their cities with those unmanned rockets, the V1 bombs."

Jack whispered something into Hilde's ear.

"They're producing those bombs with the use of slave labor," she added. "And now Hitler is developing a new threat: the Horten bomber."

Andreas looked at her in surprise. "How could you know about—?"

"I've seen it. We saw it fly overhead when we came back from Zehdenick."

Bauman seemed deeply conflicted and the look of consternation was obvious. He cleared his throat.

"Hilde, I'm a pilot, a Luftwaffe officer, and Reimar Horten's friend. I can't just forsake my oath to Germany and to Adolf Hitler. I don't like being thrust in the middle of an untenable situation."

Hilde frowned, recognizing the consternation on Andreas' face. *Does he grasp what I'm trying to say?* she wondered. *Does he suspect I am helping the American to escape?*

"The more I think about it, the less I like what you're doing," he said. "Hilde, you're embarking on a course that is contrary to your beliefs, your career, and goes against your country, and yes it even impacts our relationship."

Hilde was intuitive enough to realize that this was what troubled Andreas most: their relationship. She sensed he was feeling loss and likely the first pangs of jealousy.

She observed how Andreas scrutinized the American. She also noticed that he seemed to avoid referring to him at all. Did he feel threatened by the tall Yankee? Jack was handsome, confident, and had an air of authority that Bauman somehow lacked. As Andreas sat there in silence, Hilde became alarmed. Although he was trying to appear noncommittal, he had a dangerous look in his eyes. She moved closer to him, hoping to calm him by her presence.

"What are you thinking?" Hilde asked.

"Um, I'm considering the present circumstances," Andreas lied. "I mean the American's chances of getting to the north coast aren't good. You should have considered that. The next Gestapo checkpoint could prove to be your undoing."

"What?" Hilde's soft expression abruptly changed to annoyance. "How can you say that, after what I've just explained to you?" What was Andreas up to? She knew him well and began to suspect that he had something in mind. Perhaps he would try to arrest Jack and hand him over to the military police.

She decided to try again. "Look, Andreas, I know this has been very sudden for you, and perhaps you need a little time to think it over. We've eaten, but perhaps you and I could go back to the dining car and try to sort this out. The captain will stay put. He's not going to jump from a moving train. You have my word on it."

Jack, who'd been following the conversation reasonably well, decided it was a good idea not to contradict her. He merely nodded.

Andreas seemed about to object, but changed his mind.

"Alright," he agreed. "We can do that."

Hilde grabbed her coat and followed Andreas out of the compartment, leaving Jack to ponder his options.

CHAPTER XXI

An Unlikely Hero

"Dammit!" Jack cursed to himself. He knew things had gone too smoothly so far, and sure enough now they'd run into a crisis—a big one. He tried to calm himself, aware that panic wouldn't accomplish much. He came up with one plan after another, but ended up dismissing them all; they were all too risky or had too little chance of success.

He felt the train slow, interrupting his thoughts so that he glanced outside. As it came to a stop, he spotted several smaller buildings and a prominent sign. Greifswald. And there, further along the tracks, was a water tower.

What could be the problem? He nearly jumped out of his seat at the sound of a knock at the door. It was the conductor. The man apologized and explained they'd been signalled to vacate the main line in favor of a military train carrying troops.

Once he was alone again, Jack half-expected Andreas to return, hemming him in, but all he heard was the other passengers emerging to stretch their legs. Here was an opportunity to escape, and he instinctively felt he should take it.

Without further thought, he grabbed his small attaché case and left his compartment, leaving his suitcase behind. As he walked through the train, he detected no sign of Andreas. Just ahead, the conductor was speaking to an older couple. Jack nodded and with a *pardon,* squeezed past them and made it to the end of the car, where he stepped outside and inhaled the cool crisp air.

What he saw next made him stare in wonder. Another train was stopped on the adjoining track. It wasn't a troop train, but neither was it a passenger train. *A supply train?*

No sooner had the thought left him than the explanation presented itself. This train consisted of seven or eight brown cattle cars, but they were carrying human cargo: POWs.

Jack leaned over the railing for a better look and what he saw astounded him. Men were disembarking and lining up in ranks against each car, assembled in groups of fifty or so and held in check by soldiers brandishing submachine guns. Patrolling the perimeter were more guards, some holding guard dogs in check that were straining against their leashes.

The conductor had spotted him and motioned for him to get back inside. Not far behind him was Andreas, a look of fear and apprehension on his face. Jack heard a shrill whistle and the sound of the expected German troop train as it thundered by on the other side of the tracks.

Suddenly, the familiar click-clack of the train wheels was drowned out by another sound, this one depressingly familiar—the shrill descent of a falling bomb.

Several things occurred almost simultaneously. Bauman called out to him, Hilde screamed, and an American fighter plane zoomed overhead. The bomb it had dropped exploded nearby, wiping out an anti-aircraft battery and catapulting a truck onto its back, exposing its undercarriage like a hippopotamus' underbelly. One of the fuel tanks ruptured, spewing gasoline on the ground. As the P-51 Mustang climbed out from its low-level bombing run, a second fighter appeared from the right and lined up for a strafing run, its bullets savagely ripping apart a second battery. It continued past, not more than ten feet off the ground, flying a diagonal intercept course for the departing German troop train.

The engineer must have disengaged the drive lever and

deployed the brakes, as the train appeared to slow. The Mustang caught up to the troop train in seconds and the pilot unleashed a salvo of cannon-fire that tore at the camouflage tarp of the freight car directly behind the tender. The wind found its way under the sheeting and ripped the tarp off, revealing a massive Tiger tank and a smaller Panther tank in front of it. The Mustang gained a little altitude and executed a gut-wrenching tight turn, returning with speed and losing a bomb that decimated the Panther, sending shrapnel flying everywhere.

The concussion snapped the tethering chains on the Tiger like they were made out of string. The flatbed holding the two tanks listed dangerously, with the wheels on the right side of the car leaving the steel rails. The Tiger, no longer chained to the flatbed, gave way to gravity, toppled off its mooring, slid onto the gravel bed, and took the remains of the Panther with it, ploughing into the gravel bed and sending a shower of rocks onto the next flatbed, which was occupied by two soldiers manning gun positions. Both men ducked behind their gun shields, desperately hoping to escape the barrage of rocks. One of the rocks struck a glancing blow, spinning one soldier's helmet off like it was a Frisbie. Had the strap been properly secured, it would likely have broken his neck.

The flatbed's rising action uncoupled the car from the tender, leaving the locomotive to labor on by itself. The P-51 fighter then pulled up, while its twin joined the attack and let go a salvo destined for the locomotive itself. A hail of bullets tore apart the engine's boiler. Boiling water escaped its confinement and spewed out of the aperture with deadly accuracy, mercilessly showering the engineer and coal-tender. The men, powerless to stop the onslaught of the gaseous water mixture, froze in place. Superheated steam and scalding water peeled the flesh from their unprotected faces and throats, throttling their pleas for mercy. They collapsed where they stood.

The engine, bereft of human guidance and, more importantly, losing steam pressure—the lifeblood of a steam locomotive—abandoned its forward momentum. The flatbed, free of its cargo, hovered precariously at about a forty-five-degree angle, still attached at the rear to the boxcar. There, two soldiers hung on for dear life, hoping for some miracle that the flatbed ahead wouldn't derail. They watched in wonder as the flatbed slowly lowered itself and crashed down onto the far rail. The wheels, almost motionless, spun furiously and fought to catch up to the train's momentum. Sparks flew in all directions as the car continued on as if nothing had happened.

While the second Mustang was inflicting damage on the slowing train, the first returned to the station siding to render further damage until it ran out of ammunition.

In no time at all, the first fighter had made a tight turn, and positioned itself for a second attack run. The prisoners standing in ranks in front of the freight train, hit the ground in the hopes of protecting themselves from the indiscriminate bullets.

That's when it hit Jack—those POWs from the freight train were captured American soldiers! During the next few frenzied moments, Jack distinguished a few English words escaping the frightened men. They were close to panicking. Only the orders from their officers kept them from bolting.

There was carnage all around. The truck that had been attacked first still burned, thick black smoke spewing into the air, reminding Jack of an unintentional grease fire he'd once observed at a local garage back home. Germans were running, some dragging fire hoses while others were frozen into inaction.

Jack felt himself drawn to the plight of his countrymen. As a pilot, he knew that the P-51's main objective was to attack the troop train. The train would need to stop to allow its soldiers to escape the attack. But once the fighters had inflicted sufficient damage to the train they would likely return.

As if heeding his thoughts, the second fighter appeared

over the treeline and let loose a hail of bullets, striking several fortified German positions, but also hitting Allied soldiers nearby. Jack heard an American officer screaming orders for his men to brush the snow from on top of the freight cars. The train carrying the POWs had arrived earlier at the siding and consequently had been there longer. The slow-falling snow had covered the white-painted markings on the roof, making it a target for the Mustangs.

Shit! Jack thought. *Our own men are getting killed by our own pilots.*

As he watched the scene unfold, a tall, muscular black soldier, a sergeant, scrambled to his feet and ran for the closest boxcar.

"Halt!" a sentry stationed next to the boxcar challenged, but the American sergeant ignored the warning and kept running. Thinking that the POW was intending to escape, the sentry fired. He missed.

Yet before the POW was able to reach the car, a second shot rang out, striking him in the left shoulder. With a painful cry the man fell to the ground.

"Damn!" Jack exploded as he cursed the offender. To his chagrin, he spotted a German officer holstering his sidearm.

The P-51 was coming back around. Jack acted on his own volition. Forgetting about his own safety, Jack jumped from the trestle and ran toward the train. Since he was dressed in civilian clothes, he reached the car unimpeded.

By sheer miracle, he spotted a broom, probably discarded by a frightened railway worker. He scooped it up, scrambled up the ladder of the nearest box car, and frantically started brushing the snow from the carriage's roof. But he didn't find what he was looking for: three all-important white letters proclaiming to the planes that these cars contained Allied POW's.

Oh God, he thought, *please let there be letters on one of the cars.*

Undaunted, he kept sweeping. Nothing.

When the firing started again, it wasn't cannon fire from the P-51s. Rather it originated from down below. Jack glanced over his shoulder and was about to yell at the German who was taking pot shots at him. It wasn't just any soldier, though. It was Andreas Bauman.

Jack couldn't believe the man's stupidity. Or was it just stupidity?

Ignoring the bullet that whistled past him, Jack abandoned the current freight car and ran to the next one, jumping the gap and sliding on the freshly fallen snow. Wielding the broom like an out-of-breath acrobat, he somehow managed to maintain his balance. Suddenly, he flashed back to third grade, sliding on the sidewalk outside his school during recess to see who could make it the farthest without falling. Back then he was encouraged by laughter and good-natured banter, not threatened with shouts and bullets.

He stopped and spotted a trace of white paint near his shoe. He attacked the snow with the broom, working up a fury that would have made any seasoned janitor proud just as one of the Mustangs was lining up again.

"Dammit, man!" he grunted. "Give me a few seconds. That's all I ask."

The scene was surreal, almost comical, if it weren't the life-and-death situation. Here he was, a captain in the U.S. Air Force attired in civvies, madly sweeping the snow away, while facing off against a rapidly advancing killing machine, piloted by a young man, probably no older than twenty-five, flying the colors of home.

Jack redoubled his efforts and had barely managed to remove the last of the snow, to reveal those bright white letters—P O W—against the dull brown of the freight car. The P-51 was moments away from opening fire again. Jack thought about jumping onto the next car, but time was against him. He had done what he could.

Nearly out of breath, he stood in the middle of the freight

car and waved the broom over his head, like a chimney sweep who had gone berserk. He waved and prayed, prayed and waved.

And he wasn't alone. Down below, a mass of uniformed men, huddled together and unified in purpose and prayer, stared in terror at the advancing fighter, pitting their hopes on one man, an unknown man, one wielding not a weapon but an ordinary broom. Whether it was the collective prayer or his frantic waving, it worked.

As the Mustang zoomed overhead, the Rolls Royce V-12 Merlin super-charged engine roared with pleasure, yet the Browning 50 caliber machine guns, which just a few moments ago had spat out fierce destruction in their wake, remained deathly quiet, as if an unseen hand had stayed further mayhem. Jack thought he saw a grin on the pilot's goggled face. Or was it just his imagination?

Swaggart's courageous action hadn't gone unseen. At the last second the Mustang pilot was alerted by Jack's frantic waving and spotted the crudely painted white letters. He made a split-second decision, thus averting further casualties—not killing his own landsmen.

Jack dropped the broom, which only seconds ago had been elevated to a life-saving instrument, now returned it to its former use, no longer a fitting weapon to ward off an attack. He faced the cheering men spread out below. Out of the corner of his eye, he spotted the two departing Mustangs, each one waggling its wings as it headed northwest.

Looking back down at the cheering men, Jack saw a captain raise his right hand in salute, acknowledging his actions. How Jack would have loved to spend a few minutes with these like-minded men, men who spoke the same language, men who held to the same ideals as he … but it was not meant to be.

All too soon, the gawking German soldiers, summoned into action by their officers, instilled order and began rounding up the prisoners, firing warning shots into the air. The Allied soldiers had no choice but to reassemble.

Jack scrambled down from his lofty perch and would have liked to have said a few words to the nearest men. Although the threat for the assembled men was over, his was still very much at play. He sensed Bauman was still lurking somewhere and wasn't finished with him yet. He had to get away.

Clearly Bauman had crossed the line by firing at him. *What the hell was the man thinking?* he asked himself. *What did he hope to accomplish by killing me?*

Jack had to relinquish his anger and focus on matters at hand. He spotted the attaché case he had discarded and thought of heading for the station house. The German soldiers were busy rounding up POWs and were hardly paying attention to him or the other civilians.

Unmolested and breathing a sigh of relief, Jack rounded one of the damaged freight cars, only to come face to face with an incensed Andreas Bauman. Jack stopped dead in his tracks.

Bauman, armed with fresh resolve in his eyes and a pistol in his right hand, didn't have to say a word. With the muzzle of the pistol pointed at Jack, he motioned him to turn around and head back, presumably to their train. Jack didn't know what Bauman had in mind, but he could guess that it wasn't in his best interest.

Fighting defeat, Jack felt he should try one more time. "Please, Herr Bauman, can't we discuss this like civilized—?"

"Nein!" Andreas cut him off. "No talking. My name is Lieutenant Bauman. *Verstanden?"* Obviously, the man wasn't interested in discussing the situation. The line had been drawn. *"Zurück!"* Andreas hissed, this time prodding him with the pistol.

Jack recognized it was futile to try and reason with him, and he certainly couldn't do so out here in the open, surrounded by the enemy. He was about to capitulate and follow Bauman back towards their car when the German grunted and collapsed in a heap. Jack spun around, bewildered to see Bauman lying on the ground, motionless. Next to him stood his friend and co-pilot, Charles Boyer, still holding the brick he had used to knock Bauman out.

Boyer looked like the closest thing to a guardian angel Jack had ever seen.

"I thought you could use a little help, Jack."

Without saying a word, Jack advanced two quick steps and hugged his friend. The two men embraced, each man knowing their encounter wouldn't last long.

"It's good to see you, Chuck. But how did you know—?"

"You mean, how did I spot you?" Chuck asked, grinning. "Easy as pie. You on top of the freight car. Man, was that a sight! You were going at it like a madman. But it worked."

Jack nodded, sore from his frenzied efforts. "You couldn't have shown up at a better time." Jack glanced down at the prostrated Bauman. "Chuck, we have to get him out of sight."

Each man took hold of an arm and dragged Bauman under the nearest abandoned railcar. Jack removed Bauman's belt and tied his hands behind his back, ensuring he wouldn't get free too soon. As an afterthought, Jack took the man's handkerchief from his pocket and stuffed it into his mouth. He pocketed the pistol.

"Who is he?" Chuck ventured. "Gestapo?"

Jack was tempted to laugh, but he stifled the outburst. "No, he's not with the Gestapo. The funny thing is, he's also a pilot, with the Luftwaffe. It's a long story, Chuck."

As they faced each other, they knew their reunion would be short-lived. The Germans were rounding up the POWs, and time was short. Jack worried that he himself would be found out, and any hard-nosed interrogator would quickly realize he was no German bureaucrat.

"How are the men?" Jack inquired.

"Actually, not bad. We're all together. As you've probably guessed, we're heading to a *stalag* in northern Germany. It was supposed to be Neubrandenburg, but they had an outbreak of typhus there. So, we're being shipped further north."

Jack nodded. "Chuck, I don't have much time to explain,

but I need to get back to England. I've got vital information that I need to—"

"Halt!" shouted a sentry, interrupting their tête-à-tête.

The soldier rounded the corner and first spotted Boyer. Seeing the POW in conversation with a civilian momentarily confused him, but it didn't prevent him from removing the rifle from his shoulder.

"*Schon gut, Gefreiter,*" Jack addressed him, taking Boyer's arm. "*Nehmen, Sie!*"

The soldier seemed to accept the situation at face value, assuming Jack was either an undercover policeman or with the Gestapo. He shouldered his rifle again, took hold of Boyer's arm, and propelled him forward back toward their train.

Jack watched in bitter silence as his friend was taken away.

He hoped Boyer would understand his actions. There was so much he would have liked to say, but it just wasn't possible. He had to get back to his own train. The further away he got from Bauman, the better chance he would have of making it to London. He suppressed his frustration at not being able to help Boyer, and with purposeful gait walked back to the passenger train. He saw that Allied soldiers were being herded into loose ranks. Jack spotted Boyer among them. Boyer circumspectly raised his right hand in quasi salute.

Yes, Jack realized with relief. *He understands.*

Jack retrieved the hat and overcoat which he had discarded earlier and got ready to board the train. He was about to enter the carriage when he nearly ran into a frantic Hilde on the platform.

"Jack, thank God you're here," she blurted out in English. As she did so, she cupped her mouth in horror, realizing her faux pas. Fortunately, the German soldiers were occupied with rounding up the POWs and her indiscretion went unnoticed.

"*Alles in ordnung?*" Jack asked if all was fine, his concern genuine.

"*Nein* ... actually, yes," she reassured him. "But I can't

find Andreas anywhere."

She hastily recounted the details of her own adventure, how after the Allied fighters started firing, Bauman had instructed her to go back into the compartment. She had wanted to go looking for Jack, but Andreas had insisted that he would take care of it.

Jack took hold of her arm and guided her back to their car, trying to reassure her, wondering all the while what he was going to say, and how much he should reveal about the confrontation with Andreas. One thing was certain though, things were bound to get far more interesting.

Back in their compartment, Jack sat in his seat opposite Hilde. He was grateful that she didn't press him for details about Bauman.

The car jerked forward as they resumed their journey. The train's wheels spun in place until friction took hold and the locomotive began to pull the cars, heading north. Relieved that he had escaped Bauman's clutches, Jack gazed out the window at the approaching dusk. He couldn't see the POW train on the opposite side, but his heart was with his countrymen, especially his own crew. He was grateful he had seen Boyer, to know he was alive, and that he had understood his actions.

As the train picked up speed, Jack's mind returned to the present. He reached across and picked up Hilde's gloved hand, startling her. She pulled it back, whether out of nervousness or embarrassment, he couldn't tell.

"There's something I need to tell you, Hilde," Jack began. "It's concerning Andreas."

He had considered how to approach the subject and how much he should tell her. In the end, he'd decided that the truth, the whole truth, was the best way to proceed. And so, putting on a brave face, he outlined what had happened outside the train, how Bauman had shot at him while he scaled the freight car to brush the snow off the roof, revealing the white letters that ended up saving countless lives.

At first Hilde looked at him with skepticism, but her disbelief gradually changed to wonder, then admiration.

"You mean that you spared Andreas' life?" she hesitated, her eyes moist. "Even though he deliberately confronted you a second time?"

Jack nodded.

This time Hilde reached out and took Jack's hand in hers. "You Americans continue to amaze me."

Jack grinned, happy that Hilde saw his actions in a positive light. "It was nothing," he managed, looking embarrassed.

It was Hilde's turn to smile. "And you don't take enough credit for your actions."

‡

Andreas Bauman's head ached like it had been wedged between two stone plates. In the distance he heard what sounded like a millstone screeching as it crushed kernels of wheat. In reality what he heard was the sound of freight cars being uncoupled and moved to another siding.

Andreas stirred, trapped between semi-consciousness and a dream-like state. For a moment his mind drifted to thoughts of Hilde, of walking with her in the park—

"Hey you! What are you doing under there?"

Bauman forced his eyes open, realizing that he wasn't in the park with Hilde, but in some sort of railway yard. As he took in the carnage around him, the events of the day came back to him. He had been chasing after the American pilot as they came under attack by Allied fighters. He recalled spotting Swaggart and firing at him, but the rest was blank. He wanted to touch the back of his head but for some reason wasn't able to.

A uniformed soldier hovered over him; indecision written on his face. Andreas tried to speak but all that came out was a muffled garble. His mouth felt funny and, sensing something foreign in his mouth, Andreas worked his jaws until he could free himself of the obstruction. He took a deep breath.

"I'm … I'm Lieutenant Bauman—Luftwaffe," Andreas said in a tone which he hoped sounded convincing. "Help me up …"

The soldier, no more than eighteen years old, took him at his word and shouldered his rifle. "Right away, sir," he said getting down on his knees. He untied Bauman's hands by removing the belt, rolled him over, and helped him to a standing position.

"Danke," Bauman said gratefully. He stretched and instantly felt pain at the back of his head. Shaking it off, he took the belt out of the soldier's hand. He slid it through the loops in his trousers and pocketed his handkerchief.

"I'm alright now. Which way to the station house?"

The private pointed the way. Bauman nodded and headed for the building. He felt in his coat pockets, relieved to find his billfold and papers were still there. Holding his handkerchief against the back of his head, he walked into the station's lobby. The room was crowded, men in uniform competing for space with all sorts of civilians—mothers doing their best to hold on to small children, older siblings running through the crowd in games of tag, a woman in a gray dress with a Red Cross patch on her sleeve …

Bauman watched the nurse, noting how skillfully she applied a dressing to a young girl's bruised arm. The pigtailed girl, no more than ten, seemed to be more in shock than injured.

Once she spotted her parents, she smiled at the matron and skipped off after them. Bauman watched the activity in the lobby, and after a decent interval he asked the matron if she would look after his injury. She nodded, assuming that he'd been injured by flying debris during the attack. As it turned out, there was little to be done. She cleaned the wound, bandaged his head and even cleaned the bloodstain from his overcoat.

With a grateful smile, Andreas excused himself and sought

out the harried station master. He learned that a southbound train would be heading to Neubrandenburg within the hour. He thanked him and headed outside where he hoped he might find an unoccupied bench.

Andreas needed to be alone. He needed time to think. He suppressed his hostile feelings toward Jack Swaggart, about whom he could do nothing, and tried to concentrate instead on Hilde. Would she forgive him for his ill-conceived inter-vention? Did she still love him? These and many other ques-tions plagued his mind.

Fortunately, the train steamed into the station as predict-ed. People rushed out and clamored for a place on the plat-form, robbing him of any more peace and quiet, but also absolving him of further recrimination.

CHAPTER XXII

The Plot

Horst Kloster purposely walked into the hangar and his attention was immediately drawn to the Ho 229 prototype, He barely paid any attention to the man beside him, Colonel Siegfried Knemeyer, the head of RLM's program.

When he got closer, he noticed a mechanic kneeling inside the cramped cockpit. The man seemed to be checking the integrity of the wiring. *No doubt examining the cables for defects, perhaps trying to figure out why Ziller died,* Kloster thought to himself wryly. *They'll never learn the real reason.*

The mechanic noticed the two officers and quickly completed his inspection, closing the plane's canopy.

"Alles in ordnung?" Kloster demanded.

"Yes, sir. All is in order." The mechanic nodded as he replaced his tools in a nearby tool chest. "I've completed the inspection and just have to finish the requisite paperwork."

The man nodded to the two officers and hastily left the room.

Kloster watched him leave, then turned to appraise the bomber in the gleam of the bright overhead lights.

"What do you think of her?" he asked looking over at Knemeyer.

"Indeed, a fine-looking airplane," Siegfried agreed. He glanced over his shoulder to make sure the technician had left. "But will it be able to perform as expected?"

"I don't see any reason why it shouldn't. It's ideal for the job, and the proposed modifications to the fuselage will ensure the bomb bay can accommodate the payload." Kloster hesitated. "Sir, I'm still not clear on that part. What exactly will be the payload?"

"Ah yes, the payload," Knemeyer mused, a faraway look in his eyes. "Don't worry about that for now. Just make sure the modifications are completed in time."

Kloster nodded, though not entirely satisfied. He thought back to that all-important telephone call from Knemeyer during which he'd asked Kloster if he would be interested in serving the Fatherland in a more *meaningful* way.

Of course, that had gotten his attention.

"I'll see to it that this project gets top priority," Siegfried stated, bringing Kloster back to the present. "Well, I need to be going," he smiled. "I have an important meeting with Kurt Diebner, you know, the Director of the Nuclear Research Council. If you have any concerns, you know where to reach me."

Knemeyer grabbed his overcoat and headed for the door and, before Kloster knew it, had climbed in the back of his Mercedes, with his chauffeur smartly closing the door behind him. Kloster looked on with irritation, again reminded of his own driver's lack of attention.

⚑

Walter Horten eyed his brother Reimar with disbelief. They were still coping with the aftermath of Ziller's untimely death. The mechanic's revelation caught them by surprise, heaping more responsibility onto their shoulders. His news seemed incredible. No, unthinkable. To use their newly-designed bomber to drop an untested and massive explosive charge on London would bring untold pain and suffering on the English people. It seemed beyond belief. Yet here they were, the recipients of bad news, supplied by one of their trusted mechanics. The man was honest to a fault and they had no reason to doubt his report.

The mechanic had related how, when he'd completed his inspection of the Horten bomber, two officers had entered the hangar. He had excused himself and headed for the lavatory. Thanks to a nearby vent that amplified sounds, he became privy to a most private conversation carried on next door, the details of which raised the hair at the nape of his neck.

Each brother was absorbed with his own thoughts, trying to imagine what was at stake and, furthermore, what they could do about it.

One thing was certain: they couldn't go to their immediate superiors—they would be questioned, perhaps arrested on the spot. Colonel Knemeyer, they both knew, was not a man to be trifled with. He carried a lot of clout and authority. Worst of all, this entire scheme seemed to have been sanctioned by the Führer. Now that they were privy to the information, could they just ignore it? But what was to be done? What could they do?

Walter was first to find words. "I'll have to give this more thought."

Reimar nodded pensively. "You're right. This is out of our hands. Besides, we have unfinished design work."

⸸

Jack managed to sleep fitfully, the rocking motion of the carriage having done its job. He checked his watch, a Swiss-German product given to him by Hilde to replace his American one and allay suspicion.

Sunrise wasn't far off. He stifled a yawn and glanced at the sleeping Hilde. The overhead light, though dim, illuminated her enough for him to make out her facial features. Her head rested on the coat she had bundled up and placed against the window. As the carriage rocked gently, a lock of blond hair loosed itself and fell on her cheek.

Sleeping Hilde, he thought. *More like sleeping beauty.*

With each passing moment, Jack felt himself drawn closer to her, not just by her physical appearance, but by her many attributes—integrity, honesty, bravado—and yes, she had spunk, no question about that. He chuckled to himself, as he recalled trying to explain the word "spunk" to her.

He thought back to his home, to his family, and to the woman who almost became his fiancée. Was it fate that he and Nicole hadn't formalized their engagement? He recalled that he had been anxious to announce it before his deployment overseas, but Nicole had talked him out of it. He still didn't understand her reasons. She had said it was too soon, but deep-down Jack felt maybe she had been afraid of him going to war. There was nothing unusual about that. Many girls back home agonized over the safety of their husbands and boyfriends.

But then Nicole was different, more mature. She hadn't pestered him about the war. Perhaps she had been holding back, distancing herself in case the worst happened. Although her last letter was back at Beauvais airfield, he still recalled her last words, their reserved tone, somehow less caring.

He was spared further evaluation of their relationship when he sensed the train slowing down. Sure enough, the swaying was less noticeable, and as the dusk retreated, he distinguished nearby farm yards and the odd house.

Finally, he spotted a sign marker alerting him that Stralsund wasn't far off.

Jack was about to let Hilde know when she stretched in her seat, now half-awake.

"Guten Morgen, Fräulein," he said in greeting. "We're approaching our destination."

She looked over at him and gave him the warmest smile he'd seen in a while.

"Yes, good morning. What time is it?"

When he told her, she excused herself to freshen up. Jack watched her leave and wondered about breakfast. Hilde returned in a few minutes, looking refreshed and carrying a small, silver tray with a domed silver cover. She placed it on the small table between them, and to his surprise it revealed three croissants and two cups of steaming coffee.

"I bribed the conductor," she teased.

The train soon pulled into the station, its prominent sign confirming that they had come to Stralsund. Coincidentally, Jack glanced out the window when he noticed a man jump from the slowing train and head for the station master's office. Ordinarily he wouldn't have paid such a man much attention, except this one wore a gray overcoat and fedora. He glanced not once, but twice over his shoulder. Jack couldn't shake the feeling he was looking at a Gestapo man.

⚜

Wilhelm Vogel, Kloster's underling, had been lucky in managing to get on the train just outside Berlin. *Oberleutnant* Kloster had alerted him that Hilde would likely be travelling to Neubrandenburg, perhaps further, with an unknown companion. It seemed likely this companion might be the missing American pilot.

And so, on Kloster's orders, Vogel had rushed to the Haupbahnhof, Berlin's Central Train Station, and managed to get on board. He identified himself to the conductor and stowed away in the baggage car so as not to be seen. When the train had pulled into Greifswald, and the German freight train was under attack, Vogel, unlike Swaggart, had not ventured out, and had no desire to lend assistance to the wounded. Vogel was an opportunist desiring advancement, but no hero. He was quite willing to let others do the dirty work, while he benefited from their efforts.

Getting off the train in Stralsund, he walked briskly to the station master's office and, after identifying himself, asked to use the phone to call Berlin. He had quickly brought Kloster up to speed and awaited further instructions. As predicted, it seemed that Kloster was ahead of the game, and having anticipated events had made contingency plans. He instructed Vogel to alert the local Gestapo, and, if possible, commandeer a vehicle and head to the Marien-Kirche, where they would affect the arrest. Vogel knew better than to question his superior as to the validity of the information. He hung up with a Heil Hitler and placed the next call to the local Gestapo office.

CHAPTER XXIII

The North Sea

As Jack and Hilde alighted from the train amidst the throng of military personnel and civilian passengers, Hilde consulted the hand-drawn map supplied by Rudi. Before long they had left the Hauptbahnhof and walked along BartherStraße across the Tribseer Damm, struck by the beauty of the Renaissance period. Stralsund had escaped much of the Allied bombing campaign which had been focused on the neighboring city of Rostock. The towering spire of St. Mary's Church on Marienstraße came into view, allowing Hilde to stow the map.

It was a pleasure to walk in the fresh air after the long train ride. They had just rounded the corner and were about to cross the square on the west side of the church when they noticed a young man purposely walking toward them. He was casually dressed in a tweed jacket, trousers, and scuffed shoes. He also wore a brown cap, leaving the impression that he might be a college student or apprentice late for work.

The man approached the couple and tipped his hat in greeting.

"Herr und Frau Schuman?" he asked in German.

"Ja, das sind wir," Hilde said, acknowledging it was them.

"My name is Fredrik Hildebrand and I was sent to warn you. It's not safe to go into the church." Jack took it in and gave him an appraising look.

Fredrik was pointing toward TribseerStraße. "Gestapo,"

he whispered, as if the very word would bring the henchmen out in droves. Without thinking, Hilde grasped Jack's hand.

Jack, on the other hand, wasn't so sure of their new savior. Although Fredrik looked like who he claimed to be, a student, Jack had faced enough betrayal to this point. *How had he known our names?* he wondered.

As he debated what to do, he glanced over Fredrik's left shoulder and saw a man step out of a black automobile and head for the church. There was nothing unusual about that, except that the man walked with a slight limp. Jack followed his progress until he reached the steps and met another man clad in a black overcoat and hat. As the two men conversed, the first man, seemed upset.

Once Jack got a full view of the first man's face, he gasped. What struck him was the angular head, particularly his nose, which resembled a bird's beak. There was something familiar about him, yet Jack couldn't quite place him.

Hilde must have come to the same conclusion, because her hand flew up to her mouth. "Isn't that the same man who earlier exited our train?" she exclaimed with a trace of fear in her voice.

Recognition hit Jack like a punch. It *was* the same man who had disembarked earlier, but the familiarity went deeper than that. Was this also not the same man he'd seen in the farmer's field near Zehdenick, the one sitting on the motorcycle with sidecar?

"Fredrik, I'm sorry to have mistrusted you," Jack said to their new-found guide. "Please, lead the way. Let's go, Hilde."

As they entered the alley, they came across three bicycles stacked neatly against the back wall of a brick building. Jack wasn't about to question their mode of transportation with the Gestapo waiting just around the corner. He helped Fredrik secure their small suitcases on the rack and soon they had mounted their bikes.

Fredrik pedalled fast out of the alley and maneuvered the

trio onto Ossenreyerstraße, adeptly dodging the pedestrian traffic. Jack and Hilde kept pace and to their relief soon made it onto the thoroughfare without the sound of a single shout or pursuing vehicle. Fredrik led the way until they came to the Altermarkt, a farmers' market usually bustling with activity.

Hildebrand stopped at one of the booths selling food wares and hot drinks. Jack was about to ask why they'd stopped, when he purchased three *Tüten*—newspapers rolled into a cone—and three cups with golden-brown liquid. Jack nodded his thanks as he handed one of the cups to Hilde. He cautiously tasted the inviting liquid and to his surprise discovered it was hot apple cider. Hilde handed him one of the rolled newspaper treats. Jack was far less inclined to open the strange looking wrap, but Hilde smiled as she opened hers and showed him that it contained a snack of roasted chestnuts.

Hilde popped one in her mouth and chewed with pleasure. Jack wasn't about to resist, since his stomach had started making noises of protest. Surprisingly, the taste was to his liking and in no time had consumed three in a row.

Hilde smiled at their benefactor, who had declined Jack's offer of Reichsmarks but gladly accepted Hilde's grateful smile.

Jack crumpled his now empty *Tüte* and discarded it in a nearby garbage can. All three remounted their bikes and, with Fredrik leading the way, headed north. They continued down a cobblestone street toward an assortment of old buildings. Some showed signs of damage, most likely from a recent air raid.

"Johanniskloster!" Fredrik announced, which Jack understood to be some sort of monastery. They passed through a series of brick arches, covered with creeping vines bereft of foliage. Despite the recent damage, Jack was taken in by the beauty of the structure, but there wasn't time to contemplate architecture. Fredrik stopped near what looked like an old machine shed and jumped off his bike, with Jack and Hilde

following suit.

First impressions can be misleading and such was the case here. The building's outward appearance belied what was inside. Jack and Hilde walked into a spacious and comfortable anteroom inside the shed, which was furnished with well-worn but inviting furniture.

No sooner had Jack removed his overcoat and helped Hilde out of hers than a man entered from an adjoining room. Short, balding, and in his late fifties, he had the appearance of a mild-mannered grandfather, but Armin Faust, though he was a grandfather, didn't partake in the usual grandfatherly activities. He hated the Nazis and aided the local Resistance movement whenever he could.

"Please, Herr Swaggart," he began, "come in and make yourself at home, and that goes for you as well, Fräulein Augsberg. I'm sure you have many questions."

Faust then explained how he'd been forewarned that the Gestapo had staked out the church in anticipation of capturing the American. Under the circumstances, he felt it prudent to send Fredrik ahead and divert the couple to the monastery.

After supper, Jack suggested to Hilde that they go for a short walk before curfew. The only word of warning from Faust was that they should keep their walk short.

Jack found a narrow path that jutted between a crop of poplar trees. He took off his jacket and spread it on the grass, inviting Hilde to make herself comfortable. He then sat down beside her; his back propped against a tree.

He smiled, feeling as if he'd known Hilde for years, not the few short days since the crash. She looked ravishing in her blue dress and yellow scarf, which didn't make it any easier to figure out what to say. At times like these, Jack wished he had paid more attention to his grandmother's German. If he had, perhaps he'd be able to speak a little more eloquently.

Hilde seemed to sense his dilemma. "It looks like you want to get something off your chest, Jack. Perhaps it would be easier in English."

Relieved, Jack nodded. "We men have a hard time expressing our feelings at the best of times, never mind in a foreign language. Well, here goes. Hilde, I can't begin to express how much you've meant to me these last few days. From the moment I laid eyes on you in that farmer's barn, I knew you were different … er … special …"

"My mother even chastised me for being so …" she thought for a moment, "so bold. I just knew I needed to help you, Jack."

"And I sensed that I could trust you. You've risked an awful lot to get me this far, and if all goes well, I'll soon be on a trawler, headed for Denmark. I'm going to miss you. A lot."

A moment passed, and then Hilde got up and walked two short paces away from him. When Jack stood to follow, she suddenly turned and pulled him close. Jack, thinking that was her signal to head back was about to speak when Hilde leaned forward and kissed him on the cheek. He in turn pulled her closer and intended to kiss her on the lips when they were interrupted by a man's voice.

"Come now, young man. That's not how you kiss a lovely girl. Show her you mean it."

Startled, Jack wheeled around to see the owner of the deep baritone voice: a short, older man in lederhosen. The man stood not ten feet away, an amused expression on his face. He was accompanied by a panting brown cocker spaniel. He laughed, tipped his hat in greeting, and continued walking away.

Jack flushed with embarrassment, not so much by the man's prodding but by his own timidity. *What the heck*, he thought and spun Hilde around, kissing her fully on the lips. To his surprise, Hilde responded.

Hearing more voices coming down the path, Jack suggested they head back to the safety of the house.

╫

Horst Kloster paced in his office, eagerly awaiting what he hoped was good news from the Gestapo office in Stralsund. Although he didn't have much faith in the small detachment, he reasoned they could at least affect the arrest of a lone American pilot and a civilian woman.

He was about to break the seal on a new bottle of schnapps when he abruptly decided against it. He felt he should delay gratification—for a little while, anyway. The phone rang. Forcing himself to wait until the second ring, Kloster picked up the receiver and heard his secretary's familiar voice.

"An important call for you, *Herr Oberleutnant,*" Maria Stengl announced. "I'm afraid it's not the call you've been waiting for, sir. It's from the local police."

"The local police?" he asked, surprised. They hardly ever called. "Alright, put the call through." He waited a moment, heard the expected click, and a man's voice came on the line.

"Lieutenant Kloster? This is *Kapitän Löffler, Statspolizei.*"

Kloster was about to correct the policeman for cutting him down in rank—he was, after all, an *Oberleutnant*—but stopped himself. The name Löffler rang a bell. If memory served him right, the man was actually one of the more competent investigators within the police ranks in Oranienburg.

"Yes, Captain, what can I do for you?" Kloster replied, almost graciously.

"I'm afraid I have some bad news, sir."

A thousand questions went through Kloster's unscrupulous and suspicious mind. Had Schinkel been in an accident? Had a former lover he had bedded been indiscreet? Did it have something to do with Ziller's untimely death? Kloster could have gone on, but he detected a seriousness in the man's voice that his instinct told him wasn't concerning a trivial matter.

"Alright, what is so important?"

"Otto Saufman is dead," Löffler replied curtly.

"He's what!?" Kloster practically shouted, barely containing himself. "Did I hear you right? Otto, dead?"

"Yes. He's dead. There was nothing nefarious about it. It happened right in his office. As per protocol, I was notified early this morning. Naturally, I attended to oversee the investigation."

"Go on. How did he die?" Kloster asked, envisioning Saufman's portly body slumped over his desk. "Heart attack?"

"No, nothing like that. Although I didn't see the body, I did have a look at the office. By all accounts it was an accident. He seemed to have knocked over a cleaning lady's bucket and slipped on the wet floor, then lost his balance and hit his head on an oak table. The night watchman found him."

"I see. And how does this concern my office?" Kloster added, trying to sound uninterested, though inwardly elated.

"We … er, I mean I found some correspondence." Kloster's face went pale, the color draining from his face. "I believe some documents contained your name," Löffler continued. Kloster's earlier expression instantly changed from elation to dismay. He gripped the edge of his desk, fighting to maintain control. He could guess what was coming next.

"The man was blackmailing you, sir, wasn't he?" came Löffler's reply, a statement more than a question.

Silence. Feeling rattled, Kloster gazed at his untouched tumbler, the yellow liquid once soothing now strangely unappealing. He thought about hanging up, but then thought better of it. "Are you quite certain of that, *Herr Kapitän?*"

"Quite certain, *Herr Oberleutnant.* I have the papers in my possession; however, they're not in the dossier with the official report for all to see."

Kloster's head was spinning. The fear of the truth getting out was more than he could bear. His memory went back to a phone call the previous month. He had concluded a briefing with Schinkel and had been about to leave the office when his secretary had stopped him by announcing an incoming call from the mayor's office. It had sounded important, with Herr Saufman himself on the line.

Kloster recalled the short conversation, the preamble and Saufman's pleasant-sounding voice. The man had wanted a private meeting, and when Kloster had asked him to be more specific, he had slipped in a name: Adam Rosenbaum.

The shock of hearing his nephew's name spoken aloud by Saufman had caused Kloster's throat to constrict. He'd tried to shrug it off, but clever Saufman had the upper hand. Later that day, in the back of a Potsdam bar, they had a brief but telling discussion. Saufman had ferreted out the truth. Somehow, he learned of Adam's Jewish heritage and his connection to Kloster. The boy, fifteen years old, was indeed his nephew and, as it turned out, one-quarter Jewish. Only one-quarter! But that little detail didn't matter to the Nazis.

Saufman had refused to elaborate when and how he'd learned of this, but he had made it clear that he was prepared to keep it under wraps. For a price, naturally.

Adam Rosenbaum? Kloster mused. *What will become of you now?*

"*Herr Oberleutnant,* are you still there?" Löffler asked, bringing Kloster back to the present. "Don't worry, it won't go further than this."

"What do you mean?" Kloster asked warily, not wanting to hear the reply. Yet it was true. Saufman had been blackmailing him. Would Löffler ask for a small reward, some small payment to carry on where Saufman had left off? It wasn't a pleasant thought. But before Kloster could pursue the idea, he heard the man's voice again.

"I'm prepared to deliver the incriminating papers into your hands, no strings attached. All I ask in return is that if I should call upon your office for a favour in the near future that it would be handled promptly and to my satisfaction."

"Do I have your word on that, Herr Löffler?"

"Absolutely. I'll hand deliver the papers tonight. Heil Hitler."

After the man hung up, Kloster gently cradled the receiver, thanking his lucky stars. *But can I really trust him*, he debated? He had barely removed his hand when the telephone rang again. Oh no. Löffler again with more conditions.

"Yes, Maria," he stated simply. "Who's calling now?"

"It's the call you've been waiting for, sir, she announced. "Herr Vogel is calling from Stralsund."

"Excellent. Put him through." Anticipating good news, Kloster straightened out his tie as if the act would give him a measure of renewed confidence. "So, Vogel, you've got him at last?"

The line remained silent. For a moment, Kloster thought the connection had been severed. "Vogel, are you there?"

"Yes, *Herr Oberleutnant,* I'm here," Vogel replied.

"Is everything in order, Vogel? Out with it, man!"

"I er … everything was in order, sir … right up until the moment when the local Gestapo raced ahead to the church. I gave them explicit instructions to wait until my arrival so I could point out the fugitives."

"*Scheise!*" Kloster cursed into the mouthpiece. "I take it Swaggart eluded them. Did they at least capture the woman?"

"No, sir. They both got away. The Gestapo are searching for them right now, but it's proving to be a difficult task."

Kloster slowly sank into his chair, deflated over the latest news. What was he going to tell Schinkel? Sure, it wasn't his fault that they escaped, but he knew some of the blame would be placed on his shoulders.

"Alright, Vogel, you get out there as well. Search all the *kneipen!* That means bars, flop houses, even whorehouses. Search all night if you have to. Don't let them get away. Understood?"

"*Jawohl, Herr Oberleutnant.*"

Kloster hung up, not wanting to think about the bad news.

"They had them!" he said aloud, clenching his fists while

absentmindedly turning to address the portrait of the Führer. "They were in my grasp. Damn it!"

Kloster's gaze remained fixed on Hitler, gazing into the man's black eyes. The Führer was well-known for rewarding success when warranted. And he was equally known for ranting at his generals when they failed him. *Well, at least I won't have to report to you, will I?* he mused.

He reached for the schnapps, now determined to open it, when the phone rang for the third time. He thought of ignoring it but steeled himself for what was to come. Perhaps it was good news after all.

"Yes, Maria, who is it now?"

"The *Sturmbannführer* is on the line. He's asking for a progress report on the American pilot's capture."

Kloster sank even deeper into his seat. The schnapps would have to wait. He didn't even have to tell her to put his boss through. Hell was going to be paid for incompetence and Schinkel wouldn't let Kloster off that easily.

⊹

Well past midnight, Jack glanced up at the partly cloudy sky. A crisp wind was picking up from the east, giving rise to the sea swells. No sooner had he looked at the waves than he leaned farther over the railing and retched into the water again.

He had withstood the queasy feeling of the fishing boat's rolling motion for the first couple of hours, but it had finally caught up to him. The first mate, Ulf Nielsen, waited for a moment and then slapped him on the back.

"

, get it all out. You'll feel better soon."

Jack looked at him as if he were an imbecile, but refrained from a retort. He was too sick.

"The captain says we've cleared Bock Island," Nielsen added. "Thanks to the incipient fog, we have a decent chance of eluding German patrol boats. If all goes well, we'll make Denmark before sunrise."

Jack nodded but didn't reply, not keen on conversation. Nielsen left him alone and headed back inside the wheelhouse, while Jack forced himself to take his mind off his ill-tempered stomach and reflected on the last few hours.

It was remarkable how a man like Armin Faust, the caretaker and handyman for the monastery, could accomplish so much. He had the freedom to travel and make purchases on behalf of the order. More importantly, it allowed him to collaborate—more accurately, assist the Resistance. Although he wasn't one of the main participants, his travel permitted him to function as an invaluable courier.

The resourceful Faust had arranged for his passage on a fishing trawler bound for the outer banks, northwest of Insel Hiddensee. Their goal was to travel to Nykøping Falster, a small peninsula on the southern tip of Denmark.

Jack had been thankful for the short choppy ride in the small boat as they had left a deserted beach just before midnight. Several miles into the strait, they had rendezvoused with the trawler. Jack had waved goodbye to Frederik, the only occupant of the small boat. He hoped he would make it back to Stralsund without incident.

He had been given forged documents in the name of Alexander Larsen, which should pass a cursory examination if they were stopped and boarded by sailors of a German patrol boat.

Will Hilde miss me as much as I'm going to miss her? Jack wondered, with the trawler chugging farther away from Stralsund with each passing mile. *When will we see each other again? And what about Andreas? Would he, out of spite, harm her, perhaps betray her?*

Jack caught a reflection of himself in the wheelhouse window. What he saw, made him smile as much as he permitted himself under the circumstances. Clad in gray slicks, black boots, and a yellow anorak—all supplied by Nielsen— he looked like one of the fishermen.

As if reading his mind, Jack caught a reassuring smile from Nielsen indicating that all was well. He took it as a good sign and said a quick prayer for the remainder of the trip. If only he could silence his fears for Hilde. She had risked much to help him escape, and now she would be heading back to Berlin, right into the heart of the Third Reich.

⁜

Back in London, James Buchanan sat in his friend's office, looking pensive, as they came to the end of a long evening reading over several classified memos. Bryan Shelby seemed equally contemplative.

One had dealt with information from a spy who worked at the *Gotha Wagonfabrik,* near Göttingen. He'd managed to smuggle out a drawing of a swept-back winged aircraft design, dubbed the Gotha-229.

In order to gain favor, the man had revealed details about his work as a carpenter at Göttingen, a secret German manufacturing facility.

"Quite interesting," Shelby remarked. "It's further proof that the Germans have been working on a delta-wing model. This man claims that two brothers, Walter and Reimar Horten, have been experimenting with gliders and propeller-driven airplanes for years." He scanned the memo. "But I don't see any mention of a mock-up, a full-scale prototype, or even test flights."

"Yes, I noticed that too," Buchanan reiterated. "One of their sources, a man who went by the codename Gustav, had been quite adamant that the Horten brothers had developed a prototype that was already undergoing flight-testing near Berlin."

"Right, the airfield at Oranienburg," Shelby interrupted. "The two sources seem to corroborate each other."

"At first glance, yes," Buchanan added. "But on closer examination there are differences in their reports. Don't you agree?"

"Yes." Buchanan scratched his head. "If only Gustav had photos." He flipped through the pages of memos before them. "Somewhere, one of these pages had a reference to the design. Didn't it say that the entire airframe was constructed of wood? Could that really be true? I mean, we've all heard about Howard Hughes' *Spruce Goose,* which he claims will be constructed from Canadian spruce. Could the Germans have beaten him to it and perfected the concept? I wish we had some confirmation."

They were interrupted by the ringing of the telephone, and Shelby quickly snatched the handle off the cradle.

"Shelby here." Shelby's offhanded demeanor changed instantly. Buchanan noticed how he gripped the handle tighter, as if the action would bring him closer to the caller.

"By all means, put him on," Shelby spoke into the phone. Placing his hand over the mouthpiece, he whispered to his friend, "Finally, good news. Our Norwegian friends have successfully smuggled Swaggart out of Germany. He's enroute to London now."

Buchanan beamed at the news. "Jolly good!" he said imitating his British friend. "Maybe now we'll get some answers about that mysterious aircraft."

After the call, Shelby put down the phone. He tipped back in his chair, balancing it precariously on its hind-legs while interlacing his fingers behind his head.

"So, what do you make of that?" Shelby asked. "Your American friend has managed to elude the Gestapo and is now safely in England. Apparently, he has vital news."

"Vital news?"

"Yes. The major didn't elaborate. You know us Brits. We don't blabber secrets over the phone. We prefer to spill the news over a pint at the local pub."

Buchanan grinned at his friend's joke, realizing there was more truth in it than either one cared to admit. "Alright, so what's next?"

"Well, I should imagine that we could meet up with Swaggart later today. Tomorrow at the latest. Perhaps we could lunch at a pub ... er, I mean here at the office. Do you have time to spare?"

"Sure, I can rearrange my schedule."

"Good. I'll fix it," Shelby nodded as he reached for the telephone.

CHAPTER XXIV

Haigerloch

Siegfried Knemeyer stubbed out his cigarette with his boot and checked his watch again. It was 12:30 p.m. and Kurt Diebner was nowhere in sight. *Where could he be?* he thought. *It's not like him to be late. He should have been here a half hour ago.*

Lately, things had gone from bad to worse. He was becoming more used to the constant phone calls and interruptions, all asking for one thing: progress on the latest military projects, including the secret nuclear research conducted at Thuringa.

Diebner, the head of the nuclear test facility at Thuringa, along with other prominent German scientists, had been tasked with developing Germany's nuclear program. Hitler demanded constant progress, and when told of delays he would fly into a rage. Fortunately, Knemeyer wasn't present at those high-level meetings and only heard about it from one of the many visiting generals.

Now he was waiting for Diebner, who had been delayed, likely by another last-minute scientific meeting. It was reported that he often met with Werner Heisenberg, a principal scientist in Germany's nuclear program.

Knemeyer reflected on what he knew about the two men. Heisenberg didn't flaunt his credentials, which were considerable, and he wasn't patronizing, though he was arguably the smartest man in scientific circles. Still, he had a way of getting things done—even though the SS had questioned his loyalty.

Diebner, on the other hand, liked to boast of his connections, rarely complemented other scientists, and frequently took all the credit for himself.

Hitler was well known for promoting the concept of isolating members in important research projects, thus ensuring that "the left hand didn't know what the right was doing."

Knemeyer had his orders and wasn't about to question Diebner, not wanting to risk complaints about him going back to Hitler's ears.

He knew the specifics of Hitler's secret project, but not the technical aspects. He knew not to ask too many questions. As a loyal Nazi party member, he actually preferred it that way. He looked up at the beautiful blue sky and spotted a crane flying toward the town church steeple, rekindling a boyhood memory. Siegfried remembered his time in Leipzig and how he loved to watch the cranes and storks as they came to nest in the spring time. He sighed, wishing he was back home enjoying the simpler things, rather than accommodating the snobby scientific elite.

As much as he liked to reminisce about his boyhood, the sound of a diesel engine interrupted further memories and he forced himself to focus on the task at hand. He recalled Diebner's last phone conversation outlining the latest project. The man would be arriving in person and hand-delivering an experimental device that he and his team had been developing. It was Knemeyer's job to ensure its safe delivery to a secluded airfield in northern Germany.

Kloster leaned back in his chair, staring at the untouched drink on his desk. Only moments ago, he had longed to indulge in its contents, anticipating victory, but now it seemed more like a reminder of unfinished business, of failure at the hands of incompetent fools.

He mentally replayed his conversation with the *Sturmban-*

nführer. Surprisingly, Schinkel hadn't been more upset with him. The man had patiently listened to Kloster's report, which he outlined concisely. Kloster had concluded it with his own apology, accepting the blame. Schinkel had asked few questions and then left it at that. Clearly, the whole thing, though initially handled well by Kloster, had been botched by the Gestapo in Stralsund. Kloster breathed a sigh of relief, having side-stepped Schinkel's anger.

He vaguely heard a knock on the outer door and heard muffled voices between his secretary and a visitor. He dismissed it as unimportant, but Maria's gentle knocking made him reconsider. She stood in the doorway, holding a wrapped package in her hand.

Whatever it was, it had just been delivered by messenger. Kloster took possession of the package and thanked her, closing the door behind her. He quickly tore open the brown paper wrapping, revealing a thin black book. He didn't even have to read the accompanying note, to know Löffler had been true to his word. This was Otto Saufman's blackmail ledger.

He raised his tumbler at the unseen Löffler, an unexpected ally, and allowed the warm liquid to soothe his parched throat, enjoying every drop.

Kloster glanced at the little book. It was no larger than a diary, *but appearances can be deceiving,* he mused. He could only imagine what secrets it contained. After all, Saufman had been cunning, deceptive, and resourceful—a man not to be underestimated.

He found himself still staring at the book, as if keeping it at a distance would absolve him of further responsibility. *Utter foolishness,* he nearly said out loud, and had to remind himself that he was now in possession of its secrets. The sole benefactor. Satisfaction at last.

Only then did he put down the tumbler and pick up the book. He carefully examined the spine, then the front and back covers, ensuring that no pages had been removed. Satisfied that wasn't the case, he leafed through the first pages, looking for the entry pertaining to him, and there it was: Horst Kloster—captain; it noted his previous rank. What followed were several entries, detailing payments and dates.

Seeing his name at first made him wince. But then, as quickly as it had surfaced, the feeling passed, replaced by the pleasant certainty that Saufman was finally out of the picture. Kloster proceeded to look through the diary at random, examining the various pages. He came to appreciate Saufman's tenacity and utter lack of compassion.

Well, there we have something in common, he thought with a twisted smile.

He flipped to the last few pages and came across the most recent entries. Here was a list of names still not crossed off, implying that their payments hadn't yet been received at the time of Saufman's death.

One of the names triggered a flash of recognition. *Herr and Frau Schuman? Schuman.* Suddenly he remembered. It was as if a flashlight had been flicked on, illuminating a once dark room. Schuman was the assumed name of that American pilot, Jack Swaggart, and his likely accomplice, Hilde Augsberg. Wasn't her mother's name Gertrude?

His smile widened into a fiendish grin. Thanks to Saufman's meticulous record-keeping he finally had a good lead. With his left hand, he downed the rest of his drink and, with his right, dialed his secretary's number.

"Maria," he asked pleasantly, "I need you to find the address for a family in Oranienburg: Augsberg, Gertrude Augsberg. And after you've obtained it, please summon my driver. I'll be heading out soon."

"Right away, sir."

Ten minutes later, Kloster was seated in the back of his chauffeured car, with his usual driver, Helmut Köhler, in the front seat.

"Where to, sir?" Helmut queried.

"Oranienburg." Kloster handed him the folded paper with the address.

Köhler scanned the paper and returned it to his superior. "Very good, *Herr Oberleutnant.*" He engaged the gear and pulled out into the light evening traffic, heading north toward Oranienburg.

Kloster had initially considered interviewing all the cleaning staff at city hall, but the more he thought about it, the clearer the picture became. Realistically, only two women had reason and opportunity to steal the Schuman travel papers—Gertrude and Hilde. And unlike Saufman, he was in a position to find out exactly which one had done so.

⫚

Gertrude Augsberg put away the supper dishes after enjoying a visit from her neighbor Hazel. She had seen Hazel to the door and now looked forward to a quiet, relaxing evening.

No sooner had she sat down in her favorite armchair than she heard a knock at the front door. She opened it quickly, assuming Hazel had forgotten something, and instead came face to face with an unexpected visitor.

"Frau Augsberg?" asked a man with gray, unsmiling eyes. "I'm *Oberleutnant* Horst Kloster."

"*Ja,* I'm Gertrude," she replied haltingly. He seemed familiar, but she had trouble placing his face. She instinctively knew she had seen this man before.

"Surely you remember me," Kloster replied, his tone disarming. "I was here only a few weeks ago. Your daughter, Hilde, had forgotten a hat she had purchased and I felt it expedient to drop it off. Is your daughter at home?"

"Oh yes, now I remember," Frau Augsberg managed, wondering how quickly she could end the visit. "No, I'm afraid Hilde is away."

Although the visitor was alone and not in uniform, he

commanded a presence she couldn't ignore. Kloster glanced over her shoulder, peering into the house. The dishes were drying on the counter, a tea cup with steam rising was sitting on a small table next to an arm chair, and best of all, no one else seemed to be at home.

"May I come in?" Kloster asked.

Short of offending the man, Gertrude could find no way of forestalling him.

He smiled and inched forward, forcing her to fully open the door. As he removed his coat, he glanced approvingly at the small but well-kept home.

"A nice place you have here. Now, there is something we need to talk about …"

⧈

Hazel Kravitz peered out her window for the tenth time that evening, if for no other reason than to confirm the black automobile was still parked in the lane outside the Augsberg residence. Its driver was hidden in shadow, reminding her of a scene from *The Public Enemy*, a James Cagney movie she had seen.

The driver stepped out of the car occasionally to light a cigarette, but Hazel wasn't worried about the driver; her thoughts were on the man who'd entered the house almost thirty minutes ago. But not worried to the point that she would actually leave the safety of her own house and check.

"Sit down, Hazel," August, her husband, instructed. He had spotted the look of worry on her face. After putting up with her fretting he finally decided to say something. "It's really none of our concern."

While Hazel debated how to respond, she caught a flash of movement at the side of the house. A tall man had come outside, and he was escorting Gertrude towards his car, a firm grip on her arm. The driver, seeing them approach, quickly extinguished his cigarette with the heel of his boot and hurried back just in time to open the rear door for their new guest.

The man brusquely guided the woman into the back seat. With no visible signs of protest, Gertrude took a seat, the door already closing behind her. The man walked to the far side and joined her in the back. Hazel heard the engine start up and witnessed the car drive off, the taillights receding in the darkness.

Hazel, drawing up the last of her resolve, convinced her husband to accompany her to Gertrude's house. They found the door unlocked and everything appeared in place, save for the cup and saucer lying on the floor, its yellow liquid now spread onto the carpet. Hazel gazed at the overturned cup, knowing that Gertrude, given the opportunity, would never have left the house without cleaning up the spill.

August, no fool, appeared to have formed much the same opinion, but wishing to spare his wife from unnecessary grief, kept those thoughts to himself.

"Well, Hazel, let's lockup for now," her husband said breaking the silence. "I'm sure she'll be back … later."

They quietly walked back to their own house, neither one holding out much hope.

╬

Rudi Schultz was taking a huge risk by showing up at Berlin's main train station. He'd been warned that the Gestapo might be following him, but he felt that warning Hilde was of greater importance than being watched. He reasoned that they wouldn't be keeping track of him every minute of the day.

Relying on the borrowed Luftwaffe uniform, he passed the police checkpoint and proceeded to the platform where he waited impatiently for the train to arrive.

The last twenty-four hours had been trying to say the least. He'd learned from a friend that the Gestapo had visited Frau Augsberg. The rumor mill in Oranienburg was as efficient as ever and word had spread quickly of Gertrude's late-night caller. Rudi was sure there was more to it. Had she been allowed to return home?

He'd tried contacting Gertrude by telephone with no results. After some discreet inquiries, he learned that Gertrude had been sequestered in a women's holding facility in Berlin. Rudi felt his only course of action was to intercept Hilde before Kloster's henchmen could.

At last, the train pulled into track #11, the locomotive dumping steam as it decelerated into the station. Rudi paced back and forth on the platform, scanning the crowd like a young man eagerly anticipating his lover's arrival. He spotted Hilde soon after, winding her way around a plump woman struggling with an oversized suitcase. Hilde recognized Rudi in an instant, even though he was wearing the borrowed uniform, and flashed him a warm smile.

That smile faded with each passing step as she approached him, realizing Rudi was in no mood for good cheer.

Rudi glanced nervously over his shoulder and greeted her with a handshake. "It's good to see you again, Fräulein Hilde, but I'm afraid we don't have much time. I have news. Some good, some bad."

She looked at him inquiringly, hesitant to ask. He saw the apprehension in her eyes and decided to spare her the bad news for the time being.

"Otto Saufman is … dead," Rudi announced. "He died in his office—an accident. Now, we must hurry." As if remembering something, he added. "Um, your papers, Fräulein."

Before Hilde could ask for an explanation, he took the small suitcase and identification out of her hand and turned on his heels, heading for the exit.

She tried to keep up, forcing herself to save her questions for later. Soon they'd be passing through the Gestapo checkpoint. Did they know about Jack's escape? Were they planning to arrest her? Hilde said a quick prayer, suppressing her anxiety for the moment.

Providentially, a woman with three young children was fumbling with her papers while at the same time trying to keep control of her rangy charges. The commotion formed a bottleneck.

Reading the situation perfectly, Rudi pushed past a couple to the front of the line.

"Entschuldigung, Herr Inspektor," he said respectfully but with authority. "I know you're busy, but I have to get Fräulein Augsberg through quickly. She's late for an appointment with the *Bürgermeister.*

The Gestapo official, initially irritated at being interrupted, was about to respond with indignation but then he caught sight of the Luftwaffe uniform. He cast a sideways glance at Rudi's companion and was immediately arrested by her smile.

"I, er …" The man fought to regain his composure. He swallowed the acidic words forming on his lips, and contrary to his habitual disposition, returned a weak smile. "One moment, please."

He turned to his associate, not two feet away, and whispered something in his ear. The younger man simply nodded and turned his attention to the woman with the restless children.

"Now, Fräulein," the first man said, almost agreeably, "how can I be of assistance?"

Hilde kept up the bravado, explaining that she had just returned from a business trip to Stralsund and needed to get back to Oranienburg. Her reasons were clear and to the point: Otto Saufman, her boss, had tragically died in an accident.

Hearing Saufman's name, the Gestapo officer nodded, seemingly aware of the incident and the investigation. He reached out his right hand toward Hilde, not in a gesture of comfort but of repetitive duty.

"Your papers, please."

Hilde turned to Rudi, who handed over both documents.

Outwardly she appeared calm as she forced her lips into a smile, hoping that her hands weren't shaking.

The inspector, though caught up in the moment, dutifully and carefully examined both sets. "You may proceed," he grunted as he prepared himself for the next passenger.

Once they were out of earshot, Rudi steered Hilde toward a parked car that she didn't recognize. He opened the rear door for her and deposited the suitcase inside, then situated himself in the driver's seat and started the engine. As they left the parking lot, he kept one eye on the road ahead and the other on the rear-view mirror, hoping they weren't followed.

As they traversed the next few streets, Rudi decided to depart from the familiar route, and took a road heading further north.

"Is something wrong, Rudi?" Hilde asked. "Where are you taking me?"

After they'd gained enough distance from the train station, Rudi pulled over and parked behind a delivery truck. He turned around and glanced at his passenger, her worried look unmistakeable. He then related everything he'd heard about Saufman's death.

"But there's more," he continued. "I umm … I'm afraid I have some bad news as well, Fräulein. Your mother has been arrested by the Gestapo—we think by Kloster. Late last night."

Hilde cupped her hands over her mouth. Her earlier bravado at the railway station vanished like mist, leaving her in shock.

"*Mutti* … arrested?" She pleaded with her hands. "No, Rudi, it can't be …"

Rudi didn't know what else to say and simply nodded.

He thought it best to resume their trip and pulled out into the traffic. Even though Hilde fought to get a hold of herself, tears escaped her eyes. She blinked and forced herself to calm down, and felt a little better after she blew her nose. She thought of her mother and how she would want Hilde to be strong at a time like this.

As they continued on their journey out of Berlin, Hilde peppered Rudi with questions and he did his best to answer.

Eventually, silence filled the small cabin, the gravity of her mother's arrest descending like an invisible shroud. Finally, Hilde hoping to break the spell, asked where they were headed.

"Oh, to Zehdenick," Rudi replied. "Your aunt's house. It's no longer safe for you to remain in Oranienburg."

╬

Andreas Bauman arrived at Neubrandenburg's airfield later than he had intended. He returned the loaner to the aerodrome's carpool with an apology and remembered to retrieve his holdall from the trunk. He quickly changed back into his flight suit and headed for the commander's office. He realized he'd been so consumed with thoughts about Hilde that he hadn't considered what explanation to offer the major.

Before he entered the outer office, he checked his appearance again in the hallway mirror. Armed with fresh resolve, he entered with a hearty, *"Guten Tag."* The clerk glanced up, the uncertainty evident on his face.

"I'm Lieutenant Bauman," Andreas identified himself. "I've returned to pick up the dossier intended for Berlin. Is the major disposed to see me?"

The clerk nodded and dialed the phone on his desk. After a brief verbal exchange, he hung up, opened a drawer in his desk, retrieved a brown attaché-style satchel, and handed it over.

"The major is tied up and asked that you leave when you're able." The man glanced out the window, pointing out the approaching storm clouds. "But it's not likely you'll be leaving tonight, is it, sir?"

Andreas had been too distracted to pay the weather much attention. He nodded and left the office, resigned to spending the night in the officer's barracks.

Andreas was greeted the following morning by a lingering fog. He tried to quell his impatience by taking a leisurely stroll. By the time he had pre-flighted his airplane, the fog had given way to a broken cloud layer and his mood had picked up considerably; he even found himself whistling. A quick phone call to the flight office supplied him with the latest weather information as well as his authorization for departure.

Thanks to a light schedule, he was airborne within minutes. As he climbed to his planned altitude, his thoughts returned to Hilde. He criticized his actions and realized he had been a fool and had acted deplorably, when a flock of birds came out of nowhere, narrowly missing his right wingtip. That snapped him out of his musings and he resolved to pay more attention to flying the fighter.

After landing safely in Berlin, Andreas left the aerodrome in his Opel and headed back to the office at the barracks to complete his first order of business—the delivery of the documents from Rostock. Once he'd completed his task, he returned to his quarters, changed out of his flight suit and cleaned up. He debated if he should have supper with a friend, but then came up with a different idea. He got back in his car and headed for Oranienburg.

Andreas made it to the local butcher shop just before it closed for the day. He selected a decent-sized portion of flank steak. He added a loaf of bread and with the offering drove to the Augsberg residence, arriving just before dark.

He parked at the side of the house and found it strange that none of the lights were on. Nevertheless, he knocked on the front door hoping for some sign of life. After several knocks and still no response, he tried the rear door with the same result.

While debating what he should do next, Andreas spotted a woman's head in the window of the neighboring house.

Although the woman quickly pulled back, he thought he recognized Hazel Kravitz's face. He walked the short distance to their front door and knocked.

After a few seconds of hushed activity, the door slowly opened.

"*Ja,* what do you want, young man?" the elder owner demanded.

"*Guten Abend,*" Andreas greeted. "I'm a friend of Gertrude Augsberg."

The man peered suspiciously at Bauman. "Step closer, so I can see your face."

Andreas did so and removed his hat, doing his best to give a reassuring smile.

"Ah, you're that pilot fellow, the one who's sweet on Hilde—" he stopped himself.

Andreas smiled, embarrassed, yet pleased at being recognized.

The couple invited him to enter and take a seat in the parlor. He removed his overcoat and placed his package on the floor, the loaf of bread poking out at the end. While Hazel made tea, August told Andreas what little they knew about Gertrude and her arrest by the Gestapo.

Andreas listened in horrified disbelief. The story sounded far-fetched, probably embellished by the couple to make a good-sounding tale. Even so, there was no denying the truth. Gertrude was gone—and so was Hilde. In between sips of the soothing tea, he mentally filled in the gaps and concluded that Gertrude was likely held in some detention facility, probably in Berlin.

Hazel asked Bauman to stay longer, while at the same time eyeing his package. Andreas, though pleased with their hospitality, didn't wish to engage in a whole evening of gossip. He excused himself citing he had duties back at the airfield. As an afterthought, he offered his package of food intended for the Augsberg home. Although Hazel's husband feigned a mild protest, Hazel quickly extended her hand.

Andreas left the house amidst their well-wishes, happy to have escaped.

Hilde. But where was Hilde? he asked himself. He had to find a way to make it up to her. He didn't know it, but at that very moment she was heading away from Berlin, travelling to Zehdenick with Rudi.

As Andreas drove away from the Kravitz home, an idea came to him. *What if I can find a way to secure Gertrude's release? Surely, that would count for something in Hilde's eyes.* The more he thought about it, the more it appealed to him. With Swaggart out of the way and presumably now in England, it was perhaps his last and best chance to salvage his relationship with Hilde.

Back in his barracks room, Andreas slumped pensively in his upholstered chair. When he opened the window to get some fresh air, an errant fly flew in. Andreas stared at the annoying intruder, which settled on a framed picture above the dresser. Something drew him to the picture when he realized it was taken a year or so ago at the Oranienburg airfield: a young woman of about sixteen, flanked on one side by her older brother, Kurt, and himself on the other.

Kurt. Kurt Löffler, of course! An old friend with whom he had studied at *gymnasium,* now a respected senior officer within the Oranienburg police force. Fortunately, Andreas had kept up their friendship. Perhaps Kurt might be able to help him out.

Andreas picked up the phone and dialed the number for the police station. Captain Löffler was not in, but Andreas left a message for a callback.

Roughly one hour later, Andreas had not only received the phone call, but he was having a late supper with Kurt at a gasthaus in Oranienburg. The two men rehashed their most recent experiences, with Löffler eager to share the most recent news—Saufman's untimely death and the subsequent investigation.

Andreas listened with interest and waited for an opportune time to tell his own story. He was selective, but shared enough that Kurt would feel sympathetic to his plight. He concluded with his shocking discovery that Hilde's mother had been arrested by the Gestapo.

Andreas appealed to Kurt's friendship and sense of fair play, intimating that Gertrude's arrest must have been a mistake or based on a trumped-up charge. As expected, Kurt took more than just a passing interest and promised to look into it.

Andreas couldn't have been happier and insisted on paying for their evening meal.

CHAPTER XXV
Operation Lusty

Much had to be done upon Jack's return to England. Although he was given the option of returning to the U.S., he eventually decided against it. The reason may not have been clear to everyone, but those who knew him intimately, like James Buchanan, understood there was more to it.

Like many officers, Jack took his responsibility seriously. He would have preferred to return to his unit in France, but, recognizing his leadership ability, his superiors chose a different role.On Colonel Bartsch's insistence, he was assigned to the intelligence section (OSS). As such, Jack was able to participate in some high-level meetings.

One of those was Operation Paperclip, a program that dealt with identifying, locating, and appropriating German scientists, engineers and technicians before the Soviets could beat them to it. Closely related was Operation Lusty, which also looked for suitable candidates, including test pilots and technicians from Germany, but focused more on obtaining models, prototypes, and military aircraft in flying condition.

Headed up by Colonel Harold Watson, the main objective of Lusty was to locate military aircraft. Beginning in 1944, the Americans were keen on getting their hands on Nazi technology. While the Allied forces' military arm reached mainly toward Berlin, this highly specialized and secretive group canvassed various German factories, warehouses, and even the countryside, hoping to obtain sought-after aircraft, including the highly prized jet-powered Messerschmitt Me 262 fighter, the Arado Ar 234 bomber, and the virtually unknown Horten Ho 229.

From these meetings, Jack deduced that the war in the European Theater was quickly coming to a close. To that end, he threw himself into his new assignment. Working with men like Bryan Shelby and James Buchanan made the job a little easier.

His thoughts often returned to family back home in North Dakota. He had been privileged to call his mother on several occasions. She was doing as well as could be expected after her husband's death. She taught Sunday school at her local church and, when time permitted, volunteered at the town library. Yet her main responsibility was at home; life on a farm didn't stop. Jack was relieved to hear that several close friends had agreed to help out, making him feel a little less guilty for not returning home.

He also wrote to Nicole, debating how to broach the topic of their relationship. Whereas most of Jack's fellow officers received care packages and photos from their sweethearts, Jack did not. In a brief letter, Nicole had merely expressed her condolences for Jack's father and asked about his combat unit and hardships of war. *What was missing?* he asked himself. The answer was obvious: the personal touch.

He decided to confide in his good friend. James wasn't an expert by any means, but Jack still valued the Canuck's opinion.

One evening, over a few pints at a local tavern, Jack filled him in. James listened attentively, leaning back in his chair, a faraway look in his eyes. Then he abruptly dropped the chair legs. They smacked the floor, as if signalling a decision.

"I hate to tell you, Jack, but it seems to me as if the fire has gone out. You get my drift, eh?"

Jack nodded reluctantly. "Yeah, I can see it too, but do you think there's any hope?"

"I don't see how. You're stuck over here and she's back

in the States. From what you've said, her letters have become less frequent and there's hardly been any … er, sweet stuff in them."

Jack had to admit their relationship, though promising before the war, didn't seem like it would advance much further. With a heavy heart, he penned the words that just six months ago would have seemed so foreign.

It came as no surprise when her letter in reply arrived late the following week.

Jack needed to be alone and sought refuge in a little out-of-the way park down the street from the War Office. He opened the plain white envelope and scanned the familiar flowing script discovering the message he'd expected. Nicole didn't beat around the bush with flowery words or make apologies. She agreed that it was for the best to end their relationship; perhaps they could simply remain friends.

Jack glanced up, distracted by what he thought might be a chickadee that had landed in the branches of a nearby tree. Its tiny claws embraced the limb, its head swivelling from side to side. Jack almost burst out laughing. It was impossible for the small bird to have any notion what was in his head, but Jack found its movements amusing.

He got up from the bench and smiled at the bird as he left the park. Now that he had formally ended his relationship with Nicole, Jack immersed himself in his work—but Hilde Augsberg was never far from his thoughts. The German beauty's bravery and resilience had more than captured his heart. He suspected—no, he knew deep down—she had feelings for him, but only time would tell if anything further developed.

Getting in touch with her was out of the question. It was much too risky, Jack reminded himself.

That afternoon, and back at the office, Jack was still reminiscing, when he caught his friend's questioning look.

"Let me guess," Shelby said. "You're thinking about Hilde, right?"

"Guilty as charged," Jack replied sheepishly.

He forced his mind to return to matters at hand: their latest high-level meeting with Field Marshal Montgomery, aka "Monty." It had come as a surprise when Winston Churchill himself had attended the meeting unannounced. Well, Monty had known, as had a few senior bureaucrats, but it had still been a shock when the famous, diminutive man had entered the ministry boardroom.

Their discussion had revolved around the development of German aircraft, but until they obtained more actionable intelligence, they couldn't make any definitive plans. That meant it was up to men like Jack and Shelby to procure the intelligence themselves.

Not surprisingly, and just a few days later, they happened to be sitting at a back table of a popular tavern near Piccadilly Circus, discussing various options.

"I think we need to get a closer look at one of those assembly sites," Jack offered.

Shelby raised an eyebrow. "You mean send someone into the heart of Germany and get photos?"

"I don't see any other way. The brass wants more. My sighting along the highway just isn't enough. It's not that they don't trust me, but they need drawings and photos—real proof. Without something tangible, like the location of an assembly or manufacturing plant they could attack, we're spinning our wheels."

"That's no easy feat," Shelby replied. "Security at these German facilities will be tight. There's the main assembly plant at Friedrichroda in Gotha ..." He trailed off, staring pensively as he lit his pipe. "Wait a minute, Jack. Didn't you say that one of those assembly sites is located in occupied France?"

Jack checked his notes. "Yes, it says so right here. There's one near Strasbourg. No, wait—there's an addendum. The Germans have moved the operation to Ludwigshafen for fear of the advancing Allied army. We could fly to liberated France and then parachute into Germany from there. Still, it's a risky endeavor."

Much too risky, thought Shelby.

"Perhaps there's another way," Shelby said after a moment. "I've recently come across information that may prove beneficial to our cause. As you know, a lot of information has come our way from various, non-military sources deep inside Germany. One of these, codenamed "George Wood" has been a treasure trove.

"This man, a German national, had initially approached us Brits. Regrettably, we had dismissed him outright, now much to our chagrin. At the time the brass felt he was an opportunist, full of hot air, perhaps even a Nazi plant. But the Americans felt there was something to be gained, so, on the insistence of Allen Dulles, they gave him a shot, and he produced. Heavens, did he produce. I'm wondering if we could persuade the brass in the OSS to give us access to their man. He might be able to find a way to smuggle *you* back into Germany? Sounds outlandish, right?"

"Smuggle me?" Jack queried. He stood up and walked over to the window, his gaze settling on the throng of traffic outside the pub. In his mind's eye, he tried to envision what London might have looked like if good men like him or Shelby gave up in the face of the Nazi threat. If he were to take up Shelby's suggestion, as farcical as it might seem, to go back into danger, it would give the Allies a fighting chance.

Jack returned to his table and glanced at Shelby's expectant face. "I guess it's worth a try, old boy."

He hoped he sounded more enthusiastic than he felt.

Shelby nodded sombrely. "I don't see any other way. Certainly not with the little time at our disposal. Let's ask Bartsch and get his opinion."

╬

The staff car worked its way through the bombed-out craters littering the street, eventually pulling up in front of the once impressive Air Ministry building. It had been recently damaged by American bombers.

The driver climbed out and opened the rear door to allow two uniformed men to emerge: Horst Kloster and Siegfried Knemeyer. Although they were expected, their identity cards were carefully scrutinized before they were allowed to enter. They were then escorted by two SS men to the entrance of the bunker. After surrendering their sidearms, they were subjected to a body search. Hitler was taking no chances.

A sentry led the way down the stairs, where after several lefts and rights they were ushered into a waiting room. Kloster glanced at his watch and noted they were early. Did he have time for one quick cigarette? A few pulls of it would be enough to relieve the stress.

Just when he was about to extract one from his cigarette case, a familiar figure entered the room: Martin Bormann.

Kloster had only met Bormann once in the flesh, but he was well aware of the authority the man carried. He had ingratiated himself to Hitler and been allowed into his inner circle, attaining the position of the Führer's personal secretary, having supplanted Göring, even Himmler.

"Ah, Knemeyer," he stated matter-of-factly to Kloster's companion. "I see you've arrived." He merely nodded in Kloster's direction without addressing him. "The Führer is waiting for us. Please, follow me."

The words "pompous ass" played on Kloster's lips, but he managed to keep them to himself. It was well-known that Bormann enjoyed belittling officers, making them wait unnecessarily and generally doing everything he could to be seen in a most favorable light by the Reichsführer. He was the consummate yes-man.

Bormann led them to the conference room on the lower level. Kloster tensed up when he saw Hitler at the head of the table, alongside Field Marshall Wilhelm Keitel, General Krebs, Minister Goebbels, and a man he didn't recognize who wore civilian clothing. He assumed this must be Dr. Klaus Stückner, a renowned physicist and deputy-head of Germany's weapons research program.

"Mein Führer," Bormann began, "Colonel Knemeyer and Captain Kloster, the man to pilot the aircraft."

Hitler, who was bent over and examining the documents laid out in front of him on the large table, looked up to examine the newcomers. Kloster was shocked at how much their leader had aged in the last few months.

Under Hitler's eyes were dark circles and his skin had taken on an unhealthy sheen. The man seemed weary, weakened by lack of sleep or the stress of fighting a losing cause. He seemed to have lost weight; the plain jacket didn't fit very well.

"Good, good, I'm glad you have come," Hitler announced. "Come, join me at the table and fill me in on your plans."

Keitel coughed, just loud enough to get Hitler's attention. Hitler viewed him absentmindedly and, remembering why he was there, nodded for him to continue.

"Yes, Wilhelm, please go on."

Keitel produced a folder and spread out its contents on the tabletop.

"Gentlemen, you know why you're here. The Führer has ordered this meeting so you will be absolutely clear as to his wishes and the importance of this latest mission: *Unternehmung Heimlichkeit* (Operation Stealth)." The field marshal checked around for confirmation and was rewarded by nodding heads, with one exception: Stückner. The man seemed detached— no, apprehensive, Kloster thought.

Perhaps the man was merely uncomfortable in Hitler's presence. Kloster had witnessed many ordinary Germans come under Hitler's spell. Yes, the Führer had that ability; he came across as larger-than-life, overbearing and intimidating, even when it wasn't his intention.

Yet Kloster sensed something might be different in this case. The physicist was in a position of authority, had dealt with high-ranking Nazi party members, and was no stranger to high-level meetings. What was going on here?

Then it struck Kloster: the doctor wasn't distracted or disinterested. He was afraid. *But afraid of what?* he mused. *Surely not afraid of Hitler.* No, it must be more than that, something more substantial.

As Keitel outlined the nature of the mission and its details, Kloster saw that Hitler seemed pleased with the entire plan. The physicist then contributed a few technical details before being dismissed.

A few moments later, Kloster received an unspoken message from Keitel that he along with Knemeyer were also meant to leave. He was actually happy to be leaving the cavernous confinement, preferring a more spacious environment.

As they exited the underground bunker, Kloster walked behind the two men, observing Dr. Stückner closely. It seemed to him that the man's breathing was labored as he climbed the steps.

No, Kloster discovered. The man was muttering to himself.

"Es geht nicht. Scheisdreck," the man voiced to himself, meaning it just won't work. Kloster quickened his pace. But before he could ask Stückner what was bothering him, Knemeyer stepped closer and corralled the scientist.

"Excuse me, Doctor, but what won't work?" Knemeyer asked.

"Er … I'm sorry, *Herr Oberst,*" Klaus replied dismissively. "It was nothing."

"No, go on," Siegfried encouraged. "Something is troubling you. I can tell."

Dr. Stückner glanced at Knemeyer, and then at Kloster, but he didn't say anything.

Knemeyer caught the unspoken question and turned to Kloster. "Captain, why don't you go ahead and wait by the car? I'll be along shortly."

Kloster fished a cigarette out of the pack he had retrieved from his coat pocket and simply nodded. He turned to walk down the corridor.

The last words he caught before he passed out of earshot came from Knemeyer:

"So, Herr Doktor, what seems to be troubling you … ?"

Kloster picked up his pace and quickly walked outside towards the waiting car.

CHAPTER XXVI

A German Spy

In early February 1945, Fritz Kolbe's train pulled into Bern's main station. He remained seated, while the other passenger in his compartment, an elderly Swiss woman, rose from her seat. She wore an expensive grey woolen suit, a mauve overcoat, capped with a suitor hat, reminding him of his mother's last Easter centerpiece. Her belongings included an expensive leather suitcase, a fashionable handbag, and two cylindrical containers with bowstrings, which Kolbe suspected held hats. He couldn't resist a wry smile meant for the unseen porter who would soon be laboring with her belongings.

But then his mind returned to his *raison d'être*. His expression turned serious as he clutched his attaché case. It housed important documents that he, in his role as a German diplomatic courier, had been instructed to hand over upon his arrival at the German embassy.

He wasn't concerned about the documents in the case; he was worried about the papers he had meticulously copied, and which were now taped to his right thigh, only concealed by his pant leg. If they were discovered, it would not only end his diplomatic career, but invoke an unpleasant end to his life: death by hanging—that was if he survived long enough after being interrogated and tortured by the Gestapo.

The truth is that he had long ago become disillusioned with the Nazi party, the endless demands of the German war machine, and the Gestapo's ruthless tactics—as had many decent Germans—and decided that he would no longer stand idly by, even if it meant turning to the Americans for help and spying on their behalf. He had done just that, and with great success.

He knew—almost everyone in authority knew—that the war was lost, and the best way to help Germany now was to facilitate a speedy end to the hostilities. It couldn't be allowed to drag on.

Kolbe picked up his small suitcase with his left hand and, clutching the attaché case in his right, stepped down from the first-class carriage and walked towards the military checkpoint. There he produced his diplomatic passport and, after a few customary questions, was allowed to continue into the city.

He walked the short distance to the German embassy and, after the obligatory identification process, stepped into the foyer. He opened the attaché case and handed the diplomatic pouch to an undersecretary. The man nodded and stated matter-of-factly that Kolbe could return the following morning to collect the return pouch. Standard procedure.

The official became distracted, already occupied with another task, and had almost forgotten the courier in front of him. That was fine by Kolbe. He had no wish to be conspicuous and was past the point of caressing his ego with meaningless talk.

Kolbe walked out of the embassy and headed to a local gasthaus, just in case he was being followed. After he had eaten a plain meal of sauerkraut, dumplings, and sausage, he paid his bill and went to a nearby hotel. Upon checking in, he commented to the clerk that he was going to have a rest.

In reality, a nap was the last thing on his mind.

He checked the second-floor hallway for any sign of activity, then donned his fedora and gray overcoat and left the hotel via the service entrance. He was careful to leave a do-not-disturb sign on the door handle of his room, ensuring that no one would bother him in the foreseeable future—hopefully.

Kolbe walked along the street at a steady pace, projecting the appearance of someone who had no particular destination in mind. But he did have plans for a visit at 23 Herrengasse, the lodging of Allen Dulles.

"Would you care for a sandwich?" his host asked once Kolbe had settled in. Kolbe declined Dulles' offer of sandwiches but gratefully accepted the offered coffee—real coffee.

After a brief exchange of pleasantries, Kolbe expected the American to get right down to business, but Dulles just stared ahead pensively. At last, he cleared his throat and commenced their discussion.

"My dear Kolbe—ahem, I mean George Wood," Dulles began while lighting his pipe. "What I'm about to ask of you isn't easy, but I hope you'll agree to cooperate. This is definitely out of the realm of your current, er … assignment, but it's vital to the war effort—our war effort."

Kolbe leaned forward, indicating to Dulles that he had his attention.

"Our side is very pleased with your efforts," continued Dulles, "and we wish to demonstrate our trust in you by giving you an opportunity to do something vital, something which will carry with it a fair … well, a great amount of risk."

Kolbe, by now accustomed to all sorts of risk, nodded a fraction, curious about what Dulles had in mind.

"We've become aware through your efforts, as well as from other sources, that the Germans have been working feverishly on a new bomber, hoping to put it into production." Kolbe nodded again. "One of our pilots, whose aircraft was shot down near Oranienburg, actually caught a glimpse of the airplane, the Horten Ho 229, as it flew overhead. Although it's first-hand information, his eyewitness account isn't enough. The top brass in England need schematics, pictures … something tangible to present to Field Marshall Montgomery, before he'll commit himself to ordering an air strike. To accomplish this, we need you to send a man into Germany to obtain the vital information. Can it be done?"

Caught off-guard, Kolbe coughed. The heightened danger that he would face by smuggling in an enemy spy wasn't lost on him. He glanced at the picture hanging on the wall behind Dulles, a portrait of American President Franklin D. Roosevelt.

Then he looked steadily into Dulles' eyes before replying.

"Certainly, it can be attempted," Kolbe began, "but its success will depend on many factors, not the least of which is your man's ability to pose as a diplomat. Then there's his competence with the German language."

Dulles pulled on his pipe and let the smoke out slowly, sending the aroma of tobacco smoke towards his guest. "I was hoping you'd bite," he grinned. "But the decision is entirely yours. I can't order you, not like I can order our man."

"And just who is 'our man'?" Kolbe asked, not in the least bit amused.

"His name is Swaggart. Captain Jack Swaggart, a flyer."

╬

The following morning, Kolbe went for his usual walk through the streets of Bern and, after ensuring he wasn't being followed, he once again ended up at Allen Dulles' apartment. Dulles, polite as always, offered coffee and croissants.

Although Kolbe had always been reluctant to accept such gratuities, he decided to make an exception. It seemed to be an American institution, and if he were being honest, he actually enjoyed the treats.

After a short discussion of current propaganda, Dulles steered the conversation to the matters at hand.

"So, my good Kolbe, have you thought about my proposal?"

Kolbe nodded. "I'm prepared to risk it."

"Good. Then there's someone I'd like you to meet."

Without further explanation, he left his office through an adjoining door, and returned almost immediately, followed by a tall, lanky man Kolbe hadn't met before.

"George Wood, I'd like you to meet a colleague of mine," said Dulles by way of introduction. "He's a fellow American. Captain Jack Swaggart."

Kolbe's jaw dropped as he realized he'd been manipulated. Clearly Dulles had planned this all along and had fully expected Kolbe to jump on board.

But he didn't show his frustration. Instead, he glanced at Dulles and shrugged his shoulders, acknowledging that he'd been played. He nodded to the American pilot, with his quiet acquiescence welcoming him into the dangerous game of espionage.

"Glad to have you aboard, Captain," Kolbe said. "Tell me, how is your German?"

"Es könnte besser sein, Herr Wood," Jack replied, meaning it needed improvement. "I'll have to work on it." Jack was glad he'd had the foresight to brush up on his German.

Kolbe merely nodded, not revealing if he thought it passable.

Dulles bade the two men to take a seat and over the course of the next hour went over the details of the operation. He then reached into a desk drawer and produced a manila envelope, which he handed to Kolbe. Inside, Kolbe found German travel documents and identity papers, which bore a picture of Swaggart and purported him to be a German diplomat. Kolbe was intrigued, not merely by Dulles' resourcefulness but by the quality of the forgery. He let out a low whistle. "So, when do we leave?"

"Ist Morgen zu früh?" Jack asked, indicating tomorrow would suit him.

"Then tomorrow it is," Dulles confirmed, settling the matter and concluding the meeting.

⊞

As had been arranged, Kolbe arrived at the German embassy punctually at eight o'clock the next morning and collected the diplomatic pouch destined for his masters in Berlin. Just like the day before, the undersecretary, Wilfred Leben, hardly paid him any attention.

That damned high-minded schwein, thought Kolbe, barely able to suppress his anger. *The man is full of himself and thinks he can just brush me off, like lint on his three-piece suit.*

Kolbe suppressed his irritation. *What did this man do all day anyway? He sat at his desk, taking charge of incoming mail and packages and handling phone calls. Hardly what one would consider a difficult or prestigious job.*

Still, Kolbe glanced at the man's suit and found himself admiring the beautifully handcrafted fabric, a stark contrast to the man inhabiting it. The cut and finishing suggested that it came from a reputable clothier, while he had to make do with material from a second-rate shop, all because his regular tailor, one-quarter Jewish, had been apprehended and deported by the Nazis.

For a moment he envisioned his life after the war—after the Americans had won. He hoped to be the recipient of well-deserved accolades, not to mention the benefactor of a decent apartment and a worthwhile position. By contrast, Leben would likely be rummaging through rubbish piles and looking for anything of value, having been forced to sell items like his precious suit long ago …

With a smile on his lips, Kolbe left the embassy by the front door. He took up a leisurely pace and walked the familiar route to the railway station. On this occasion, he didn't care whether he was being followed. He just tried to maintain a steady though unhurried pace.

His mind turned to the mission and his new travelling companion. It was risky enough to spy for the Americans, but an entirely different matter to smuggle a foreigner into Nazi Germany. Would Swaggart's limited German be enough for him to pass close scrutiny? He didn't want to consider the implications of being caught and dismissed the thought, not wishing to dwell on Gestapo tactics.

Kolbe passed the checkpoint and headed for the ticket counter, where he purchased a second-class ticket to Berlin. He then sauntered over to a kiosk that sold magazines and newspapers. Not far away, he spotted Swaggart sitting on a bench reading a Swiss publication. He walked over.

"Guten Morgen, Herr Kollege," Kolbe said in greeting as he sat next to the American pilot.

"Ja, ein schöner Morgen. Gut geschlafen?" Jack replied, inquiring if his colleague had slept well.

Kolbe nodded. *"Ja, danke. Ah, hier kommt unser Zug,"* he said, alerting Jack to the train's arrival.

Both men picked up their small suitcases and headed for the appropriate track. To an outsider, they would appear to be nothing more than two businessmen embarking on a journey. Indeed, no one seemed to pay them the slightest attention.

But then they were still in neutral Switzerland and Nazi Germany was a long way off yet.

╬

Hilde Augsberg glanced out the window of her aunt's house in Zehdenick. Rudi had dropped her off after their latest adventure, assuring her that it would only be for a couple of weeks. She'd been cooped up in the house for close to two months and the worst of it—there wasn't any word as to what had happened to her mother. For all they knew, she was likely confined in a women's prison somewhere in Berlin.

Hilde blamed herself for her mother's incarceration. She looked around her aunt's house, at the rooms she knew so well, and realized that she too was confined, not by concrete walls and iron bars, but confined nonetheless. She watched the softly falling rain, the small growth starting to bud in one corner of the flower garden, and wished she could be outside, breathing in the fresh air and enjoying the warm splatters on her face.

And why not? she considered. There was no one around. Her aunt had gone out to make some purchases at the local butcher's. Without giving it more thought, she donned her aunt's spare coat, covered her head with a plastic bonnet, and headed outside for a brief taste of freedom. She breathed in the invigorating spring air and splashed the puddles with her boots, bringing joy to her senses that she hadn't experienced in a while.

Hilde glanced around at the houses across the lane and, to her relief, couldn't see anyone outside them. She would have liked to spend a few more minutes enjoying her interlude with nature, but she knew she should make it quick.

Hilde spotted a young man pedaling a bicycle up the lane. She quickly turned back toward the house and disappeared inside just as he came into view. She hurried to the sitting room window and peered outside.

The cyclist, wearing a messenger's uniform, stopped in front of her house. He dismounted and scrutinized the exterior, perhaps to verify he had the correct address. Then he approached the door and knocked.

She knew she couldn't answer the door, painfully aware that the Gestapo was still looking for her. She recalled the twice weekly visits, of hiding in the basement, and her aunt's persistent denials. Still, her inner sense told her it was important. Perhaps it was news of her father, who was also imprisoned, not in Germany but in a Russian prison camp.

Then she heard her aunt's familiar voice address the messenger as she opened the door. She must have just come up the walk. He greeted her aunt politely, advising her that he had a telegram. Hilde heard an exchange of words and then saw the young man climb onto his bicycle and ride away.

She waited by the front door and opened it before Eva

could use her latchkey. Without saying a word, Eva removed her raincoat and boots and headed for the kitchen. She placed her purchases on the counter and dropped into the nearby chair, holding the unopened telegram toward Hilde.

"Here, my dear," she said. "You read it."

Hilde nodded and took the offered edict. She glanced at it but realized there was no external address, only the stamp from the telegraph office. Carefully, she slid a knife through the perforated end, and sliced it open. The message was brief.

Dear Eva. I'm well and alive. Don't worry. I'll write when I can. Your loving sister, Gertrude.

Here at last was news that her mother was alive!

Hilde handed the telegram to her aunt who read it silently. She then took Hilde's hands into hers and smiled faintly.

"There's only one thing we can do right now," Aunt Eva said quietly. "Let's pray."

Hilde nodded in agreement, and both women got down on their knees, invoking a practical and well-known tradition of seeking intervention from a higher power.

CHAPTER XXVII

Hilde Arrested

Wilhelm Vogel couldn't believe his luck. He was driving his boss' Opel through Berlin's streets on the way to the small town of Zehdenick. Apparently, a nosy neighbor had recognized Hilde Augsberg at her aunt's home. Hilde had managed to evade the local Gestapo, but that was all over now. She shouldn't have made the mistake of going outside.

Vogel grinned, reminded once again how much of the Gestapo's information came to them not by way of diligent detective work but from local informants: neighbors, busybodies, and acquaintances hoping for a reward. All too often it was an aggrieved individual seeking revenge.

He scanned the few lines on the sheet Kloster had handed him. Even though the report stated both women had been picked up without incident, it didn't tell the rest. He could envision the scene: the unexpected knock, then shock, gasps, perhaps one of them fainting.

Vogel smirked, having seen such a scene often. He knew that Eva Poller would be questioned and severely reprimanded. What possible defense could she muster? A little white lie? Ignorance that Hilde had been sought for questioning? It didn't matter. She would be held at the local Gestapo office and given a few memorable days of interrogation.

But her real punishment? She would quickly find herself ostracized from village life. Once you'd been picked up by the

Gestapo, people became scared, even reluctant to speak with you.

Besides, Vogel knew that Kloster wasn't interested in the aunt anyway; it was Hilde he wanted. His new assignment was to pick up the absconded fräulein and take her to Berlin for questioning.

Vogel walked into the foyer of the Gestapo office and presented his documentation to the Gestapo official on duty. The man briefly perused the papers, and then told him to wait while a matron went to fetch the prisoner.

Seating himself on a wooden bench, Vogel looked around the sparsely furnished outer room. He wrinkled his nose in disapproval. Aside from a dilapidated table and two wooden chairs, the only thing adorning the foyer was a mounted picture of the Führer.

A uniformed woman soon came through an adjoining door, escorting a haggard Hilde, who clearly hadn't slept much. Her hair was unkempt, and she had bags under her eyes. Even so, it wasn't enough to diminish her good looks. This was the first time Vogel had seen Hilde up close, and he wasn't disappointed. He appraised her wrinkled blue dress and noted a run in her left stocking. No matter. He looked forward to driving her back to Berlin.

Vogel nodded to the matron and took a firm grip of Hilde's left arm, in effect taking custody. The matron also handed over Hilde's small suitcase and gray spring coat, which he draped over his other arm as they headed toward the front door.

Hilde, for her part, didn't put up any resistance, nor did she inquire as to where they were going. The answer seemed clear enough in the transfer: to see a higher authority.

Once outside, Vogel released his grip and escort her to the waiting car. He mused that the scene must look like a couple out walking together.

"Have you eaten anything today, Fräulein Augsberg?" he asked, startling Hilde with his civility.

"Nein. I only received a cup of tea, just before you arrived."

"Well, we'll have to remedy that, won't we? I'll pick up a few sandwiches along the way."

True to his word, he stopped at a roadside gasthaus. Before departing on his errand, Vogel produced a set of handcuffs, cuffing Hilde's left wrist to the steering wheel.

He smiled awkwardly. "Sorry about the precautionary measures, but you're a prize that Herr Kloster doesn't want to lose for a second time."

"Kloster?" she asked, looking puzzled. "What does the Luftwaffe—?"

Vogel left the vehicle abruptly, leaving the young woman to ponder his last words. He returned shortly, freed Hilde from her confining bracelets, and offered her a wrapped sandwich. Hilde didn't have to think twice; she hungrily dug in, thankful for the little gesture.

Vogel nodded in satisfaction and unwrapped his own, joining her in their simple repast. He offered her a cold beer as well, which she declined. She preferred the warm coffee instead.

In no time at all, they resumed their journey south toward Berlin. It was a fine spring afternoon, with fluffy cumulus clouds popping up over the skyline with the sun shining brightly in between the puffy balls of white. It was beginning to warm up.

As Vogel drove, Hilde placed her spring coat in the back seat. As she did so, she twisted her upper body, allowing the folds of her dress to reveal cleavage.

Hilde quickly resumed her position and straightened her dress, but Vogel had already taken notice. He took a cursory glance at his roadmap, refolded it and placed it atop his briefcase. After a minute or so, he picked up the map again, pretending to look for a landmark. When he replaced the map, he did so awkwardly so that it slid from the briefcase onto Hilde's dress. In the act of retrieving it, his hand fell on her knee.

Hilde gently dislodged his hand.

"Don't!" he insisted, as he placed his hand against her skin.

She was about to object audibly when she caught the smirk on his face in the car's rear-view mirror. She steeled herself.

"Bitte, Herr Vogel," she said politely but firmly. "I'm not that kind of girl."

"Perhaps," he replied amused, "but that can easily change."

No sooner had he uttered those words than he bunched up the folds of her dress, revealing a nylon-stocking. The leg was shapely and smooth to the touch.

Licking his lips and craving more, he moved his right hand ever so lightly over her knee, but then inching further up her thigh.

Hilde's throat parched and her heart started racing, terrified of his advances.

"Please, don't do that," Hilde pleaded, brushing his hand away.

Vogel allowed this, only to replace the hand a moment later, now firmly resting on her thigh. In response to her protestations, he picked up the folded map and slapped her hand with it, dismissing her objections as one would an errant fly. Now he gripped her knee and refused to let go. He stroked it, while pulling the hem of her dress, exposing more stocking.

Hilde crossed her legs, attempting to discourage his efforts.

"Enough!" Vogel laughed. "Stop resisting."

Terrified, Hilde froze. Perhaps he was only playing a game, trying to get a reaction. But then he moved his hand up to her garter clip. His fingers probed and worked to undo the fastener. Not having much experience, and realizing there was little chance of success with only one hand, Vogel had to take his other hand off the steering wheel.

Hilde was scared, outraged, and felt she had to do something. Anything. Impulsively, she slapped Vogel across his face.

Vogel had taken his eyes off the road to focus on the garter belt. Her slap stunned him just as the car was entering a bend in the road. The Opel crested a small hill and, on the downward side, came face to face with a farmer herding his sheep across the road.

Panic replaced lust, shooting up his spine like a striking snake. Snapped out of inaction by Hilde's scream, his right hand involuntarily gripped the steering wheel.

The farmer tried to usher the last few sheep across the road. Vogel tried to steer around them. Failing to slow down, he braked too late. The rear of the vehicle started to skid. Overcorrecting, he sideswiped two dawdling sheep and propelled the car straight into the ditch.

The Opel ploughed through standing water in the ditch, sending up a geyser in its wake.

Hilde was quicker to react than Vogel and instinctively curled into a ball. Fortunately, the Opel didn't roll over but, in a big splash, came to an abrupt stop, with the water absorbing much of the car's kinetic energy. Hilde was thrown forward and under the dash, the carpeted floorboards cushioning her impact. Vogel wasn't so lucky. The force of the collision propelled him out of his seat so that he struck his forehead on the windshield, knocking him unconscious.

Hilde lay stunned for a moment, thankful to be alive. She gingerly unfolded herself and climbed back onto the seat. Finding that she was basically alright, with no broken bones, she eyed her tormentor. He was slumped over the wheel, unmoving. Her first impulse was to slap him again, as punishment for the deplorable way he had conducted himself. But then she noticed blood dripping from his forehead. She pulled him back so his head leaned on the headrest. Though he was unconscious, she detected that he was breathing and the gash on his forehead didn't seem too serious.

Hilde managed to open the passenger door. She pulled out her suitcase and climbed out of the sedan, only to find herself standing in a foot of murky water. She steadied herself against the side of the car and surveyed the chaotic scene. Behind her and up the grassy slope were sheep, some running in circles, others stationary and crying, and still others bleating spasmodically. The poor farmer was trying to herd them together, an impossible task if it weren't for his border collie.

She watched in amazement as the patient dog ran circles around the scattered frightened sheep, barking, nudging, and nipping at their hind legs, until it was able to corral them with the others.

Realizing she was still standing in knee-deep water, Hilde climbed out of the ditch and removed her wet shoes. By this time the farmer had rounded up most of the sheep. He left his trusty canine to finish the job and walked toward the offending car. He cupped his left hand to shield his eyes from the sun and that's when he noticed her. Seeing the angry look on his face, Hilde rightly guessed that he blamed her for his troubles.

"Entschuldigung," she offered by way of apology. "My driver, Herr Vogel, in a moment of inattention, failed to recognize the danger and reacted too late. I'm sorry he caused this mishap. Are your sheep alright?"

The farmer, a short and rotund man in his fifties, looked her over and seemed to take her at her word. He relaxed a fraction, softening his craggy face, revealing smile lines around his anxious eyes.

"Ja, ja," he muttered, "I suppose it couldn't be helped. The driver, your, er … boyfriend … I think he was going a little too fast?"

Hilde nodded. "Yes, perhaps a little fast, but he's not my boyfriend. An acquaintance …"

"Hmm. Well, it could have been worse." He pointed over his shoulder at the dog. "Birke is rounding up the last of the animals. I don't know how, but fortunately none were killed."

"That is a blessing," Hilde replied, showing genuine concern. "But what do we do now? The driver should be alright once he comes around. It's just the car …"

"Well, I'll see to him. Then, once I get the sheep back, I can telephone the police. Will that do?"

The man turned and stomped off toward the car, not waiting for an answer. Hilde was glad she didn't have to administer first aid to that reprobate. She shuddered as she recalled his unwelcome advances.

Moments later, the farmer emerged from the car and made his way back up the embankment. "He'll be fine; just banged his head, that's all. I propped him up to make him comfortable. The bleeding seems to have stopped."

Hilde was about to respond when another vehicle came around the bend, this one heading in the opposite direction. The driver, a woman, prudently slowed and came to a stop near them. She got out and approached the two.

"*Guten Tag,*" she announced. "Does anyone need assistance?"

"Not at the moment," the farmer answered. "Just a minor mishap. The fellow in the car bumped his head. My farm is just around the bend. Don't worry, I'll send one of my boys back."

"And you, Fräulein?" the woman asked, turning to face Hilde. "Why, I know you, don't I?"

Hilde took a closer look. The woman wore a gray jacket and matching skirt, overlaid with a green spring coat. With her auburn hair concealed under a fashionable hat, Hilde almost hadn't recognized her.

"Er … Frau Bresslauer?"

The woman smiled. "Why, yes, I'm flattered you remember me," said Inge Bresslauer, a shopkeeper from Oranienburg. "I'm on my way to Liebenwalde to make deliveries for my shop, Chanté boutique. Perhaps I could offer you a lift, *ja*?"

Indecision was written on Hilde's face. She owed no allegiance to her Gestapo escort, and this was the perfect opportunity to get away. But how would it look if she abandoned her travelling companion?

The farmer, seeing the consternation on Hilde's face, patted her on her shoulder. "Don't worry, Fräulein," he said reassuringly. "I'll look after him. There's nothing you can do here. Besides, you'll catch cold in those wet stockings."

Hilde, still holding her shoes, glanced down at her wet feet.

"He's absolutely right," Inge echoed the farmer's sentiments. "You come with me right now."

Hilde was about to object, and even opened her mouth to voice her concern, but Inge would have none of it; she simply took Hilde by the hand and led her to her car. Hilde climbed into the passenger side with her suitcase. As they pulled out onto the roadway, Hilde watched over her shoulder as the farmer herded the last of the sheep around the bend, his trusty dog bouncing between them. Silently, she offered a prayer of thanks to her heavenly protector for providing a timely rescuer.

The two women drove north toward Liebenwalde, and with each passing kilometer Hilde's mood improved.

"My dear, you're looking better already," Inge said, smiling.

"I don't know how to thank you," Hilde said. "It's been so dreadful the last few days. Leaving Oranienburg to stay with my aunt, after Otto …"

She cupped her mouth with her hand, realizing she had said too much.

"Don't worry," Inge replied. "I know all about the mayor. Actually, I don't feel the least bit sorry he's gone." She looked sideways to see if she'd offended Hilde. "It may sound uncaring, but I too have known about his womanizing and the way he misrepresented his office." She stifled a giggle. "Many women in Oranienburg know about him."

Feeling a little more at ease, Hilde thought she could confide a little in Frau Bresslauer.

"Then you do understand," Hilde offered. "I suppose many felt that way but were afraid to say anything."

Inge merely nodded.

"But there's something I need to tell you," Hilde added. "That man, the one driving me today, I … I didn't come willingly. He was taking me back to Berlin, for questioning—and on the way he grabbed me and tried …"

Inge must have seen the fear in Hilde's eyes. "You poor girl. It's alright now," she said immediately drawn to her plight. "You don't have to explain yourself. That's no way for a man to treat a woman. I think it was providence that brought me this way. You see, I was scheduled to come yesterday, but I was delayed … well, I'm glad I came along when I did."

Hilde cast a grateful smile in Inge's direction.

Having made it back to Berlin without incident, Fritz Kolbe locked up, left his apartment, and quickly walked the short distance to the Foreign Office, housed in a stately-building on Wilhelmstraße. He was five minutes away when the air raid sirens went off. He scrutinized the gray clouds and, not seeing anything unusual, speculated that it must be another false alarm.

People hurried past, running for the shelter, but Kolbe wasn't paying attention and suddenly found himself alone when the first one-thousand-pound bomb exploded a mere one hundred meters down the street. He was nearly knocked off his feet and scrambled into the nearest building, not a moment too soon, as the brick and stone edifice of the building next door disintegrated from a direct hit.

The concussion rocked the apartment block and propelled Kolbe forward so that he half-stumbled and half-ran down a flight of stairs to the basement. He just avoided colliding with a small boy huddled next to a wooden pillar, holding on for dear life.

Kolbe saw a few people in the dim light of a single bulb that flickered and threatened to go out with each detonation. He made it to the far end of the shelter and crouched beside an old man in a long black coat. The man nodded and tipped his hat. Under other circumstances, Kolbe may have burst out laughing, but his dust-caked face and parched throat prevented it this time. He merely smiled and pulled his own hat down over his ears.

With each successive blast, the building shook, eliciting screams from the frightened people nearby. Kolbe wanted to scream himself, but realized it would accomplish little. Instead, he silently prayed for the bombing to end. Under his breath, he cursed the Americans and the hapless bombardier who had miscalculated his target. Fortunately, the bombing subsided as quickly as it had begun.

Kolbe appraised his fellow Berliners, some hugging, others crying, but all relieved that it was over. He got up, tipped his hat to the old man again, and walked toward the stairs, where he found the small boy still clinging to the wooden support. After several attempts, he was able to loosen the boy's grip and lead him out of the basement. Once they were at street level, Kolbe reached into his pocket and pulled out an orange; he handed it to the boy in the hope that it would take his mind off the ordeal. The boy took it, still dazed.

When Kolbe walked outside, he saw destruction everywhere. Large craters pockmarked the main street like abandoned excavation projects. Many of the stately linden trees flanking the street had been uprooted or split in two, some still burning. A ruptured fire hydrant haphazardly sprayed water on one of the burning trees, leaving the eerie impression that it had intervened while awaiting the fire department's arrival.

Kolbe swept the sight out of his mind and carried on, maneuvering as best he could around toppled wagons and car wrecks. He breathed a sigh of relief when he didn't see any bodies littering the sidewalk.

He tried to collect himself as he mounted the limestone steps of the Foreign Office. He stopped at the top of the stairwell and stared in disbelief. Although he himself had been left untouched, the same couldn't be said about the building in which he worked. A whole section of the second floor had simply vanished. He saw a gaping hole in the once ornate ceiling, with scorched, twisted wiring reaching down like menacing tentacles. Clerks and office personnel milled about in confusion. He spotted two women trying to comfort a third, who sat on the floor covered in plaster dust, apparently still in shock. Papers were scattered everywhere, littering the foyer.

Along with several co-workers, Kolbe tried to salvage what documents he could. He scooped up several files and placed them onto an abandoned handcart. While moving the cart to an undamaged section of the floor, he rounded a corner and nearly collided with a burly man—a deputy minister, as it turned out—who was also pushing an overloaded cart of salvaged documents. Bracing himself for an impact that never came, Kolbe dropped a few folders.

"For God's sake, man, can't you be more careful?" the minister scolded him.

"I'm sorry, sir. Here, let me help." Kolbe bent down and picked up the dossiers, handing them to the man. Without uttering a word of thanks, the man barged ahead as if nothing else mattered.

Kolbe just shook his head, picked up his files, and headed for what he hoped would still be his small corner office. By sheer luck, it had remained untouched. To give himself a sense of normalcy, he made a cup of tea and fished a lone biscuit from his coat pocket. Relieved that his office had been spared, he sat down and proceeded to organize the files he had salvaged.

Every once in a while, chance—or providence—favors a

man that has neither deserved nor asked for it. Such was the case with Fritz Kolbe. In his haste to leave, the deputy minister hadn't bothered to take stock of his files and, consequently, left one crucial dossier behind.

Kolbe sat perfectly still, still not believing his luck. He peered down at a plain manila folder that had fallen off the deputy minister's cart, reasoning he had already pilfered so many files that this hardly constituted any new danger. Still holding the tea in his right hand, he opened the dossier with his left and glanced at the improbable title: *Streng Geheim*—Top Secret.

He squinted through his eyeglasses to make sure he'd actually read the dossier correctly. *How did the deputy minister come into possession of this document?* he pondered. It originated from a physicist named Kurt Diebner and included several schematics of an object that resembled a bomb, as well as correspondence between Diebner and a man named Siegfried Knemeyer, who worked for RLM. He recalled that RLM referred to the Ministry of Aviation.

Kolbe sat up, took a gulp of the soothing tea, and gently placed the cup back on its saucer, focusing his attention on the last name: Knemeyer. He knew that name. He leaned back in his chair and gazed out the small window of his office just as a German fighter zoomed past, its shrill engine reverberating in its wake.

The departing aircraft seemed to tweak a distant memory. The answer came surprisingly easily. Knemeyer had been involved with the Horten project. Kolbe had seen cables several weeks ago that mentioned the new Horten bomber undergoing test flights.

When the phone rang, Kolbe nearly spilled the contents of his tea cup. *Damn!* Half the second floor had been obliterated, but the phones were still working? He picked up the receiver and calmly identified himself.

"Ah, Kolbe, good that you're there," announced his superior. "I was worried about you when the bombs fell. Um … a change in plans. Your trip has been postponed by one or two days. We need your help here at the ministry. Heil Hitler."

Before he could reply the line had been disconnected.

Rather than feeling relief, Kolbe felt a knot tighten in his stomach. He sat perfectly still, contemplating the connection between Diebner, Knemeyer, and the Horten brothers. Although the dossier's few scant papers didn't specifically refer to the new bomber, it did acknowledge the "significant progress" in recent tests. There was also a mention of technical terms like fission, neutrons and something called a chain reaction. He didn't need to be an expert to recognize that the Nazis were developing another sinister weapon.

He leaned back in his chair and debated what he should do, what he could do. Certainly, he had to warn his contact, Allen Dulles, so the Americans could decide what should be done. He would have preferred to keep the dossier overnight, to study its contents further, but he surmised that the minister would eventually discover it was missing and come looking for it. So, he produced a few sheets of paper from his desk drawer and quickly copied the memos via mimeograph, reproducing the diagrams as best as he could.

After he had concealed the copies, he carefully replaced the originals in the dossier in the order he'd found them and headed down the hall. He dropped into the deputy minister's outer office as casually as he could and handed the dossier to the man's secretary, explaining that the minister had inadvertently left it behind in the hall when they'd bumped into each other.

The secretary, while nodding at the explanation, barely glanced at Kolbe and, as expected, relieved him of the burden. Without further ado, Kolbe returned to his own office, happy over how smoothly the transaction had gone.

CHAPTER XXVIII

Desperation

On a dreary spring day, Horst Kloster sat in the back of the Daimler limousine, gazing out at the tree-lined street. What had once been the pride of Berlin, Göringstrasse was quickly turning into an urban wasteland. Russian forces were closing in from the east, while Patton's army pressed from the west. Months of Allied bombing had slowly been reducing the city to rubble.

How much longer can we hold out? Kloster wondered, holding a cigarette between his fingers. He glanced across to the vehicle's only other occupant—save the uniformed driver—and noted how calm Colonel Knemeyer appeared.

Kloster then examined his new uniform, evidence of his fresh promotion to captain. He now looked every bit the polished Luftwaffe officer again, with his formal tunic, pressed pants, and highly polished boots.

They drove on, passing Neuendorf, heading north toward Oranienburg. Kloster became lost in his own thoughts as the Daimler negotiated burnt-out wrecks and immense bomb craters. It was evident that the public works had been frantically trying to repair these damaged streets but couldn't quite keep up.

The car turned off the main highway toward the airfield. The military support services had not been idle here, and for good reason: the airfield was vital to the war effort.

Although Kloster had been briefed on the destruction, he was still unprepared for the devastation he witnessed as the car pulled up. He nearly gasped. Several of the buildings had been virtually levelled by the raid of American B-17 Flying Fortresses several days before. Many military aircraft had been destroyed, too, the overworked ground crews working feverishly to remove their remnants from the tarmac.

As instructed, their driver bypassed the main access road and continued northwest towards several plain buildings that resembled small barns rather than hangars. Knemeyer had been careful, perhaps even overcautious, in ordering that the last working Horten prototype be moved here to escape the systematic bombing of airfields.

What if the jet had been manufactured en masse in 1942 as planned, Kloster mused, rather than delayed by political wrangling and Hitler's stubbornness of insisting that the fighter, die Schwalbe, be converted into a fighter-bomber? Ah, the possibilities ...

Kloster resisted getting drawn into meaningless self-recrimination that would only serve to get him internally worked up. *Those incompetent fools ... never mind. No, the futility of war and all those what-ifs will be debated by historians for years to come.* He sighed, prompting a side-ways look from Knemeyer. They pulled into a vacant space between two buildings, just as the sun peeked through the broken cumulus. *Well, at least it's going to be a good flying day,* he mused.

Two workers in overalls came around one of the buildings and slid open the doors of the closest building. The lights had been switched on. Both men could see an aircraft situated in the rear, as if hiding in the shadows, an aircraft with gray camouflage paint. Kloster eagerly stepped forward with Knemeyer close behind. As the opening increased, the Horten bomber filled their vision.

Knemeyer seemed to be taken aback. The colonel was a former pilot himself, and he appraised the bomber with a critical eye. Still, the look on his face told Kloster he was duly impressed.

"If only ..." Knemeyer murmured.

Kloster raised an eyebrow at him.

The colonel sighed, but also looked angry. "If only we had implemented this design sooner."

While Kloster walked up to the airplane, a uniformed captain hurried over to Knemeyer. He saluted smartly, clicking his heels.

"Guten Morgen, Herr Oberst." He introduced himself to the colonel. "I'm Captain Kurt Dönitz. I was informed to expect you at 8:30 sharp." He motioned to the aircraft. "As you can see, we haven't been idle."

"Is everything in readiness?" Knemeyer asked.

"Of course, sir. The aircraft has been fuelled and pre-flighted, as per your instructions. I was informed that a He-111 transport will land shortly. It was supposed to have been here yesterday, but due to the heavy damage inflicted on the runways by the American bombers, we only have one runway that's serviceable, and that only barely."

"I understand. Well, let's go inside. I could use a good coffee. A real coffee. We can wait there while the pilot changes into his flight suit and goes through his pre-flight briefing."

"This way, Colonel," Dönitz beckoned.

Knemeyer stepped into the small building adjacent to the hangar, removed his coat and gloves, and took a seat in the chair that Dönitz had offered him. The colonel glanced around and deduced that the small structure must have once served as a supply room or storage facility; it had only been converted into an office as a matter of necessity. He appreciated the display of German ingenuity.

As if reading Knemeyer's mind, Dönitz re-appeared from the back, removed his coat, and seated himself behind the desk. The captain then picked up the telephone and instructed to be connected with Operations. A conversation ensued about the current weather forecast and reports of imminent enemy formations.

After several minutes, Dönitz hung up and smiled at Knemeyer.

"The gods seem to be favoring your mission, Colonel," he offered. "No reports of enemy sightings. However, it doesn't eliminate the possibility of single fighter incursion by the Americans or the British. As you well know, we've been prone to frequent raids by British Spitfires."

Knemeyer nodded. He'd read the reports. The British had been especially adept at devising strategy against the formidable Messerschmitt fighter and had devised the tactic of congregating near German bases, then following unsuspecting Me 262 jets back to their airfields, attacking when the jets were most vulnerable during landing mode.

A soldier walked in carrying a simple tray loaded with biscuits, steaming croissants, and a pot of coffee. As Knemeyer took the first cup of coffee, he smiled at Dönitz's resourcefulness, confirming it was, indeed, real coffee.

Dönitz acknowledged the unspoken complement. It was a simple pleasure during war time. By the time they finished their meagre breakfast, the Ho 229 had been wheeled out by a small utility tractor. The jet was now situated on the pavement outside the hangar, looking ominous to any casual observer.

Knemeyer turned a wary eye to the sky as if a British fighter might materialize. He spotted two Me 109 fighters crisscrossing the field at about five hundred meters. It seemed Dönitz had arranged for the overhead protection.

Knemeyer realized that Captain Kloster was already seated inside the cockpit, going over his start-up procedure. Kloster had been briefed and knew what was expected of him. He would take off under escort of two Me 109 fighter aircraft, and head northeast to Hamburg, where he would land and take on the Führer's special package.

A junior officer discretely walked up to Dönitz and whispered in the man's ear. Upon hearing the report, the captain dismissed him and turned to Knemeyer.

"Sir, I've just been informed that the Heinkel transport has landed and will be ready to depart within the hour. I've arranged for one of my men to lead your driver to the serviceable part of the airfield where the aircraft is being refueled."

"Very good, Dönitz. I'm impressed with your efficiency. It won't go unnoticed."

Knemeyer stood up and left the office, making his way down to the tarmac. He wondered if he would see the Ho 229 and its pilot again. Only time would tell.

He turned and followed a subordinate to the waiting Daimler, which transported him to the far side of the airfield where an He 111 aircraft was being refuelled next to a hangar that had been miraculously spared by the recent Allied bombing.

Knemeyer emerged from the backseat just as another vehicle pulled up. Two men emerged and Knemeyer immediately recognized First Lieutenant Andreas Bauman.

"Ah, Bauman, I'm glad you've made it." Knemeyer pointed to the newcomer. "Your wingman?"

"Yes, *Leutnant Schlopf,* from my former squadron."

"I know it was short notice," Knemeyer added, "but I needed two experienced pilots to accompany us on this trip to Hamburg." He turned around and addressed his driver. "Corporal, fetch their bags and stow them in the transport."

"Jawohl, Herr Oberst," the man replied as he headed to retrieve the officers' duffel bags. Meanwhile Bauman and Schlopf headed toward another hangar, where camouflage netting was being removed from two Messerschmitt fighters.

Five minutes later, the Heinkel transport rumbled down the runway, bouncing occasionally over a hastily filled crater and slowly lifting off, banking and settling on a north-easterly heading.

╬

Next to a small shack situated a short distance from the

main hangar, Fritz Kolbe watched the proceedings with interest. A gust of wind whipped around the corner, nearly stealing his hat and blowing it down the tarmac.

Before he could reflect on the departing aircraft carrying Colonel Knemeyer, he heard something much more interesting—the roar of a distant jet engine. He glanced at the far side of the airfield just in time to witness the takeoff of a strange-looking delta-wing aircraft.

Kolbe had read of its development but had never before seen the real thing and he marveled at the spectacle. *So, this is what the Horten brothers have been working on.*

"Herr Kolbe, your car is waiting," his driver announced.

"*Danke*, Bruno," Kolbe replied. "Please take me back to my office. In all the haste this morning, I forgot to bring my suitcase."

Seated comfortably in the backseat, Kolbe contemplated the significance of Knemeyer's send-off. But he couldn't focus on that. He had to get back to the German embassy in Bern and, in the process, deliver his concealed report destined for his American contact, Allen Dulles. The outcome of the war may hinge on it. Even though the Luftwaffe was beaten back daily, the Horten bomber was still a formidable threat.

╬

As Kloster lifted the aircraft off the runway, he diligently monitored the instruments for any warning indicators. Even Hitler's express orders wouldn't let him compromise his own safety by getting ahead of himself and thereby missing some crucial blinking light, oil pressure drop, or landing gear malfunction.

But all appeared normal. The compass registered north, the altimeter continued to show a positive climb, and the needle of the airspeed indicator inched slowly up the dial.

He watched through the Plexiglas canopy as the airplane climbed steadily into the beckoning clear blue sky. He would have preferred a cloudy day, so that his aircraft would blend in with the clouds. He winced at two Me 109 fighter escorts flanking him, one of which was sliding in behind his right wingtip. He cast a glance to his left, and sure enough, the second plane moved into the reciprocal position.

Kloster returned the wave of the fighter's young pilot, wondering whether these escorts had been ordered to protect him or ensure he flew as instructed to his destination.

No matter. He needed to concentrate on flying the plane and getting to Hamburg in one piece. Knemeyer had been explicit that there was to be no radio communication, no chatter to give away his presence to the enemy. He set course for Hamburg, dialing in the magnetic compass heading while comparing his position to the map on his lap. He scanned the instruments again and allowed himself to relax a fraction. Everything looked the way it was supposed to.

Then an idea popped into his head, and without a second thought he carried it out. Kloster advanced the throttle with his left hand to eighty percent power, the Jumo turbojets responding instantly and accelerating smoothly. With a little back pressure on the control stick, he climbed to five thousand meters.

He checked the airspeed indicator and noted that he was passing 680 kilometers per hour—an impressive 430 miles per hour. With satisfaction, he glanced to his left, and then his right, noting that both fighters were dropping back, unable to match the Ho 229's superior performance.

Kloster couldn't suppress a grin. He quickly banked to the right, settling on a new heading, and watched as the fighters tried in vain to keep up. He entered a small cumulous cloud, then quickly throttled back and, once clear, watched with glee as the two fighters shot past him, unprepared for the sudden change in tactics.

Kloster then opened the throttles and caught up to the two startled pilots, falling in behind them. Both men automatically dipped their wings to create separation between the aircraft, not wanting to play his dangerous game. Having earned a measure of respect, Kloster waggled his wings and continued on his original course, inviting the two fighters to fall in line behind him.

⸸

After the mishap with the farmer's sheep, Frau Bresslauer had been true to her word, passing Hilde off as a niece and finding temporary accommodations for her. But she hadn't stopped there. Hilde was reunited with her mother, not in Oranienburg, but in a more private setting—a quaint cottage in the town of Liebenwalde.

Gertrude recounted her ordeal at the hands of the Gestapo, only in part. She still shuddered when she thought back to the damp confining cell, the meagre rations, and the lonely nights. But the worst part was not knowing what else was in store for her.

In hushed tones, she told how in early February she had been moved to another facility, one that was less harsh, less confining. Then, inexplicably, after only four days, a matron collected her and brought her to the reception area. She had been instructed to collect her purse and coat and sign a release form.

Dumbfounded, Gertrude wasn't going to argue, but she did have one question: who authorized the release? The matron didn't answer but pointed to the signature on the document. There, along with the official stamp, was the signature of *Oberleutnant* Horst Kloster.

Roused from her musings, Gertrude heard a knock at the front door. She glanced at the wall clock and then at her daughter with a now-who-could-that-be kind of look, but in the end, she put aside her knitting and rose from her chair.

"It's Rudi," Gertrude announced from the foyer. "And he's brought someone with him."

For a moment Hilde envisioned Andreas Bauman standing next to Rudi. She sighed, not looking forward to being reunited with the man she had once been certain she loved.

"Hilde, are you coming?" her mother's voice was laced with amusement.

"Coming, mother." Hilde steeled herself to face Andreas.

First, she spotted Rudi on the doorstep and pecked his cheek in greeting. She couldn't help but notice a bemused, even conspiratorial look on his face.

"I thought you said Rudi had brought—"

Hilde was interrupted by the appearance of a tall, handsome man who had been lurking just outside the door in the shadows. And not just *any* tall, handsome man.

"*Guten Abend,* Fräulein *Augsberg,*" Jack Swaggart greeted.

"Jack! How did … ?"

She couldn't get the words out. The rest of her sentence trailed off as she fell into his arms. Jack embraced her and spun her around, once, twice, even a third time, before setting her back down.

"Well, my dear," Gertrude chided, "are you going to keep your American friend outside where he'll catch cold?"

"Of course not, *Mutti.*"

Hilde dragged Jack into the kitchen, while Rudi and Gertrude followed, closing the door behind them.

Jack had barely removed his coat, before Hilde bombarded him with all sorts of questions. She wanted to know everything that had happened since his departure by boat from Stralsund. Jack managed to find a seat at the kitchen table, and in between bites of home-made *apfelstrudel*—a delicacy supplied by Gertrude—filled her in about the dangerous crossing by trawler, omitting only his bout with seasickness, erroneously believing she'd think less of him.

Hilde ignored her mother's offering of strudel and leaned forward to catch every word, laughing with delight.

Jack went on to relate his experience of being cooped

up in a small plane, a two-seat English Westland Lysander, of trying to converse with the pilot, whose British cockney accent was virtually impossible to understand. They'd landed in a field near the small town of Tønder, Denmark, close to the coast. They had only stopped to refuel and stretch their legs, before taking off again and heading over the North Sea to England. That flight, fortunately, was without incident, and by mid-morning they'd landed at a British airbase near Great Yarmouth. From there, he'd been whisked away by motorcar to London.

"That was a miraculous escape, Captain," Gertrude noted. "How was all that arranged?"

It was Jack's turn to smile.

"Although I'm not at liberty to disclose all the details, since much is classified, I can tell you that I have a benefactor in London who was looking out for me."

Jack turned to face Hilde. "Without intervention from this lovely fräulein, or her mother for supplying the passes," he cast a grateful glance toward Gertrude, "I would not be sitting here today. Who knows? I might be rotting in a Gestapo cell somewhere."

Rudi nodded thoughtfully. "A few of my friends have been rounded up by the Gestapo, suspected of being Communists or Jew sympathizers." Gertrude shuddered, remembering her ordeal. It cast a sombre mood on the group.

Hilde was first to break the spell. She slid her chair next to Jack's, took his hand in hers, and leaned her head on his shoulder.

"I wish I could keep you here until the end of the war," she whispered.

Gertrude sensed that the two wanted to be alone. She prompted Rudi to help with clearing the table and washing the dishes. Hilde led Jack into the small parlor where they could be alone. She knew he wouldn't be able to stay long. Whether through a nosy neighbor or other informant, his whereabouts always seemed to find its way to the authorities. Jack couldn't risk compromising the Augsbergs' safety by staying overnight. It was risky enough staying with Kolbe.

Hilde gazed longingly into his eyes. There was so much she wished to say, but time was against them. She leaned in and kissed him passionately, only to release him after a fleeting embrace. She watched him walk out into the night, then wave before he got into the sidecar of Rudi's motorcycle. Hilde bit her lip and wondered if she'd ever see him again.

CHAPTER XXIX

A Temporary Reprieve

Andreas Bauman, flying escort for the Ho 229, was torn between his love for his country and his allegiance to the Luftwaffe. Considering the state of the war, he reasoned it would be expedient to go against Hitler and his crippling policies. The war now seemed to be a lost cause.

But it wasn't that simple. His emotions made the decision more complicated. Upon takeoff from Oranienburg, their itinerary had called for a direct flight to Hamburg. However, once they were airborne, there had been a last-minute change in the schedule. Due to recent Allied bombing raids, an alternate location was selected: Bremerhaven Army Airfield. The port city of Bremen and the Bremerhaven aerodrome were far less conspicuous than a major airfield, thus less prone to fighter attack. They would serve as an ideal jumping off point for the Horten mission.

Bauman watched as the Horten prototype landed mid-afternoon at the army airfield, then began his own descent. Everything was going according to schedule as he landed close behind the bomber, followed by his wingman.

Once on the ground, a flagman in blue coveralls signalled the prototype's pilot to taxi toward a plain gray hangar. There was no sign of aircraft around. Bauman even detected dandelions gracing the lawn, adding to the illusion of inactivity.

Another signalman appeared and motioned both escorts

to veer off to the left and park outside on the north side of the hangar. Meanwhile, the Ho 229 had rolled to a stop and its pilot was shutting down the engines.

A technician positioned a metal access ladder along the side of the fuselage for Kloster to exit the cockpit. First, Kloster had to complete the process of shutting down the avionics and performing a final check.

The technician climbed up and slid back the canopy. "Is all in order, *Herr Kapitän?*"

"No, everything is not in order," Kloster replied with irritation. He studied a yellow light on the instrument panel and cursed. "*Scheise!* It's the fuel-flow warning light for the starboard engine. I need to know if it's the light itself or something worse. Get to it!"

"Right away, *Herr Kapitän.*"

As the technician assisted Kloster with disconnecting the oxygen supply and freeing him from the shoulder harness, a tractor appeared from a nearby building and chugged toward the aircraft. A mechanic stopped beside the airplane and jumped off. He retrieved a tow bar and expertly connected it to the nose wheel.

Once Kloster had climbed down from the ladder, he walked beside the tractor, keeping a watchful eye on the workers' progress as they wheeled the prototype into the hangar. Out of the corner of his eye he also noticed mechanics securing the two escort aircraft and covering them with camouflage netting.

Kloster recognized Andreas Bauman, the taller of the two escort pilots, but had never seen the other pilot before. The two pilots began walking toward the hangar, prompting Kloster to smile as they were confronted by a group of four elite soldiers.

"I'm sorry, sir," Kloster overheard one of the soldiers bark at the startled pilots. "Authorized personnel only. On express orders of *Reichsmarschall* Göring."

In the same instant, a lieutenant appeared and informed

Kloster of some changes to the schedule. Their respite here in Bremerhaven was to last considerably longer—at least three days longer—on account of unexpected repairs.

The Ho 229 starboard engine's combustor wasn't functioning one hundred percent. An experienced mechanic explained that a temporary fix was possible but risky. He recommended replacing the whole set of fuel injectors. Unfortunately, this particular model of fuel injector wasn't readily available in Bremen, or even Hamburg.

Kloster shot the mechanic a withering look. He grudgingly climbed the steps to an office to place the necessary telephone calls, hoping to locate the correct parts in Berlin.

He had to use considerable influence to persuade the clerk in charge of parts procurement to ensure priority consideration.

When Kloster heard from a clerk that they intended on shipping the injectors via train he nearly lost his composure. He had difficulty convincing the dumbfounded clerk that it was of the utmost priority. The clerk apologized and said he would relay the request to his lieutenant. Kloster took a deep breath and swallowed the outburst poised on the tip of his tongue. He knew the routine all-too-well and advised the clerk that he would call back.

Kloster slammed the receiver down, the sound resounding in the small office. He had only one option: wait for Knemeyer's arrival, the man who had the necessary clout to move the wheels of bureaucracy.

Desperate for a cigarette, and with nothing else to do, Kloster walked back outside and fished out second-last of his *Lucky Strikes*. He cupped his hands around a gold lighter and lit the cigarette, allowing the smoke to draw deep into his lungs, while at the same time expelling his frustrations.

Kloster noted the picturesque blue sky, with nary a cloud in sight. He wondered if he would enjoy such a splendid view again, pending the outcome of his mission. As if on cue, an

He 111 overflew the aerodrome. He looked up to see the massive landing gear being lowered as the plane made a wide sweeping turn, lined up with the grassy runway, and touched down. The transport pulled off the end of the runway and lumbered toward the hangar.

Once it had stopped, a mechanic hustled over and placed an apple crate under the exit door. Kloster silently commended him for his foresight. The door opened inward and two soldiers disembarked, followed by Knemeyer.

Kloster quickly extinguished his cigarette by squashing it on a dandelion leaf and walked over to greet his superior. As expected, Knemeyer appreciated the urgency for the prototype's fuel injectors. The colonel immediately headed for the administrator's office to place some telephone calls.

Kloster paced outside the office and lit another cigarette, hoping it would distract him, or at least calm his nerves. The cigarette had long gone out when the door opened and Knemeyer strode out. He good-naturedly patted Kloster on the shoulder.

"Come, come, Captain. There's no need for that worried look. I made doubly sure that we will receive those parts. The fuel injectors will arrive sometime tomorrow, not by train but by aircraft. I've commandeered a Messerschmitt to deliver them."

Although appeased, Kloster still had reservations and the frown showed on his face. As if reading his mind, the colonel nodded toward the hangar.

"Don't worry. I've brought an experienced mechanic with us. He'll oversee the installation of the fuel injectors and ensure the Horten is airworthy." He clapped his hands together. "Now, Horst, I've had a long flight and I'm thirsty for a good German lager."

╬

Lieutenant Börser hung up the telephone, a sense of unease spreading through him. He had just been chastised by a senior officer—and not just any senior officer: Colonel Siegfried Knemeyer from RLM.

He still winced from the rebuke. What had started off as a relatively minor problem—a request for aircraft parts—had morphed into a huge issue. First, a captain had called, outlining his urgent request. Then he'd called back a second time, *demanding* that the part be located and shipped as soon as possible.

Börser had assured the man that they would do their best and ship it by train the following morning. Upon hearing this, the captain had nearly blown his top. Börser hadn't known what to say except to repeat that they would do their best and try to find a better shipment solution. What more could be expected?

Then the captain's voice had turned ice cold. "Not good enough, Lieutenant," he stated and abruptly hung up.

Roughly thirty minutes later, Börser received another call, this time from Colonel Knemeyer himself, telling him in no uncertain terms that he had better procure those engine components that very day and have them sent by air in the morning. No excuses.

Börser was livid from the brow-beating, but he saw no way out. He assigned the task that afternoon to three of his clerks, hoping one of them could obtain the fuel injectors on such short notice.

Finally, after a number of inquiries, one of his men, Rolf Pilser, succeeded in locating the appropriate fuel injectors. Börser then made arrangements to have them shipped to their facility.

Börser's telephone rang again, and the tone in his secretary's voice told him the incoming call was quite urgent. He didn't realize just how urgent it was until he heard the unmistakeable voice on the other end. A deep, menacing voice.

"Jawohl, Herr Marschall," Börser's voice croaked. "I'm doing everything I can. As a matter of fact, we have just received

word that the fuel injectors are being delivered to our facility this very afternoon."

Börser listened with trepidation as none other than *Reichsmarschall* Göring laid out a series of explicit instructions.

"Of course, *Herr Reichs* ... yes ... I will expedite the request and send the parts ... certainly, sir ... I understand ... yes, spare no expense. Very good, sir. Heil Hitler!"

Börser hung up the telephone and slumped into his chair like a man who had run a marathon—exhausted and sweaty. Pilser, who had been completing the pertinent documentation at his desk, poked his head inside the office and looked quizzically at his superior.

"Forgive me, sir, but I couldn't help noticing. Who was that man on the line? Colonel Knemeyer again?"

"You're not even close. The call came from Göring himself. Can you believe it? The man is positively incensed over our incompetence. I've never heard such harshness in a man's voice. I'm still shaking."

Pilser, for the first time, seemed to take the whole matter seriously. He picked up the documents and scanned the details. It seemed to be a fairly standard request. The form provided the specifications for a Jumo jet engine, and correct replacement parts for the ...

He checked again to make sure he'd read it correctly. Apparently, these engines belonged to a new type of aircraft, one he'd never heard of before.

"Lieutenant." He roused Börser from his stupor. "Is this information correct? It looks like a mistake to me. What's a Ho 229? Is that a part number for some new combustor?"

Börser glanced up. "Um, I'm not supposed to say ... but since you've helped in locating the parts, I suppose I can tell you. The Ho 229 is an experimental plane, designed and built by the Horten brothers. They say it rivals the Messerschmitt jet."

Before Pilser could get any more out of his superior,

the man left to secure a plane to transport the fuel injectors as promised.

‡

It was early evening when Rudi Schultz ventured out of his small apartment in Oranienburg's west end and headed to a little pub, hoping to join a couple of friends for a pint of German brew. He had recently learned of a friend's arrest by the Gestapo and needed to shake the cobwebs from his head. The best way to do that was to indulge in some good old *gemüttlichkeit*. After finding a table, he was soon joined by a couple of friends, including Franz Pfalz.

Pfalz, used to driving dignitaries, seemed relieved to have the evening off, and before long they were caught up in discussing a pair of Hollywood movies, they'd seen featuring James Cagney and Clark Gable.

Several other men came in after and seated themselves at a nearby table. They were young and boisterous and, judging from their attire, employed as clerks. If Rudi had to guess, he'd say they were affiliated with a branch of the military.

Rudi's chair was a little closer to their table and thus he became privy to their boasting. After a couple of rounds, the men became more vocal.

The main speaker was a fellow named Rolf Pilser. It seemed Rudi was right about him being a clerk. The man revealed he worked for a military procurement office in Berlin. Pilser was a natural-born talker and seemed more than happy to fill in his mates about the latest gossip at the aerodrome.

Before long, his friends were roaring with laughter.

"Yea, but there's more," Pilser insisted. "My lieutenant is really a mouse and jumps at anyone who barks at him. Well, today he got several unexpected phone calls. A couple were from some captain—I didn't get his name—but the next one was from a colonel up in Bremen. The man was adamant that we locate fuel injectors for a jet engine—now! Not only that, but he wanted them delivered the next day. Doesn't he know there's a war on?"

This was greeted by further laughter.

"Anyway, the officer was very insistent and wouldn't take no for an answer. Although I didn't hear the conversation, I take it he expected updates throughout the day. Here's the best part ..."

Pilser paused to make sure he had their attention. Rudi had been about to excuse himself and head for home, but he was caught up in the story and decided to hear the end.

"Well, sure enough, not one hour went by before our secretary put an urgent call through to my lieutenant." Pilser grinned, getting ready for the punchline. "Börser's face went white as a sheet when he heard the voice on the other end. I thought he was going to faint. He just kept stammering, 'Yes, sir, ... of course, sir.' So, guess who was on the line?"

His friends shrugged their shoulders. Rudi was tempted to guess Knemeyer, but he wisely kept the thought to himself.

"It was the *Reichsmarschall* himself—Göring!"

Rudi nearly jumped up in surprise, barely catching himself. He forced himself to remain calm and look away, despite having to strain his ears to catch more.

There were calls of surprise from around Pilser's table.

"Rolf, what could be so important that Göring felt compelled to call?" asked one man.

"That's exactly what I was thinking," agreed Pilser. "Obviously it has something to do with those components. I don't understand it all, but they're being shipped out tomorrow so they can install them the same day. The airplane, the, er ... the Horten ... well, it's slated to leave the day after tomorrow."

Rudi couldn't believe his luck. There it was, that one word on which his world seemed to hang—Horten.

He took another gulp from his stein and then excused himself.

"Where are you off to in such a hurry?" Pfalz asked.

"Um, I'm tired and I need to get home. I'll see you tomorrow."

Rudi left some money for his beer and headed out, looking for the nearest public telephone. He needed to alert his contact.

⚜

Fritz Kolbe returned to his apartment and started packing for his trip to Bern, Switzerland. But before he'd gotten very far, Jack Swaggart walked through the open study door, grinning at him.

"What's so funny?" Kolbe asked.

"You Germans are so … deliberate," Jack offered. "So … organized. I've watched you carefully fold each item before placing it in your suitcase. We Americans have dispensed with that long ago, preferring to simply toss our belongings into a holdall."

Kolbe peered closer and noted that Swaggart had already finished packing. He shrugged, but before he could respond, the telephone rang.

Both men looked at the instrument, uncertainty written on their faces. It rang again.

Kolbe walked over, allowed it to ring a third time, and then casually answered.

"*Ja,* Herr Kolbe here. What can—?"

He listened with concentration, nodding several times before hanging up with a habitual "Heil Hitler."

He turned to face Jack.

"As you've probably guessed, that was my superior, advising me of a change in plans," Kolbe explained with a frown. "I will no longer accompany you to Bern. They want me instead to go to Bremen."

"Then it's up to me to meet with Dulles and deliver the papers alone."

"It is indeed, my friend. Our hope rests on you getting through."

There was much more to be discussed, but they were

once again interrupted by the shrill ringing of the infernal telephone.

"Now what?" Kolbe said with annoyance. "Don't tell me they've changed their minds already …"

He picked up the receiver, expecting to hear his boss' insistent voice. Instead, he listened for a moment, the look of concern on his face deepening. Kolbe cupped the phone and whispered, "It's Rudi Schultz." He listened with interest, nodding a few times.

"I see. Is it really that urgent? Alright, it's now …" he said, consulting his watch, "… just after seven o'clock. Depending on the Gestapo check points, I should be able to get there in less than one hour. Goodbye."

Kolbe hung up and turned to face Jack.

"Rudi has some vital information and naturally doesn't want to discuss it over the telephone," he said. "He wants to meet me at The Church of St. Nicholas. Tonight."

Jack raised his eyebrows, but not being privy to the conversation didn't reply. A moment passed between the two men.

"Do you want me to accompany you?" Jack offered.

"No, it's too risky. I'll fill you in when I get back to Potsdam."

✠

Rudi Schultz entered The Church of St. Nicholas just as the parish priest concluded his homily. Although Rudi entered quietly through the side door, his entrance didn't go unnoticed.

Father Hiller, who was officiating the service, appeared to recognize him. The priest was holding a golden chalice in preparation for the Eucharist. He smiled at the latecomer while tapping his forehead.

Rudi looked questioningly at the priest, but then caught the unspoken message. He smiled sheepishly and quickly removed his hat as he found a place at the end of a pew. He looked around and even though there were less than twenty parishioners, he couldn't spot Kolbe among them.

He unobtrusively checked his watch.

Rudi followed the service with detachment, his mind occupied with earthly things and not the sacraments. He looked at his watch again, as if the action would speed up the man's arrival. Still no sign of Kolbe.

Rudi eventually picked up a hymnal and absentmindedly leafed through, hoping Kolbe hadn't been unnecessarily detained. He needed to advise him of recent developments.

Just then, the object of his worries entered through the same side door he had taken earlier and took a seat near a pillar. A much less conspicuous seat than the one Rudi had chosen for himself. When the priest had turned his back, Rudi got up and shuffled over to the pew directly behind Kolbe.

"I don't have much time," Kolbe offered without turning around. "I saw a Gestapo car cruising past just as I entered."

Rudi glanced at the side door, half-expecting the feared secret police to walk inside.

"Thanks for coming," Rudi whispered, taking a deep breath. "I was in a local tavern during the supper hour this evening when four men entered. They had a few beers and quickly got caught up in boastful talk. One of the men, someone named Rolf, started talking about a work-related incident, a last-minute order. Apparently, he works in one of those military procurement depots." He looked around and continued.

"A high-ranking officer called and insisted that the delivery of a vital jet engine part be expedited. Here's the interesting part. One of his friends asked what was so vital, and the man said it was for a new jet, a Horten. Naturally, I—"

"Shh!" the voice of a female parishioner interrupted, silencing Rudi temporarily.

Both men slid a few paces further away to continue their conversation.

"The Horten bomber?" queried Kolbe. "We've been trying to get word on its whereabouts all week."

"Right. And I know where it is."

"Where is what?" asked a strange voice.

Rudi looked up to see the church's deacon hovering over him, not pleased that the young man would be speaking while the service was underway.

"I'm sorry," Rudi said. "I was telling my friend about a new butcher shop."

"Uh-huh. Well, this is a house of God, not a meat market," the deacon replied. He then walked to the front to assist the priest with the distribution of Communion wafers.

Once they were out of earshot again, Rudi hastily added, "the clerk blabbered the location where the Horten is undergoing repairs. They're shipping the parts to a small aerodrome in Bremerhaven, near Bremen—tomorrow."

Kolbe nodded. "Excellent. Thanks, Rudi. I need to go."

He quickly headed for the side door. Rudi wanted to hurry after him, but thought it best to wait a minute or two, not wishing to disrupt the distribution of the wafers.

A few minutes later, Rudi walked out into the cool evening air as dusk was falling on the city.

"Just where do you think you're going in such a hurry?" a voice challenged from the recesses of an alcove in the church's exterior wall.

Startled, Rudi squinted his eyes to spot the caller in the failing light as he was grabbed from behind by two strong arms.

"Your spying days are over, Schultz," the gruff voice announced, spinning him around.

Rudi recognized the determined face of Wilhelm Vogel.

⚜

Jack Swaggart was sitting by himself in a second-class carriage. He had stowed his overnight case in the luggage bin above him, but kept the attaché case close, tucked up against the arm rest. As another passenger, an elderly woman, entered the compartment, he involuntarily gripped the case tighter. The woman, looking every bit of German extraction and dressed for travel, nodded curtly and sat down opposite him without speaking.

Jack acknowledged her unspoken greeting with a slight nod and then turned to face the window acceding to the customary formality of strangers who wished to be viewed as polite yet refrained from unnecessary conversation. He hoped she would follow suit and was relieved when the woman pulled out a magazine. Judging by its cover, he was sure it would occupy her interest for the next hour.

His mind wandered to his travelling companion, Fritz Kolbe, now seated in the car of a different train. They had greeted each other at the railway station, but then parted company. The Gestapo men were everywhere, on the hunt for deserters, constantly harassing civilians with the irritating phrase, *"Papiere, bitte!"* Jack, supplied with excellent forged documents, was reasonably certain of passing scrutiny, and Kolbe had assured him the recent bombings had created chaos in Berlin. Many of the telephone lines in the Foreign Ministry were down, and those that had been restored were reserved for priority calls, not minor inquiries, such as questions arising from a bureaucrat's travel documents. By the time an inquiry could be made, Jack would be safely out of Berlin and well underway to Bern.

As if following the woman's example, Jack produced reading material of his own, the *Berliner Statszeitung*, a daily paper preferred by most Berliners. Jack wasn't interested in its slanted news about the war effort, though. He was all too familiar with the poor state of the German economy and that it was in shambles. Many other countries faced with the same situation—fighting a war on two fronts—would have capitulated long ago, but the Germans were a proud and determined people. Despite the nearly daily bombings of the Third Reich's capital, the general populace refused to give in and pressed on with a dogged determination that even surprised him.

No, Jack was only interested in the handwritten notes now taped to his thigh—the notes given to him by Kolbe about Germany's latest weapon. After much thought, they had decided to split up the documents so that if one man was caught or detained by the Gestapo, the other had a chance of getting through. Although he flipped through the newspaper, his mind was on the information Kolbe had gathered.

Jack realized that Kolbe and other like-minded men were already thinking of a new, post-war Germany, a Germany that would rise from the ashes and become vibrant and productive once again. Jack just had to ensure this vital information made it back to England, to be seen by the right people.

The importance of the mission was riding on his shoulders, on him getting back and out of Nazi Germany. Once he was safely in Bern, Switzerland, Allen Dulles would make the arrangements to get him all the way to London. The hard part, when dealing with bureaucracy, is convincing superiors they need to act sooner rather than later.

While Jack Swaggart was heading south, Fritz Kolbe found himself travelling north toward Hamburg, where, if all went well, he would catch another train, this one heading west toward Bremen, his intended destination.

His boss hadn't been very specific about the current assignment. The man was scheduled to go himself, but had to defer the trip when another more pertinent issue had arisen within the ministry.

Kolbe was initially disappointed not to accompany Jack to Bern, but over the course of the last day he'd thought better of it. Maybe this trip to Bremen would present him with other opportunities, and perhaps he could even take a little side trip to the nearby seashore.

He happened to have an aunt who lived in the small village of Tossens, on the Butjadingen peninsula. He hadn't seen her for some time, but the fact that she lived close to Bremerhaven was not lost on him.

In the meantime, he would do as ordered: deliver the documents concerning troop deployment to the authority in Bremen. According to Rudi Schultz, the Horten bomber currently sat in a hangar in Bremerhaven, undergoing repairs. The good news was that Kloster wouldn't be leaving for at least two days, giving the Allies more time to come up with a plan to thwart the upcoming mission.

But what sort of contingency plans could the Allies come up with in that time span? Kolbe smiled ruefully. If the past was any indicator, those plans would almost certainly involve him. He sighed. *Well, if not me, who then … ?*

William Sochalski was roused earlier than usual. The normally reserved *kapo*—the Nazi collaborator who brought them their meals—seemed agitated and left as quickly as he'd arrived. Something wasn't right.

The prisoners had barely finished their meagre breakfast when a guard barged into the barracks and ordered them all out. They were herded into ranks and then marched away from the tunnel, heading out of the encampment. Sochalski, like his fellow mates, was surprised at the change in routine. He felt uneasy, unsettled, because no one—save the guards—seemed to know where they were headed.

The morning was cold, with the sun occasionally peeking through the broken cloud layer. Sochalski was thankful it wasn't raining. By the hundreds, they continued their trek northwards. William, on speaking terms with one *kapo*, managed to coax a bit of information out of the man. He learned that the Allied troops were on the verge of overrunning the Dora-Mittelbau camp, thus explaining their hasty departure.

Barely two rows ahead of him, Sochalski saw a man stumble and fall over a prisoner who was probably already dead. Rather than helping him up, those following stepped over him, not willing to expend needless energy on a fellow prisoner. He had seen it before. Men unwilling to help each other for fear of being punished by the guards. Sadly, it was every man for himself.

Sochalski, however, unwilling to subscribe to that ideology, stooped down to help the fallen prisoner rise to his feet. What he saw shocked him. The man's face was bruised, almost to the point of no recognition, every square inch covered with black and blue welts, evidence of a recent beating.

"Danke," the man managed after he rose, trying to keep up the pace.

"Sure, anytime," William replied. "My name's William. William Sochalski. And yours?"

"Rudi," he managed through a split lip. "Rudi Schultz."

"My God," William exclaimed. "Rudi, it's me, William. You brought me to The Church of St. Nicholas, remember? Who did this to you? Surely not one of the barrack guards."

Rudi did his best to smile ruefully. "Nein. Not here. In Berlin—the Gestapo."

During their walk, Rudi related how he'd been arrested, interrogated, beaten, and lastly sent by train to Dora-Mittelbau to serve out a life sentence. They traded stories of survival, and it didn't take much prodding for Rudi to fill William in on their mutual friend, Jack Swaggart.

Rudi explained how he'd helped the downed American flyer elude the Gestapo's clutches and how he had arranged his escape on a fishing trawler bound for Denmark, only for Swaggart to return weeks later posing as a German bureaucrat.

"And that's only the half of it," Rudi grinned. "Honest!"

Sochalski was stunned and speechless. He considered Jack a friend but had no idea what had actually happened to him when they had been separated. He assumed Jack had eventually been caught and taken to a POW camp.

"Please, Rudi," William pleaded. "Tell me all you know."

But before Rudi could elaborate, an overzealous guard slammed the butt end of his rifle into William's back.

"No more talking, Jews," the guard bellowed.

When Fritz Kolbe arrived in Hamburg, he discovered that the westbound train was already in the station awaiting its next allotment of passengers. He wasted little time boarding the train, found a compartment with a window seat, and settled himself in for the two-hour journey to Bremen.

Fortunately for him, the train only stopped twice: once to allow passage for a troop train, and the second time for an air raid alert at a substation. Fortunately, the attack never materialized and the train was allowed to proceed.

Once in Bremen, Kolbe quickly disembarked and cleared the Gestapo checkpoint without being hassled. He headed directly for the building in town that housed the government offices. He discovered the turn-of-the-century structure surprisingly intact despite the report of recent Allied bombings.

He mounted the front steps and supplied his credentials to the sentry on duty. The ministerial clerk inside advised that he wouldn't be needed for at least two days, perhaps three, and directed him to the local hotel where a room had been reserved under his boss' name.

Kolbe once again was reminded that rank had its privileges. He was thankful that at least he had a place to stay and wouldn't have to go looking for a room at the last minute.

The following morning, after a decent breakfast of eggs, buttered toast, and real coffee, Kolbe headed back to the government office and sought out a clerk so he could obtain transport from the motor pool. It would be a perfect day to drive to the seaside.

He was in luck, as an older model Opel had just been returned. Using his boss' authorization, he signed the necessary papers, making sure to obtain a gas ration card. Equipped with purpose and a full tank of gas, Kolbe drove out of the compound and turned northwest to meet the coastline.

He had brought a small suitcase that contained a change of clothes and a hidden compartment that housed a rudimentary wireless, courtesy of Allen Dulles. He wouldn't need it on this excursion, but he couldn't very well leave it behind at the hotel. After all, Kolbe had agreed to take one back from Bern at great personal risk. If he were caught, he knew that he wouldn't be able to provide a plausible explanation for having one in his possession.

Kolbe wasn't big on family reunions, but a part of him looked forward to the visit with his aunt in Tossens. They hadn't seen each other or spoken in at least two years, and her presence here gave him the perfect alibi for travelling to the area. Kolbe would use her abode as a sort of home base from which to scout out the nearby towns.

As expected, his Aunt Greta was thrilled to have a visitor. A large woman, she bombarded him with questions about life in Berlin and doled out generous portions of dumplings and *apfelkuchen* until he feigned a full stomach to extricate himself from culinary torture.

Bright and early the following day, Kolbe loaded up his loaner with a basket of German cooking, along with his small suitcase, an easel, and a painter's kit. He recalled that Greta used to paint occasionally and as an afterthought had asked to borrow her paintbrushes.

Kolbe drove around the peninsula to reacquaint himself with the locale. Later in the day, he headed further inland and stopped for a simple lunch in a pub in Aurich.

Next, he headed toward the coast and investigated the

area of Norden, a quiet seashore hamlet. Armed with the easel and paint paraphernalia, he parked just off the main road and ventured toward the dunes, breathing in the fresh sea air. He found a comfortable spot and plopped down his field stool. He set up the easel and prepared the oil paints.

As his paintbrush hovered over the canvas a few moments later, he was struck by how much he missed landscape painting, having been taught by his aunt when he was just a boy.

After a couple of hours, he reluctantly packed up, not because he was tired but because rainclouds had begun forming in the west. Kolbe liked the small town and decided to spend the night rather than impose on his aunt's hospitality. He checked in at the Hotel Norddeich and, after a delicious meal of sauerkraut, fried potatoes and bratwurst, he secured a spot on the veranda and immersed himself in a copy of Karl May's *Unter Geiern*.

Later that evening, as the rain drove him inside, he allowed himself an aperitif of Jägermeister and retired to his room.

The next day's weather forecast promised more rain, so Kolbe returned to Tossens to spend a little more time with his aunt. He arrived around lunchtime and parked just outside the farmyard, not wanting to get his car stuck in the mud, newly softened by the recent rain.

To his surprise, he found the yard strangely bereft of activity. Instead of the welcoming sign of the old German shepherd dog Bruno, Kolbe spotted a black Daimler parked next to the farmhouse, and inside the car were two men he didn't recognize.

One of the men opened the door and emerged from the front seat. Kolbe watched as the man yawned and stretched, revealing a shoulder holster hidden beneath his coat.

Kolbe's heart nearly stopped. He ducked behind a tree and surveyed the scene again, this time watching as the second man emerged from the auto and lit up a cigarette. Neither man presented a favorable or comforting impression. The astute Fritz Kolbe needed no explanation. The men were obviously from the Gestapo. Why were they here? And where were Greta and the farmhands?

Kolbe doubled back to his car and hurriedly drove off, hoping he hadn't been seen. As he travelled back to Norden, he thought back to his most recent conversation with Rudi in the church.

Then he understood. He had let it slip that he intended on spending a little time with his aunt Greta on the Butjading-en peninsula after his arrival in Bremen. It wouldn't have been too difficult for the Gestapo to track her down in the village of Tossens.

Kolbe cursed to himself. Because of his momentary slip—his carelessness—he'd put Greta in jeopardy. Tears welled up in his eyes as he reflected on what must have happened to poor Rudi. If his theory was correct, the young man would have been interrogated and tortured. He didn't want to believe it, but he could think of no other reason for the Gestapo to have come to the out-of-the-way hamlet of Tossens.

Kolbe steeled himself from further recrimination as he returned to his hotel.

Later that evening, he immersed himself in his Karl May book, hoping the familiar pages would distract him from further feelings of guilt. He debated placing a telephone call to the ministerial assistant in Bremen, but dispensed with it, reasoning that the Gestapo would be expecting him to call.

The following morning, Kolbe rose early and checked out after breakfast. As he loaded up his car, he debated what to do next. A part of him wanted to head back to Tossens and make inquiries about his aunt, but the logical part—that which had kept him alive so far— overruled his heart, reminding him why he was here: alerting the Allies of the Horten bomber's departure from Bremerhaven.

Reluctantly, Kolbe headed back to the seashore. As on

the previous day, he lugged his easel and paint case out to the dunes. This time he also brought the small suitcase containing the wireless set; he couldn't risk leaving it in the car.

It was a cool, windy day, one that he hoped would lessen the chance of visitors coming out to the coast. He found a suitable spot near a vacated lifeguard platform. Rather than pull out his oil paints, Kolbe took out a sketchpad and began to draw the windswept dunes.

Around midday, he stopped sketching and fished out a thermos of coffee and some sandwiches. As he was about to take the first bite, he heard an unexpected sound, high-pitched and shrill.

The unmistakeable sound of an approaching jet aircraft.

He turned away from the sea and glanced over his right shoulder. What he saw nearly took his breath away. The Horten bomber, replete in camouflage paint, flew nearly directly overhead, flanked by two Messerschmitt fighters, all three aircraft heading northwest, undoubtedly bound for England.

Kolbe dropped his sandwich and scrambled to open his suitcase. He hastily retrieved the portable wireless set and propped it up beside the lifeguard chair. He unwound the flexible cable, attached one end to the set, and climbed to the top of the chair. He fastened the lead to the metal pipe that, in better times, would have held the lifeguard's umbrella, substituting it for a make-shift antenna.

He furtively glanced over his shoulder, hoping that no elicit lovers or patrolling guards would happen across his hastily erected transmitter. He seemed to be alone.

Kolbe pulled out his codebook and dialed in the prescribed frequency. Once everything was set, he took a gulp of his coffee to calm his nerves. He then wrote a concise message and, satisfied that it made sense, transmitted his initial code, hoping he was being received.

Almost immediately, Kolbe received confirmation that they were ready on the other end. He commenced to transmit his vital message.

The entire operation took less than five minutes, but there was no time to await a response, as he knew that German anti-espionage teams monitored continuously for unauthorized transmissions. As he retrieved the cable and packed up his gear, he said a silent prayer that the operator had received and deciphered his message. From there, it would be up to Commander Shelby to alert the Allies.

One thing was certain: the Horten bomber was on its way. God help the British if Kloster managed to drop his ordinance on London's unsuspecting populace.

Kolbe picked up the suitcase and calmly walked back to the car. No one seemed to be around. He drove the car to the edge of town and abandoned it near a store, minimizing the risk of being spotted. He then sauntered back toward the beach, looking for an out of the way spot. He found a little hillock and sat down beside a beech tree. One thing nagged at him though. Assuming that the Gestapo were looking for him, should he dare send out another message? Kolbe needed a little luck.

He looked around the deserted beach and made up his mind. He retrieved the wireless set from his suitcase, rigged up the antennae, and sent out a message. His hope now rested on Shelby to convince the "brass" to send a trawler or other watercraft and pick him up before the Germans found him.

He donned his earphones and patiently waited for the set to start receiving. He nearly jumped when the Morse code popped up in his ears, the familiar beep-beep reassuring him he hadn't been forgotten. The decoded message was brief:

"Your request under advisement. stop. Expect reply at 21:00. stop. Shelby. stop."

He dismantled his set and stashed the suitcase in nearby bushes. He then walked back to his knoll and settled back into his chair. He smiled, picked up his pencil, and concentrated on his sketch of the seashore.

CHAPTER XXX

Attack on London

At last, the promised parts arrived at the Bremerhaven aerodrome via military aircraft. Kloster monitored the installation of the fuel injectors on the Ho 229 and wasn't satisfied until the mechanic had closed the engine cowling and nodded affirmatively.

Later, Kloster supervised the loading of the bomb, despite the fact he still knew little of its functionality or capability. He mentioned as much to Knemeyer but wasn't given much of an explanation.

"Leave it to the scientists," Knemeyer told him. "Your job, your only concern, should be the delivery of the bomb. The plane's unmatched speed will be your best chance to get safely away afterwards."

Kloster wasn't completely satisfied, but he knew he had little choice in the matter now.

The following day, Kloster sat in the cockpit as the Horten bomber flew steadily toward the English coast, now better than half-way to his target. Two hundred meters to the rear and on either side were his escorts, the same two Me 109 fighters, each one carrying a three-hundred litre drop tank for the long flight to England.

In one of those fighters, Andreas Bauman watched as the Horten began to accelerate. The reason became abundantly clear: enemy aircraft. An American P-38 Lightning appeared on the horizon.

The P-38 was a widely used single-seat fighter and commanded respect by Luftwaffe pilots, some of whom had come to label it a "fork-tailed devil," a reference to its twin-boom tail. It was coming directly toward them, seemingly from the English coast.

The Lightning made a dangerous sweeping turn and, using its height advantage, fired a burst at the nearest Me 109, piloted by Lieutenant Schlopf. Bauman needn't have called out a warning to his wingman since he'd already detected the threat and taken evasive action.

Jack Swaggart, piloting a B-26 Marauder, had purposely held back from engaging in the imminent situation. The plan had been for two P-38s to attack and engage the two Me 109 escorts, thereby distracting them from their chief mission: flying escort for the Horten bomber.

Jack was waiting for a tactical advantage to present itself—and when it did, he had every intention of attacking the Nazi stealth plane. Information supplied by Fritz Kolbe suggested that the Horten's pilot was none other than his old nemesis, Horst Kloster.

Meanwhile, Kloster apparently had no desire to engage the enemy and so he continued on, leaving it to the Me 109s to safeguard him and his mission. Bauman fought to remain airborne, as he watched Schlopf execute a series of tight turns, momentarily eluding the Lightning. Eventually, though, he was the recipient of a well-placed burst from the American fighter's main gun. The .50 calibre shells practically disintegrated half of his starboard wing.

Bauman cranked his head to witness the damaged Messerschmitt flip over onto its back and spiral down toward the gray sea. There was no indication that the pilot had jettisoned the canopy, much less bailed out.

Alone and helpless, Bauman had no time to agonize over his wingman; he had to focus on his own plight as a second

P-38 was zeroing in on him, having dropped out of the stratus cloud layer.

Both aircraft twisted and turned, each pilot seeking an advantage, but the Messerschmitt was slowly losing ground to the twin-engine Lightning. Although Bauman made a valiant effort to elude his pursuer, the Lightning's pilot got off a lucky burst that shot holes through his left wing, puncturing the fuel tank. Fuel droplets immediately streamed out, negating Bauman's ability to remain in the fight. Witnessing the German drop out, the Lightning decided not to finish off his adversary. Instead, it changed course to pursue the Horten.

Although there was no love lost between Swaggart and Kloster, Jack's inner sense of fairness, his call to duty, and his honor and integrity, compelled him to try to convince Kloster to abandon his plan.

"Kloster!" Jack's voice invaded the Germans' frequency. "Cease and desist. The Russians are advancing on Berlin as we speak. It's over."

"Damn you!" Kloster's angry voice reverberated in Jack's headphones. "You Americans are always sticking your noses where they don't belong."

Bauman was listening in on the exchange and thought he recognized the voice. "Captain Swaggart, is that you?" he asked, sounding dumbfounded. "This is Andreas Bauman."

"Yes, Bauman," Jack replied. "Don't worry. We're not here for you—"

Jack stopped transmitting. Whereas the Ho 229 had been in view just a few seconds ago, flying level toward the coast, now it was nowhere to be seen. Jack was horror-stricken as he realized they'd lost sight of their target. During his exchange with Bauman, he'd allowed Kloster to slip away.

James Buchanan, flying co-pilot for Swaggart, was no less shocked. The Horten bomber had vanished without a trace.

Bauman turned his damaged fighter around and headed back toward the mainland, but as he glanced at his fuel gauge, he realized he'd never reach Germany. Although the prospect of spending the last few months in a POW camp wasn't thrilling, it was better than being dead.

Jack cursed to himself, scanning the horizon, while his co-pilot switched frequencies and tried to raise the pilot of the second Marauder, still some distance away from the fight. Nothing but static.

"Lame Duck calling Gray Goose, over," Buchanan spoke into the mike. Nothing. "Bosch, Fred, are you guys there?"

In the pilot's seat, Jack searched the vast sky ahead and checked his instruments. Nothing! He looked over at his co-pilot, finding apprehension on Buchanan's face. He wondered if his own exhibited the same.

Buchanan tried again, hoping and praying to raise the other crew, but static filled his headphones. They both knew what was at stake. To make matters worse, it as if both Lightnings were missing, too. James couldn't reach either pilot.

Seconds ticked by, followed by a full minute. Then another. Jack considered his options. Should he contact Allied Command and advise that they had lost their target? It was unthinkable.

He put the Marauder into a gentle turn, maintaining his altitude of three-thousand feet above sea level. He reasoned that Kloster wouldn't have climbed to a higher altitude. If he had, he would have burned precious fuel and become visible from below. No, he had probably dropped down to sea level. That way his gray camouflage paint would blend in with the water, making it almost impossible to distinguish. Jack was about to share his thoughts with his co-pilot, when Buchanan began pointing excitedly out the forward window.

"There!" he shouted. "I see something down there—just below us!"

Jack followed the Canadian's outstretched arm and found nothing. But as he gazed intently, he spotted it too. Something orange. Incredibly, a small orange life raft, looking no bigger than a postage stamp, was bobbing up and down in the channel. And the best part—it wasn't empty. A man wearing a yellow life jacket was huddled inside, hanging on as the life raft was tossed around by the swells.

Jack breathed a sigh of relief. That must be Bosch, the pilot of the second Marauder. Jack had trained with him back in the States and he was a father of two. Jack was grateful he wouldn't have to write that dreaded letter to Bosch's wife. Instead, he envisioned Bosch—a guy with a gregarious personality and talent for telling jokes—reliving his escape from death.

"I can just imagine the tales he'll tell us over a few pints," James said, as if drawing the same conclusion. "Bosch must have pursued the Horten bomber and undoubtedly met his match."

"Right," Jack ventured. "But where are the Lightnings? The last I saw, both were in pursuit of the Horten bomber—"

Jack cut himself off, having spotted a P-38 come out of a cloud and fly a slow circle above the downed airman in the water. The aircraft appeared undamaged, except for the bluish smoke trailing the right engine's exhaust nacelle.

As if on cue, the pilot came on the air and hailed the Marauder.

"Hey, Cap. Sorry to be a spoil sport, but that Nazi pilot got off a lucky shot and damaged the liquid cooling on the starboard engine. I'll be lucky to make it to the coast."

"For sure," Jack responded. "Just make sure you get home in one piece. We have one downed pilot in the water."

At least everyone was alive—so far. Before he could utter the order, Buchanan was already on the radio, alerting Command that they needed to pick up one airman in the water. He supplied the coordinates.

Jack put his aircraft into a slow turn as he circled Bosch to alert him that he'd been spotted. How he wished he could remain 'on station' until a trawler or destroyer picked him up.

Instead, he gave a farewell salute by waggling his wings, then resumed his northerly course and offered up a quick prayer for their safety.

Jack's mind returned to his objective: spotting and intercepting the Horten bomber. At this point it was like looking for a needle in a haystack. Kloster would undoubtedly play it smart. After engaging and quickly dispatching the other Lightning, he would have dropped down to the deck—and Jack ruefully had to admit, he would have done the same.

Nothing needed to be said between Jack and his co-pilot. They knew what was at stake. Jack's eyes swept the vast expanse of water below, searching for that glimmer of hope, a glimmer that would transform itself into a flash when light bounced off the prototype's canopy.

But there was nothing.

Still Jack flew on, refusing to give up.

Several minutes passed and Jack was about to change course when he saw something—a speck, no bigger than a fly, but it was moving ever so slightly below them. No more than a mile ahead, it was skimming the tops of the waves. The gray camouflage paint allowed it to blend in perfectly. Almost motionless, it seemed to hover like a bird of prey, ready to pounce on its next victim. But that was just an illusion.

"We've got him," Jack shouted exuberantly, startling his co-pilot.

Without waiting for a response, he advanced the throttles and the bomber surged ahead. Kloster, alerted to the threat, didn't wait for the Marauder to catch up to him. He accelerated his aircraft.

"Dammit!" Jack cursed, shaking his head. "How could he possibly have seen us?"

The Horten started to climb, imperceptibly at first but then in a more pronounced fashion, pulling away from its pursuer.

Jack wasn't willing to give up without a fight and so he pushed his throttles to the stops. Coupled with his descent, he was able to squeeze a few more miles per hour out of the old bird. But as impressive as that was, with the airspeed indicator climbing past three hundred miles per hour, it wasn't enough. His two Pratt & Whitney radial engines, each producing a respectable 1900 horsepower, were no match for the thrust of the Jumo turbojets.

With each passing second, the German bomber not only pulled away, but clearly outdistanced its pursuer—and doing so while climbing.

With his mouth open, Jack watched in disbelief as he gazed at Germany's marvel of aeronautic engineering. He had, of course, seen the stolen schematics Kolbe had supplied, and he'd studied them in detail, but nothing could have prepared him for this. This truly was a remarkable feat of innovation, designed, not by proven engineers, but by two unknown brothers.

"Four bogeys at nine o'clock," James alerted Jack, snapping him out of his trance. "No, wait. I don't think they're *Jerry.*"

Indeed, the four aircraft turned out to be British Supermarine Spitfires. One of the pilots, Greg Phillips, had been out on reconnaissance patrol when he spotted activity below. At first, he wasn't sure what he'd seen and was about to dismiss it, thinking it was a fishing trawler. But then there was a break in the clouds, and what he saw made him straighten up. Had that been an explosion? He alerted Beckett.

"I didn't see anything, Greg," Beckett replied. "Alright, you'd better have a look."

Phillips dropped his right wing and began a slow, circling descent, hoping to make sense of what he'd seen. He descended through five thousand feet, eventually spotting debris in the sea, debris that could have come from an aircraft.

Confirming his suspicions, the distinctive twin-boom momentarily bobbed up, the unrelenting sea not completely in possession of its prey. The tail swayed from side to side and seemed to wave farewell, as if alerting Phillips to its plight. The next billow swallowed the empennage and the plane disappeared into the depths.

Then, miraculously, an orange dinghy surfaced.

Phillips dropped the next two thousand feet quickly, looking for survivors. Rewarded for his optimism, he spotted one Mae West next to the dinghy and a man desperately clinging to the sides of the dinghy.

He keyed his mike to inform Beckett. "I've found one downed airman. Luckily, he managed to climb aboard a life raft. I think I can—wait, what the hell is that?"

Silence.

Rather than outrun the English fighters, Kloster still had a few tricks up his sleeve. Relying on the Ho 229's impressive speed and maneuverability he climbed directly at the descending Spitfire, catching the pilot off guard.

"Holy crap!" one of the pilots blurted out. "Did you see that?"

The Horten bomber zoomed past a startled Phillips and banked sharply to come up behind him.

"Oh my God!" Phillips blurted, his voice losing all control. "He's coming around."

"Who's coming around?" asked Jimmy Hooper, one of the other Spitfire pilots.

Phillips tried to make sense of what he'd seen. "A Nazi plane ... I've never seen anything like it before. He's coming after me. I'm not sure—"

The transmission was cut off. Beckett strained to spot his wingman, and there it was, the Nazi warplane, little more than a shadow, streaking below the cloud layer in pursuit of what he supposed must be Phillips' Spitfire.

My God! he thought. *That thing, whatever it is ... it's fast!*

Beckett dropped his right wing to get a better look. What he saw sent a tingling down his spine. Phillips was maneuvering to get distance between him and his pursuer, hoping to escape into the safety of the thickening cloud layer, but the German pursuer clearly had a speed advantage. Phillips banked his aircraft and the German followed suit, closing the gap at an alarming rate.

Just as Beckett was getting his first glimpse of their new nemesis, Hooper's Spitfire appeared out of nowhere and opened up, catching Kloster off-guard. However, the Australian misjudged the German's speed and the bullets sailed harmlessly past his right wingtip.

Kloster abandoned his pursuit of the original Spitfire and pulled a tight, gut-wrenching turn to engage his new adversary.

"Jimmy!" Beckett shouted into his mike. "Get out of there. He's coming around and has his sights set on you. Move it!"

Hooper advanced his throttle and banked left, but the warning was both unnecessary and too late. The German aircraft came up behind him so quickly that for a moment Beckett thought the Spitfire's engine had stopped working.

But that was only an illusion.

In the next breath, the delta-wing plane spat out deadly cannon fire, tearing apart Hooper's left wing. The Spitfire lurched ahead, but with the loss of lift it staggered in the air, pitched forward, and spiralled toward the sea.

Beckett forced himself to look away.

"Heads up lads," Beckett radioed, dismayed. "That German isn't finished with us yet. Keep your eyes peeled and stay in formation."

Just then, the Horten bomber screamed past them at their nine o'clock, no more than two hundred feet below the three remaining Spitfires. It was both mesmerizing and unnerving. The German pilot could have fired another burst but had decided not to engage them. His message was clear: I have the superior aircraft—don't mess with me.

Still flying at five thousand feet, each man strained in his harness to catch a glimpse. None of them had ever seen such a machine before. The sleek, delta-wing shape, painted in camouflage color, presented an eerie futuristic image.

A strange craft indeed, thought Beckett. *What have the Germans dreamt up now?*

He hadn't detected any armaments, although clearly it was equipped with machine guns. Not able to view the undercarriage, Beckett supposed it must be a prototype of some kind, used primarily for reconnaissance. He dreaded to think what havoc three or four of these superior aircraft could inflict on them. Pity that the only Spitfire equipped with an onboard camera was earlier forced to head back.

"Flight leader to station Delta," Beckett alerted his base operator. "I've spotted a new type of German aircraft, apparently on a reconnaissance flight. It's a delta-wing design, powered by what appear to be two jet engines, and it's incredibly fast. Over."

But before the operator could confirm, another voice cut in.

"Flight leader, this is Captain Jack Swaggart. We're also after the German prototype. It's not a recon flight. He's heading for London—to bomb it."

Jack had been monitoring the action and continued on his course, hoping against hope that somehow Kloster might have been slowed down. Jack's plane was vectored toward Kloster's last known position. Jack looked at the fuel gauges and winced. As a result of pushing the engines to better than 75% power, they had consumed a significant amount of fuel. They were down to less than a third in both tanks.

"Command, I have a further update," Beckett said as he watched the Marauder pursue the Horten. "The unidentified intruder engaged us and shot down one of my aircraft. He's headed for the coast with superior speed. We don't have a hope of catching him. Besides, we're running low on gas and need to return to base. Good luck, Yank."

CHAPTER XXXI
Providence

Horst Kloster couldn't have been more pleased. He continued on, confident that he'd not only reach London but deliver his payload. He relaxed a fraction and thought of the praise he was going to receive from the Führer—if he survived.

He dismissed the thought and turned his mind back to the mission. He first scanned his instruments and then, even though he had dispatched the Spitfire, kept a sharp lookout for enemy fighters. He searched the vast sky, and as he approached the coast, he spotted a strange shape below the clouds. He throttled back and descended a few hundred meters to get a better look. The vertical and elliptical shape morphed into a familiar sight: an observation balloon.

Kloster swung the bomber into a slow lazy turn, intending to fly past the lone, unarmed observer. His pride and belief in German superiority had persuaded him to flaunt the Horten jet, allowing the English observer to marvel at Germany's latest feat of engineering while unable to do anything about it.

The balloon was tethered to the ground via a long connecting cable and its occupant, a red-haired lad of fifteen or sixteen, gaped wide-eyed at the circling Nazi war machine. He followed the progress of the bomber as it made a wide circling turn.

Kloster circled the balloon twice and, rather than fire a salvo, decided to perform a close flyby and depart in a bold climb-out, giving the British a sight they wouldn't soon forget. He advanced the throttle and roared past the balloon at an impressive 650 kilometers per hour, startling the observer.

As he roared past, he banked his airplane to get a final look over his shoulder. What he saw made him laugh into his oxygen mask. The impromptu flyby had caused chaos. The jet blast had upset the balloon's equilibrium, sending the basket pitching from side to side like a rowboat bobbing in hostile seas.

The boy hung to the sides for dear life, having nearly been tossed from his lofty observation post. He swore at the departing aircraft with curses the German pilot couldn't possibly hear.

The youth stopped his tirade midstream, alerted by something the German hadn't detected. The observer's scowl transformed into a wide grin.

A Nazi V1 rocket, a so-called "doodlebug" had come into view, its pulse motor working efficiently and propelling it to its ultimate destination: London. Yet this one was flying erratically, one of the onboard gyros having malfunctioned. The rocket abruptly pitched up to a thirty-degree angle, climbing steadily.

Having satisfied his base desire of besting the British, Kloster rolled out of the turn and throttled back. He levelled off and was occupied with scanning his instruments—but that one decision, to check his instruments instead of scanning the sky, brought him onto a collision course with the rocket.

It was as if an unseen hand had manipulated the rocket's magnetic compass, altering its trajectory and sending it directly into the Horten's path.

Kloster finally looked up and, as if relying on a sixth sense, stared at the advancing rocket with disbelief. Most pilots would have frozen in terror, unable to react in the face of certain death, but he was no ordinary fighter pilot. His narcissism, his self-preservation, and his devil-may-care attitude had enabled him to escape death before.

His brain ignored the monumental odds. Instinctively, Kloster pulled back on the control stick and applied left aileron control, flipping the Horten onto its back. Coupled with his low airspeed, the aircraft buffeted and stalled. The Ho 229's wing passed dangerously close to the doodlebug's narrow wingtip, disrupting its airflow. The rocket's onboard gyros received conflicting messages and plunged the V1 bomb on a downward trajectory, where it splashed into the sea, impacting with a tremendous explosion.

‡

Jack spotted the doodlebug race past his airplane and noted its erratic course. He followed the rocket's progress, then in the distance spotted another aircraft circling what looked like an observation balloon.

He rubbed his eyes to make sure what he was seeing was real. Jack couldn't believe his luck—or providence. Astonishingly, the Horten bomber was flying tight circles around the manned balloon, threatening to topple its observer.

"I see it too," James blurted out. "Has he lost his mind? Doesn't he see the doodlebug?"

They witnessed Kloster's near miss, the inevitable stall, and his frantic efforts to regain control of his aircraft. The pilot had his hands full just trying to stay airborne, and in the process, he failed to detect the approaching Marauder.

In those few seconds, he became vulnerable to attack. This would be Jack's last and best opportunity to catch Kloster. Jack shoved the Marauder's throttles to their stops in the hopes of intercepting the Horten.

If Kloster managed to recover from the spin, he could conceivably continue on his mission and drop his bomb on London. Jack wasn't about to let that happen.

With practiced skill, he honed in on the bomber, anticipating where the Horten would come out of its spin.

Meanwhile, Buchanan climbed down into the nose turret

and strapped himself into the seat. "Jack, I'm in the turret bay. I'm ready."

Jack, his own heart rate elevated, readied himself for the finale. He was intense, focused on the task at hand. Someone would fail to return to base, but whether it was the Horten or the Marauder was yet to be determined.

When Jack had achieved the optimum firing angle, he shouted at Buchanan to let loose a volley. James crouched in the cramped turret bay, released the machine gun's safety, and fired several well-placed bursts at the spiralling Horten.

The first few shells narrowly missed the Horten's right wingtip, but the next twenty or thirty rounds found their mark, shredding the top of the wooden wing. Strips of plywood peeled off like they'd been attacked by a jackhammer. James followed up with another burst, this time striking the starboard engine. The bomber seemed to stumble in midair, black smoke billowing out of the exhaust nacelle.

The Marauder, its engines still developing full power, roared past the now-crippled Horten like it was standing still. Jack eased back on the throttles and commenced a tight turn to port as he lined up for another sortie. With the Horten's right engine out of commission and the right-wing hampering flight, the Horten was a sitting duck.

Buchanan fired another burst for good measure, striking the fuselage.

Whether Kloster had inadvertently activated the bomb bay release lever or the bullets had damaged the control mechanism, the doors swung open, exposing a strange-looking object within the cavity. Jack had little doubt that he was looking at a new sinister weapon, a bomb unlike anything he'd seen before. He only had a fleeting glance, yet the gray cylindrical device sent a shiver down his spine. From the little he'd learned from Kolbe's pilfered drawings, he knew he was staring at some sort of experimental atomic weapon, capable of immense destructive power.

Buchanan fired another burst, hoping to hit the other engine, just as the aircraft flipped over. Several rounds struck the Plexiglas canopy, shattering it. Jack flew past and made another tight turn. On his next pass, he spotted Kloster's lifeless body, still strapped into his seat, his helmet covered in crimson. Jack smiled grimly, knowing Kloster would never receive Göring's accolades.

Reduced to twisted wreckage, the once streamlined Horten airframe had lost most of its forward momentum and plummeted, slowly spiraling toward the brackish estuary below, accompanied in its ungraceful fall by indistinguishable chunks of debris. What had once been a marvel of German engineering had been reduced to a pilotless metal carcass.

Jack looked up at the sun, whose rays had just penetrated the cloud, sending a cascade of beams streaming all around. Curiously, the rays were a reminder of God's providence and he thought of one of his favorite hymns, "Blessed Assurance" by Fanny J. Crosby.

Yes, he had the assurance of a higher power, that when things were at their worst, at their most threatening, God was there in their midst, still in charge.

He turned to his co-pilot. "Well, James, let's call it a day and head back to base, shall we?"

Buchanan, still stunned by the devastation of the Horten, was at a loss for words. He simply nodded, relieved they had come through unscathed and still alive.

∾

Several weeks had gone by since Rudi Schultz's arrest. Reclining in his study, Alfred Hiller hung up the telephone with his brother-in-law, Heinrich Schinkel. He smiled with smug satisfaction, pleased with the good news he'd just received.

Schultz, long suspected of being a communist sympathiser, had been interrogated by the Gestapo. They had been richly rewarded. Schultz had been forced to reveal that he'd been instrumental in supplying information to the Allies. Even better, he had implicated several other traitors, Fritz Kolbe among them.

Hiller would have liked to have seen Schultz's face, when he was being shoved onto a freight car headed for Dora-Mittelbau, the notorious Nazi concentration camp.

He was enjoying a cup of tea when he heard a knock on the door. His ministerial assistant Matthäus soon entered and handed him a sealed envelope.

Once he was alone again, the priest opened the envelope eagerly, wondering what it contained. To his surprise, he found two items—a hand-written note and a second, smaller envelope bearing the insignia of a local law firm.

He scanned the note's few lines and saw that it was signed by Kurt Löffler, captain of the Oranienburg police. The note stated that Löffler had been entrusted with the last will and testament of a man named Horst Kloster.

Hiller nearly dropped his tea when he read that name. Heinrich had told him that Kloster had been seconded to the Luftwaffe on instructions from a high-ranking officer, Colonel Knemeyer. Indeed, it seemed that Kloster had recently participated in a secret mission, but had, in the process, lost his life in an airplane crash. That was two weeks ago.

Now he was the recipient of Kloster's will. *Was this a joke?* he thought.

Next, he studied the envelope carefully, but then recognized the law firm's name. He unwound the string and opened the clasp. He pulled out several sheets of typewritten paper and began to read. The first page was nothing more than legalese, confirming that the signatory was of sound mind and had left instructions to be carried out by the firm.

When he progressed to the second page, Hiller let out a low whistle. He had to read the bottom paragraph a second time to make sure he'd understood it correctly. It stated that the Church of St. Nicholas was to be the recipient of a substantial amount of money—but only if certain conditions were met.

He couldn't believe his luck. The parish was in desperate need of funds to carry out overdue repairs to the roof. The diocese, aware of his plight, had problems of their own and couldn't help.

Hiller quickly turned to the third page and read the conditions. They dealt with finding a suitable administrator to handle the funds and determine what they could be used for.

Then he came to the caveat, right there in black and white: in exchange for receiving the funds the clergy had to take on the responsibility of caring for and raising an orphaned child: Adam Rosenbaum. As he continued reading, he realized the boy was Horst Kloster's nephew, and he was one-quarter Jewish.

The papers floated to the ground, as Hiller was unable to hold them any longer. The priest slumped over in his chair, clutching his chest. He appeared to have sustained a heart attack.

EPILOGUE

Six Months Later

Jack sat in the driver's seat of a grey military Jeep. He had dismissed his driver, preferring to drive himself on this occasion. As he drove through Berlin's streets, he looked around at the destruction, the burnt-out buildings, and the remnants of tree-lined streets. But he also saw hope and determination in the eyes of the Berliners around him.

Jack slowed, avoiding an old man who pushed a handcart filled with broken bricks. He carefully drove around bombed-out buildings and craters that were being attended by myriad local workers.

Jack was amazed to see how the German populace, though defeated only a short time ago, got back to work, salvaging bricks and materials, rebuilding the damaged buildings, in effect, rebuilding their lives. Hitler had done the Allies a favor by ending his life early, bringing a conclusion to the war in Europe and avoiding the public spectacle Mussolini had endured.

Yet life managed to go on, and Germany's determined people were no exception.

Jack had just concluded a briefing with Allen Dulles, the interim head of the OSS in Europe. He'd been briefed on a number of events, not the least of which was the important role Fritz Kolbe had played.

But as much as Kolbe's story had interested him, he was

far more interested in his next meeting. Hilde's house in Oranienburg had suffered extensive damage from Allied bombing, and so she, along with her mother, had sought refuge with her aunt in Zehdenick, at least until their house could be rebuilt.

Once he had established contact with her, which wasn't too difficult since Hilde had secured a job with the occupying forces, he managed to arrange for a pass and the necessary funds, allowing her to travel by train to Berlin.

Although they had exchanged letters and talked several times over the telephone, they hadn't seen each other since April.

A lot had changed since then. Berlin, and the rest of Germany, had been split into four main jurisdictions, each overseen by one of the occupying nations: France, England, Russia and the United States.

Jack had been requested to remain behind, tasked with many of the logistical problems in rebuilding the war-torn country. There was even talk of instituting a court to address the many war crimes committed by the Nazis.

Yes, a lot had to take place to bring Germany out of the devastation caused by a handful of madmen. And it would certainly take a lot of time and resources to rebuild.

But that wasn't the real reason Jack chose to stay behind. His motivation centered on Hilde and his affection for her. If he were being honest with himself, he had fallen in love with the beautiful blonde.

And here she was, coming out of Berlin's Hauptbahnhof. Jack smiled, realizing that he'd arrived just in time. He parked the Jeep and jumped out.

Hilde looked stunning. Wearing a fashionable yellow dress and white pumps, a brown handbag slung over her shoulder, she walked out with the crowd. He hoped she was scanning the throng for him.

He dashed up the steps to catch Hilde before she reached the sidewalk. She walked around a merchant selling apples and began to descend the steps when she caught sight of Jack in his handsome American uniform.

They met halfway.

"*Guten tag, Herr Kapitän,*" she proclaimed. "How are you doing?"

"Very well, Fräulein?" Jack replied in kind. "So much better now that you're here. And you?"

"Well, good, except for one thing." Her smile slowly faded.

"Your father?" Jack asked intuitively guessing what she was thinking.

Actually, Jack had asked a fellow officer to inquire about her father's incarceration. At first the man had been doubtful he could find out anything worthwhile from the Russian sector, but he'd promised Jack he would look into it. Jack hadn't heard anything for three weeks, but then the fellow officer had called unexpectedly and said the search had taken a promising turn.

He had called in a few favors and been informed by one source that Hilde's father's regiment had been relocated to a camp that was touted as being less severe than others.

The Russians were in no hurry to send German prisoners home. And for good reason. One, they were paying them back for the brutality their own countrymen had experienced at the hands of the Nazis. Two, they were using foreign workers to rebuild their infrastructure at virtually no cost.

Although the scant information wasn't what Jack had hoped for, it was better than nothing. He hoped the news of her father's welfare would at least be a comfort to Hilde and make her a little less anxious about his fate.

As they looked into each other's eyes, he hesitated, not knowing if this was the right time. He'd been mulling over the best time to propose and hadn't come to a decision.

He reached into his pocket and pulled out a little box.

"Don't just stand there, you bloke," a familiar voice urged, breaking the silence. "Kiss her!"

Hilde turned to the source of the interruption, an officer in uniform, leaning on a cane.

"Chuck!" Jack blurted out as he mounted the steps.

He ran past Hilde, then stopped, unsure what to do. Instinct took over. He hurriedly kissed Hilde on the lips. Before she could respond, he pressed a little box into her hand and ran up the remaining steps.

He hugged Boyer as if he were the prodigal son himself, giving him the affection that had been meant for Hilde.

Hilde stood there, baffled yet smiling, holding the open box with tears running down her cheeks. She clearly needed no explanation. After all, Jack had told her about his friend and co-pilot, Chuck Boyer, while on the train to Stralsund. And now, here they were, reunited at last. Hilde couldn't have been any happier for them.

She climbed the last two steps and joined the two men, who at least had the sense to part just enough for her to squeeze between them.

Hilde's smile was dazzling, confirmation that she had accepted Jack's unspoken proposal. Chuck pulled back a fraction and gaped at the open jewellery box in Hilde's hand. The diamond ring sparkled in the bright sunshine.

Amidst all this, a third man stood nearby, close enough to see the reunion but far enough away not to intrude in their merriment. After a decent interval, the man emerged from behind the column that had been shielding him and coughed discreetly.

Jack was first to notice him.

"Colonel Bartsch, I wasn't expecting to see you here."

"I know. Actually, I've come to say goodbye. I'm scheduled to return to the States." Now that he saw Hilde up close, he couldn't help but grin. "So, this is the beautiful fräulein. It seems she has captured … er, more than just your imagination."

Jack nodded, unable to suppress the grin that was slowly spreading across his face.

"Congratulations are in order, sir," Chuck offered. "They've just become engaged."

"Well now!" Bartsch beamed. "In that case, I might as well contribute to the good news."

All three looked at him expectantly.

"Congratulations on your engagement, Major Swaggart."

Jack was speechless, not knowing what to say. "The promotion and details are back in the office, on my desk. There's no point in delaying the news. Um ... Major, could I have a word with you?"

Not waiting for an audible reply, Bartsch took Jack by the arm and steered him off to the side.

"I have more good news," he began. "As you know, our boys have been diligently searching for wreckage of the Horten bomber. One of the recon flights spotted an object resembling the wreckage of an aircraft in the Thames estuary. Thinking it was just one of the many crashed airplanes from the end of the war, it didn't get immediate attention. Eventually, a Navy patrol came by and sent two divers down. After a fruitless initial search, they sent another team down—only yesterday."

He paused, took a deep breath, and continued. "They located the remnants of what we believe is the Horten bomber ... *and* its payload. Both the bomber and the experimental bomb have been shipped off to London for further inspection."

Jack took it in but didn't interrupt.

"We're not completely certain yet, but initial findings confirm that it was a sophisticated bomb," Bartsch added. "Nothing like the explosive experts have seen before."

He looked around conspiratorially before whispering in Jack's ear. "I'm not supposed to say anything because it's top secret. But, what the hell. I can tell you since we all owe you a debt of gratitude for stopping the Nazi plot." He paused, more for effect than secrecy.

"I've been informed by a highly respected physicist that what the Horten bomber was carrying is what we laymen would call a 'dirty' bomb. A radiological weapon, that as far as the expert could tell wasn't carrying fissionable material but was instead designed to act as a 'dispersal' weapon, in effect meant to contaminate everything in the blast radius."

Jack's eyebrows furrowed in concentration as he tried to absorb what he heard.

"Thank God Kloster never reached his destination," Jack finally replied.

He looked at Bartsch and felt the man knew far more than he was letting on. But then Jack looked over his shoulder and caught the look on Hilde's face, signalling that it was time for them to leave. He waved at her, acknowledging the unspoken message.

Yet, there was something that still puzzled him.

"Colonel," he started, "I just—"

"Gregg. Call me Gregg," Bartsch interrupted him.

"Alright, Gregg, there's just one thing that puzzles me. After we alerted you of the Nazis' plan with the bomb, how did you know … I mean, how did you know when to scramble the P-38s to intercept the Horten bomber? The Germans were very secretive, their itinerary known to a handful at most."

It was Bartsch's turn to grin. "Ah yes, I was wondering if you'd come around to asking that. Actually, we can all thank one man. Just a few—"

They were startled by a booming sound which forced both men to look up at a B-17 Flying Fortress passing overhead. The drone of its engines momentarily drowned out any conversation.

"As I was saying," Bartsch continued, lowering his voice, "few men dared to do what he did, and he did so at great personal risk."

"Do you mean my German friend, Fritz?" Jack nearly whispered.

Before Bartsch could continue, a man in a trench coat and fedora hat came around the corner of the building carrying a briefcase.

"*Guten Tag, Herr Mayor*," greeted Fritz Kolbe. "It's a lovely day, don't you think?" He turned to address the colonel. "Herr Bartsch, we should get going, right?"

Kolbe touched his hat in salute and descended the stairs before Jack could formulate a reply. They watched him climb into the back of a waiting car, the rear door remaining open, a signal for Bartsch to follow.

"Speaking of survivors, you might want to tell your fräulein that a certain pilot by the name of Bauman is alive and well," Bartsch added with a sardonic smile. "It seems he ditched his Messerschmitt in the English Channel and was picked up by a British patrol. He was then sequestered in a POW camp in the north of England, courtesy of His Majesty's government. I believe he was released and returned home not two weeks ago.

"Oh, what the hell!" Bartsch exclaimed. "I've let the cat out of the bag, so I might as well tell you the rest."

"The rest, sir?" inquired Jack. "Good news, I trust."

"Yes, this seems to be the day for it. Well, a friend of mine, a captain with the U.S. Army Chaplain service happened to assist the British Army Corps. You see, the Brits were the first contingent to liberate the infamous Bergen-Belsen concentration camp, in mid-April. They came across deplorable conditions, with many inmates half-starving and barely alive, while a typhus epidemic raged through the camp.

"All available personnel were enlisted to save as many lives as possible. What was interesting was that two men who were seemingly inseparable, one Jew and one Catholic, worked together, side-by-side, assisting our troops with whatever was required. The Jew went by the name of William Sochalski and actually spoke quite good English. The other man, Rudi Schultz, I suspect, is more familiar to you."

Jack's jaw dropped at the sound of the names.

"He asked my chaplain friend if he could do them a favor and make inquiries with the U.S. Army regarding a certain Captain Jack Swaggart," Bartsch continued. "It seems they had played some role in the captain's rescue."

"Heavens! But those men—"

"Don't worry, Jack," Bartsch cut in. "My friend managed to obtain the particulars and how you can get in touch with him." He handed Jack a folded paper.

Jack, though caught up in the moment, was perceptive enough to catch that Bartsch had used the singular tense.

"Him?" Jack asked. "You mean only one?"

Bartsch nodded. "I'm sorry. Only one survived. During the course of their work, both men had contracted typhus. Although they were given the best of medical care available, only Sochalski pulled through."

But before Jack could respond, Bartsch had already turned and headed down the steps toward the waiting car.

Jack took a deep breath and then looked at Hilde's ravishing face, all the while mindful that it could have been Bauman standing next to her instead of him. He reflected on the circumstances that had brought him thus far: a crash-landing in a farmer's field, meeting the resourceful Hilde Augsberg, being an eyewitness to the Horten bomber in flight—it all could have been for naught had he been captured by the irrepressible Horst Kloster. Certainly, teaming up with the spy, Fritz Kolbe—cleverly arranged by Allen Dulles—proved to be a good idea. Even if Jack had tried, he couldn't have worked it out any better.

He rejoined Chuck and Hilde, who seemed to sense everything wasn't quite right.

"Is something wrong?" Hilde asked.

Jack looked uncomfortable, still holding the folded paper in his hand.

"I've just received word that William Sochalski, my former

stable mate, is alive and well, now assisting the Brits in Hanover. Sadly, your dear friend, Rudi Schultz, who had worked alongside William, had contracted typhus and died."

Hilde pressed her hand to her mouth, clearly saddened by the news. After a moment, she looked up, eyes glistening with tears but a smile returning to her face. "I feel we owe them our gratitude. Well then, perhaps we can help William."

LIST OF CHARACTERS

Hermann Göring. Real life persona and a WWI flying ace. He joined the Nazi party in early stages and was considered Hitler's right-hand man.

Jack Swaggart. American bomber pilot, 30ish, stationed in northern France. After getting shot down, he finds himself on the run, pursued by a relentless Gestapo officer.

Horst Kloster. Former fighter pilot in the Luftwaffe. He's a risk taker, flamboyant, unpredictable, and quite ruthless. He's Jack's nemesis.

Hilde Augsberg. Only twenty-five years old, she's unmarried and employed as the mayor's secretary in Oranienburg. She is a people person, but also organized, resourceful, and dependable.

James Buchanan. Hails from Winnipeg, MB, joined the RCAF in 1943, now attached to the War Office in London. Like many single men, he's shy and reserved, preferring to tinker with mechanical things.

Otto Saufman. An egotistical Nazi. Ambitious, opportunistic, and dangerous. Worse yet, unhappily married, low moral standards, and in pursuit of Hilde.

Gertrude Augsberg. She lives in Oranienburg and is Hilde's mother. She becomes instrumental in helping Jack escape the Gestapo.

Charles "Chuck" Boyer. Not to be confused with the famous French film star. Chuck is Jack's co-pilot. A natural leader with a non-nonsense approach, he's dependable, heroic and not one to step away from a challenge.

Heinrich Schinkel. He stems from pure Aryan lineage, but a lower-class background. Through sheer determination, he attained the rank of major in the SS. A stickler for rules, he loathes insubordination. He's Kloster's boss.

Alfred Hiller. 50ish and mild-mannered, is a Roman Catholic parish priest at presides over the Church of St.Nicholas. parish. He is Schinkel's brother-in-law, and supports the church's position of co-operating with the Nazi regime.

Fritz Kolbe. Forty-five years old and short in stature, Fritz is a German bureaucrat, but by no means diminutive in his accomplishments. He loathes the Nazi party and spies for the Allies.

Andreas Bauman. A Luftwaffe pilot and in love with Hilde. Smart, generous, but emotionally reserved. Naïve to the political situation in Germany, he becomes torn between his loyalty to the Führer and a crumbling Germany.

Siegfried Knemeyer. A colonel in the German military. He is under immense pressure to develop and implement *wunder* weapons capable of inflicting horrendous damage.

William Sochalski. Only15 years old, mature beyond his years. He's a Jew living under Hitler's threat. He managed to escape a train bound for a concentration camp and fortuitously met up with Jack.

Erwin Ziller. Real-life person. Erwin is a fighter pilot and was accepted into the Horten test-pilot program, much to Kloster's chagrin. He's an all-around good guy, but fails to recognize Kloster's vindictiveness.

Bryan Shelby. A Navy man and seconded to the War Office in London. A Lieutenant-Commander in Britain's Navy, he works alongside James Buchanan.